# THE
# HOUSE
# OF
# HIDDEN
# MOTHERS

# THE
# HOUSE
## OF
# HIDDEN
# MOTHERS

*Meera Syal*

SARAH CRICHTON BOOKS

FARRAR, STRAUS AND GIROUX   NEW YORK

Sarah Crichton Books
Farrar, Straus and Giroux
18 West 18th Street, New York 10011

Printed in the United States of America
Originally published by Transworld Publishers, Great Britain
Published in the United States by Sarah Crichton Books / Farrar, Straus and Giroux
First American edition, 2016

Library of Congress Cataloging-in-Publication Data
Names: Syal, Meera, author.
Title: The house of hidden mothers / Meera Syal.
Description: First American edition. | New York : Sarah Crichton Books /
    Farrar, Straus and Giroux, 2016.
Identifiers: LCCN 2015039002 | ISBN 9780374172978 (hardback) |
    ISBN 9780374714963 (e-book)
Subjects: | BISAC: FICTION / Literary. | FICTION / Family Life.
Classification: LCC PR9499.3.S975 H68 2016 | DDC 823/.914—dc23
LC record available at http://lccn.loc.gov/2015039002

Our books may be purchased in bulk for promotional, educational, or business use.
Please contact your local bookseller or the Macmillan Corporate and Premium
Sales Department at 1-800-221-7945, extension 5442, or by e-mail at
MacmillanSpecialMarkets@macmillan.com.

www.fsgbooks.com
www.twitter.com/fsgbooks • www.facebook.com/fsgbooks

1  3  5  7  9  10  8  6  4  2

For Sanjeev, Milli and Shaan, my North Stars

'Each of us holds in her lap a phantom, a ghost baby. What confronts us, now the excitement's over, is our own failure. Mother, I think. Wherever you may be. Can you hear me? You wanted a women's culture. Well, now there is one. It isn't what you meant, but it exists. Be thankful for small mercies.'

*The Handmaid's Tale,*
Margaret Atwood

# CHAPTER ONE

R ELIGION IS FOR those who believe in hell, spirituality is for those who have already been there.' Shyama had to squint slightly to read the laminated sticker on the side of the receptionist's computer. It must be the light, she consoled herself. She shifted slightly in the queue, catching a whiff of perfume from the woman in front of her – something woody and expensive, blended with a scent she recognized intimately, a musky aroma with a bitter undertone: the familiar smell of desperation. The woman exchanged a few hushed words with the receptionist and then took a seat on a faded chintzy sofa, giving Shyama a better look at the owner of the computer.

A new girl. She was young – too young, Shyama felt, for a place like this, a discreet Harley Street address where women under the age of thirty-five ought to be banned. With a faint nod, Shyama handed over her appointment card and stole a longer look at her. Sun, sin and saturated fats had not yet pinched the skin around her eyes or spider-legged their way around her smiling mouth. She was a natural redhead, with that translucent paleness and a smattering of tiny freckles, dusting on a freshly baked cupcake. How could this snip of a girl have ever had a glimpse of hell, as her sticker proclaimed? Then Shyama spotted her earrings: silver discs with the Hindu symbol 'Om' engraved on the surface.

1

'Do take a seat, Mrs Shaw,' the young girl said. 'Mr Lalani won't be long.'

There was a moment's hesitation while Shyama considered commenting on those earrings. But that would spark a conversation about where Shyama came from and yes, she was Hindu, but no, born here, and no, she hadn't been to half the ancient sites that Miss Cupcake had visited, and yes, isn't it humbling that the Indian poor have so little yet they would give you their last piece of chapatti and, despite living knee-deep in refuse, how on earth do they always seem so happy? Then there would be some more chat about the charming guest-house the receptionist had found in Goa or the unbelievable guide who had practically saved her life in the teeming, chanting crowds of Haridwar, or that moment when she had watched the monsoon clouds rolling in over Mumbai bay, dark clots curdling the horizon, the air turning metallic and tart to the tongue.

Shyama had done all those things, many years ago, before motherhood and divorce and laughter lines – though frankly, when she looked at herself in a magnifying mirror nowadays she wondered if anything could have really been that funny.

They could have swapped life-changing anecdotes, Shyama knowing she would always be able to trump the earrings simply by pointing to her skin. 'The real deal, see?' Though she knew she wasn't. She hadn't been to India for years. The only branch of the family she had ever been close to were now not speaking to her, and it seemed highly unlikely that she would be going there in the foreseeable future because every penny of her savings had gone on this clinic. The clinic where the redhead with the Om earrings was now staring at her.

Shyama flashed her a warm smile, wanting to reassure her that she wasn't one of those bitter women who would give her a hard time simply because she had youth and insouciance on her side – no sir, not she – and she sat down heavily on a squishy armchair, trying to steady her nerves.

She started as a metallic ping announced that a text from Toby had just arrived. 'U OK? Phone on vibrate next to my heart . . .' She knew the dots denoted irony. They did a lot of that: self-conscious romantic declarations, inviting each other to join in and trample on the sentiment before it embarrassed them both. It was cute, it was becoming habit, maybe she should worry about that. There might come a point where one of them would need to say something heartfelt and sincere without being laughed at. She texted back, 'Glad phone vibrating next to heart and not in trouser pocket as usual. Not gone in yet . . .' It was only after she had sent the text that she realized she'd ended with dots too. Surely he would know that they denoted a resigned sigh, rather than an invitation to let the joshing begin. Oh well, it was a test. If Toby misunderstood and texted back with some quip, she would know that they weren't really suited and that it wasn't worth carrying on with any of this time-consuming, expensive grappling with Nature. Best to walk away with a sad smile and a good-luck-with-the-rest-of-your-life kind of wave. Then she could just let go. Let the belly sag and the grey show through, and blow the gym membership on vodka and full-sleeve tops to cover up the incoming bingo wings.

A text from Toby. A single unironic X.

'Mr Lalani will see you now.'

Shyama stood up at exactly the same time as the woman who had come in before her. Smart suit, perfect hair, pencil-thin, one arched eyebrow raised like a bow.

'Mrs Bindman? Do go through.'

The eyebrow pinged off an invisible arrow of victory and Shyama sat back down, repressing an urge to bang her heels against the chair like a truculent toddler. There was so much waiting in this game and yet so little time to play with. Her life was punctuated with mocking end-of-sentence dots. All those years spent avoiding getting pregnant, all those hours of sitting on cold plastic toilet seats in student digs/shared houses/first flats, praying for the banner of blood to declare that war was over, that your life would go on as before. And then the later years, spent in nicer houses on a better class of loo seat – reclaimed teak or cheekily self-conscious seats like the plastic one with a barbed-wire pattern inside (her daughter's choice, of course) – still waiting. But this time praying for the blood not to come, for a satisfied silence that would tell Shyama her old life was most definitely over as, inside her, a new one had just begun.

On impulse she dialled Lydia's number, exhaling in relief as she heard her friend's voice.

'Any news?'

'I haven't gone in yet,' Shyama whispered, getting up and going out to the corridor so she could talk at normal volume.

'You just caught me between my 11 o'clock bulimic and my midday self-harmer. Great timing.' Lydia's cool, measured voice felt like balm.

Shyama's shoulders dropped an inch. 'Think I need a free session on your psycho-couch right now.'

'That's what last night was for. Therapy without the lying-down-and-box-of-tissues bit. And as I told you then—'

'I know.' Shyama sighed. '*Que sera sera* and all that. Out of my hands. It sounds more palatable in Spanish somehow.'

'Oh, hang on a minute, Shyams. Got another call coming through . . . stay there . . .'

Before she could tell her that they could talk later, Shyama was put on hold. She looked across the corridor at her fellow patients, absorbed in old copies of *Country Life*. They were all, as the French so politely put it, women *d'un certain âge*, maturing like fine wine or expensive cheese, ripening into what might be regarded in some cultures as their prime years, when the children had flown the nest, the husband had mellowed, and the time left was spent in contemplation, relaxation and generally being revered. She, Lydia and Priya had talked about this very subject last night at their local tapas bar, the three of them hooting gales of garlicky laughter.

Lydia had started it. 'Did you know that some Native American tribes actually used to hold menopause ceremonies? A sort of party to celebrate the end of the slog of childbearing?'

'A party?' Priya said doubtfully, wrinkling her perfectly pert nose. 'Must have been a laugh a minute.'

'Oh, I can see that,' Shyama chipped in. 'Dancing round a bonfire of all your old maxi pads. Bring your own hot flush.'

Priya snorted a considerable amount of white wine out of both nostrils, grabbing a serviette to mask her splutters. She looked a decade younger than Shyama, though she wasn't. She managed a huge office, two children, a husband and ageing in-laws who lived with her, batch-cooked gourmet Indian meals and froze them in labelled Tupperware, and always wore four-inch heels. She would have made Shyama feel resentfully inadequate if it wasn't for her expansive generosity and her frank admission of several business-trip affairs.

'A little respect, please, for the wise women who came before us,' Lydia intoned, mock seriously. 'Apparently feathers and drums featured heavily, plus some spirited dancing and the imbibing of naturally sourced hallucinogenics. The point was, they didn't see the menopause as this terrible curse, they welcomed it, celebrated it. Because it meant you were passing into your next and maybe most important phase of life – the powerful matriarchal elder, the badly behaved granny, take your pick.'

'Dress it up how you want, honey.' Priya was filling her glass again. 'No amount of druggy dancing is going to make me feel any better about intimate dryness.'

'They saw it as a beginning, not an end. Imagine, a whole tribe of cackling, don't-give-a-toss hags proudly sailing their bodies into old age. Who's up for it?'

They had decided they would do just that, once that hormonal watershed had been crossed. Find a leafy spot on Wanstead Flats, gather a tribe of fellow crones – the three of them plus a few of the game birds from their Bodyzone class – choose a full-moon night and chant defiantly at the skies, 'What do we want? Respect! Adoration! Our right to exist as non-fertile yet useful attractive women! When do we want it? As soon as someone notices us, thanks awfully, sorry to bother you.' Or something a little more snappy.

But it wouldn't be like that, Shyama realized now, the phone still to her ear, humming with electronic silence. It would rain, someone would tread in dog poo, they would have to fight for a spot amongst the cottagers and illicit couplings, and after two minutes of embarrassed mumbling, Lydia would suggest they repair to a nearby wine bar where they would crack self-deprecating jokes about their changing bodies over a shared bag of low-fat crisps. Besides, nowadays no one had to have a real menopause. You could just ignore it, take the drugs which keep a woman's body in a permanent state of faux fertility and parade around in hot chick's clothing, long after the eggs had left the building. A whole phase of life wiped away, glossed over, hushed up, for as long as you could get away with it. And given how society treated older women, why the hell not?

'Shyams? Still there?'

'Lyd – I think I'm next . . .'

Shyama stood aside as Mrs Bindman exited the consulting room. Shyama noticed that her skirt was slightly askew, a child-like muss of hair at the back of her head confirming a session on Mr Lalani's examination couch. Oh, but the smile she carried, softening every angle and crisp crease of her. It must have been a good-news day.

'Got clients up until five, then I'm all yours,' Lydia got in quickly.

Shyama muttered a brief goodbye and returned to the desk, where she waited until the receptionist looked up brightly.

'Do go in, Mrs Shaw, and so sorry for the wait.' And then more softly, 'It was a bit of an emergency appointment, thank you for being so patient.'

Shyama forgave most things when accompanied by impeccable manners. She hesitated, then said, 'I always thought hell would turn out to be some kind of waiting room. Sort of weird that this is in here.'

The receptionist looked confused.

'Your sticker?'

'Oh, that!' The receptionist laughed, and it really did sound as if Tinkerbell had fallen down a small flight of steps. 'That's not mine. I'm just filling in for Joyce. She's off sick.'

Shyama had never known Joyce's name but remembered the middle-aged, comfy woman who usually greeted her with a doleful smile.

'I just thought . . . your earrings.'

'Oh, these!' The receptionist briefly touched one of the engraved silver discs. 'My boyfriend got them in Camden. Pretty pattern, isn't it?'

'Mmm. Anyway, sorry to hear Joyce's off. I'll discuss my spooky-sticker theory with her when she's back.'

The receptionist hesitated, then lowered her voice. 'I don't think she'll be coming back. Poor Joyce. Who'd have thought it?'

Shyama battled with an image of matronly, sad-eyed Joyce standing on a pile of self-help books whilst looping a dressing-gown cord around her neck, all the way down the corridor and into the hushed beige of Mr Lalani's private consulting room.

'I wish I could give you more encouraging news, but I want to be completely honest with you, Mrs Shaw.'

Mr Lalani held her gaze; he really was absurdly good-looking with his mane of salt-and-pepper hair and limpid brown eyes – Omar Sharif in *Doctor Zhivago* but with better teeth.

'No. I mean, yes, I appreciate that.'

She always put on nice underwear for her visits here, pathetic as that was. Like the old joke about the busy mum who gives herself a quick wipe with a flannel before her gynae appointment; once she's on the couch, her doctor clears his throat (why are they usually men?) and tells her, 'You really didn't need to go to so much effort.' She has used the very flannel her four-year-old employed to wash her doll that morning with glitter soap. It was amusing the first time Shyama heard it. She had heard it several times now, attributed to different people, some of them famous. One of the urban myths that she and her fellow travellers shared in their many waiting rooms. Except she wasn't one of them any more.

'Mrs Shaw? Can I get you some water, perhaps?'

'No. Really, I'm fine. I'm just . . . surprised. Because, well, I've managed one before, haven't I? A child, I mean.'

'Yes, of course. And I hope that's some comfort, though I know this isn't what you wanted to hear. But you had your daughter nineteen years ago. Your body was very different then. And, of course, I am pretty certain at that point you did not have the problems that . . .'

Mr Lalani became pleasant background noise, though Shyama remembered to nod knowingly as she caught the odd word drifting by – 'Laparoscopy . . . endometriosis . . . ICSI . . . IUI . . . IVF . . .' – soothing as a mantra in their familiarity. She had a strange and not unpleasant sensation of floating above her body, looking down at the smartish, attractive-ish woman in her casual yet edgy outfit, looking rather good for forty-eight (because of her Asian genes, you know – black don't crack, brown don't frown) and feeling surprisingly calm. Ridiculous to expect there wouldn't be some issues at her age; women half her age had issues. There were plenty of other options, surely?

'. . . very few other options available, I'm afraid.'

Shyama blinked, came back to earth with an uncomfortable lurch. 'What? Sorry, I missed that last . . . paragraph, actually.'

Mr Lalani's eyes softened. Only on men could wrinkles look empathetic. 'I'm sorry if I'm not being clear. Let me discard the jargon for a moment.'

His archaic use of language and impeccable grammar hinted at expensive foreign schooling. She had been seeing him for over a year, the third expert during two years of trying, and still knew nothing about his life. The discreet gold band confirmed a wife, presumably a family. How many children had he fathered, or helped create? How many women had sat here in this chair and received his judgement like a benediction or a curse?

9

'. . . very little point in pursuing IVF or any other kind of assisted reproduction. Even seeking donor eggs would not solve the issue of your inhospitable womb and the dangers of attempting to carry a child yourself.'

An inhospitable womb! There, she had been looking for a title for her autobiography. It was a game she played with her girl-friends; every so often, usually when one of them was going through a particularly challenging life phase – rebellious children, a recalcitrant partner, money slipping through their fingers like mercury. So far her favourite title had come from Priya, who had proffered *In These Shoes?* Later on, Shyama found out that 'In These Shoes' was the title of a song, but still, coming from Priya at that moment, it had seemed like poetry.

'Of course, it is always your choice. You can get a second opinion, many women do. But the medical facts remain as they are. I am sorry.'

'So it's me, then?' Shyama exhaled. 'I mean, I know Toby has passed all his tests with flying colours. Well, he would, wouldn't he? Thirty-four-year-old men, that's their prime, isn't it? And he loves red meat, though we try and limit the lamb chops to once a week. Or is it zinc you have to eat? Is that in eggs? Eggs have good cholesterol now, don't they? And after all the warnings they gave us . . . so doctors can be wrong. You just find out way after the event, usually.'

Mr Lalani let the silence settle, mote by mote, like fine dust. He had been here many times before. He knew not to argue or over-sympathize. He knew it is always best to let the woman – and it is almost invariably the woman – talk and cry and vent her rage at the world, at Nature who has betrayed her. At forty-eight, the betrayal was almost inevitable. Not that he would ever say that out loud.

'As I said, Mrs Shaw, please feel free to seek a second opinion, I assure you I won't be offended. I just don't want to raise your hopes and see you spend even more money.'

'Well, there's not much more of it to be spent, I'm afraid!' Shyama attempted a breezy chuckle, which sounded more like a ragged, repressed sob. 'Toby's got some temporary work, but he's looking for something better . . .'

She knew how this sounded. It sounded exactly as her mother and some others presumed it was. Silly older woman of modest means falls for predictably handsome younger man without a steady career. She gets an ego boost and unbounded energy in bed; he gets use of the house and the car, and the soft-mattress landing of her unspoken gratitude. He kisses the scars left from a disastrous marriage – there's not much that youthful tenderness cannot mend. He says he loves her, he wants a life with her. Above all, he would love a child with her. He is kind towards her daughter – he treads that fine line between friend and guardian, but never tries to be her father. (She has one of those, occasional as he is.) There are only fifteen years between Toby and Tara – why on earth would she want to call him Daddy? Tara didn't call her own father that.

'Mrs Shaw? Maybe you want to discuss this further with your husband before making any decisions? Perhaps you and Mr Shaw would like to make an appointment to come and see me together?'

Shyama ought to tell him now – this gentle man who had navigated his way around her reproductive system like a zealous plumber, undaunted by the leaks, blockages and unexpected U-bends that confronted him – that she was not, in fact, Mrs Shaw. Never had been. That in a fit of misplaced modesty she had assumed Toby's surname when they had begun this whole process four years ago. She had hurriedly reassured Toby that this was not some devious feminine wile to trap him into marriage, as she was pretty sure she never wanted to marry again – nothing personal. But she had to admit that some part of her felt, well, embarrassed to be publicly declaring their fertility issues as a co-habiting couple. She knew it was one of the few traditional tics she had left, stemming from the part of her which she always imagined to be a middle-aged Indian woman in an overtight sari blouse and bad perm, standing at her shoulder clucking, 'Chi chi chi! Sex and babies and no wedding ring? And none of your clever-schever arguments about Indians doing it all the time and everywhere and look at population and old naughty statues. Kama Sutra was always meant for married peoples only!'

Shyama often wished her Punjabi Jiminy Cricket wasn't so lippy. And spoke better English. Besides, Toby had pointed out several times that declaring themselves to be a married couple wouldn't guarantee them a faster or better result.

'I mean, look at who gets knocked up the quickest. Pissed teen-agers under a pile of coats at a party. I'm pretty sure marriage is the last thing on their minds . . .'

'That's because they're teenagers, Toby. Youth is the one thing we can't put on the overdraft.'

The elephant in the room had woken up and scratched itself, sending a few ornaments crashing to the floor. There, she had said it out loud. They both knew that it didn't matter how many sit-ups and seaweed wraps and nips and tucks a woman went through to pass herself off as a decade younger. In an age where you could cougar your way around town with a wrinkle-free smile, inside you were not as old as you felt, but as old as you actually were.

'Mrs Shaw?'

Shyama rose unsteadily, the room swimming into focus.

12

She gathered herself, layer by layer, each one hardening into a protective skin. She and her inhospitable womb left the building.

Outside the world still turned, the sky a torn grey rag pulled apart by a restless wind, behind each jagged seam a glimpse of blue so bright that Shyama had to look away. She walked blindly past the gracious four-storey mansions, like rows of faded wedding cakes with their tiered creamy façades and stucco doorways flanked with pillars, once rich family homes with servants in the basement and attic. Now the airy drawing rooms welcomed international medical tourists and the locals who could afford to pay, the basement kitchens where floury-armed women used to dice carrots and stuff chickens now given over to hi-tech equipment and strobing green screens, where bodies were tested and assessed.

The wind buffeted Shyama across the A40, the main arterial road running east to west, always pulsing with traffic, the steady drum and bass of London throbbing in time to her own heartbeat. She found herself in Regent's Park as a weak sun finally broke through, starkly yellow against the heavy clouds, the light so fluid in the breeze she wanted to open her mouth and take great gulps of it, willing it deep into her body, the body that had let her down.

Shyama found a space on a bench, next to a mother trying to persuade her apple-cheeked toddler to take a sip from a fluorescent plastic beaker. The child, almost rigid in her quilted snowsuit, all four limbs starfish-spread, shook her head slowly and gravely from side to side, as if she was frankly disappointed with her mother for even trying this on. Everywhere there were children swaddled in warm layers, being wheeled in buggies, trotted after on tricycles and scooters or waddling along like demented ducklings, giddy with freedom, entranced by their own feet and shadows, squealing with joy, all the pre-schoolers whose carers needed to exercise them like puppies to avoid tantrums at bedtime. Shyama could just about remember Tara at this age, sensory memories mostly: the smell of her after a bath, nectar-sweet and kiss-curled; sitting in her stripy booster seat at the table, mashing spaghetti between her fingers with fascinated concentration; her laugh, which sounded unnervingly like her crying. There were so many occasions when Shyama had rushed upstairs expecting to find her trapped under the wardrobe or missing a digit, only to discover her sitting in a circle of her soft toys, serving up tea in plastic cups and chuckling loudly like an over-eager dinner host. Tara's own favourite memory – and she claims it is her first – is when she was about fourteen months old. She had cut her two bottom teeth and Shyama suspected the top two were also trying to push their way out, so she told Tara to open wide so Mummy could have a quick feel of her gums. And as soon as her finger was in, Tara clamped her mouth shut.

'It was like being savaged by a piranha, honestly!' Shyama said, dressing it up a little just to see Tara's delight in the retelling. 'I mean, whoever thinks babies aren't strong . . . the power in those little jaws – I couldn't get it out. And the worst thing was you thought it was a game. The more I yelled and said let go, the more you laughed and laughed. But without letting go. You laughed through clenched teeth like some mad little goblin. That was the disturbing bit.'

'No,' said Tara. 'I knew it wasn't a game. I remember thinking, that's hurting Mummy but I can't stop. It's too much fun. That's the really disturbing bit, wouldn't you say?'

Tara then tossed her hair, or rather her hair plus the extensions she'd insisted on adding to the defiant bird's nest perched on her head. Shyama had made the mistake once of telling Tara her theory that an Indian woman's virtue was measured by her hair. Respectable women – in the movies and paintings, on the street – always had long straight tresses untouched by perm or primping, tamed into matriarchal buns or thick tight plaits hanging heavy like stunned black snakes. Only wild 'junglee' women or women in mourning uncoiled the serpents and set them free. The shorter and wilder the haircut, the looser the morals, wasn't that the inference? It was only a theory, but within days Tara's hair seemed to have grown up and out by several inches. Shyama's, meanwhile, was getting longer, as if she was trying to blow-dry her way back into respectability. Well, too late for that now. Divorced, toy boy in tow and a stranger for a daughter. Who would have seen that coming?

An ice-cream van pulled up at the park entrance and chimed out 'The Teddy Bears' Picnic', the dissonant notes dancing into the park and sprinkling on the shifting wind. It worked. Every child suddenly stopped mid-activity, ears pricked, sniffing the air expectantly. They are like little animals, Shyama thought as several of them started galloping towards the siren call, pulling adults with them. Others less fortunate were told Not Before Tea and the coordinated wailing began. The fury of injustice made them cry louder, but No Means No and Life Isn't Fair – best you learn that one early. Shyama's mother had told her that when that jingle sounded it meant that the ice-cream man had just run out of ice cream and was on his way home. For years, Shyama wondered why he always seemed to finish his supplies just as he reached her house. When the truth finally dawned, she couldn't decide if she was horrified by her mother's cruel lie or impressed by it. How odd it was that children believe anything we tell them

15

for years, and then one day mistrust every word that comes out of our mouths. Why did she want to do this again?

A faint beep sounded from the depths of Shyama's overstuffed handbag. She rummaged amongst her usual debris of tissues and vitamin-pill bottles and a half-read newspaper until she found her mobile. A text from Toby. 'All OK?' She hesitated. She didn't want to talk to him yet. She wasn't quite sure what she was going to say or even how she felt . . . Doomed and defiant in alternating waves. Of course, she could call him back and quote him any number of women who had defied the odds and given birth way past their medical sell-by date: that woman who was a judge on some dancing talent show, she was forty-nine when she popped one out, wasn't she? With a grown-up daughter, like Shyama herself. Probably all those years of pliés kept her fit and flexible. What was her name? Then, of course, there were all those OAPs who Zimmer-framed their way to that notorious Italian doctor who got them pregnant, though she recalled that one of them had died before her daughter's fourth birthday. She had been a single parent, too. What had happened to that child, she wondered? Who would explain to her that Mummy had spent her savings having her in her sixties, had brought her into this world only to depart it soon after from cancer, rumoured to have been triggered by the amount of drugs and hormones she'd imbibed in order to create and sustain a life she would not see into double figures. Shyama's finger hovered over Toby's number. Why did she want to carry on with this?

And then, on cue, because the universe sometimes works that way (or at least we like to think it does, so we create patterns from random collisions and see omens and signs in every coincidence, otherwise what's the alternative? Accepting that we are merely random specks flicked around by the gnarly finger of

16

indifference?), the apple-cheeked toddler returned. She was still in her buggy, but now holding an ice-cream cone triumphantly between her fat fists. It was already beginning to melt; vanilla tears were making their way down the rippled orange cone on to the little girl's fingers. As her mother braved an approach with a wet wipe, the child looked up and smiled the way only children can – in the moment and with unadorned purity. Shyama's guts clenched, holding on to nothing, muscles contracting around an empty space waiting to be filled. In a year's time, she would look back at this moment and tell herself, there, that was the brief window when you could have recognized this yearning for what it really was, the ten seconds when you could have made a different choice and walked into a different future. But instead, she picked up her bag and wandered over to the playground, her phone to her ear, waiting for Toby to answer her call.

'Ew, sir! Sir! That pig's dead, innit?'

Toby looked up from the sty to face a row of schoolkids with their faces pressed against the iron railings, wild delight in their eyes at the prospect of seeing a real-live dead thing.

'There! In the corner! Can we touch it?'

Toby whirled round, dry-mouthed. Christ, maybe he'd inadvertently stepped on one of the piglets – he had been so distracted since Shyama's call. A quick glance at Priscilla confirmed she was still sprawled on her side, eyes shut, whilst her recent litter fought their squealing, desperate battle to find and hold on to a teat. It was an undignified scramble with piglets kicking each other's snouts and climbing over each other's heads to get to the milk. It reminded him of the buffet queue at a Punjabi wedding that Shyama had dragged him to, not long after they had first met.

'This,' she had told him, 'is what's known as a trial by fire. Not unlike the one that Sita had to walk through in order to prove her purity to Ram. Don't ask now, we're doing Hinduism on Wednesday. Today is Meet the Family day – all of them in one place, plus all their friends, acquaintances, hangers-on, people we don't like but have to invite because we went to their kids' weddings, and anyone else who will want to gossip about us, which is everyone. This is what's known as the one-rip-and-it's-off approach.'

'You're not going to make me take my trousers off and pretend it's some ancient Indian custom, are you?' Toby was only half joking.

'No, though that's tempting. When you have to take off a plaster, there are two ways, aren't there? You can pick up a teeny corner and try to peel it off really slowly, wincing and hurting all the way. Or—'

'One rip and it's off?'

'Exactly. Me and you becoming an item is possibly the biggest scandal on the Birmingham kitty-party circuit since Uncle Baseen's son announced he was gay two days into his honeymoon and ran off with the cocktail waiter.'

'I'm not sure we could top that.'

'Well, you're the wrong colour, you live in a bedsit, and wait till they find out how old you are.'

'You don't have to tell them, do you?'

'No, I don't have to. I just want to. Ready?'

They were standing at the rear of a purpose-built banqueting suite, a low-roofed concrete building that from the back could have been a factory or a modest shopping mall, except for the garlands of fairy lights festooned over every available inch of outside wall. 'The only man-made structure in the West Midlands visible from space,' Shyama told him as they pulled into the car

18

park, her ancient hatchback out of place amongst the Mercedes and Lexuses with their personalized number plates. Now they were standing outside the car, trying to ignore the slight drizzle that had just started, and Shyama was waiting for Toby to say yes. Or go home. Those were his choices. Toby had never liked an ultimatum; he reached decisions slowly, almost unconsciously, letting the seeds of the pros and cons settle into the primal mulch in his back brain whilst he got on with something physical like chopping logs or mucking out a sty. Then hours later, when he was thinking of nothing in particular, the answer would bud and unfold, and it was always the right one because it came to him. He didn't chase it. He wasn't prepared to chase this woman he had only known for six months either.

Their meeting had been like one of those moments you read about or see in cheesy films but never think is actually going to happen to you. Not to someone like him, at least, who didn't even like surprises. It had been six years ago, not long after his twenty-eighth birthday. He had been clearing out one of the stables. Then he had heard this voice, this guffaw, deep and full-throated enough to make him turn. She had been laughing at the rabbits, a child at either side of her. Not hers but Priya's, he found out in due course. An hour later, she'd asked for his number and in a daze he'd given it. Dates followed swiftly, increasingly; she always suggested the venue or event: restaurants he had never heard of, bars he would never have gone into without her, films he would not have chosen but usually loved. She took the lead, but subtly, without ever making him feel he didn't have a choice. And he kept choosing to say yes.

And now here they were, in a car park in Birmingham, on the verge of their first and maybe last row. She stood, hands on hips, only a couple of inches shorter than him, but in this mood seeming feet taller. Her normally unruly hair was a straight sheet of dark brown with red streaks. ('I nearly did the full Sharon Osborne after the divorce,' she told him. 'Short and traffic-light scarlet. But I haven't got the guts. Or the cheek-bones.') She was wearing a sari, red and black shot through with gold thread, very dressy. He was used to seeing her in work clothes: casual suits, mannish jackets. It sounded stupid, but he hadn't thought of her as Indian until now. The sari – what was it, just a long piece of material? – clung to her generous bust and revealed a waist and hips he knew by touch rather than sight; the jewels at her neck and on her wrists imitated the raindrops caught like tiny prisms in her hair. She looked so . . . foreign, like one of the busty beauties pouting out of the painted mural in his local Indian restaurant. What used to be his local – in fact, the only one within a twenty-mile radius of the Suffolk village he used to call home. Eating an occasional chicken tikka masala was the nearest he had ever come to Indian culture. And now her. Doe-eyed, firm-jawed, angle-browed, soft-curved, older than him, dark to his blond, pugilist to his pacifist – too many contra-dictions to work. Then he caught a glimmer of something in her eyes. Those eyes; he wasn't a poetic man but they made him think of chocolate, fresh earth and twisted sheets. Beyond the brown was something he recognized from years of tending to unwanted animals, a kind of fear or maybe a resigned accep-tance that however much you barked and spat, in the end some-one was going to kick you where it hurt. He realized she didn't want to fight. She wanted to get in first before he disappointed her. I never want to disappoint you, was his first thought, and his second caught him by surprise. That he loved her already.

'Shall we?' He smiled, offering her his arm with a self-consciously gallant swoop.

20

She raised one eyebrow, Bollywood style. 'Don't say I didn't warn you, sweetie.'

'There! In the corner! Nah, behind you! Behind you!'

Feeling like an unwelcome pantomime dame, Toby peered into the far corner, where sunlight couldn't penetrate the overhanging tin canopy, and saw the outline of a motionless prone piglet. He scooped it up in one fluid movement, shielding it from the little darlings now baying for blood.

'Is it dead then? Can we see?'

The piglet was barely breathing; each tiny inhalation seemed a mighty effort.

'Fighting for life' made sense to anyone who had held the runt of any litter, battling its early and inevitable demise. He'd seen so many of them and still didn't understand why Nature bothered creating them in the first place. What was the point, throwing together a weaker, smaller version of a species just so its mother could reject it, its siblings bully it and some other passing predator get a free and easy meal? Maybe it was the Darwinian equivalent of the naughty step, a way of warning your kids to behave, of reminding them how hard life could be and how lucky they were. Maybe Priscilla had lined up all her piggy kids this morning before opening hours and pointed a quivering trotter at their unfortunate brother, coughing in the corner.

'If you don't listen to Mummy and eat all your swill, that's where you'll end up. All eighteen of you. Take a good look. That could have been you.'

The piglet gave a little quiver as if he was reading Toby's thoughts. He wouldn't last the night, not unless they chucked money, time and resources they didn't have at him. In any case, not intervening was policy at Broadside City Farm.

'We want the children to have as authentic an experience as we can give them,' Jenny Palmer, the farm manager, had told him on his first day. Jenny was an earnest, friendly sort and had tried very hard to look as if she lived on the premises and was up at sparrow's fart to milk the herd. But Toby had already clocked the designer wellies and the line where the fake tan ended and her neck began. What did he care? He was grateful to have a job, even a temporary one such as this.

'You have to remember,' Jenny continued, 'that many of these children have never even seen a real cow or a pig or a horse. They have no idea that vegetables come from the ground. Many of them don't even have gardens . . .' She shook her head sadly.

Toby tutted in what he hoped was a sympathetic manner.

'So that's why we have to let them just come here and be. Explore. Breathe. But this is a working farm. We sell our milk and eggs and meat, as you know, and we don't want to shield the children from that either. They need to know how we make our food – that all those cute little piggies will end up as bacon. And if an animal is sick or dies, well, we let them see that too. I mean, if it happens during opening hours, obviously. Otherwise we put it on the website. The most important thing is, we let Nature take its course as far as possible and we don't interfere.'

Toby wanted to ask what 'as far as possible' actually meant. If a fox broke into the henhouse and they caught it in the act, would they just sit back and enjoy the majesty of a good feathery massacre? Could they shoot or poison rats? Or drown the kittens they couldn't give away? He knew the answer to the last one: kittens were cute, and nothing cute deserved death, apparently. Just the under-achieving uglies that no one really wanted anyway.

The children's whooping stopped as Toby turned round and

made his way carefully towards the gate of the sty. They vied with each other for a good look at the piglet. Some of the girls oohed and aahed, wanting to stroke it. The boys laughed, pointing at its tiny spiral of a tail, its muddy snout. The boys always laughed, at least the ones over the age of eight, when it seemed to become deeply uncool to show any kind of emotion other than mockery. But when no one was looking, they were all the same, all these hard-nosed, urban, feral kids on their school trips. Alone and unobserved, they talked to the animals, private crooning conversations, offered them inappropriately sugary snacks from their lunchboxes, ventured tentative strokes of furry ears and velvety muzzles. Toby knew that under all the bolshy backchat, their first instinct was to be kind. Maybe that's why runts were created, he mused. Not to encourage us to kill the weakest, but to help them.

'He's not dead,' Toby said loudly as he eased his way out of the swinging iron gate, careful not to jostle any of the chattering schoolchildren, all runny-nosed and red-cheeked.

'He looks rough, man!' laughed one lad at the back.

'Can you make him better?' asked a voice at his elbow.

A young girl – mixed race, Toby guessed. He'd learned not to say 'coloured' any more after Shyama had threatened him with violence the first time he'd used the term in front of her.

'*Coloured?* Sorry, have we just slipped through a hole in the time and space continuum and landed in 1971? Maybe you'd like to call me Little Lady and smack my arse while you're at it.'

He would have quite liked to do both, but he guessed that would also be a big mistake.

'Listen, there weren't any col— different races of people where I grew up . . .'

'Except those nice smiley Bengalis in the local curry house,' Shyama sneered.

'Well yes – except they weren't Bengali. They were Kashmiri. And they couldn't go home – lots of trouble there, apparently. Riz left a wife behind. Awful story. My mum was always inviting him over. He always came but he never ate much except for the chips. Probably a bit too bland. My mum thought brown sauce was a step too far. He's a bloody mean darts player though, Riz . . .' He trailed off, wondering which bit of his story had offended her most.

Instead she pulled him to her and kissed him so hard, his head swam.

'You're a good man, Toby. And the nice thing is, you don't know you are. Hope it lasts.'

That was in the early days, when they danced around each other, pulled and pushed by lust and longing, wondering and dreading who would walk away first. Though if ever there was a time to cut and run, Toby guessed this might be it. Before they started a process that would tie them together irrevocably.

'Can you make him better?'

This girl was stunning, blue eyes against burnished skin, hair like a dandelion clock, so full and fine he wanted to blow on it and see if it would break into feathery seeds and fly away. Is this what his children with Shyama would have looked like? People said that mixed-race kids were especially beautiful, maybe getting the best of each gene pool. He didn't know why, but he liked the thought of it. And the thought that he might never have a child with Shyama made him feel so weak and empty that he stumbled for a second, provoking a good-natured cheer from the slowly dispersing audience.

Toby sat on a nearby hay bale to steady his breathing. Where

24

had that come from? He'd never wanted a kid before, even when confronted by one as adorable as the little girl who was now back at his side, staring at the shivering piglet. He'd never been one of those men who had an urgent desire to scatter their seed far and wide to ensure their immortality. He'd had one scare, some years back now, with his first long-term girlfriend, who had run out of their small shared bathroom in a fury, waving a plastic stick in Toby's face.

'Negative! See? You can't even do that properly!'

What had annoyed him was that he hadn't even known she was trying to get pregnant. She had just assumed that because they had got engaged and were discussing wedding plans, why not? He called the relationship off the next day, horrified when he imagined what would have happened if her plan had worked. There would have been no paternal outpouring of joy, no swelling of his manly breast at the news that his boys had got in there, done the job and done it good, he was sure of that. Maybe he had spent too long around animals, watching reproduction in all its messy, grunting reality and clinical efficiency, attended by bored farmhands and busy vets, where it was merely a process that would keep mothers breeding and babies coming so bills could be paid.

The little girl extended a gentle finger and stroked the piglet along its heaving back. Her clumsy tenderness stirred a kind of yearning in Toby, full and bittersweet. He had always considered himself to be an ordinary man in every way: average at school, OK-looking, modest ambitions, not the kind of bloke you'd notice in a room full of people, but if you had a drink with him, the kind of bloke you might want to see again. 'Solid' was an adjective he provoked in others, steady and unexciting as timber. He had always assumed he would find a regular job in some branch of

25

animal husbandry or agriculture, settle down with a nice local girl with dimpled knees and cheery common sense and live a contented, uneventful life. Good enough for most of the human race. But then, what was that Chinese curse? 'May you live in interesting times'? Since colliding with Shyama's unapologetic sun, everything he had mapped out was thrown into stark relief; the world he thought he had created and occupied so fully had revealed itself to be a mere speck of leaf litter eddying on a fast-flowing river. Time wasn't linear or graded, as he had always assumed, it was unpredictable, relentless motion. This was a lot to take in for an average kind of man. This is what he wanted to tell her, but he never found the words, and on the rare occasions he did, his mouth was too busy kissing her.

The day they did Hinduism – and yes, it had been a Wednesday – Toby had been flicking through a child's picture book of Hindu gods (she had told him not to take this too personally) and had paused at one illustration of a blue-skinned deity with heavily lidded, blissful eyes. What struck Toby, however, was his mouth, half open, a tiny galaxy of stars, moons and comets within it.

'What's he swallowed?' Toby asked her.

She paused, looking up briefly from the family photo album that had diverted her attention. 'He hasn't swallowed anything. He holds it in his mouth.'

'What?'

'The universe.'

She then spent another ten minutes trying to explain how the gods were both part of everything and yet also created every-thing, but he wasn't really listening. He was too astounded by this image of a universe within a mouth, the infinite residing within the ordinary. He knew this was important, maybe the most important thing he had ever discovered in his life, if only he could articulate it.

He still couldn't, but remembering that feeling led him quite easily to name the one that overwhelmed him now. And he realized it was true that he did not want *a* baby. He wanted his and Shyama's baby. And if they had to seduce Nature into cooperating with them or pummel her into submission, so be it. Despite today's bad news, they would keep trying. Anything.

'He won't die, will he?' the child at his side asked anxiously.

'No,' said Toby, in a blatant violation of company policy. 'He will be fine.'

As Shyama reached her front door, it swung open to reveal her mother, Sita, with a tea towel in her hands, as always.

Sita cocked her head on one side like a small bird, neat, bright-eyed, her silver hair coming away from its loose bun. 'You're early! I was just doing some tidying.'

Shyama ignored the subtle rebuke – the breakfast dishes were rarely cleared before she and Toby dashed out of the house in the morning – and instead gave her mother a swift hug. She was shocked to discover that her mother seemed to have shrunk, her head barely reaching Shyama's shoulder, and that beneath the comfy leisurewear top her bones felt brittle and delicate. One hard squeeze and she might shatter. Shyama followed her mother into the kitchen, noticing the slight curve in her shoulders and her gentle, uneven gait.

'Your back playing up, Ma?'

'Oh, you know. How about nicecuppatea?'

It always tickled her, hearing her parents peppering their conversation with what they imagined to be casual English banter. It was even funnier when there was a group of them, when the cards club or kitty-party stalwarts met up, their loud Punjabi spliced with Enid Blyton slang such as 'That takes the biscuit!' or 'Mind your business, loafer!' or 'You hop it, bloody fool!'

'Oh and Tara's friends are here,' Sita added pointedly.

Shyama sighed. She had planned to flop on the sofa and eat her way through the biscuit tin. Instead, Tara and an assortment of her student friends were doing just that.

In amongst the tangle of limbs and empty crisp packets she recognized a few familiar faces – the pretty blonde girl and her razor-cheekboned surly boyfriend – Tara sitting between them and some god-awful show at full volume on the television. Tara barely looked up at her mother's loud hello, glued to the screen, where a group of silicone-busted, orange-skinned young women were watching two other luminous-toothed girls trying to pull each other's hair extensions out.

'Sorry!' Shyama raised her voice, not sorry at all, but actually bloody fed up and in need of a good cry. 'Could you . . . ?'

Tara huffed loudly and grabbed the remote, reducing the volume by one bar.

'Hi, everyone.' Shyama made an effort to sound friendly, though she barely got grunts in return. 'Thought you had a screening today?'

'Four o'clock. We're going in a minute . . . ohmygod, did you see that?'

The whole sofa erupted in whoops and cheers. One of the orange women had decided to join in the fight, her pneumatic mammaries strangely motionless as she administered some ineffectual slaps with tiny taloned hands.

'So this is part of your course, is it, watching these crappy reality shows?' Shyama enquired.

'Yes, actually.' Tara shot her a brief glance. 'And it's called Structured Reality, as it happens.'

'What's structured about it?' asked Shyama. 'It just looks like a cat fight in a strip club.'

'Maybe, but it's real.'

'A reality show, like I said.'

'No, actually, because what the producers do is get a bunch of real people and create storylines and situations out of their real lives, so Becca and Tiggy have been actually dating the same guy for weeks and they've only just found out.'

'So they don't watch their own programme then?'

'Well, I dunno, maybe it was filmed ages ago, but anyway, Mindy's the real bitch in all this because she's only stirring it because she's after Ade herself and they made her blurt it out in the bar in front of everyone.'

'Who's "they"?'

'The producers. More dramatic, isn't it? Otherwise she would have just put it on social media, like normal people.'

'So it's producers manipulating abnormal yet real people pretending to be very bad actors?'

'No, it's the next stage in the evolution of the documentary genre,' sighed Tara, rolling her eyes at her mates, who were all studying the same Media and Culture course as she was, although, unlike her, most of them lived away from the parental home. Tara had rejected any thought of leaving London to study, saying it was pointless as she only intended to live and work in the capital when she graduated. That's if she didn't get a job in New York or South America. She had ambitious and admirable plans for the future; however, what she hadn't planned on was being turned down for university accommodation as the family home was too close to her college. So she had ended up living at home and commuting for study. Just like school, but with more unexpected playdates and sleepovers with her mates whenever they fancied a bit of home cooking and all-night TV.

'You know, I could just drive you down to the local psychiatric ward and you could have a good laugh at the looneys.'

Finally everyone looked up at Shyama. She had meant it as a joke. She wanted to explain that this was a reference to how the Victorians got their kicks from watching the mad and the maimed, and how such programmes seemed to be an extension of the same soulless voyeurism. (It wasn't her theory, she'd read it in a Sunday supplement in one of her endless waiting rooms.) Clearly this gathering was not impressed in the slightest. Who was she kidding? This was the generation who were defined by their new-media narcissism. Without an audience somewhere, they simply did not exist. I tweet, therefore I am. And at this moment Shyama suddenly saw herself in Tara's furious eyes: a sour-faced, middle-aged woman who didn't know when to shut up.

Tara flicked off the television and on cue the gaggle rose up, murmuring their thanks as they sloped out.

'See you later,' Tara muttered as she tried to push past Shyama.

'Have you spent any time with Nanima today?'

Tara stopped at the door, waiting till her friends were well out of earshot. She turned to her mother, talking slowly in the same exaggeratedly patient tone that Shyama herself had used on her daughter years ago.

'Yes, as I have been here all day and you haven't. And yes, I have keys and money, and yes, I will text you on my way home. Anything else?'

The bird's nest on her head had grown; it had graduated from the size of a sparrow's cottage to something approaching an eagle's luxury apartment, held up by various butterfly slides and sparkly pins. Shyama hoped to God her daughter never got nits again.

'No,' Shyama said, and then, 'I, er . . . went to the doctor today.'

She had no idea why she was broaching this subject with the one person who had always been completely uninterested in it. But she felt so alone; a cold damp grief seemed to be seeping into every bone. She would have liked to hold her child – the only one she would ever have now – and comfort herself that she at least had her.

Tara's expression didn't change. 'OK.'

'And, well, the IVF thing, it's not going to work. I wore my bits out having you!'

'So it's my fault then?' Stung, Tara flicked the intended joke back at her.

'Don't be silly, that's not what I meant.'

'So that's it then, is it?'

Shyama chose to ignore the tiny flame of hope flickering in her daughter's eyes. She knew Tara had spent twenty years as an only child – Shyama's best years in terms of strength and youth – her main focus and only joy during a sad and slowly dying marriage. And instead of flying the nest, her daughter had built one on her head and stayed put.

They stared at each other for a moment. Somewhere in the background Sita clattered pans and hummed an old Hindi film song to herself, the soundtrack of Shyama's childhood, when choices were simple and mostly involved food. They stood in the cluttered hallway, mirroring each other's stance, hands on hips, chins tilted defiantly, each waiting for the other to break the silence.

Only the grandmother of the house, who now hovered in the kitchen doorway holding a dripping colander, could see the ironic

31

symmetry that bound both these women. It was at moments like this that Sita wondered how life might have turned out if they had not left Delhi, but had raised their children as pukka Indians. Shyama might have settled with some nice Army officer with a waxed moustache and a pension, and now be busy arranging Tara's marriage, instead of the two of them standing there shouting at each other like village sweepers. Then again, if they had stayed, she herself would have ended up in a joint family home, cooking for three generations at every mealtime and watching her husband be slowly drained of cash and confidence by his needy family. Easy to be sentimental afterwards about what you might have missed, easy to forget how much worse it could have been. And look at how bad it was now – even from five thousand miles away, their beloved relatives had behaved like dirty snakes in the grass. If it wasn't for her bad knee, she would kick every last one of them up the *bund*. Secret thoughts, delicious and dreadful, that she would keep to herself, for now. She had to behave like a proper matriarch, and with the practised ease of all women who were expected to sacrifice personal desire for public duty, she said, 'What's the matter with you two?'

Tara raised an eyebrow at Shyama, who swallowed a prickly ball of shame. Her mother had no idea that she and Toby had been trying for a baby and this didn't seem the right time to drop that particular bombshell on her sweet silvery head.

As it happened, Shyama didn't have to.

'Mum and Toby were trying for an IVF baby, but it's not going to work, apparently. See you later.' Tara flounced out of the front door, which slammed heavily behind her.

Shyama turned to her mother, who regarded her with a puzzled smile.

'A baby?'

# CHAPTER TWO

IT WAS THE arrival of the tip-top luxury silver fridge that got tongues wagging again, soo-soo-soo, all over the village. Mala first heard it from Cuckoo, a one-eyed, stick-thin boy, who spotted the delivery van huff-chuffing its way along the dirt road. She knew it must be coming to them because the road didn't lead anywhere else. As it got closer she could see that it had some fancy name on its side in red and gold letters, wedding colours all glittered up and showing off, catching the sunlight and throwing it back at them even brighter, just to impress them. Of course, Mala was impressed, though, unlike some of the other slack-jawed idiots in the village, she would not be showing anything other than boredom on her face.

Her husband's mother, Bee-ji, heaved herself up from the charpoy and left her mother-in-law-shouting-at-daughter-in-law TV drama to watch the van chug into the village square, coughing clouds of dust into their mouths like a newly arrived relative.

Mala knew who the delivery was for. Everyone did. It was for the only person in the village who did not come running out to see the *tamasha* but lurked behind her new blue-painted bug screen, shivering in the fierce blast of her new AC unit, all icy cool and waiting.

Two men got out of the van, city sahibs with their Brylcreemed hair and tight trousers, sweating and dusted with red earth, asking for water. Pogle sahib, as village elder, pointed to the well. He wasn't being impolite, Mala understood, no one was going to waste time running indoors to fetch cups and suchlike. Who knows what they might miss? One of the men drank loudly, gulping like a buffalo, the other unrolled some scrunchy paper, pointing to the name everyone already knew was written down there. Pogle sahib stroked his wispy white beard and pointed a bony accusing finger at *her* house, with its gleaming new bricks and proper roof, the only house with a wall around it. Not that it stops anybody knowing everything, Mala reflected bitterly, because even a private belch in your own bed is being sniffed and discussed next door in moments.

And then the back of the van was rolled up like a steel chapatti and the city men trundled the new fridge out on a standing frame that somehow reminded Mala of her papa's funeral stretcher, when the men had had to stand him upright to get him down the bank towards the foaming river. She thought he would fall off, roll all the way down, his white shroud unrolling and unwrapping like the winter rug when they shook out the silverfish. But they didn't drop him, they burned him, and Mala and her mother and sister watched from afar. As women, they were not allowed near the funeral pyre, but they were still close enough to see his skin blacken and crackle like roasting meat and his fingers – the fingers that had fed Mala laddoos and picked leaves from her hair and poked the dimple in her left cheek and called it Shiv-ji's kiss, a blessing on her face – she watched as those same fingers curled in on themselves like sooty claws trying to hold on to them and their old happy life that would never come back.

And so, months later, when Ram said he would take pity on

fatherless Mala with her cursed widow of a mother and unmarried sister, Mala didn't feel she could complain. He was taking her on with virtually no dowry, just a wooden trunk full of second-hand saris and stainless-steel pans. Six months later, there was nothing left in the trunk except the one coconut that wasn't broken at the wedding ceremony, lying at the bottom, poking out of an old tablecloth like the wrinkled brown head of a long-dead baby.

A few of the kids, shoeless, grinning monkey-boys who had clambered into the neem tree from the stone bench at its base, clapped their hands when the fridge finally came out, its shiny steel surface smooth as a mirror. Mala's lip curled at their open-mouthed, silly, greedy faces gasping in its reflection. But she managed to twist the grimace into a sort of smile before anyone noticed. Bee-ji might claim she could not see well enough to make it to the toilet, but she could read Mala's face as expertly as a farmer reads the skies, never missing any passing cloudy look or rainy-day eyes.

The fridge-wallahs didn't manage to reach the house before the husband emerged: new kurta top, new leather chappals – everyone saw them, but pretended they didn't and that they certainly didn't care. He nodded at the men almost sadly, not meeting anyone's eyes, and yet the way he patted the fridge before he beckoned them inside was as if his favourite cow had finally come home.

The new steel gate cling-clanged behind them, and five minutes later Mala heard the kick and kerang of their new generator starting up, which meant that everyone else's electricity would have just cut out. Mala stared at the shiny steel gate, willing Seema, the lucky wife beyond it, to show her face just for one moment, so that she could shoot her a swift, sneaky death-stare. In that look Mala wanted to say to her, 'Our electricity is gone off but in your house there will never be darkness again. There will never be milk that curdles while your back is turned, or ghee that overflows its earthen jars and pools into yellow crusted rivers, or almond-bursting wedding *barfi* that you bury in shade and hope will last but still becomes a sugary palace for tickly bugs, and every one of your drinks will sing with the clink-kiss of crystal-clean ice cubes.' But Seema never appeared.

Mala remembered how Seema used to be before whatever it was happened to her. She would come down to the river to wash clothes with all the other women. Washing was only the background for the real work of talking: who's marrying who, who's fighting or travelling or cheating or hitting. Nothing surprised them. Mala had once visited Chandigarh for a cousin's wedding, startled and energized by the speed and vigour of the city, but surprised at how many doors were shut at night. Even next-door neighbours would smile and disappear inside to be with their widescreen TVs. It was then Mala realized that in the village they saw more real-life non-TV stories than the city-wallahs ever did, because here, there was nowhere to do your business other than your small house or the fields, and people will be people, after all, so you just learned to turn your face away, from your own shame or theirs. It was exactly like when people passed through on the train and saw the farmhands shitting at the side of the tracks, balls to the wind. The passengers looked away, not the labourers, whose doleful faces seemed to say, 'Who asked you to look anyway?'

Mala reflected that Seema must have been a first-class fool if she thought that no one would notice the difference in her. Or spot the lies. She and her husband had said that they and the two children were going all the way to Delhi for a wedding, even though Pogle sahib said he knew their entire family over three

36

generations and no one had ever mentioned any relatives in the capital. When they returned a few weeks later, something had changed. They were all different, as if they had brought back with them an uninvited guest or a very bad smell, and suddenly Seema was fainting in the heat and avoiding unripe mangoes and all the women knew what that meant. Yet Seema did not say a word to anyone, she just came down to the river as usual, and if Mala noticed that she did not scrub the clothes as vigorously as usual or thwack-smack them against the river-glistening stones as forcefully as before, she assumed this was because of the secret hiding in her stomach.

What was unforgivable was that Seema refused to share any details of the wedding, nothing about the paleness of the bride or the height of the groom or how much gold was exchanged or how many starters were served or was it plastic compartment trays or sit-down servant-waited tables or how much the girl cried when prised away from her family with beetle pincers by her new in-laws, smacking their lips at the banquet bride, bringing the last of her family's savings with her. She said nothing. And as if that wasn't impolite enough, then Seema disappeared again weeks later, just like that, a dustball blown away. Her husband stayed behind, working his small scrub of land, and told Mala and everyone else who asked that their Delhi relatives loved Seema and the children so much they had insisted that all of them go and stay with them for a few months, for a holiday. A holiday! Mala snorted at the memory. This from the man who made his wife walk four miles with his lunchtime roti so he could eat it hot from the tiffin.

And then months later, just when Mala was wondering whether Seema had met some urban misfortune, killed by a runaway three-wheeler or kidnapped to service lorry drivers in some backstreet brothel, she reappeared. She arrived in a taxi, she and the children in new outfits, still with the price sticker on the soles of their chappals. She had hardly raised her eyes to acknowledge the curious gathering crowd, and had entered her house, slamming the screen door behind her.

Days later, the first of the expensive treasures began arriving. But Mala could see that Seema had left something of herself behind, as if the city had nibbled quietly, softly at her plump corners, and everything fat and free about her had been swallowed up. The kids also, they came back to school but their eyes were filmed over with something that had made them grow up bamboo-fast, too fast.

'Did somebody die?' Mala asked her one day at the river, before the washing machine had come but after the bricks for the new house had arrived. The only explanation that made sense to her was that some rich old relative had left them something in his will. The other women chirruped and clucked at Mala's shameless tongue, even though they were all grateful she had had the guts to ask what they had all been thinking.

Seema paused for a breath, almost as if she was going to say yes, but she said, 'No. No one died, Mala.'

And she threw the sodden saris at the stones with such fury that Mala expected to see cracks show themselves in the sad old boulders.

Of course, there were so many stories – some filthy, shameless ones, although Mala noticed that in all of them Seema was the dirty wrong-doer and never her husband. She knew this was the same old crappy talk but still, she stopped talking to her too.

And then something even stranger happened. Mala's husband and Seema's husband suddenly became friends. Mala caught them laughing together several times, smoking under the neem tree, muttering at the water fountain; even across the fields she recognized her husband's tall stork-stepping legs and Seema's husband's stout hooves keeping time together as the sun started to dip and the crows settled in the trees, like rotten fruit hanging blackly from the branches. But it was when Ram started to behave like a complete *oolloo* that she knew she had to do something.

At first she kept catching him looking at her much as he had done in the month after they were married, like a starved dog salivating at the meat of her backside. This wasn't an unpleasant sensation. After all, who doesn't like it in the first year, before any children have come along? It's a new thing, after all, completely free and allowed. So she waited for him to pull her on to the charpoy, waited to hear the creaky song of its weave under them, punctuated by Bee-ji's pneumatic snores. But he didn't touch her. He just looked and looked, staring at her breasts beneath her blouse, swinging in time with the chapatti dough she kneaded angrily because she knew he was looking and doing nothing, the drooling idiot. She felt his gaze on her back as she squatted over the fire, breathing it into life, his eyes moving down in time with the sweat snaking along her backbone; he watched her ankles and thighs as she hitched up her sari to sweep the courtyard, trying to poof-poof the dust right into his stupid smiling face. At night she lay next to him, burning like a dying fire. She tried throwing her ankle over his, pretended to roll in half-sleepy moans into his back, pressed herself into his trembling thighs. Mala could feel his desire and knew he was tying it down like an unbroken animal. She told herself, it cannot be me. Not yet, not this soon.

At one time she thought he might be angry with her, wanted to punish her for not managing to keep her first pregnancy. It

39

must have been a child conceived on their first night together. They had barely got used to the idea of themselves as a married couple, let alone as parents, when the blood and clots plopped and pooled out of her as she was squatting on the riverbank with ropes of wet saris coiled around her arms, waterlogged iridescent snakes. She had been in her fourth month, when all should have been safe inside. Instead, she became like the river, an unstoppable tide flowed from her, the banks of her womb too weak to hold it.

The other women had helped her home. One of them held her face hard, turning it away from the thing she had already seen caught in a rock pool, the too-tiny baby curled in on itself, a bloody comma, a pause in the paragraph of her life. The women soothed and sang to her, clucking loud reassurances as she cramped and cried in the windy heat. Hai, why so many tears? This is nothing, this happens, this will happen again. Some children are not meant to stay. You are young! But Mala had not been crying with grief, just relief. She thought Ram would see this in her face, but instead he sat at her side every evening for a week, ordering his mother to bring her ginger tea and *pinny*, sweet balls of spiced gourd stuffed with secret herbs supposed to tighten a woman's insides like a drawstring. Maybe he was already preparing her for the next time.

Yet still Ram kept talking to Seema's husband, and she noticed the more he talked to him, the more he day-looked and night-trembled and left her lying choking on her own desire, blowing on her own simmering skin when really she wanted to bite into it and taste her own blood.

That's when Mala decided. It was Seema's husband's fault, all of this mess. And then she knew she had no choice. Who cared what the other women would think? She had to talk to her.

# CHAPTER THREE

TOBY ARRIVED HOME still smelling of mud and pig. He had been so anxious to leave that he had forgone his usual end-of-work shower in the small mouldy staff cubicle, and had jumped on the first bus going east.

Alighting at the end of their road, he began to walk steadily, distracted by the lights in various front rooms, glimpses of other lives before curtains and blinds shut out the approaching night. It was a mild winter and the air felt stale and thick. He missed the cleansing bite of frost. He still hadn't got used to this suburb on the edge of London, despite everyone telling him it was going up. In his opinion, that was the only direction in which it could possibly go, but he also knew as a yokel child that any place without a grassy view and a clear horizon would probably disappoint him.

As he approached Shyama's house, he was struck as always by the contrast between its squat, red-brick exterior and what was inside. 'Deceptively spacious,' she had teased him when he first visited. And he liked the feel of it: the dark, tiled hallway leading into high-ceilinged, airy rooms with their original coving and fireplaces; sliding wooden doors that you could pull across to divide a room and make a space cosy; old wooden floors, scuffed and pocked with age but still as solid as the day they went down.

Most of all, he liked the way Shyama had subverted the English rectitude of the architecture with her ethnic sass: many-armed statues bursting out from alcoves; framed fragments of old saris hanging on the walls, intricately embroidered, their seed pearls and sequins catching the light and throwing it back in fractured shards; a wall painted burnt orange. It made his lone Lamborghini poster in his bachelor bedsit look tragic. He had somehow fallen in with a mature woman with a grown-up house and a grown-up child, and even now, after six years of being together, four years after moving in with her, he still felt like a visitor.

He kicked off his mud-encrusted boots in the hallway, shrugging off his fusty-smelling windcheater, and paused halfway to the kitchen. He recognized Shyama's mother's gentle murmur, inter-cut with her daughter's staccato bass tones. He liked Shyama's parents – it was hard not to, they were always smiling, always polite – but he knew he confused them. He would catch them looking from him to Shyama and then at each other, disguising their disappointment with exaggerated hospitality. What was this blond boy doing with their divorced, too-much-older daughter? (He noticed they said 'die-vorced'. Shyama told him that was a guilt trip disguising itself as a mispronunciation.) There had been a brief flare of hope when they thought Toby was a vet as opposed to a glorified farmhand, and they still didn't under-stand why someone would want to spend their time tending to beasts of the field unless they received handsome payment in return. Sita had tried to cover their disapproval by sharing her own childhood with Toby, proud to be the daughter of a Punjabi farmer, regaling him with tales of how she and her sisters would walk back from school gathering food from the land that they owned, bright peacock-hued *chunnis* fluttering from their necks against the emerald green of the endless fields. So many English

42

people thought India was an uncivilized desert or a waterlogged swamp because that's what they saw on the news. Did he know Punjab was called the granary of India because it was fed by five rivers, Panj meaning five, Ab meaning rivers? Her family sent their wheat and beets all over the land, did he know that? No, Toby certainly didn't, and he remarked how satisfying it must have been to turn the soil in ancestral meadows. Sita had stared at him. 'Well, of course, we didn't do that. Our workers did. Our family were owners, not labourers.' She ended her sentence with a little laugh and a warm smile, but Toby knew he had opened his big Suffolk gob and put his size tens firmly in it. He had smiled back, knowing they were killing him with kindness.

He hesitated in the hallway, aware the women were in mid-conversation. It sounded urgent, secretive, drifting through the half-open kitchen door.

'A baby is so much work . . . you need so much energy to look after them properly.'

'I'm fitter than a lot of women half my age.'

'I know, darling, you look very nice. But honestly.'

'Women in India have kids well into their forties. Look at Kamla Auntie, she was forty-eight when she had Vippu.'

'Yes, but he was her seventh. She had lots in between. God knows why, the woman should have used up her energy getting a job instead of lounging around eating chocolates and watching TV melodramas. But what I'm saying is her body knew what to do, and her older ones helped her with the baby.'

'I have Tara.'

A brief pause. They let that one go.

'Anyway, Mama, like I told you, I won't be having a baby – any baby. I can't, and that's that. So we might consider adoption or—'

'Adoption? At your age? Why do you want to start all that

hard work all over again? This is the time you should be relaxing and going on cruises. Anyway, how can you adopt? You're not married.'

'It doesn't matter nowadays.'

'Well, it should. We are modern, but not stupid. What happens if you adopt a baby and your Toby runs off with someone younger? Someone more like him? You want to be a fifty-year-old on your own with a little one?'

'Marriage doesn't stop husbands buggering off. Remember?'

So Shyama had told her mother. Toby initially felt confused, then slighted. She had insisted on keeping their IVF a secret from her parents for the last four years, so why choose to tell Sita now when it wasn't going to happen? And how had adoption filled that gaping loss so soon? He heard a chair being scraped back, a tap turning as the kettle was filled, then silence descended. If he left it much longer, who knows what he might hear next? So he cleared his throat and walked into the kitchen.

'Hey!' Toby sang cheerily, making straight for Sita first, hands together in a respectful namaste.

'Namaste, Sita-ji,' he intoned solemnly, making Sita giggle like a schoolgirl. It always worked. He had fretted over how to address Shyama's parents for ages. Shyama had vetoed any kind of Mum/Dad/Mrs/Mr business – one too formal, the other reserved only for bona fide son-in-laws, and they'd had one of those who had turned out to be a thoroughly bad sort. So how about the all-purpose suffix of respect for those older or more important than you, one word merely added on to the end of the name. Ji. It made Toby feel like an over-impressed American from the fifties, wanting to add 'Neat' and 'Swell' to the rest of the sentence. But it covered a million cultural potholes and it was, after all, one very small word.

Sita slapped him playfully on the shoulder. 'Funny boy. Cuppatea?'

'Lovely, thank you.'

Toby glanced at Shyama, cradling her mug between her hands, who shot him a small tight smile. She looked tired, with smudges of shadow beneath her dark lashes, and the pain clouding her eyes made his chest ache. He laid a hand over hers and gave it a small squeeze – there wasn't much else they could say now with Sita there. It didn't matter, telling her mother, mentioning adoption, she had needed to talk and he hadn't been there. He would have liked to throw his arms around her and carry her upstairs, but Shyama discouraged him from being too lovey-dovey in front of her parents. 'It's a cultural thing,' she had explained, which was no explanation at all. He considered it for a second, tempted to see if Sita would throw a bucket of cold water over him in response.

'Toby, would you mind if I call Prem over? He has some more papers to sign. We were wondering—'

'Mama, he's just got in,' Shyama interrupted.

'He doesn't mind. You don't mind, do you, Toby?'

'No problem, Sita-ji. A pleasure.'

As Toby added milk to his cuppatea, Sita picked up the phone and made a brief call in Punjabi. A moment later, a gate at the end of Shyama's garden swung open and her father strolled through it, a bundle of files under his arm and his ever-present pipe clamped between his teeth, each step punctuated with a puff of smoke as if he was being power-steamed towards the back door.

Shyama greeted her father with a hug and got up to make his tea, very strong, a splash of milk, piping hot, the way he liked it. His kindly face and the tufts of hair above his ears reminded Toby of a koala bear.

45

Prem dropped the papers on to the kitchen table and slapped Toby manfully on the back. 'Toby sahib!' he joshed. 'How are you?'

The first time Toby had visited this house, Shyama said to him, 'You know how English people have fairies at the bottom of their garden? Well, I have parents.'

Once he had got over the surprise of Mr and Mrs Bedi occupying the ground-floor flat of the house that backed on to Shyama's, and once he had reassured himself that there wasn't any possible way they could see him defiling their daughter in the master bedroom, he had accepted it surprisingly easily. Extended families were common in farming communities when he was a lad. As Sita placed the obligatory plate of biscuits before him, he remembered his own mother's wind-reddened hands producing scones and bread warm from the oven, her satisfied half-smile as Toby and his father and brother fell upon them with barely a thank-you. The memory brought a lump to his throat.

'You OK, *beta*?' Sita enquired. She called him 'son'. The lump got bigger. Toby felt Shyama's eyes on him. He had to be the strong one; that was the deal now.

'Long day, Sita-ji.' He smiled and patted the chair next to him. 'So, Prem-ji, what have you got for me this time?'

Prem sat down with a sigh and gave an apologetic glance at the untidy heap of papers before him. 'We have another court date!' he said jovially, as if this wasn't the sixth in as many years, all of which had come to nothing.

Toby sat beside Prem and cast an eye over the first few pages, the usual tiny print and legal gobblededook they had come to expect from these official missives. He wiped his palms on his sweatshirt, conscious of the smell of manure rising from his clothes, and flicked through them quickly.

'So, five weeks away then, the next court hearing. Have you made sure your lawyer has got all the right papers this time?'

'Oh, the lawyer had the right papers all right.' Prem smiled at Toby. 'It was the clerk in the court. He had brought the wrong file.'

'You're happy with your lawyer, Prem-ji? It's just . . . well, this has been going on a long time and . . .'

'The Indian courts. They're a mess. We are lucky we even have another hearing. Sometimes the file disappears altogether and you have to start again. At least we have another chance.'

There was a brief pause while everyone in the room nodded and sighed, not daring to meet each other's eyes, not wanting to see the resignation or recrimination residing there. The story was a long and painful one, the kind Prem imagined telling a gaggle of wide-eyed grandchildren around a blazing fire, epic in scale and mythic in theme, brother against brother battling over land and property. Told a few generations on, he hoped it would reveal itself to be a valuable moral fable and not the sordid paragraph of everyday betrayal it was now.

Five years before his retirement, seven years before hers, Prem and Sita decided to invest their life savings in a piece of Back Home, a three-bedroom flat in South Delhi not far from either the centre or the airport, close to Prem's favourite brother's place, the idea being that Yogesh could keep an eye on the property until Prem and Sita occupied it. A small flat near family, perfect for their retirement: the summer months in England with Shyama and Tara, the winter months in Delhi, eating *falooda kulfi* at their favourite café, wandering around the Lodi Gardens reliving their college strolls when even the brush of a hand could send Prem into a tailspin of unrequited longing, playing *taash* in shaded dhabas over a peg of whisky with the old friends who had decided to stay, those who were left.

Of course, they both knew it wasn't the India they had fled. How could it be? Why should it be? Connaught Place was now a grubby concentric car park, overrun with American-style eateries and confused, sweating tourists dodging the bloody sprays of betel-nut juice spat out by bored shoeshines. You couldn't stroll through the Lodi Gardens without being knocked down by some mad jogger (jogging in India! What was wrong with a brisk walk?), and the old friends had to live near enough (or be strong enough to brave the insane Delhi traffic and mish-mash of flyovers, half-finished bridges and endless, never-progressing roadworks) to be persuaded to come out to visit them.

But, unlike most of his contemporaries, Prem did not fear progress. During his many trips over the last few years, often at short notice to attend some legal hearing or sign some incomprehensible form, he had watched with growing wonder as the Delhi skyline had transformed from sleepy small town to skyscraper city, the horizon crowded with glittering fingers in concrete, steel and glass, aggressively pointing up, up, up. That's where we're going, buddy, Third World, my ass! His childhood haunts were almost unrecognizable; it was like looking at an old familiar face and finding not wrinkles and pouches but taut new skin, a reconstructed jawline, a smile too white and wide. Time hurried forward at breakneck speed, having been held back for so long, and they had to run to catch up. And they would soon overtake, judging by how much the flat had increased in value in the last ten years or so. Almost quadrupled. Their modest investment had turned out to be an accidentally smart business move, a large three-bed in a prime location. Such a shame, then, that they could not get into it.

Sita broke the silence. 'Look what happens when you do people a favour.' She shook her head.

'Mama . . .' Shyama began. She was in no mood to hear the whole sorry saga again, but for Sita, the constant retelling of it reaffirmed the injustice.

'I said to Prem when Yogi asked us' – she turned to Toby, knowing he would at least pretend to listen – 'when Yogi said, oh my poor daughter and her family, they need somewhere to stay just until their house is finished, I said to Prem, this is a mistake.'

'The flat was just sitting there, empty, what could I say?' Prem said for maybe the thousandth time.

'I knew as soon as Sheetal and her useless husband moved in, they would never leave. First they stopped paying rent, after just one year.'

'Sita, they know all this!' Prem attempted a breezy chuckle, rolling his eyes at Toby as if to say, it's nothing, this is nothing.

'And then,' Sita ploughed on, 'they build an extension there, they have two children there, and during this time Yogi has got rich enough to buy two flats of his own which he could have given them to live in, no? And then your favourite brother's daughter sublets the garage – our garage – to a bicycle-repair-wallah, making money from our property whilst they are refusing to give it to us.'

'Hah, of course, that was naughty,' Prem conceded. 'Another biscuit, Toby?'

'Naughty?' Sita stared at him. She bit back what she wanted to say so hard she tasted blood. 'Fifteen years we have been asking, begging them to leave, ten years of fighting in the courts, and you call your niece *naughty*?'

Prem swallowed hard; the plate of biscuits he held out to Toby shook slightly in his hand. Sita knew she had gone too far, but oh, how much more she could say about her stupidly soft-hearted husband, who could never say no to family. All the times he had dutifully dispatched money to pay for sisters' weddings, nephews' graduations, medical bills, over the years. He was the second eldest son, he would remind Sita, as she watched helplessly whilst the bundle of precious, sweated-for notes was sent away without even touching her hands. There goes the new fridge, she told herself, the central heating, the repairs to the car, the remote, longed-for possibility of a holiday. There goes any thought of private education for their only child, when so many of their friends' *oolloo* kids had got to university only because they had the money to pay someone to wring exam results out of their spoiled, vacant heads. There it all goes. And here sat her husband, with a plate of biscuits in his shaky hands, and she felt her own heartburn churning under her breastbone like an acrid sea. They had spent their retirement years fighting for the home they had wanted to retire to, and now they were older and more tired and maybe – but she could not face this thought head-on – maybe it was already too late.

'He is my brother,' Prem said softly, placing the plate carefully back on the table. 'Yogi touches my feet when we meet.'

'Hah, and he also left you all the restaurant bills when we ate!' Sita laughed bitterly, patting Prem's arm as she rose, filling the kitchen with activity, collecting mugs, flicking on the kettle again. Punjabi therapy – hot tea and changing the subject – worked every time.

They ate together, as was usual whenever Sita and Prem came by at this time of day. It was taken for granted that Sita would bring a carrier bag full of food in Tupperware boxes, or often the pans themselves, still gently steaming with rice, daal, biryani, whatever she had thrown together in her seemingly effortless way.

The meal was a quiet, strained affair, Shyama picking at her food and chewing listlessly, Toby cleaning his plate so fast he had to suppress a series of spicy burps, ungraciously hoping that Sita and Prem would hurry up and leave so he could digest what was really ailing him. Nearly half past nine already. He had to be up early to open the farm for their weekly hay and feed deliveries. Shyama could sense his restlessness without looking up. She, on the other hand, wanted to draw out this meal for as long as possible, knowing that the moment Toby said, 'It doesn't matter,' she would howl like a madwoman at the moon. She needed noise, distraction.

'Mama?' Her voice sounded unnaturally loud to her ears. 'Didn't you say this has happened to loads of your friends as well?'

Sita paused halfway up from the table, plates in each hand. 'What happened?'

'You said lots of them have had property stolen from them by their families?'

'Oh, yes! For example, Rishi Bhaga, you remember him – consultant, three kids, all of them doctors too, married to Rani, lives in Gerrards Cross? Well, he hired the Dorchester for his daughter's wedding.'

'Who could forget?' said Shyama drily, exchanging a fleeting smile with Toby which flooded him with relief. She was still in there, still glowing.

'He told his grandfather to let out his top floor to a second cousin. That was fifty years ago, and can you believe the lying cheaters are still there? They have never paid poor Bhaga sahib a penny. When his family go to India, they have to sleep on blow-up mattresses in the same house, one floor below, or fork out for a hotel!'

Prem tutted and slurped his tea, happy in the knowledge that there was always someone worse off than them.

'Bhaga sahib says these people have even built their own

entrance round the back. He said – remember, darling, so funny he was – he said, "We have Partition in our own damn house!" '

'And Kailash, didn't she?' Prem knew the story backwards, but also knew that Sita would provide the melodrama the telling required.

'Hai, her papa had just died, she knew he had given her the house in his will, being the only child and all, and her *thaya* – that's her father's elder brother,' she said with a kind nod to Toby, 'he sold the house without telling her, while she was in hospital having a hysterectomy.'

'And Jaggi and Mohini also.' Prem helped himself to another biscuit, grateful for his wife's animated relish in others' misfortunes.

'Hah! They bought a brand-new build in an NRI complex – non-resident Indians, Toby, like we are now.' Sita paused for breath.

Toby nodded, warmed by Shyama's stifled smile across the table.

'They thought they would be safe, you see? Security gates and twenty-four-hour guards, but when it was all finished and they flew over, they went there straight from the aeroplane with their bags, all ready to move in, and when Jaggi put his key in the lock it just wouldn't fit! At first they thought there was something wrong with the key. Then they found out one of the labourers from the next block had just walked in with his family and changed all the locks. They even waved to them through the window, laughing at them as if to say, you left it empty, what do you expect?'

'They used to burn down English holiday homes in Wales,' Toby piped up.

Sita stared at him, nonplussed.

'The Welsh nationalists?' Toby added. 'They were angry the foreigners had bought up all these properties, pricing local people out of the area, and then just left them unused for most of the year. I mean, you could see their point, I suppose.' He stuttered slightly under Sita's unwavering gaze. 'It's sort of the same problem, isn't it?'

'Not the same at all, Toby, no,' Sita said firmly. 'If you had heard Kohli sahib's story, you would never say that.'

None of Prem and Sita's friends would ever forget Kohli sahib's story, shared during the monthly kitty party which had suddenly become an impromptu therapy session, where, one by one, each couple spat out their shameful family betrayals over spiced cashews and lamb samosas.

'I had already sold the farm when we were about to leave.'

Everyone had turned to look at Kohli sahib, a man of few words who sat gripping his whisky tumbler like a light sabre, both hands around it, ready to fight. His wife placed a warning hand on his arm, which he ignored. He was already back in the room in Jullundur with its peeling turquoise walls and slowly revolving ceiling fan barely stirring the warm soup of the evening air. He had been flushed with achievement and imported whisky, filled with love for his family in this room with him – his brothers, their wives, the children still running in a tumbling pack, playing hide and seek in and out of the carved wooden screens and folding doors. His wife had been worried that the brothers wouldn't take it well that their *bhaiya* from the UK wanted to sell one of the farms to release cash for his daughter's wedding. But no one had objected, no one was being left homeless, it had always been the agreement in the will, and here they were, sharing crispy, just-fried jalebis with syrupy-tipped fingers to the night orchestra of crickets and gossipy cornstalks exchanging their secrets, a sports bag at Kohli sahib's feet containing the proceeds of the sale. It was too much money to be carrying around so they were going to drive through the night and deposit the whole lot in a bank first thing. His brother's son sat next to him, refilling his glass, a big strong youth built for land work, tendons rippling as he banged the whisky bottle down. His nephew put his arm around him and whispered in his ear like a lover, 'Leave the money where it is. Just get up and go now. You are still here in five minutes, we will kill both of you.'

Kohli sahib's hand had trembled as he remembered and beads of sweat popped up on his forehead like bubbles breaking on the surface of his skin, an eruption deep inside.

'I looked up at my brothers – both of them were looking back at me. And I knew they would do it. And no one would ever even find our bodies.'

His wife, next to him, her voice low, devoid of emotion, added, 'He didn't tell me until we were ten miles away, just threw me into the car. I left my best shawl behind. I thought he was having a heart attack or something. His face was like a sick moon.'

There was a respectful pause for a story like this one, dredged from the sediment of communal memory. They all carried this ache in some form; it was the legacy of leaving, they knew this now. But not back then, when pastures new and fast money and oh, more than anything, opportunities for their children were the prize. Who knew then what the price would be years later?

'They want to punish us,' Kohli sahib had said finally. 'When we escaped, they resented us, the ones who got away. They thought we were all millionaires, so they asked us for everything. And we gave it, because we were rich, compared to them. And we felt bad for having abandoned them. But not now. Now the gap is closing. We can never afford to buy there again, those days are gone. I think that's what they wanted. You left us, so now we don't want you back.'

Much later that evening, as Prem and Sita picked their way home through the garden, Shyama was already heading for the stairs. Toby caught up with her in the hallway, pulling her into his arms. They stood there for a while, not saying anything, their breathing gradually finding each other's rhythm.

'I'm sorry,' Shyama began, her voice muffled, her head on his chest.

'None of that,' Toby whispered. 'We'll find a way.'

Shyama raised her head, studied his face in the half-light. 'I thought . . . This is it, isn't it? I'm forty-eight.'

'Only just.'

'Doesn't matter. Beyond forty-five everyone thinks you've moved from brave to keep trying to just deluded. I saw it in Dr Lalani's face. I wish I could let go. It's just so hard to give up hope.'

'Oh, there's always hope.'

'Adoption? I thought . . .'

'You know what, Shyams?' Toby stroked a stray tendril away from her forehead. 'Let's not think about anything tonight. Not your ovulation chart or taking your temperature before we take our clothes off or propping your legs up with pillows afterwards. We don't have to do any of that crap any more. Can we remember how to do it just because it's fun?'

Before Shyama could answer, Toby bent his knees and scooped her up in his arms. She gasped in surprise, then laughed throatily as Toby staggered slightly, making her grab for a handhold on the bannister.

'Shit,' Toby cursed, 'Shyama, can you—?'

Shyama tumbled on to the stairs as Toby tried to straighten up. With a sharp intake of breath, he clutched his side.

'Think I've pulled my rib angle . . .' he muttered through gritted teeth.

'Your what?' Shyama felt slightly giddy.

''S OK,' he hissed. 'Done it before. Hot and cold compresses, ibuprofen . . . be fine.' He raised an eyebrow at Shyama. 'Maybe you shouldn't have had that extra chapatti.'

'Shut yer face.' Shyama heaved herself to her feet. 'Here . . .'

She stood next to him, taking his weight, gently massaging the flesh where his hand lay, feeling the knots under the skin, taut muscle, not an inch of fat, youth pulsing through him like a warm river.

'I've always been a healthy girl,' she said in her mother's sing-song accent. 'Which, of course, is the Indian way of saying fat.'

'You're not—' Toby winced, unable to finish. Shyama kneaded her fingers more gently, slipping into storytelling mode, the best distraction when Tara had been hurt or scared as a little girl.

' "Healthy" as used in the matrimonial placements in the *Hindustan Times.* Or Shaadi.com now – I suppose even arranged marriages are online. I love reading the ads families put in, all the euphemisms . . . If someone's described as "homely", that means plug ugly, "wheatish complexion" means could pass for white and looking for similar so as not to pollute the family hue, "modern" means smokes and drinks for a bloke and she's definitely not a virgin for a woman, and "healthy"? Usually means the parents' beloved child is a bit of a porker.'

'It's not like that, actually.' A voice rang out loudly from the sitting room.

Shyama swung round towards the open door and discovered Tara's head poking out from the depths of the sofa.

56

'I know loads of people who've met online on Asian dating sites and their parents have nothing to do with it.'

'What are you doing, sitting in the dark? I didn't even know you were back!' Shyama blustered, recalling Tara's last words to Sita before disappearing off for the evening.

'Clearly,' Tara sniped back. She stood up, a half-open family-sized bag of cheesy snacks in one hand. With the other she furiously brushed luminous orange crumbs from her front while avoiding any eye contact. 'It's called assisted marriage now, anyway. Only the really fundy families monitor the meetings. Usually people put their own profiles up, date as long as they want and only tell their families if they want it to go further.'

' "Fundy"?' Shyama enquired. She could feel Toby tightening up next to her, tensing beneath her touch.

'Fundamentalists.' Tara finished her tidy-up, having simply moved the mess from her clothes to the floor.

'Didn't realize you were so up on the Asian dating scene. So, anything you want to tell me?' Shyama teased, hoping this would end the conversation on a truce, that Tara would remove herself so she could turn back to Toby and finish what they had been trying to begin.

'Not now. Not ever, actually. '

Tara pushed past them and then leaned in to Shyama, exhaling a cloud of cheesy-smelling breath. 'And next time you're going to do it on the stairs, warn me first so I can shoot myself.'

She stomped up every step to her room and slammed the door for good measure.

As Shyama flew up the stairs after her, she barely registered Toby calling after her, 'Shyama, leave it. Shyama!'

She didn't bother knocking. Tara stood facing the door, waiting for her. She knew exactly what she was doing, which enraged Shyama even more.

'How dare you?' Shyama began.

'How dare I?' Tara shot back. 'Isn't it bad enough you've been trying to get up the duff, without shagging like teenagers?'

'That is none of your business!' Shyama sputtered. The sprint up to the attic had left her breathless. She wanted to roar fire instead of panting like a geriatric. The irony was, she felt as defiant and exposed as a sixteen-year-old caught on the sofa half undressed with her spotty tumescent consort. Everything she wanted to scream at her daughter would sound like adolescent whining: It's not fair! You always ruin everything! What about me? If she had the oxygen and the patience, she would sit Tara down, take her hand and try to explain how those long years with Tara's father had felt. How he would treat her with charming deference in front of their friends and family, who would comment on how lucky she was to have such an attentive husband – and how then, later on, he would lie on the very edge of the bed with a contortionist's ease to avoid even an inch of their bodies touching. How many nights had Shyama spent smothered in supposedly irresistible perfume, squeezed into underwear which had holes and wires in all the wrong places, steadying her breathing so he wouldn't guess how much she longed for just one look or caress that would make her feel wanted, or even noticed. She didn't dare instigate anything herself; the one occasion she had attempted to 'take the initiative in the bedroom', as the magazine headline had screamed at her, she thought the poor man was going to leap out of the window. Later he'd said she had caught him by surprise. It had been on the tip of her tongue to shout, 'Yes, that's the bloody idea, isn't it?' But by that time she had eaten most of a tub of cookie-dough ice cream and had gotten back into her tracksuit, so it seemed the moment had indeed passed. She had thought she was an aberration, a freak. Men wanted sex all the time, didn't they? It was the women who feigned headaches. What was so wrong with her that she managed to buck the trend like some accidental Medusa, shrivelling a man's desire with one desperate look? It had not even occurred to her that this particular man was too tired to oblige as his sap was being expertly milked elsewhere. She would have liked to tell Tara that it does something to the soul, this benevolent and gradual amputation of affection, of touch. And that this kind of spontaneous fumbling on the stairs was not only what she needed, it was what had finally healed her.

'If it was none of my business,' Tara spat, 'why even tell me about all the IVF crap? Did I ask? No. Do I care you've stopped when I didn't know you'd started? No again.'

'I thought you'd want to.'

'What? Share the love? Mum, there is no part of my brain that even gets why anyone your age would want a kid. So yeah, thanks for letting me know you've given up. At least I don't have to worry about dying of shame seeing you pushing a buggy up and down the high road.'

'Maybe I haven't given up.'

The moment Shyama said it, it became true. Her anger receded, leaving cold calm resolve, which not even the slight tremor around Tara's mouth could dissolve.

'You're joking.' Tara shook her head slowly. 'OK, for the record, just stop including me in any more baby chat, we both know it's pointless.'

'Fine. If that's what you want,' Shyama said evenly.

'It's what *you* want, Mother. We done now?'

Meanwhile, in the ground-floor flat opposite, Prem sat on the carpet in front of the television with the sound turned down, one eye on the recorded cricket highlights, paperwork spread before him. Next door he could hear Sita gently snoring. He had waited for her to fall asleep, pretending to read his newspaper until he could slip back out to the sitting room and begin the familiar task of reordering their legal papers, ready for the next round. He had decided to make a definitive list of the various stages of their ten-year struggle to repossess their flat. It made sobering reading, as he knew it would, which is why he hadn't wanted Sita to see it.

1. March 2002 – eviction order granted in Delhi High Court with order for Yogesh Bedi to vacate within six months. Order ignored.
2. November 2002 – arrived at flat with bailiff. Yogesh Bedi refuses to vacate, bailiff says not legally allowed to use force and tells us to forget it. Yogesh Bedi seems very friendly with bailiff, not sure why.
3. January 2003 – lawyer asks for new eviction date with new bailiff and is told original paperwork is lost and he will have to reapply all over again.
4. April 2004 – lawyer reapplies for new eviction order.
5. December 2004 – new court date given: January 2005.
6. June 2005 – new eviction order granted.
7. January 2006 – date fixed for eviction in October 2006.
8. October 2006 – eviction halted as Yogesh Bedi's lawyer argues we do not intend to live in flat but to sell it to someone else. This is because we are apparently too old to climb the stairs.
9. January 2007 – application for new eviction order.
10. May 2007 – date given for new hearing: November 2007.
11. November 2007 – eviction hearing. We discover that judge

who was handling our case has been changed, he has retired or moved court, no one is sure. We are told we have to refile all over again.

12. February 2008 – lawyer reapplies for eviction order. Clerk points out there is a mistake on the court records. Flat has been noted as number 14, not 14A. Case halted as new records have to be filed, even though we showed them ownership papers and it was their fault, not ours.

13. November 2008 – lawyer reapplies for new eviction order in front of new judge. Eviction date given for March 2009.

14. March 2009 – day before eviction, Yogesh Bedi's lawyers claim eviction illegal as no paperwork received from chief inspector of police to sanction eviction. Lawyer swears he had it lodged with the court but now somehow it cannot be found. Eviction postponed.

15. October 2009 – new eviction date given for February 2010.

16. February 2010 – lawyer informs us whole court building dealing with our case has been relocated from original site in Thri Nazar to new site of Patiala House, resulting in delay of all cases as all records need to be moved to new site. He will inform us when new court is up and running.

17. August 2010 – lawyer informs us Maharajah of Patiala had objected to one of his buildings being taken over by government for court purposes and has lodged appeal. Very sorry, nothing to do with him.

18. January 2011 – Maharajah of Patiala wins his appeal. Court shifted back to original building.

19. November 2011 – lawyer sorrowfully informs us that in the move our papers were somehow mislaid. Have to refile case.

20. February 2012 – lawyer reapplies for eviction order, given date of March 2012.

Prem considered himself a happy man, but these last ten years had sorely tested that belief. Joviality was the lifebelt to which he had clung through decades of stormy seas, a cultivated cheery manner which had seen him through the trauma of Partition, months in a refugee camp, years of struggle and poverty – not the kind of poverty people moaned about here: oh-why-can't-I-have-a-wide-screen-telly, we-only-get-one-holiday-a-year type of complaining – but the kind of hardship that gnawed at you every waking day. Trying to keep your one shirt and trousers clean, calculating how little you could survive on today so your brothers and sisters could eat too, studying under street lamps because the electricity had gone whilst mosquitoes flew joyfully into your borrowed spotlight and dive-bombed your face. Then a menial Indian government job, his pay almost gone before he got it, the family grateful for good son Prem, the worker, the trier who never complained and always smiled, even when treading water furiously, head just above the waves, gulping for breath.

Landing at Heathrow airport in 1962, during one of the harshest winters on record, when the entire country was snowbound and blizzard-beset for two months, he knew he had left part of his heart behind. It had fractured as he touched his mother's feet in farewell, splintered as they took off into bleached-white skies; fragments had been sucked into the aeroplane's vents and released into the air above Delhi, where they would find their way back to the ground-floor flat in the old city and land like tinkling glass in the open courtyard by the spreading tulsi plant. And yet, heart cracked and teeth chattering, as he stepped out into the icy maw of his new country, it felt like finally reaching the shore. He practised the smile which froze on his face and stayed there. It fooled everyone, and most of the time he believed it too.

As he climbed back into bed next to his beloved wife, he shut out the whispers of regret and the missed opportunities, the suspicion that their kindness could have been read as weakness, that his belief in justice might turn out in the end to be a childish fantasy.

Shyama, in bed next to Toby on the other side of the garden, rubbed liniment into his twisted muscles and silenced regrets of her own, the wistful scenario of having met this man when she was younger, when they would have had more choices. But now the idea of an unnamed, unborn child hummed between them like electricity, and later on they would lie together talking it all through, all spark and hope again.

# CHAPTER FOUR

MALA WAITED UNTIL dusk, just as the red bled into blue, then black-blue, like the bruises she pinched on her own thighs in the dustbowl of her marriage bed. She hurried through her daal, finishing before Ram, who sat chewing like a patient goat, mouth open, champ-chump.

Mala started clearing up around him, sealing the lids on the clay pots of yoghurt and pickle, shaking the basket of crumbs far from the door to lead the ants away, taking the pans to the tap which spewed out just enough water to get them clean. Mala scrubbed and sighed, remembering how proud they used to be of having their own tap. One in every home in the village! Pogle sahib boasted, telling anyone who would listen. Now he and everyone else felt a little poorer, and a little more foolish for their pride, because of Seema and her hot-and-cold-running house. These two rooms and small courtyard had felt world enough to Mala when she was brought here after the wedding. Lucky girl, everyone had said, no father, hardly any dowry, and a man only five miles from your village agrees to take you off your widowed mother's curse-carrying hands. And only ten years older than you. You could have ended up like Madhu or Sona, those teenagers tied to bandy-legged, one-toothed greybeards. Mala had smiled dutifully, lowered her eyes and replied, yes, I am lucky, but she thought to herself, my mother had to sell half the little land my father left to seal the match. And even when I was listening in from the kitchen, his family were dropping hints, like crumbs on the cushions, about claiming the other half also! Mala's mother had managed to brush them aside gently, reminding his family that she still had one more girl to marry off, and they had let her off. If only they could have seen Mala herself, the blushing virgin bride-to-be, on the other side of the paint-flaked door, her one good vegetable knife in her hand, ready to run in and make a masala mix of their guts if they lifted one more claw towards her father's fields. Or that's how Mala had imagined she would have reacted in the Technicolor movie in her own head.

As Mala stacked the pots and plates, she wondered why the price of women like her, her sister, even her mother, had gone down instead of up. After all, they were running out of girls, everyone could see it. One glance at the children in the village school confirmed it, sitting with Master-ji under the peepul tree in their too-white uniforms with their dusty slates: twenty-three boys, ten girls, Mala had counted them. She had stopped counting the bodies she found on her stolen solitary walks, abandoned in dried-up wells or washed up on the riverbank or hidden like death presents in thorn bushes, the hours-old baby girls still with the stump of their mother's cord on their tiny bellies, their mouths sometimes packed with sand or dirt, or their eyes and skin bleached and pinched with whatever poison they were given instead of Mama's milk.

Each time, she remembered her own almost-baby curled up in its rocky riverside cradle, the fleeting glimpse of him, her, she would never know. Would it have mattered? Of course, to everyone else.

'*Munda hai!*' the cockerel-proud cry would have gone around the village. 'It's a boy!' Bee-ji would have limped her way around personally to each and every house, scattering sweetmeats as she went, puffed out with pride as if she'd given birth to the grandson all by herself. Other men would back-slap her husband, that special big-man slap with growls and head cuffing, the secret signs that men use when they want to remind each other that they are the best and the most special and always will be. Other women would come with food and false smiles – at least, those with no sons, faces as green as unripe wheat. Well done, you! Lucky you, *theklo*, the pressure is off now. Healthy son, duty done. No wonder mothers lined their boy babies' eyes with kohl as soon as they could open them, tied black thread around their chubby wrists to ward off all the evil eyes jealous at their good fortune. The inky line around the eyelid, the dark bracelet, all for show: a visible imperfection on their perfect baby to stop the gods or anyone else from taking him away. To be fair, many mothers did the same for their daughters also. But there would be fewer sweetmeats given out, the crowing would be quieter, getting more muted with each subsequent daughter until you ended up like Jinder. Five daughters, and still they kept trying for the longed-for boy, Jinder getting weaker and sadder with each birth until the sixth one killed her. Another girl. Their father drifted around the village like an embarrassed ghost, treated like a king at home by the six daughters he knew he could never afford to marry off to anyone decent. His was the cleanest house in the village, the one whose shelves groaned with home-pickled vegetables and hand-baked buttery biscuits, whose frontage exploded into noisy blossom each spring, whose gate was always open and greedy for any passing visitor. They hung from the doorway like wedding garlands, those six beautiful girls, always smiling, keeping themselves busy, polishing their small prison till it shone. Because wasn't that what it was? Mala knew it, so did they. Ripe for the picking and withering on the stalk, one by one, the eldest gradually appearing less often, smiling less, followed by the next sister and then the next, as they realized that no amount of smiling and cooking could change the system that had remained in place for hundreds, maybe thousands of years. Girls cost money, no matter what they may give you back in kind.

All around the area, engagement offers were taking place earlier and earlier, boys' families wanting to reserve the best girls, like booking a train ticket early, to save having to travel too far away to find one later on. On the riverbank, the women had swapped hushed stories of the girls that ended up being kidnapped and defiled, soiled by the thief so no one else would want them anyway, like dogs pissing on their territory.

With all this going on, Mala's mother had reassured her two daughters, 'It will be like that year the bees started dying. Honey cost as much as gold! Remember? It will be the same with girls – less to buy, more expensive, more special. You will see.'

But she had been wrong. Mala could see that even though their numbers went down, somehow their price got lower. And so she was still finding the bad investments dumped in the bushes, to save their parents the price of a crippling dowry. Maybe better than letting them grow up and get married into one of those snake-eyed families who would torment them for years or burn them in an 'unfortunate kitchen accident', the daughters-in-law who were never forgiven for not bringing a fridge freezer or shiny motorcycle into their new joint family home.

But Mala knew that it was not like this everywhere, that be-yond her dust-defended village there were glimmers of change, thanks to a story she had spotted in one of Pogle sahib's discarded newspapers. She had been carefully collecting them before he threw them away, telling him she liked to keep the TV pages for Bee-ji. He had no idea she took away the English newspaper also. Not even Ram knew she could read and write English so well, top of her class every time. Mala's father had wanted to send her to college, even though he knew there would be snorting all around. Waste of time and money, giving that one even longer words to be big-mouth-*bai-sharam* with! But Mala's father knew who she was. '*Thithuli*,' he called her, a butterfly, too witty-flitty to settle, wanting to taste every passing blossom before the sunset. The only time he had ever shouted at her mother was when he had opened the rusty trunk looking for candles and found all the silk suits and embroidered linen she had put aside over the years for Mala's dowry, layered like a sweet silk pastry. 'You sold your earrings for this?' he had roared, lion-like, tearing the tissue paper and flinging it around their heads. Mala had caught a flake on her tongue, thinking it might taste like snow.

'Look at her!' He had grabbed his wife and turned her round to see Mala skipping with her mouth open like a frog catching flies. 'She's a child. You are already writing her future? And shutting it up in a box?'

Then he had locked the trunk and told Mala he would put money aside for her for college if she worked hard and came top in every subject.

But later on, she had had to break open the trunk and sell everything inside to pay for his funeral. As she had unwrapped each intricately patterned suit, the few pieces of simple jewellery, Mala realized that gold is worth nothing unless someone spots its glitter in the mud and digs it out to clean it up.

It was the photograph in the newspaper that had first caught her eye, a while ago. It was of a young woman, pretty enough, smiling shyly at the world. But it was the image of crowds of women around her that had moved Mala to rescue the page from the mouth of a knock-kneed baby goat and have a better look. Her name was Nisha, that much she could remember now, that pretty-enough woman, but what she had done! That was what had drawn all those crowds of women to her door, faces open to her like sunflowers, drinking her in. Just days before that photograph was taken, this is what had happened: Nisha, a nice middle-class girl from Delhi, was standing in her red-and-gold bridal sari, waiting to take her seven steps around the holy fire with her respectable, handsome, government-job-with-pension husband, when he and his vulture parents had asked for more money. Just like that, just before the ceremony, when, of course, many lakhs of rupees had been handed over already. But they knew, this government-job-with-pension boy and his family, that this was the perfect moment for blackmail: that they could demand anything, with all the gold-bedecked guests watching and waiting and three video cameras recording the whole *tamasha*. More money, another car, whatever it cost to stop them from calling off the wedding, for wouldn't the public shame and humiliation dumped upon this girl mean she would never get the chance to marry again? Apparently, Nisha's papa tried to plead with them, these people whom he had thought would become his family too, whom he had believed would love and cherish his daughter, as he had all his life. He told them he had given them all he could afford. That is when the boy's father hit him, full in the face. And then Nisha, the pretty-enough girl, calmly asked for her cellphone and called the police to arrest her government-job-with-pension almost-husband and his very surprised family. Because – and this is the paragraph that Mala had to read again and again, just to make sure she understood

69

the English perfectly – apparently it is illegal to demand dowry from a girl's family anymore. Against the law, written down and everything. But in the same way that doing a U-turn on a motorway to avoid a cow or driving the wrong way down a one-way street is also illegal, but everyone turns a blind eye and no one gets arrested, because the police would be arresting people all day long and have no time to do the important things like catching murderers, everyone still asks for dowry. At least where Mala lives. Because no one thinks anyone would be foolish or barefaced enough to call the police. Like Nisha did. No wonder she became a superwoman, an 'international heroine', said the newspaper, with tributes and wedding proposals coming to her from all over the world. Which also meant, Mala had realized, while squatting over the latrine reading the newspaper as if it was some tip-top dangerous secret book, that there were *men* out there who thought Nisha was a heroine also. Mala's insides churned with confusion. She rearranged her sari and hid the newspaper clipping in the lid of a masala tin.

She remembered that woman now, as she snapped the plastic lid on to the dented tin of ghee and returned it to its shelf – Nisha from New Delhi. She realized it was not the impossibility of sex that would keep her awake tonight, it was the possibility of a different life just beyond her reach, out there in the big cities where an ordinary woman could finally say no and someone might listen, and things might slowly-slowly change.

That's what Mala thought had happened to Seema. That she had gone to Delhi to make her own hard choice and undergo irreversible change; that Seema, or her husband, had arranged to have her unborn daughter sucked out of her, all nice and neatly. She knew that in the cities they had machines that could tell you whether you were carrying a future prince or a girl worth less than gold or honey. Better than going through the whole nine months praying and hoping, only to give birth to disappointment and the dull realization that you would become a birth-giver and a murderer all on the same day. Yes, this is what must have happened, nothing else could explain Seema's strange behaviour, and very soon she, Mala, was determined to know everything.

She felt Ram's eyes upon her as she moved around. Flecks of curd were caught in the tips of his moustache, and she glimpsed flashes of pink tongue, all baby-soft, as he chomped and swallowed.

'Can't you wait till I finish?' he asked. 'What's the hurry?'

Mala avoided his gaze, already on her way to the tap again. 'Bee-ji wants to go for a walk.'

Ram glanced over at Bee-ji, who was snoring buffalo breaths in front of the TV. Mala knew there was hardly any point in lying, he would eventually find out where she was going anyway. But she found herself enjoying the confusion on his face, enough to stop him mid-chew.

'Well, she asked me before. About a walk. So I will go anyway.' Mala clattered a pan to show she meant business.

'On your own?'

'Why? You got anything in mind to keep me here?'

Then she looked at him properly. His confusion drooped into shame and she knew she had won.

'You know how to make up Bee-ji's bed, don't you?' Mala said as she walked past her almost-new husband and wrapped herself in the ancient velvet shawl of the night.

# CHAPTER FIVE

S O, NOT SO much of a glue baby, more like a middle finger in the face of mortality, maybe?'

Lydia lit up another herbal cigarette and blew out a cloud of what smelled like smouldering tyres on a dungheap.

'Do you smoke when you have proper patients?' Shyama asked irritably, paddling her hands in front of her face.

'Clients, actually. And of course not!' tutted Lydia, struggling with the sash window until it finally creaked upwards with a wooden groan. 'And they're not allowed to smoke either. Or eat or drink anything other than water. It becomes displacement activity. But as I'm giving you the benefit of my insight for free, you may have to, as our cousins across the pond say, suck it up.'

'Could you at least smoke a proper fag then? These healthy ones make me retch.' Shyama coughed, adjusting her position on the faded brocade couch. 'You haven't answered my question yet.'

Lydia smiled, unfurling herself on the window-sill. There was something feline about her slanted playful eyes, her bendy androgynous body, the kind Shyama always envied. She'd have loved to have someone call her lithe, gamine even, be one of those women who could go bra-less without looking like a camel-smuggler, wear cigarette pants and a simple white shirt, pausing merely to muss her cropped hair and spritz herself with Chanel.

A quick glance at the women in her family told her this would be genetically impossible. 'Cankles' featured prominently amongst the various India-based matriarchs; at least she'd escaped those, but even her much smaller, shorter mother had once had the solid legs and cushioned hips of work-horse women. They had clearly been designed to walk long distances and bear heavy loads, possibly carrying the luggage of the irritating gamine brigade skipping far ahead with their pert, unfettered breasts. I'm an ox, Shyama thought, from an old culture built for survival and endurance. Lydia's a sleek weak European cat. And no wonder she had an amazing body, she'd never endured the irreparable car crash of childbirth. Thus Lydia and her adoring husband, Keith, were free to spend their considerable double income on exotic holidays, theatre and concerts, and, in Lydia's case, a personal Pilates trainer who visited her at home thrice weekly.

'Shyama, do you think Toby will leave you if you can't give him a baby?'

'No, I don't. Stop doing that weird look, I really don't.'

'What weird look?'

'You know, your I'm-hearing-a-lot-of-denial-right-now-in-the-room look that you do on your patients.'

'*Clients*. They're not ill.'

'Clients, customers, instant karma purchasers, whatever. He knew how old I was when we got together. It's not a deal-breaker or anything.'

Lydia raised an eyebrow.

'See, now you're doing the eyebrow thing!' Shyama yelled.

'What eyebrow thing?'

'The I'm-letting-you-speak-only-so-I-can-say-Really?-in-a-faintly-sarcastic-way-afterwards eyebrow thing.'

'Really?'

Shyama threw a cushion at Lydia's head. She batted it away in one graceful arm sweep and still managed to take a drag of her cigarette at the same time.

They both cracked then, big unashamed belly laughs which rolled back the years until they were students again, drunk and lazy-limbed on saggy mattresses, candles sputtering in cheap wine bottles, swapping embellished stories like Scheherazade trying to hold back the dawn. Shyama gulped for air, her sides aching; it was a while since she had laughed out loud. It felt like she'd had a workout but without having to wash her hair afterwards.

'Now I know what the Laughing Guru was on about.' She sighed, wiping her eyes.

'You've made that up.' Lydia sighed back, resettling herself on the window-sill before stubbing out the cigarette on the brick-work outside.

'I swear, I saw him on Juhu Beach, years ago now. He believes – or believed, I have no idea if he's still around – that laughing is as good for you as meditation. Better, in fact. It purifies the soul, apparently. He gets his followers to stand in a circle and they all just guffaw their way to nirvana.'

'What happens if you don't feel like laughing at that particular moment?'

'Someone tells a dirty joke, they get out the holy custard pies, I don't know. It looked like fun for the first ten minutes, quite infectious really. And then . . .' Shyama dredged up the memory, sunlit and salty-tasting. 'Then it looked quite creepy. Thirty-odd people laughing to order, not allowed to stop until he said so. I had a similar feeling when I visited an all-year-round Christmas shop. "Where every day is Christmas." The elf behind the counter looked clinically depressed.'

'Too much of anything, however pleasurable or exciting, will eventually bore or depress us,' Lydia mused. 'One of the major reasons people come and lie on my couch is to be able to cope with some life-changing event. And yet, change is essential for our growth and understanding of what pain and pleasure are. It's all relative. So, for example, if you hadn't married your first husband . . .'

'I wouldn't have properly appreciated the many talents of Toby Toy Boy?'

'Exactly. But don't mix up appreciation with obligation. You don't owe him a baby as a thank-you for sticking around an old bag like you.'

'I know that too.'

'Then why?' Lydia paused delicately. 'You're forty-eight, Shyams . . .'

'I know that, thanks.'

'You've nearly drained your glass in the last-chance saloon, don't you think? And aren't there other things you want to do with your life right now?'

Shyama sat up and looked Lydia straight in the eye. 'You don't approve, do you?'

'It's not about me endorsing your decision, Shyama. It's just . . .' Lydia shrugged. 'I see a lot of women your age twisting themselves into agonies about the babies they should have had, can't have. Let's put aside the women who actually have kids who are driving them potty . . .'

'I know that one, too.' Shyama smiled weakly.

'Right. But be thankful you're not in the other camp – our generation who thought we could schedule in babies, and then found out ovaries don't follow a time-management chart. Not that I think that was wrong. I would have been a miner's wife if my granny had had her way.'

75

'Yeah, I can just see you in a pinny, wiping up the coal dust and sputum from the hearth . . .'

'More importantly, because of our sacrifices – and there were many – we can offer our daughters the luxury of choice.'

'You don't have a daughter,' Shyama sniffed, 'so you don't know.'

'Know what?'

'Most of her generation don't even call themselves feminists. Apparently it's a swear word implying lesbian tendencies and a predilection for denim boilersuits. They defend topless models as empowered women making a smart career move; they drink and swear and shag like the worst kind of bloke and call it being equal and liberated . . .'

'And that's all of them, is it? Every woman under thirty thinks that way?'

'Maybe just the ones I hear in my house.'

Lydia uncrossed her limbs and jumped lightly down from the window-sill. Outside her window stretched the Flats, acres of green fringed by semi-wild foliage which extended a couple of miles into the next borough and almost to the end of Shyama's road. Lydia had often jogged between the two houses for an impromptu coffee; Shyama inevitably drove round in her car. Recently, a flock of wild parrots had been spotted swooping over the treetops, noisy jewelled immigrants claiming their patch of the suburbs. It had even prompted an article in the local newspaper, inspiring Tara to purchase a bagful of birdseed which she scattered on the tiny balcony outside her room. She hadn't said anything to Shyama, who, weeks later, had had to climb out there with the Hoover and tidy up the rotting heap of uneaten husks.

'Tara is a lot smarter than you give her credit for,' Lydia said lightly, snapping on the kettle. 'Tea?'

'No, thanks,' Shyama said, getting to her feet. She noticed she emitted a slight noise as she did so, something between a groan and a sigh. This was definitely one of the first signs of ageing. Being in a room full of her parents' friends at going-home time was like listening to an arthritic symphony, a veritable orchestra of 'Hai!'s and 'Ooff!'s – and her favourite, 'Oeeeweeesh!', which had made Shyama and Tara flee the room, fists stuffed into their mouths. And now she too had joined the Osteoporosis Choir. She flexed her back for a moment, checking nothing had actually slipped off its axis.

'You know I adore Tara,' Shyama said, waiting for Lydia's response. Lydia carried on rattling teacups. 'It's just . . . is it awful to say I love her but sometimes I find her – or at least some of her attitudes . . . disappointing?'

'And you reckon you've never disappointed your mother?'

Shyama grinned. 'OK, I think this session's well and truly over. I've got to get back to work anyhow. And by the way, I don't intend to actually carry a baby myself. In fact, medically I can't. So that's that.'

She enjoyed the look of surprise on Lydia's face, and spotted something else there too. Relief maybe?

'Right. Well that's . . . well, I have loads of contacts in adoption, Shyama, if that's—'

'No, we ruled that out once we found out the length of the waiting lists round here. It's even longer if you want to use donor eggs. By the time we were near the top of either list, I'd be . . . a lot older. And getting a baby – I mean any child under three – is also really difficult.' Shyama saw Lydia take a breath, but ploughed on. 'And I know there are loads of older kids who need a loving home, but many of them need really patient, specialized parenting because of what they've been through, and Toby and I felt . . . well, it wouldn't be fair. On Tara, especially.'

'Is that what Tara thinks?'

'I don't know what she thinks, exactly . . .' Shyama hesitated. 'Every time I try to mention anything to do with babies, adopted or otherwise, she looks like she wants to vomit on me.'

'Sorry, I'm confused here.' Lydia paused. 'Aren't you worried that Tara doesn't seem to be at all receptive to the idea of a new sibling? You know, it doesn't matter how old you are, there will always be issues of jealousy, displacement.'

'Get to the point, Lyd, I'm late already. Confused about what?'

Lydia sighed. She wondered how much she should tell her dear friend about the frequent late-night chats she had with Tara, mostly on the phone, sometimes in her kitchen when Tara had turned up, tipsy and tearful, raging against the mother-stranger she lived with. Keith never questioned the intrusions, retiring discreetly to his study or returning to bed, understanding that for Lydia this was not work, it was something she regarded as familial duty. Tara would ask Lydia the questions that only Shyama could answer: why had she never been encouraged to keep in contact with her father? Why was she expected to babysit her grandparents whilst her mother was out having fun with Toby? Why did her mother make her feel inadequate all the time? Why was she so convinced that Tara would never really understand the struggles and politics of her mother's generation, because Tara and her friends had all had it far too easy? ('Oh, you want to talk about racism? Well, just listen to what we had to put up with!') Ditto sexism ('I nearly went to Greenham!'), self-image ('At least you have role models now. Who did we have?'), and educational pressure ('I was considered a freak because I couldn't do science!'). Tara moaned to Lydia that it was like some twisted game of generational Top Trumps, where any experience or complaint she might have was automatically bested by her mother, who had got there before her and apparently suffered so much more. And even though Shyama encouraged Tara at regular intervals to 'plug into your mother culture', it was in a preachy, take-your-medicine-it's-good-for-you kind of way. She'd direct her to the Mughal Miniatures exhibition at the British Library, the Indian classical-music concerts on the South Bank, various India-based news websites cataloguing the latest political scandals, the rise of the burgeoning middle classes, the hot new filmi actresses, the marches against the acid attacks on women who had dared to turn down their suitors, who then returned with plastic bottles of living death to fling in their faces.

'I mean, I know she thinks I'm not . . . I mean, if she wanted me to be more Indian, why hasn't she taken me to India? Kept me in touch with family there? Why didn't she teach me Hindi? I only know a few Hindu prayers because of Nanima, not her! If she thinks I'm . . . inauthentic, it's mainly her fault, isn't it?'

Lydia might have privately agreed with Tara, but she felt unqualified to mine this particular cultural seam. Jewish issues she could do – most of the people who had trained her were Jewish and she thought she had a handle on the guilt-mother-communal-trauma-heritage stuff. But this, this was her friend whom she loved, and her friend's daughter, who was suffering, and she felt torn and compromised. Maybe now was the time to put that right.

'I'm confused, Shyams, because you say you want a baby, you say you've ruled out adoption, yet you're still going ahead with . . . What? Something. And Tara's still not part of this massive decision. Shouldn't she be?'

'Lyd, I have spent the last twenty years putting Tara first. I gave up my job for her for years, I put up with a shitty marriage for her for years. I went without so much so she could have the kind of education my parents couldn't afford for me. I may not have done the best job with her, but I did *my* best.'

'Right. So, honestly, do you think that possibly you want a baby because you're hoping to do a better job with the next one?'

Shyama thought she must have misheard, but Lydia's steady gaze confirmed what she had just said. Now she remembered why they had stopped taking holidays together – because there was always a point where Lydia's heavy social drinking tipped over to sullen, determined self-destruction, a point where kind, measured Lydia turned into a viper-tongued virago, lashing out at anyone nearby, but mostly at herself. Ken had seen his wife through two stints of rehab and her adoring clientele knew nothing of her bouts of self-medication. And Lydia's friends kept a quiet eye on their social boozing and prepared themselves for the occasional bouts of drink-and-dial she would inflict upon them during the early hours of some endless night. But it meant she stood on shaky ground when she decided to tell her nearest and dearest exactly how they were screwing up their lives.

Shyama became aware of her own accelerated breathing, and she briefly wondered whether beneath the fury simmered a layer of skin-prickling shame.

'Well.' She finally found her voice. 'Thanks for the free session. Just glad I caught you sober.' She paused at the kitchen counter. 'I've been talking it through with Priya anyway, and it was her idea. We're going to find a surrogate.'

The sound of Lydia's cup smashing into the sink coincided nicely with the slamming of the door.

Shyama was still shaky when she parked in her usual space on the forecourt of Bhupinder's Khalsa Stores and hurried past the shopfronts with their wares displayed outside: iridescent garlands of bangles; boxes of sparkly stick-on bindis, including the triple-layered Big Macs, as Tara called them; food stalls offering up cones of buttered lemon-tanged sweetcorn and plastic tumblers of freshly crushed sugar-cane juice; hardware stores stocking appliances you would only find in this part of town: circular metal spice boxes with snugly fitting little pots inside them, one for each masala; grainy black griddles, slightly curved to give breath to every chapatti; an orgy of Tupperware, because there's no such thing as a leftover; a cornucopia of serving dishes and novelty-shaped plates with different compartments for various nibbles; alarm clocks that sang out the call to Allah; mini elephant-headed Ganesh gods to stick on your dashboard (double insurance in case of accident); holy threads and bootleg Bollywood, and every staple half the price of the supermarket.

The pavements were already thronged with shoppers. Five years ago this area had been considered a no-go ghetto; now it had been repackaged as a vibrant pocket of London's multicultural heritage, with the help of some strategically placed murals – mosaic elephants always went down well – and a glossy leaflet urging visitors to 'Follow the Spice Trail!' which led them to the doors of the businesses that had paid for the leaflet in the first place. But nevertheless, it had worked and Shyama was grateful for it.

She still felt that nudge of pride as she rounded the bend and saw the distinctive red-and-gold logo of the Surya Beauty Salon like a beacon up ahead. The business – *her* business – was doing well, although it had been a huge risk, investing what little savings she had left after the divorce in a new venture. But she had seen what other places were charging for traditional treatments such as threading and sugaring and knew she could undercut them, if only she could find the right location. And it had come up: a former chemist's right here in Little India, as the area was now called in various tourist guides trying to big up East London and its many attractions. She had found the right staff – young women from India who wanted to make some real money on a short visa, who worked hard, knew their stuff and were so fast they could have threaded a gorilla in under ten minutes.

She paused at the large picture window, taking a moment to watch her staff work their magic on the row of customers seated in their leather chairs, their faces tilted to offer up an eyebrow or an upper lip. Beside them, the girls held their thread between their teeth and one finger, heads bobbing like chickens as they expertly found each rogue hair, trapped it between twisted thread and yanked it out by the root. Their skill, coupled with the reasonable prices, now brought all kinds of women through the salon's frosted-glass door. The Indian girls were training up other young women Shyama had found locally – she liked the mix of *desis* and homies. Her workplace was a noisy female retreat where a woman could walk in wearing the stubble of the world and walk out feeling like a million rupees. Thank God for my hairy sisters, Shyama thought as she pushed open the door.

Shyama knew Priya was in the salon as soon as she walked in. From one of the cubicles at the back came the sound of furious expletives, inconveniently raising the eyebrows of all the women sitting in their soft leather chairs, whose threaders had to pause at every 'Shit!' and 'Bollocks!' that shattered their concentration.

'How far gone is she?' Shyama muttered to Gita as she hurriedly removed her coat and flung it over the stand near the reception desk.

'I think just half a leg left,' Gita whispered, her index fingers still wound round with thread as her customer sat patiently, a palm placed on either side of her eye socket, stretching the skin in preparation. Gita fired something off in Hindi and a few of the other girls giggled companionably. They could have been sisters, her employees, these round-faced, sloe-eyed women, all with long tied-back hair, neat centre partings and a tiny red bindi nestling between their perfectly shaped eyebrows. They all wore short white Nehru-style jackets over their own shalwar kameezes, saris and jeans – no logo other than a small embroidered sun over the breast pocket. Surya had been Shyama's first choice of name when she knew she was carrying a girl. She liked the idea of calling her daughter after the sun itself, a child full of light, warmth and fiery goodness. But her husband had vetoed it, wanting something more 'user-friendly'. After an emergency Caesarian, a blood transfusion and liberal doses of morphine, Shyama would have said yes to anything. But she had compensated for her own missed opportunity by naming her salon Surya, thus proving Tara's pointed observation that her business was the child she'd always wanted.

Shyama roamed a practised eye over the room as she made her way towards the treatment cubicles at the rear, from where Priya's swearing had now subsided to a generalized sort of wounded moo-ing. She smiled apologetically at the regulars who were in varying stages of treatments: women mummified under thickly caked face masks, or turbanned in towels like patient Nefertitis.

Gita tapped her on the shoulder gently, a spool of thread in one hand, a thin folder in the other. '*Didi*? That info you wanted on the Moroccan argan-oil products?'

After so long together, Gita still never called Shyama by her name, only ever addressing her as *didi*, respected elder sister, a habit Shyama found touching and ageing all at once. The bond they shared went beyond that of a boss and employee; they had

83

met when Gita had come in one day all those many years ago for a leg wax. Despite Gita's careful efforts to conceal them as she undressed, Shyama had spotted straight away the bruises mottling her thighs and wrists. She was as frail as a bird, all thin-boned and hunched against the gale of her husband's daily abuse. Having just been through her own divorce, Shyama found it impossible not to listen, then advise and finally encourage her to escape the marriage that was erasing her. As is so often the case, the main reason Gita stayed and endured was money: she couldn't afford to leave her husband. Not until Shyama offered her a job, and found beneath the droopy feathers a skeleton of steel and a ferociously loyal heart.

And then, gradually, word must have been spread by Gita amongst her network of friends and their acquaintances, because women started to trickle in looking for something more than a threading. Maybe seeing that Shyama had been able to walk away from her own marriage without becoming a crack-whore or being struck by lightning had provided the nudge these other unhappily married women needed to flee theirs. Customers would call her over and enquire in hushed tones if she could recommend a cheap counsellor or a good lawyer or, in more extreme cases, a nearby refuge where they could take their children. Who would have thought there were so many of them? Amongst all the plucking and preening, so much suppressed sorrow, so much anger or regret or just never-before-asked questions, which came to the surface in that space where women finally stop and breathe while their hair gets washed and their scalps get massaged and their faces are treated with gentle respect. Maybe the very act of beautifying themselves made them think, who is this for? For someone who has not seen my worth for many years? For myself? How can I justify spending money on apricot scrubs and French manicures when I willingly lay my face in the dirt as soon as he walks through the door?

Shyama had felt powerful in her role as beautician/confidante, it suited her aggressively self-sufficient lifestyle at this single-and-proud stage in her life. Now, looking into Gita's placid eyes, she wondered what her reaction would be when she found out what her *didi* was planning next.

Shyama smiled her thanks at Gita, hurried to the last cubicle at the back of the salon and knocked gently before entering. Priya lay spreadeagled in matching lacy underwear as Neha disposed of a heap of pink wax strips, each one furred with small black hairs.

'She's evil!' Priya moaned, raising a shaky finger towards Neha. 'I think she drew blood this time.'

Flipping the pedal bin expertly with a dainty foot, Neha rolled her eyes. 'You're worse than the kids who get their ears pierced! Next time I'm gonna give you a lollipop to shut you up!' Neha's cockney glottals, mingled with a Punjabi twang, always caught Shyama by surprise, so at odds were they with her serene classical beauty. 'God knows how you had kids, innit?'

'Darling girl,' purred Priya, running her fingers over her baby-smooth legs, 'that's what drugs are for. For our next session I may just book an epidural.'

Priya reached into her mammoth handbag, unpeeled a note from a whole roll and handed it to Neha, who snatched it appreciatively before hustling off to her next client.

Priya lay back on the treatment couch and stretched lazily. 'It's bloody agony, but I feel so clean afterwards. What's the face for?'

Shyama hadn't been aware she was scowling. The sight of Priya's perfectly toned body didn't help her mood. She was all honeyed limbs and gym-honed muscle, the only imperfection the barely visible Caesarian scar curved like a rueful smile just below her navel. Shyama herself had always rather regretted that she had ended up not giving birth naturally; certainly her NCT teacher had made a point of congratulating all the mummies who'd managed to squeeze their babies out without medical intervention. All she said to Shyama was, 'Never mind. Next time, eh?' According to Priya, both her kids had needed emergency Caesarians – 'One was stuck and the other was just bloody lazy!' – though Shyama suspected the real emergency had been Priya's panic at the thought of having a vaginal cavity as big as a bucket. 'Too Punjabi Princess to push' should have been written on her admittance form.

'I've just had a bit of a row with Lyd,' Shyama muttered, nudging Priya sideways so she could slump on to the couch beside her.

'Ah, told you she wouldn't take it well.' Priya sighed. 'What did she say about the surrogate idea?'

'I don't know, didn't give her a chance. She said . . . she implied . . . doesn't matter. Didn't know she could be that mean without alcohol.'

'I hope you didn't say that. Shyama?'

'I can't stand it when women judge other women, when they should know, more than anyone else, how bloody hard it is!'

'Have you forgotten already?' Priya stifled a yawn. 'Who gave you the hardest time after you split up with Shiv? You thought it would be your dad's weirdy-beardy mates, shouting for you to shave your head and padlock your pants.'

'I'm sure some of them were thinking it.'

'But the ones who actually said it to your face? Their wives, right?'

'Not exactly. It was just . . . they didn't know what to do with me. Divorced single mother, the first in their circle. I think they were worried it might be infectious.'

'How times have changed, sweetie!' Priya laughed. 'I think you started a trend.'

'I remember once going to this party with Mum and Dad. It was only a few months after he'd moved out, and the hosts were so embarrassed at having to find a single place at the dinner table, they actually put me in the TV room with the teenagers and kids, with a tray on my lap.'

'Nooo!'

'It was either that or sit in the extension with all the old widows massaging their feet and waiting for their pureed samosas. And I had dyed my hair the day before – remember when I went literally scarlet 'cos I left it on too long? I was like an installation, "Woman on Fire with Pissed-Off Face".'

'And they just left you in there? The whole evening?' Priya sat up and reached for her clothes, layers of silk and cashmere whispering over her body.

'The host auntie came in with dessert – I think it was ice cream in a Disney bowl – as I was sneaking out, 'cos by then . . . well, you can imagine. And this woman, she cornered me and said something along the lines of, "Stop feeling sorry for yourself. If *we* all had to put up with shitty marriages, why shouldn't you?"'

'She said "shitty"?'

'Like I said, I'm paraphrasing, but it was . . . surprising. And really sad. She didn't hate me. It felt like she envied me.'

'Bet she did. Don't you think loads of our mums' generation would have run for the hills, given half a chance, high heels in one hand and what was left from their dowry in the other?'

'Funny, me and Lyd were just discussing that. How lucky we are to have choices. I suppose for that generation it was either a lonely marriage or lonely independence, because remarrying was out of the question. For women, anyway.'

'I love being a woman,' Priya declared, zipping up her tailored pencil skirt. 'It all becomes simple when you stop trying to second-guess what men want and realize how basic they are. If you'd had a son, you'd know what I mean.'

'I had a husband, doesn't that count?'

'No, no, it's too late with a husband because you don't see them in their young, raw state. With Luka, watching him grow up was like a light coming on, honestly. Here's the thing, they have all this bluff and bluster and they want to go out and fight dragons and win at everything and are obsessed with their winkies . . .'

'I'm with you so far.'

'But they can't do any of it without constant approval. Without this drip-drip "Yes, you're the best at everything and king of the world and yes, I'm looking at you, and just let me know when you need a hug-break and a biscuit." If they have that, they can do anything. Without it, they're bloody useless.'

Priya was at the mirror now, pulling a strange crinkly face so she could ascertain how much she had aged in the past half-hour.

'But every kid needs reassurance, Priya,' Shyama shot back. 'I'm no Lydia, but I think I could have worked that one out.'

'No, it's not the same with daughters. Of course, Maya needs me to be there for her, but . . . I dunno, you look at your daughter and you know she's as smart and wily and strong as you are. There's a sort of mirror thing going on. When the mood swings and the self-loathing crap kick off, you know how that goes because you've been there. You know how her body feels. You know she loves you but also can't wait to not be like you, right?'

'The Queen is dead, long live the Queen, sort of thing?'

'Right. But with boys – and men – the real shocker is not how complicated they are. It's how simple they are. Full tummies, regular sex and timetabled ego stroking, and no one would ever need to go to Relate again.'

Shyama wondered if Priya's regular extra-marital affairs had anything to do with the apparently happy marriage she extolled at every opportunity. In their early days, Priya would regale her and Lydia with spicy tales of illicit couplings in various hotel chains around the country. Gradually the hotels got more expensive and foreign, as did the men, and her stories became less detailed, less tinged with uneasy wonder; maybe Priya sensed from her audience that what had sounded daring and bohemian at thirty-five sounded a little more habitual and jaded at forty-five. Not that Shyama had ever judged her friend, not consciously. By then she knew that nothing was as inexplicable as other people's marriages; hadn't she seen the look of incredulity on their faces when she'd relayed her latest awful anecdote from her own marital car crash? And who knew what arrangement had been agreed to in Priya and Anil's marriage? Maybe he played around too. Maybe he turned a blind eye to her dalliances, accepting them as some kind of reciprocal payment for his wife's devotion and her care for his ailing parents, her über-mater marshalling of their children. Priya's presence in the world confirmed to Shyama that there were two kinds of people: those who bent and bullied life into submission, who accepted nothing as inevitable, predetermined or fated; and those who made plans, tried hard to keep to them, but knew when to shrug their shoulders, let go painfully and walk away with some dignity intact. Shyama knew which camp she was in, and at times like this, she was thankful that her friend was in the other.

At that moment, Priya reached into her briefcase and slapped a bulging file on to the couch. 'I've researched all the ones we liked the look of. And I think I've found the perfect place for you and Toby.'

'Where?'

'New Delhi. You're going home, baby!'

As the soothing music began drifting from Priya's laptop, Shyama burnt her tongue on her steaming cup of chai latte. Priya turned the volume down and pulled Shyama further back into the velveted booth. The Tip-Top Café was heaving this lunchtime. Shyama remembered the days when they had sat here on plastic seats at Formica-topped tables and been served their chai in metal beakers, which had scalded the palms of the uninitiated. But last year, the premises had been taken over by some baby-boomer City dropout, a smart Punjabi guy who had made his millions working for The Man and decided to take early retirement to indulge the artistic yearnings he'd been banned from exploring as a student. He knew that Bollywood-themed eateries were now passé, and instead had exploited the childhood nostalgia into which his contemporaries were retreating, the first-generation immigrant kids who fondly recalled sofas covered in plastic film, concreted-over front gardens with rusting swingballs instead of flowers, and fridges containing ice-cream cartons deceptively concealing leftover curry. So Tip-Top, named after a synthetic-cream topping used on the pudding of choice in the seventies Indian household – tinned fruit cocktail – was now an *homage* to that decade: leather sofas and loud textured wallpaper; rush table-mats and light-up Taj Mahals; nests of tables around tiled mantelpieces where home-fried snacks were served in period dishes; framed film posters of the era, a time when stars had rounder bellies and luxuriant, bouffant hair; even framed black-and-white photos of the extended family – *whose* family was irrelevant as everyone looked the same back then – a row of unsmiling, stiff-backed relatives obscuring whatever monument or achievement they were meant to be celebrating: Trafalgar Square, India Gate, Bitoo's new moped, a beloved son or daughter emigrating, perhaps forever. All this, coupled with the undoubtedly excellent food – reasonably priced, always hot – made Tip-Top one of the places to hang out in the East End, although the local families who used to visit were now drifting away, unable to turn up and get a table, edged out by the trustafarians and edgy boho-clones eager not to miss out on the next undiscovered hangout. Luckily for Shyama and Priya, their mutual friend Kate happened to be married to the owner, Joshan, so they had their own regular booth that was always available to them, excluding rush hours and private-party bookings.

'You have to see the clip they've posted, it gives you a good idea of what the place is like.'

Priya clicked on it and waited as the music snapped off and the face of a fine-boned, almond-eyed Indian woman filled the screen, the swathes of grey at her temples at odds with the healthy youthful glow emanating from her face.

'Hello, I'm Dr Renu Passi. Welcome to the Passi Clinic,' she began in a deep husky voice more suited to a chocolate advert than a surrogacy clinic. 'We are one of India's leading centres for ART – that is, Assisted Reproductive Technology – and we hope by the end of this short presentation you will see why.'

Dr Passi's dulcet tones narrated the story of how she had resigned from her previous post as a consultant obstetrician at one of Delhi's leading private hospitals to found the Passi Clinic, which had always been 'a special dream of mine', fuelled by the misery she continually encountered from the infertile couples seeking her advice. 'In India we now have an infertility rate of fifteen per cent and climbing, though still lower than the average rate in the Western world.' Dismayed by the rising rate of unwanted pregnancies amongst the poorer, uneducated women she treated, she had the idea that surrogacy would be the perfect and humane solution for both parties.

'This is a life-changing and life-enhancing experience for everyone involved: for the couples who long for a baby, and for the women who carry the child for them. The fees that our surrogate mothers receive enable them to transform their lives: to buy their own homes, educate their children . . . it gives them financial independence they could not get any other way. As for our couples, who visit us from all over the world, because India is now the world centre for ART, they not only get the gift of a longed-for child, but they also know that their money is going to help the woman who has given a new life to them.'

The picture suddenly sped up as Priya fast-forwarded with a perfectly buffed nail. 'You don't need to know all this boring info, she's just basically saying the clinic adheres to the newly implemented government guidelines on ART. Not all of them do.'

'What guidelines, exactly?' Shyama was irritated, frustrated by the glimpses of gleaming white labs and PowerPoint presentations that jumped across the screen. In between the flashes of techno-speak, she saw snatches of a low-roofed white building surrounded by lush gardens, what looked like a modest hotel lobby, and a smartly furnished bedroom with a widescreen TV in the corner.

'Basically, surrogacy is unregulated in India right now, that's why it's cheap. There are guidelines laid down rather than laws, so it varies from clinic to clinic. I chose this one because they seem to be long-established and well-organized, have a good success rate and are pretty strict in their parameters: all the surrogates have to be married, have a clean bill of health and medical history, to have had two healthy births themselves, agree not to have sexual relations during the pregnancy . . .'

'Nine months with no sex?' Strange how unfair this now seemed to Shyama, whereas during her marriage it would have struck her as perfectly reasonable.

'I know!' chimed Priya, her eyes still focused on the screen. 'I mean, nine months not shagging your husband, fair enough, but they have to promise not to do it with anyone. That's dedication, huh? And they have to have a signed permission form from their husbands to offer themselves up for surrogacy at all.'

'That's a bit dodgy, isn't it? What about the woman's right to choose, own her own body and all that?'

'It's India, darling. And most of these women are from rural areas. I don't think it would go down too well with the local menfolk if they snuck off and came back up the duff with a foreigner's sprog. Even if it will pay for a new tractor or what-ever. It's for their protection, at the end of the day.'

'Whose, the clinic's?'

'The woman's . . . oh, you don't need this section about egg retrieval either, right? Because you won't be using your own.'

'No,' Shyama said quietly, flinching at a sudden image of her ovaries spread out like two burnt trees with bunches of shrivelled eggs swinging creakily from their branches, a mournful wind moaning through the cavern of her inhospitable womb.

'Lucky you!' breezed Priya. 'Because it looks bloody vile, the whole thing. You have to have three days of really painful injections which pump you full of hormones that make you bloat and gag, and then hang around for two weeks until they harvest them – they actually say "harvest", like you're growing watermelons or something. And there's no guarantee you'll produce any class-A eggs anyway. And of course it pushes the cost up, the longer you stay – if you use donor eggs you can get away with a three-day trip. But they offer all the options if you're both infertile – you can still make the baby, it's just that it won't actually be genetically yours. But that's the same as adoption anyway, isn't it?'

Priya's voice was getting louder and more excitable as she continued scrolling through the film. Shyama was relieved to see a waiter approaching with their food order, the loaded plates trailing spicy wisps of steam behind them. As he smiled and bent towards the table, Priya looked up at Shyama. 'But you'll still be using Toby's sperm, right?'

The waiter's smile fixed itself to his face like a frightened leech and his tray wobbled slightly, just enough to send a buttery tide of sauce over the lip of each plate.

'I am so sorry, Madam,' he stuttered, reaching for a pile of paper serviettes which Shyama grabbed off him.

The waiter scuttled off thankfully as Shyama reached round and plucked Priya's hand from the keyboard. 'Stop it!'

Priya's eyes flashed for a second, then softened as she took in Shyama's mortified face. She squeezed her friend's hand back.

'I'm taking over, as usual. I get it.' Priya rose, grabbing her handbag. 'I'm going to freshen up, make a few calls. Just browse the site and tell me what you think, OK?'

Later on, with Toby in the privacy of their bedroom, Shyama kept returning to the same section of the promotional film. It featured a roomful of surrogates, all plump with pregnancy, sitting on their single beds in their shared dormitory. But for the colourful batik bedspreads and the swollen bellies straining under bright saris, it could have been tuck-box time in a modest girls' boarding school. As each woman spoke to the camera, subtitles appeared below. They were mostly shy, some of them covering their mouths with their saris, and most were dark-skinned, that rich burnished brown that comes from hours of hard work under a hot sun. But they were always smiling.

'This is my third time here,' one woman with an enormous golden nose piercing told the camera. 'It is not allowed to give more than three babies so I feel sad I cannot come again. Dr Passi is so kind to us. And after this baby, my own three children will be safe for the rest of their lives.'

Shyama paused on her use of the word 'safe'. Her three children would be safe because she was willing to hand over three babies she had carried with her for nine months each. An eye for an eye, almost literally.

'We are looked after very well,' another woman mumbled behind her hand, though her eyes danced mischeviously at the camera. 'Always good food, fruit, all the tests and medicines . . . and we have classes sometimes – reading, writing, making cushion coverings.'

Dr Passi's melodic voice cut in with a question; the woman paused then replied, 'Yes, we can meet the couples we have the babies for, if they want it. Some don't, you know. And we can stay in contact every week during the pregnancy. Sometimes with phone or on the Skype. And they get all the ultrasound pictures also.'

She said 'ultrasound' and 'Skype' as easily as Shyama would say 'facial' and 'leg wax'. The woman continued, 'We sign a contract to say we do not want to see the child again after we have returned it to the parents.'

Again, Shyama was struck by her use of the word 'return'. Stressing that the baby was never hers to begin with. She wondered if that's what this woman had actually said, or if something had been lost or added in translation.

Toby exhaled loudly, watching next to her intently.

'That's good to know. I mean, that's what I'd worry about, that she'd change her mind about handing over the baby or come back in a few years wanting access or something.'

'I know,' Shyama agreed. 'That was my biggest worry, more than any of the legal or medical stuff. If someone had turned up when I was lying on the delivery table and said, "OK, hand her over because she's not really yours" . . . I think I'd have killed them first. But then, it must feel different, if it's not your baby.'

Shyama moved the cursor to a headline entitled 'Your Legal Rights' and quickly skimmed through it.

'Basically each surrogate signs away all legal and parental rights after the birth. Even if the child decides at eighteen they want to trace their birth mother, all they will be given is a name. No address, no other contact details.'

'Right, right, could I . . . ?' Toby took over the mouse and clicked on the legal section, while the promotional film continued playing uninterrupted in the background.

Shyama remained silent for a moment as he read, watching the mischievous woman being replaced by another smiling face, this one with an impressive overbite which gave her the air of a friendly rabbit.

She found herself holding Toby's other hand, running her fingertips over his calluses, reading the Braille of his bones. Toby planted an absent-minded kiss on her head, a fatherly kiss that made Shyama imagine the shadowy, unformed child whose creation they were discussing. That old saying, 'Oh, that was before you were born, when you were still a twinkle in your father's eye!' came to mind. Is that when a child really

began – when the yearning began? When the planning and speculating and plotting the ovulation calendar began? Then times
had changed. It wasn't a twinkle any more. It was an obsessive,
hungry gleam. She saw it in her own face now, reflected back at
her in the dark edges of the computer screen. Toby, still reading,
tapped the mouse as he began speaking.

'It's a very normal worry, according to this. But they are
saying – here it is – the surrogate will only be given the choice to
terminate if there is a problem with the pregnancy and in
consultation with the intended parents. And there's a scale of
compensation for us if the mother miscarries, or there's something wrong with the . . . foetus so they have to terminate the
pregnancy for medical reasons. I mean, they seem to have covered
every eventuality.'

'And if she changes her mind?' Shyama pressed him. 'Doesn't
it say—'

Toby anticipated her response, nodding his head. 'Yup, she
doesn't get paid. And in this clinic, she may even be asked to
repay some of the money that has been spent on her medical
upkeep, because "for your protection, we would regard this as a
breach of contract".'

'For our protection,' murmured Shyama.

'Well, it's not likely, is it?' continued Toby, still fixated on the
screen. 'They couldn't afford to pay anything back – that's why
they're doing it in the first place, isn't it?'

Shyama nodded. She knew it was ridiculous to shy away
from the bare fact that this was a business transaction, fundamentally. Money made it possible, money was the incentive.
Supply and demand, the basis for all successful trading. India had
fertile poor women; Britain and America and most places west of
Poland had wealthy infertile women. It had begun with companies

moving their call centres towards the rising sun, so what was wrong with outsourcing babies there too, when at the end of the process there was a new human being and a woman with financial independence? It was a win-win situation, wasn't it?

Toby's voice sounded gentle when he asked, 'So, how much is this actually going to cost?'

He braced himself. He'd already spent an hour poring over his accounts before sitting down to watch this with her. At the last calculation, they had enough between them to fund one more cycle of IVF, though, of course, they now knew this would be a complete waste of money. What he hadn't told Shyama was that he had gone up that day to see his brother, Matt, who now ran the family farm. It was the first sickie he had ever pulled in his life. He had hopped on a train from Stratford, startled at the monolithic shopping mall that seemed to have sprung up when he wasn't looking. Beyond it, the London Olympic Park, the red twisted strands of the fabled Corkscrew Tower just visible, like a monument to an abandoned fairground. Within two hours, he had been at the family table, scarred oak stained with a thousand cups of tea, asking his big brother for money. When Toby refused to tell Matt what the money was for, Matt stared at him for a while before asking, 'You're not in trouble, are you? Or . . . sick? Or . . .'

'No, it's nothing to worry about.' Toby returned his gaze steadily. 'It's a . . . business investment. With Shyama. I'm just asking for a loan against my share of the land. So if I can't return it, you keep whatever acreage it adds up to.'

Toby's phrasing implied a demand more than a request. Matt's curiosity was outweighed by the prospect of clawing back the fields Toby had insisted they left for livery horses. Daft idea, Matt had told him so at the time. Hosting Pony Club events and having the lane clogged up with four-wheel-drives when parents dropped off their little darlings to tend to their horses was not his idea of farming. He'd barely nodded his head before Toby was up and heading towards the door.

'I have to get back at the usual time. Shyama doesn't know I'm here.'

And that was the only apologetic note sounded in the whole of their brief meeting.

He'd met her a few times, this Indian bird of his brother's. Not bad looking, but far too old for him. He watched Toby heave open the courtyard gate, only then wondering whether he should have offered to drop him off at the train station. Well, he hadn't asked. He rarely asked Matt for anything, so this must be important to him. 'Not my business,' Matt had muttered to himself as he drained the dregs of his tea. 'Just hope she's worth it.'

'How much?'

Shyama shifted uncomfortably on the bed. 'Basically the couple – you and me – we would decide the exact fee with the . . . surrogate and the clinic, but it's around . . . between six and nine thousand pounds, on average.'

'Is that all?' Toby's face broke into a beam of relief. 'Blimey, that's not much more than two rounds of IVF! We can afford that easily, can't we?'

'Six grand? That's immoral.'

Shyama and Toby swung round to see Tara standing in the doorway, a mug of tea in each hand.

'Can't you knock?' Shyama said, her embarrassment making her sound angrier than she felt.

'Firstly, can't you shut your door, Mother? It's wide open. And second, I brought you both some tea. So you can toast my new manufactured sibling together. Enjoy!'

Tara dumped the mugs on the dressing table and made for the door.

Shyama called after her, 'Tara! We were going to sit down with you and discuss this! Tara?'

'You're going to do it anyway, so what's the point?' Tara's voice cracked with unshed tears, she was trembling with the effort of holding them back. She wanted to run straight down the stairs and into the street and keep running, just as she had done when she was eight years old and had found out that her father would not be living with them anymore.

'Tara? If you don't want us to go ahead with this, we won't.' Toby had stood up.

Tara paused in the doorway, her fists clenched.

Shyama turned her Punjabi-mother death-stare away from her daughter and focused its full beam on Toby. Tara's antennae were finely tuned to her mother's silent moods, and this was very interesting, seeing her mother's obey-me-or-die ray harmlessly bounce off Toby's broad shoulders. Tara had perfected her own filial armour over the years: she had learned to deflect any maternal manipulation and had even reached the stage where she was able to saunter away whistling a happy tune. But it always gave her a stomach ache. Toby seemed calmly unaffected. For the first time, Tara looked at him with some respect.

'So, if I said to you right now that I'm not happy about this, you'd stop? Really?'

Shyama opened her mouth to answer.

Toby got in first. 'Yes, really. This whole thing is about creating a family. Not just for us. So you will have someone else when we're gone. I know there will be a hell of an age gap and it may not mean much now but, well, your mum's an only child. I know she never wanted you to be one too.'

Both women regarded Toby with amazement: for Tara, it was the longest speech Toby had ever made to her which didn't contain the words 'manure' or 'feed'. For Shyama, it was the first time that Toby had ever presumed to speak on her behalf or interpret her feelings for her daughter's benefit. She wasn't sure she liked it.

The silence was broken by a sudden bestial lowing coming from the computer screen, from a slippery just-born baby being held up by Dr Passi, her distinctive soothing tones unmistakeable behind her green surgical mask. She cradled the mewling child expertly in the crook of one elbow and with the other hand smoothed back strands of hair from the rabbity mother's glistening brow. The woman lay prone, eyes glazed with exhaustion, her glance flicking to the baby and then away again quickly. Jump-cut to another room where a white couple stood expectantly in their green hospital gowns. As the door opened, they grabbed each other's hands, their surgical gloves emitting a muffled squeak. Dr Passi moved towards them. She might as well have been invisible, however, because both of them had their eyes fixed on the child in her arms.

'Congratulations! You have a healthy baby boy!'

The baby was fair skinned with a faint fuzz of coppery hair. There was clearly nothing of the woman who had just given birth to him in his genes. The couple moved forward as one. The woman reached out and took the baby, who fitted perfectly into the cradle of her arms, his cries fading slowly to whimpers as he sniffed the air, mouth open, rooting for milk blindly.

Toby had witnessed this many times before, in musty stables and dark, rain-sodden fields, and it never ceased to amaze him how a baby mammal of any kind took its first breath and immediately began its furious fight for survival. That's all we are, he thought, this human animal with its glorious, unstoppable greed. A muffled sob sounded next to him. Shyama was fixed on the screen, tears coursing down her cheeks.

'Look at them,' was all she could say.

Joy was too short and stale a word for what illuminated the faces of the two newborn parents: a religious wonder, the relief of laying to rest years of pain and worry, the hope of a rewritten future.

Shyama looked up at Tara, still in the doorway, and whispered, 'That's how I felt when I had you.' She held out her arms towards her daughter.

Tara took a step forward, then paused. At that moment, she loathed herself almost as much as she loathed her mother.

'If you want to go ahead with this, I'm fine with it, Mum. Really.'

Shyama and Toby watched Tara leave, listened as she headed up to her loft room, waited for her door to close before they dared to exhale. Consequently they both missed a few moments of the film, turning back just in time to see Dr Passi handing the rabbity mother a cup of tea. She was now sitting up in her dorm bed, her hair brushed, wincing slightly as she took the china cup and saucer awkwardly; they trembled slightly in her hands.

'So, you have done so well you will be back with your own children the day after tomorrow! We have already called your husband to collect you. Isn't that good?' Dr Passi's translated words scrolled across the bottom of the screen.

The mother nodded, and took a small sip of tea.

'They were so happy. You have done a wonderful thing. You should be very proud. We are all proud of you, Gowri.'

Her name was Gowri. She was too busy concentrating on her tea to register the two circular patches blooming on her sari blouse as her milk finally came in.

Up in her room, Tara locked her door, opened her window and rolled a cigarette, flicking off the light before she lit up. If she sat on the left-hand side of her window-sill, her feet resting on the balcony, she had a perfect view of her grandparents' ground-floor flat. This proved very useful as it gave her plenty of time to dispose of tobacco and alcohol products should either of them decide to wander over.

At first, Tara had kept it from her college friends that she lived in a clichéd Asian extended-family set-up, since most of them were in shared digs, enjoying the obligatory drunken parties and messy communal cook-ins. But they inevitably came to know of her living arrangements, and she was surprised by their reaction: it turned out that most of them were planning to move straight back in with their parents as soon as they graduated, realizing that even if they were one of the lucky few to actually find a job, they would still not be able to afford to rent in London. Many of their parents were already planning loft conversions or digging down into their cellars to accommodate a generation of dependent children who might never leave home, stuffed indefinitely into reclaimed attics or subterranean dens, waiting to pay off their debts.

'Lucky cow. Think of all the money you're saving.'

'Food and laundry on tap? You're laughing.'

'You've got an en suite? You will never know the grim shame of having to smell other people's shit every morning.'

That was Charlie. He was the department wit, or so he thought. He had cultivated a floppy fringe and what he assumed to be a snappy cheeky-chappie patter which had most of the girls in stitches. Except for her. When Tara deigned to respond to him, she generally wiped the floor with his sorry arse. That was the huge advantage of being an angry young woman: sarcasm came as easily as breathing. Although lately, the line between irony and sincerity was becoming increasingly blurred. When Tara had heard the chorus of moving-back-home stories, she'd muttered, 'Well, what do you know? We're all Indian now.' And was confused to see her friends all nodding their heads sagely in agreement.

It had started in her mid teens, this blurred boundary between what was said and what was meant, and she traced it back to when she had first gone online. Having moaned at her mother for months, she had finally been given her own computer, one of the last in her class to have one. (And even then, only after her father had sent her a particularly generous Christmas cheque to make up for missing her birthday that year.) The glee at having her own Facebook page soon wore off as she found herself having to learn what felt like a complicated new language. Not just the myriad abbreviations, they were easy enough, but how to negotiate the layers of insult and innuendo that accompanied this collective faceless community. After every cruel barb exchanged online, every throwaway comment about X's fat thighs or Z's general sluttiness, all you had to do, apparently, was add 'LOL' and a smiley face and claim you were only having a laugh. It was a joke! Older and more net-wise now, Tara had learned to filter out and block the teasers and the trolls, but she wondered if she had lost something else along the way: how to read a face for sincerity, how to vocalize a line that rang true.

A quick glance at her laptop screen confirmed a number of friends were trying to get hold of her: several missed messages on her Facebook page, a few more on Twitter, informing her that the gang were already gathered at the uni bar for someone's birthday. Trending right now: a school shooting in France; an ex-footballer's new underwear range; a dog from Canada who saved a baby from choking by performing a canine version of the Heimlich manoeuvre; a female movie star's slow public decline into insanity. A world of invitations and possibilities just waiting for her to log on and jump in, and if she didn't hurry, they'd simply carry on without her, forget she even existed.

A light snapped on in her grandparents' kitchen. She recognized the slow lilting gait of her grandmother carrying out her usual night-time rituals of wiping down the surfaces and checking that all the electrical appliances were off. Behind her, as always, was her grandfather in his kurta pyjamas, a sheaf of files under his arm, just there for the company, the routine. She remembered that she had promised to pop round to collect some papers they needed to scan and email to their lawyer in India. If she left now she would catch them before they settled down in bed to watch the news on the Hindi satellite channel. Tara grabbed her coat and handbag and made her way down the stairs. As she paused outside her mother's bedroom, she wondered who her tears had been for – the couple who had gained a baby, or the woman who had given one away. Certainly not for her own daughter. She called out briefly, 'Popping out – back by twelve. My phone's on.'

She didn't quite hear Shyama's muffled reply.

Outside the house, she rolled another cigarette before running towards the approaching bus that would drop her right outside her uni bar.

# CHAPTER SIX

EVEN THOUGH SEEMA cried constantly, Mala could not stop eating. The more Seema sniffed and dripped, the more food Mala piled on to her plate, as if she could concentrate better whilst chewing. If she could have eaten the plate itself, she would have done. It was so wafer-thin that when she held it up towards the light, she could see her fingers on the other side. Around the edge was a regular looping design, which on closer inspection revealed itself to be a chain of tiny elephants, each holding on to the tail of the one in front with its trunk. The detail was so clever and delicate, the folds and wrinkles of their hide hanging like just-washed winter blankets, their sad rheumy eyes, the tender pink tips of their trunks. How many hours must it have taken to paint even one, Mala marvelled, before she dumped another handful of colourful pastries over the pattern.

It was clear that Seema had not had many visitors, if any, since her return from the capital. The eager desperation with which she had unpacked boxes of expensive sweetmeats had embarrassed Mala, until she took in the obvious trophies around the room: a new sofa and armchairs in a floral pattern, all with polished wooden legs that reminded Mala of Bee-ji's arthritic bowed knees; a nest of tables, daddy, mummy and baby size, all fitting inside one another, all with smoky-glass tops and lethally sharp corners. Four new lamps over-illuminated the room, one in each corner, with heavy-fringed shades in which a couple of fuzzy moths already fluttered helplessly, trapped in the silken fronds. The new fridge freezer sat against a wall, emitting a low-pitched, absent-minded hum, like a simple relative who had come to visit and been forgotten about. And the purchase that really made Mala draw breath, although she had been trying to look unimpressed: up on the wall, with several wires hanging from its frame, hung a huge thin television screen, like a window into another world, still dark and waiting to be opened.

'My husband can't work it yet.' Seema sniffed as she pushed another sugar-coated snack at Mala.

Mala ate it in one gulp and, finally satisfied, licked her glittered fingertips and settled back into her chair. The room looked odd, overstuffed with Seema's new purchases which seemed to be pushing against the uneven walls. There was no space to breathe properly, emphasized by Seema's snatched, shuddering breaths, which were finally beginning to subside. *Bas*, no more nicey small talk, Mala decided. When a woman opens her door and weeps a monsoon before a namaste has left anyone's lips, it is best to be blunt.

'So you went to Delhi and they took your baby away?'

The shock of Mala's question finally stopped Seema in mid flow. She opened her mouth, closed it, then nodded her head, her tears threatening to start all over again.

'Either cry or speak, you can't do both,' Mala snapped.

Seema wiped her nose on her sari. 'How . . . Who told you?'

'*Bas*, no one had to tell anyone anything. Everyone saw you were pregnant, you went to Delhi, you came back with no baby and a new handbag.'

'He told me not to tell anyone.' No need to say who *he* was, the *he* was the same in everybody's lives. 'It was his idea, the whole thing. But then I said yes also. I mean, he didn't force me.'

Mala made one of those all-purpose non-committal *hai-haa* noises that might encourage Seema to spill some more details. Especially the most important one: where all the look-at-me presents had come from.

Seema emitted a gentle watery burp before continuing, 'Afterwards, I felt glad. But also too sad, crying all the time. Stupid, hah? I should be happy . . . with all this.' She waved a limp hand around the room. 'And now we can send the children to the proper school in Bessian. And college also, if they work hard at their studies. And we can give my Babbli a good wedding when the time comes.'

Mala's toes curled with curiosity. Just how much money did this mouse-quiet mumbly couple have?

'I know people must be saying dirty things about me,' Seema said softly. 'It is a strange thing to understand. Even for me, sometimes.'

'What is not to understand?' Mala retorted. 'It happens all the time.'

'Does it?' Seema asked, her eyes wide with disbelief.

'Hah, of course! It is just you did it with a proper doctor. At least this way you won't bleed to death like a halal chicken afterwards, like poor Jassi in my old village.'

Seema looked confused. She was one of life's *lalloo*s, Mala observed – one of those sweet fools who drift on the wind, never making their own luck but letting it settle on them, good or bad; never prepared, always a little bewildered. Now if this kind of luck had blown my way, thought Mala, this room would look completely different. In fact, I would not even be living in this room. I would have bought a flat in Delhi itself with a balcony and a dining table on a ledge, a room attached to the main room but only to be reached by two-three steps. And this leaky long-face spends it all on electrical goods. What a waste! Mala would have gone on spending the money in her imagination for some time, but then something Seema said made her sit up and listen properly.

'What? What did you say?'

Seema looked up at Mala, eyes tinged with wonder. 'It was a girl. With blue eyes. So bright blue, like a peacock's neck.'

'But how could you—'

'When I was crying afterwards, my husband said, you are just the nest, not the egg. The bird gets strong and then flies away. What is there to be upset about? Especially when these people are giving us so much paisa. But how would he understand? He did not feel her knees making bumps in my belly. He did not see his skin jump like the river when the rain falls on to it, when she got hiccups. He did not feel her flip like a fish under my ribs whenever Pogle sahib sang one of his loud wedding songs. He did not have to push her out with legs so far apart that one foot is in life and the other in death, did he?'

Mala nodded, her lips clamped shut, fireworks blooming noise-lessly in her head. Five minutes later she had the whole picture, every detail. Once uncorked, Seema could not be stopped, so Mala had to do little else but listen. And as she listened, she began to understand, finally, why her husband had been spending so much friendly-time with Seema's husband, why he would not touch her any more, why he looked at her the way he did, not seeing her breasts and belly as his, but as valuable treasures for hire.

'You won't tell anyone, will you?' Seema pleaded with Mala as she hovered at the gate.

109

'Oh-foh, woman! Even if I did, they would not believe me, would they?'

Seema placed a tentative hand on Mala's shoulder, afraid it might be swatted away.

'They were so happy, the American parents, they wept like babies themselves. Even though I gave them a girl. That's what the doctor told me. They felt blessed.'

'How much did they give you?' Mala asked gently. Several eddies of emotion scudded across Seema's watery face, suspicion ebbing into childish vulnerability, a trickle of shame halted by the dam of Mala's hardening stare. Seema's breath was warm and pickle-scented at Mala's ear as she whispered a sum of money which made Mala inhale the night air in one astonished gasp that left her dizzy, overwhelmed by the layered odours of night jasmine, open fires and baked manure.

Seema's face, when Mala returned to it, was almost kindly, as if she felt sorry for the bitter knowledge she had passed on. It was an old look, one Mala recalled seeing in her mother's limpid eyes when Mala had left her childhood home to follow her husband to his, not knowing if and when she might return; a look of yearning, of bittersweet joy for what is to come and will not stay long, and guarded grief for what must be endured. A shared sense of sweet corruption when women see their fears, their frailties and perhaps their futures mirrored back at them.

As Mala swayed back towards her house, the moon hung low and heavy, a blood-orange earring pulling down on the night's taut skin. Fireflies flitted amongst the peepul-tree boughs, leaving luminous trails behind them which burned sharp and bright before slowly fading away, like the fleeing remnants of a vivid dream. In the distance, the slow pulse of the river throbbed through the darkness. Mala could feel it as she heard it, as if she and the coursing waters were one, being pulled towards the ocean, where she would disappear into its vastness, the speck of her life swallowed up as if she had never even existed.

She entered the house without announcing herself, startling Ram, who stood up too quickly from the charpoy, his metal cup of spiced tea spilling on the floor and absorbed hungrily by the pressed red earth it anointed. Mala began to untie her sari, unwrapping herself slowly like an unexpected present.

'What are you doing?' Ram stuttered, backing off as his eyes devoured each inch of flesh deliciously revealed, layer by layer. 'Mamaji might come in.'

'Let her,' Mala said calmly, the night air greeting her flesh with a warm sigh, her skin rising up, swelling to meet its embrace. She felt dizzy with power, intoxicated by this body that had brought her so much shame. Tch, a girl! A burden to be carried and disposed of as quickly as possible, whose curves had to be disguised or hidden to keep away the predators and silence the gossips. But now, she breathed into Ram's ear, now I am a goddess, hena? I hold worlds within my womb and now, you trembling, wet-mouthed, dry-throated, knee-shaky man, now you need me more than I ever needed you. The groan she tore from his throat as she placed his hand over her breast made her smile, a smile that he ate from her lips like a starving dog.

# CHAPTER SEVEN

O N THE THIRD morning in their hotel in New Delhi, Shyama opened the glass doors leading on to their small balcony and came face to face with a plump brown monkey, which looked up from the oversized brassiere it held in its paws. It barely reacted to Shyama's cry of surprise; in fact, it looked somewhat annoyed at the interruption. Toby wanted to feed it some banana from the modest fruit bowl they had found in their room, but Shyama snatched it out of his reach.

'They're vicious, these street monkeys, and they're crawling with rabies.'

'You don't crawl with rabies.' Toby smiled, making a lunge for an apple. 'That's fleas. Besides, he's holding a bra. How tough can he be? Not yours, is it?'

'Since when have I gone for purple nylon underwear, Toby? Back off! It's like going to hug a hoodie – he'll mug you for your fruit and probably chew your shoes off for good measure.'

Toby backed down and, at Shyama's insistence, tried to shoo the monkey away with loud claps and noisy stamps. The monkey scratched its bottom, threw the bra at Toby's head and leaped into a nearby tree with a yawn.

Shyama and Toby stood on their balcony for a while. Five floors up, they could see pockets of South Delhi in between the treetops and office blocks: dual carriageways and flyovers snaking around a mossy ruin of an old religious site; students streaming out of a nearby college with backpacks and bicycles; a sports stadium of some kind, its long-necked spotlights craning at each other in a perfect circle.

Later on, lying on the bed under the revolving ceiling fan, the air-conditioning unit thrumming at full blast, Shyama told him how a group of these frisky rhesus monkeys had broken into the Indian Ministry of Defence offices some years back and had thrown about top-secret papers whilst looking for food. They'd even broken into the Lok Sabha itself and run amok, terrorizing MPs, inevitably inspiring reams of column inches inviting readers to 'Spot the Real Monkeys!' Plus raising more serious questions about national security and the dignity of government.

'They're a real problem in this city. They attack people, break into houses; they can open fridges and everything, run off with kids' packed lunches. I remember the last time I came here, my auntie kept a pointy stick on the porch, she called it her *bander dhi lukurd.*'

'Which means?' Toby stroked Shyama's damp hair away from her eyes.

'Monkey stick.'

'Does what it says on the tin.' Toby snuggled into Shyama and rested his chin on her shoulder.

'It got so bad in the area around parliament, they hired these other monkeys, bigger ones, to chase away the smaller ones. Langurs, I think. Scary-looking, huge teeth.'

'Like *Planet of the Apes.*'

'Well, not really . . . I don't think the monkeys are going to rise up any time soon and enslave the good citizens of Delhi.'

'No, I mean in the film there's a pecking order. Amongst the apes. Or rather, the apes are at the bottom, they're treated like the dumb strong workers, and the brainy chimps are in all the managerial jobs. And the orangutans are the professor types.'

Shyama raised herself up on one elbow. 'You've really thought about this, haven't you?'

'I was imagining the last scene, you know, where Charlton Heston finds the head of the Statue of Liberty buried in the sand and realizes he's not on some freaky faraway planet, he's actually on Earth. But in the future. That somewhere along the way, human beings have messed up and it's too late to do anything about it. Except in our version, he'd find the top of the Taj Mahal, wouldn't he?'

'Now I'm worried. Must be the heat. Mad Dogs and Englishmen.'

Shyama kissed the tip of Toby's already sunburnt nose. She had warned him before they left that a natural blond like him who had never been anywhere hotter than Devon was going to suffer in the sun. And yet what surprised her was how easily Toby had adapted to the chaotic swell of her mother country.

The first time she had visited India with English friends, way back in her college days, she had underestimated or maybe just forgotten how even stepping out of the plane was like being slapped in the face – emotionally, physically, sometimes literally, if you got caught in the pack of passengers determined to get ahead in the passport queue. Somewhere over the Middle East, these fellow travellers, who had stood politely and patiently in line at Heathrow, had shrugged off the stiff jackets of their *angrezi* manners and slipped back into their *desi dhotis*, louder, loose-limbed, ready to push their way through any barrier, as queueing was strictly for foreigners now. Shyama still remembered the fear on her friends' faces as they realized that no amount of 'excuse me's and pursed lips would help them. It carried on as they left the airport, immediately besieged by taxi drivers and porters fighting for their luggage, which they clung to like driftwood in a sweaty storm of cheerful humanity. It got worse as they sat in the back of an incense-filled cab, its dashboard adorned with beatific smiling deities, who seemed to mock their terror as they swung in and out of the suicidal traffic, gaping as whole families perched on one moped cut them up on one side, articulated lorries decorated like wedding carriages on the other. It was when the begging children appeared at their cab windows, tapping on the glass, pointing to their mouths, that they finally cracked.

'Sister . . . Mummy . . . hungry . . . please . . .'

Shyama had looked up to see both her friends crying, one of them with her purse already out, the whole of her spending money on show.

'Don't!' Shyama said instinctively.

She hadn't meant, don't give money. Rather she was warning them to hide their money in case the beggar boss around the corner decided to send one of these children to their hotel later on. She had wanted to advise her friends not to give hard cash, which would be snatched away from those little hands the minute they rounded the corner. Rather they should get out of the cab and take the kids for something to eat, fill their bellies and then give them enough to keep them from being beaten up later. But she didn't have time to say any of this. The taxi had zoomed away, leaving the children coughing in a dustcloud, their hands still outstretched and her friends staring at her with undisguised contempt.

This single incident had overshadowed the whole holiday. Every so often, Shyama would catch her friends giving her a peculiar sideways glance, one that seemed to say, you are not the person we thought you were. She didn't know how to express what she knew instinctively: that their judgement of her was somehow linked with a whole deep-rooted colonial past, where they were the good guys and she the savage who had reverted to her true primordial nature. She didn't know how to explain that in order to survive here, as opposed to just passing through, you had to find strategies to preserve your sanity. Otherwise how does anyone get the washing done and work and laugh and dream, unless there is some way to live alongside death, poverty and truly terrible traffic? This was how her relatives had expressed it, in those years when she had visited India every summer, determined not to lose the thread that connected her to her extended family. That was, until the whole issue around her parents' stolen apartment had arisen.

The hotel phone rang, and Shyama reached over Toby to answer it.

'Oh, hi Mama . . . Sorry, did you call before? OK, just let us know. You've got my Indian mobile number, haven't you?'

Shyama replaced the receiver and rested back on Toby's chest.

'They've got legal stuff most of the day. Mum says she'll buzz us later if they can make supper.'

'Didn't she want to know what we were doing?' Toby enquired teasingly.

'Well, she's still doing the Indian-mother thing; if you don't mention it, it's not really there.'

They hadn't planned on telling Prem and Sita about the purpose of this trip, until it transpired that they would all be in

India at the same time, the latest court hearing coinciding with their clinic booking. As Sita and Prem had insisted on travelling on the same flight as Shyama and Toby, and recommended hotels for them near Prem's older brother's place, where they would be staying, Shyama realized they would have to confess all. Dry-mouthed, with Toby at her side, she finally sat them down on their first evening in Delhi and announced their surrogacy plans. The first couple of minutes went well – innocuous enough stuff about why they had chosen this particular route, how they had chosen this particular clinic, how they would manage their finances. It was when Shyama came to the actual mechanics of the process that she began to falter.

'So, well . . . it's a very common procedure . . . I mean there are literally hundreds of clinics in India that do this.'

'Do what exactly?' Sita had looked up innocently from her cuppatea.

'Well, they take an egg from another woman – the donor – and they combine it with one of Toby's . . .'

Shyama simply could not say the word 'sperm' in front of her mother, her mouth refused to move. Toby put his farming head on and manfully took over, running through the explanation with breezy efficiency, even inviting questions from the audience afterwards. Prem said nothing, but puffed at his pipe so vigorously that he sat in a cloud of fug, no doubt thankful for the smoky camouflage.

Sita was silent for a while, then dusted a few crumbs off the table and said, 'Well, in our day, if you couldn't have a baby, your sister or brother would give you one of theirs to bring up. No one minded very much. As long as you loved the baby, they grew up fine. But I suppose as Shyama is our only child, now you must pay for that . . . service.'

117

'Yes, exactly!' Shyama said, relieved. 'That's a good way to look at it, Mama.'

'Except, of course, there was none of this taking a bit from here and a bit from there. Like cooking with leftovers. But if that's what you both want . . .'

A small shrug of the maternal shoulders and that, apparently, was all Sita was going say on the matter.

Leaving the salon in the capable hands of Geeta and her team had been the easiest part of Shyama's to-do list. Toby had so many weeks of holiday owing to him that his sudden sabbatical wasn't opposed. And now here they all were – all of them bar Tara, who'd declined the offer of a free trip, citing coursework pressure. Shyama was ashamed to admit to herself that she'd been mightily relieved not to be dragging her daughter along too on her let's-get-pregnant holiday. Particularly as she had been feeling so unsettled since they had arrived in India. Sense memories hijacked her at odd moments: the smell of the *rath-ki-rani* garlands outside the roadside temples; the cool citric fizz of the *nimboo pani* she had yearned to drink on her arrival, achingly familiar, buried deep, making her feel both a stranger and a re-turning exile at the same time. What would they think of her now, her old lefty student friends, coming back as a fertility tourist? Was she now the colonial memsahib? The benevolent bringer of bounty, or the ruthless trader, smiling her way back home?

In their hotel room, Toby began slowly unbuttoning Shyama's top, kissing her neck. Outside the irregular honking of car horns was overlaid with the cries of vegetable sellers, temple bells, the soaring violins of a Hindi film song.

'The real reason they will never get rid of the monkeys,'

Shyama mused, shifting so Toby could reach the last stubborn button, 'is that people keep feeding them. Every Tuesday, my Auntie Neelum used to lug a huge bag of fruit and nuts over to Raisina Hill and join all the other good Hindus making their offerings to Hanuman.'

'The monkey god . . .' Toby murmured.

'Gold star for you. She'd always make a big deal of how religious she was, my auntie – joss sticks and mantras every morning, dragging us all to the temple when all we wanted to do was shop. Making up her packed monkey lunch like she was going on some pilgrimage: Hanuman helped Ram defeat the ten-headed demon Ravan, therefore I will go and throw peanuts at the street monkeys in case one of them reports back to their boss and I skip a few reincarnations up the scale towards nirvana.'

Toby was taking his T-shirt off hurriedly, his face filled with familiar blind purpose.

'And yet she's the same thieving old bint whose daughter has stolen my parents' flat. Marvellous, eh? Do you remember, for your bonus point, what Hanuman is the god of?'

Toby was by this time lying across her, bare chested, face flushed, about to tackle the complicated machinery of her bra fastening. He could have done with some assistance from the cross-dressing monkey. 'I don't know! Jumping?'

'Not far off, actually. Wrestlers. Athletes. He's a protector of boundaries, the supreme example of a devoted disciple. And sometimes seen as an icon of fertility.'

Toby glanced at Shyama, a strange smile twisting her face. He noticed the fine lines fanning out from the side of her eyes, a weary droop around her mouth that he had not seen before. He had a sudden glimpse of how she might look in ten, twenty years' time. The flesh at the top of her arms, which he held now, felt soft

119

and sagged slightly in his hand. He knew that when he finally removed her bra, he would have to lift her breasts with careful tenderness, like handling warm, just-laid eggs. It had never bothered him before. He didn't want to think about it now. He wished she would just stop talking. But she continued, 'Maybe we shouldn't have chased that monkey away.'

Dr Renu Passi had a very full timetable, as always. Two of her ladies looked as if they would be delivering over the next few days – it was time to alert the expectant parents to hop on to flights from California and Israel in order to welcome their babies into the world. She could not recall any parents who had not made it in time, even with the unexpected early deliveries. Somehow these people always had the cash and flexibility to drop everything and present themselves, sweating with nerves and smelling of aeroplane, at her clinic's door.

A more pressing issue was Kamini, who even now was crying into her freshly laundered pillow, eight months pregnant and threatening to leave as soon as her husband could reach her. Dr Passi had huge sympathy for those very few women who got attached to their surrogate babies. Hadn't she carried three children herself? She would tell them, stroking their oiled hair and mindful of their heaving, ungainly stomachs, you would not be human if you did not feel protective towards this child, if you even loved it a little, for haven't you grown this little seed from its first planting, knowing you will not get to see it blossom, take root and thrive? (She always found it helpful to use agricultural imagery, as the majority of her ladies came from rural villages. They, more than anyone, should understand the relentless, amoral march of Nature.) But then, after the women had calmed down a little, sipped some sweet tea and nibbled the cardamom biscuits she kept for such occasions, Dr Passi would have to reiterate the terms of their contract.

'*Theklo, beti,*' she would say, insisting on eye contact so there could be no misunderstanding. 'It is true we cannot make you give this baby away if you don't want to, God strike us dead if we were such monsters to do that. But you signed a legal contract that you will have no contact with or connection to this child after the birth, and if you refuse, you will not get any payment. In fact, you will owe us some money for everything that has been spent on your medical care here. This is a lot of money – money you do not have, I think?'

At this point the woman would usually nod, sniff, and avert her eyes from Dr Passi's kindly gaze.

But Dr Passi would continue, 'And then there's the question of whose baby it actually is – where would it belong?'

This could either be a very short conversation or a longer one, involving diagrams and much patient repetition. This was usually the moment at which Dr Passi marvelled at how far reproductive technology had advanced during her career. In some cases, the women were incubating embryos that had been fertilized elsewhere, not even in India. These could be any combination of the man's sperm with his partner's egg, the man's sperm with a donated egg, the woman's egg with donated sperm, or even an embryo created with donated egg and sperm, so that the surrogate and the parents were equally unconnected genetically to the child they all thought of as theirs. (In fact, it was recommended that the surrogate should have no biological connection to the child at all, even if she were to offer up her own eggs, purely to avoid situations such as this one.) Although Dr Passi's clinic provided a one-stop service, with a healthy balance of sperm and donor eggs in its bank, specialized agencies had sprung up in dozens of countries to source eggs and sperm and create the embryo in the commissioning parents' country, which some much preferred. These agents would then transport the frozen fertilized embryos in what looked like village-style metallic milk churns, to be defrosted and implanted in Dr Passi's clinic, and many others, in India. It wasn't so very different from the people whom Dr Passi's own parents had used to pay to queue up for them in interminable lines at post offices, bank counters and government offices. Time is money, *hena*, so if you have the money to save some time, spend it on those who don't mind doing the running round and form-filling and are themselves making a living in the process. Everyone gets what they want and the wheels of this flourishing industry keep on turning happily. A 2.5-billion-dollar industry at the last count, all of it helping the Indian tiger economy to stretch its jaws, flex its flanks and leap even higher, snapping at the sun.

Not that Dr Passi would say any of this to the occasional weepy lady with cold feet. Would she understand that without her cooperation, no one above them in this huge pyramid would be able to continue, to survive? No, once her ladies had been alerted to the small print, to the reality of giving back money they did not and would never have, of plodding back to their villages with a changeling baby tucked beneath their sari that would become at best an object of curiosity, at worst an outcast, they soon calmed down. They just needed reminding how important they were, how much joy they would bring to those who could not go anywhere else for a child, how many karmic blessings they would accrue for their next life in this, the most selfless of humanitarian acts.

Dr Passi scrolled quickly through her new emails whilst dragging a brush through her wiry hair. The chaos of her desk belied her ruthless competence in every other area of her life: gold-medal winner at medical school; head of the Obstetrics and Gynaecology department at a leading Delhi hospital; all three children through medical school themselves, and a loving husband whose frequent business trips afforded her the time and energy to focus on her clinic. She caught herself sometimes regarding the surrogates almost as an alien race, their lack of education and opportunities, and their diminished status as women so far from her own experiences. As a woman, she had never felt, not for one minute, that there was any area of life closed off to her. Her parents had positively revelled in her ambition and achievements, had never once worried that she would not marry well and happily (although they did make some slight grumbling noises when she reached the age of twenty-seven without having expressed any need to settle down). Dr Renu Passi enjoyed every aspect of being female. If some stupid men out there regarded her as less capable than them or in need of taming, well, that was their problem. One of the happy consequences of her job was that she was reminded on a daily basis of the astounding miracle of birth, of how wondrous women actually were, able to sustain and deliver another human being. She recalled the exhibits she had pored over at some museum on one of their European jaunts – maybe the Uffizi? Or was it the Louvre? Anyhow, the children had opted to go shopping instead, insisting her husband accompany them with his credit card, and she was left alone for a delicious few hours to enjoy an exhibition entitled 'Fertility and Birth: A Sacred Mystery'. In every engraving or painting, in each statue or carving – some life-size, some as small as a month-old foetus – there was the attempt to express what each artist, probably male, must have felt as an incompetent witness to the act of birth: a helpless sense of terror and awe.

123

Rotund female forms with pendulous breasts and spreading legs; buxom, drum-bellied goddesses, like ripe pods about to burst; open-mouthed, screaming women bearing down to gasp at the emerging head between their thighs; razor-toothed, wild-haired women, clawing the air, baying for blood and revenge as the pain of labour ripped through them. Even through the agony, Dr Passi could see in their ancient faces a twist of triumph that they had escaped death to create life. What must the first man have thought, wrapped up in his mammoth skin, poking around in his smoky cave fire, when that fur-clad woman over there in the corner suddenly squatted down and produced his future? They should damn well worship us, mused Dr Passi, grimacing as her brush caught on a particularly persistent knot in her hair. But why, then, did all the reverential iconography stop? You could see plainly in the timeline of the exhibition that the fecund, naked women gradually became smaller, neater, clothed, decorative and deferential. What had happened to the men to curdle their fearful admiration into fear itself? What made them cross that blood-speckled line between devotion and denigration?

Dr Passi's musings were halted by an email marked 'URGENT' from her lawyer, Vinod Aggarwal. Vinod marked virtually every email he sent her as urgent or extremely urgent; she appreciated his efficiency and it certainly made her read his emails immediately, but much of the time the contents were not at all urgent, merely another swell in the tsunami of paperwork she had to navigate on a daily basis. In the face of an as-yet-unregulated industry, where the Indian government had established guidelines for surrogacy as opposed to laying down actual laws, the contract between surrogate, commissioning parents and clinic was everything. A signed contract was all you needed to proceed and was your only protection should things not go according to plan. This necessitated enough paperwork to wallpaper the entire clinic and kept Vinod Aggarwal very busy and very well paid.

Dr Passi scanned Vinod's email and saw that, whilst it wasn't urgent, it was certainly very worrying. She checked her appointments: Kamini had to be seen, obviously; she had two interviews with potential surrogates and a meet-and-greet with a couple just in from London. Of course, she had been in contact with Mr and Mrs Shaw for some weeks, arranging the necessary medical visas, liaising with the embassy about the future registration of the surrogate child, who would need a valid passport before entering its adopted country. All these boring, time-consuming procedures were now at least underway and she could concentrate on finding them a suitable match. They seemed good people, friendly, responsive, always prompt in their replies. Checking the computer's clock, she realized she only had five minutes before her schedule kicked in, so she quickly called Vinod's mobile.

He answered on the second ring, sounding quite out of breath. 'You got my email then? . . . Oof . . . Sorry, one second.'

'Vinod? Are you climbing the stairs or what?'

'I'm in the gym . . . God, how do you switch this goddamn machine off? It's trying to kill me, I swear . . . OK. I've escaped. Go ahead.'

'So this latest bill is definitely going ahead, is it?' Dr Passi asked, plunging straight in.

'That's the rumour,' Vinod panted, trying to steady his breathing. 'But given it's been hanging around for years, debated by lots of fat old men without a womb between them, shouting loudly at each other across parliament, who knows? Hai! Just let me sit a moment . . . *Hahn-ji*, look, the government's under pressure to do something now with the press and the religious brigade

125

snapping at their heels, so it's looking likely it may become law soon . . . Renu?'

'I'm here, just thinking . . .'

Dr Passi slumped into her ergonomic office chair. The sudden relieving of pressure on her feet made her realize she hadn't sat down for hours and had probably missed lunch again. The Assisted Reproductive Technology Bill had been knocking about since 2008, when it became apparent that India was fast becoming the world centre for surrogacy. Not surprising, considering the expense and restrictions facing childless couples in so many other countries. Dr Passi could list in her sleep the many advantages of coming to her instead – it was the section of their website that received the most hits. A service which would cost you around ninety to one hundred thousand dollars in the US or Canada would cost between ten and eighteen thousand dollars in India. She knew that the majority of her clients came from countries such as the UK, where both egg donation and surrogacy were strictly voluntary gifts offered by a few good-hearted women for no profit. Childless couples were not even allowed to advertise for a surrogate, let alone offer payment; they were dependent on the surrogates to come forward themselves. And all these women could expect in return for weeks of debilitating hormone treatment and painful operations for egg retrieval, or nine months of carrying someone else's child to term, were basic medical expenses. Also, there were many countries where surrogacy itself was actually illegal, or where the law banned single people or gay couples from the entire process. True, at first, some of her staff had found dealing with the lesbians and the gay men somewhat bemusing: she had lost one very good midwife early on, who had stood open-mouthed when Dr Passi had introduced her to Joel and Luke, two Canadians who had arrived to claim their newborn son. Their mountainous proportions and gingery beards hadn't helped matters: they had attracted crowds of gawping children whenever they ventured out of their hotel, sunburnt giants wading through a brown sea of giggling Lilliputians. But Dr Passi could only remember their sweet natures and the image of a sleeping baby in the hammock of their huge arms. The midwife had walked out moments later, clutching her handbag to her chest like a shield and interspersing Hail Marys with doom-laden mutterings about unnatural abominations and the incoming tidal wrath of God. Dr Passi paid her off; she had never understood bigotry. She felt a surge of pride when she reflected that here in India, the largest democracy in the world, famed for its tolerance and mix of so many different religions, the parental doors were open to all. But it looked as if that was about to change.

'What's really put a firework up their asses,' Vinod continued, his daily and ever-increasing Americanisms grating on Dr Passi, 'is all the problems around visas and citizenship for the children once they're born. I mean, all the *tamasha* with that Norwegian woman, the worldwide coverage made us look like disorganized idiots – and cruel idiots at that. So they're panicking and have gone too far the other way maybe, but until we get some sort of unified legislation across all the participating nations, it's going to keep happening and I think . . .'

Dr Passi zoned out for a minute, as she often did when Vinod got over-excited by legal techno-speak, remembering instead the haunted face on the news of that woman who was not able to take home her twin girls, successfully born to an Indian surrogate. Having subjected her to DNA tests which proved she had no genetic link to the children, the Norwegian embassy refused to issue the children with travel papers. Officially they did not belong anywhere, these stateless little girls, which meant that they and their adoptive mother were stranded in India for two years whilst she fought her way through the labyrinthine legal system for some proof that these children did in fact exist in the eyes of the law and deserved to go home with her. In the same year, a gay Frenchman returned home with his newborn twins in tow, only to be arrested on arrival. As surrogacy was banned in his country, the children were forcibly removed from him and placed into foster care whilst he launched a lengthy court battle, which for all Dr Passi knew was still going on right now.

'. . . and of course the Baby Manji case is quoted time and again in all the campaign literature, although I suspect they love throwing this around because it involved wicked parents getting divorced rather than focusing on what happened to the poor kid.'

'I knew them,' Dr Passi blurted out.

'What, you knew the couple who . . .'

'No,' she corrected him. 'I knew the people whose clinic they used in Rajasthan. They're good people. They told me the commissioning parents seemed very stable, solid, you know? One was Indian, the other Japanese, can't remember which. Anyway, they were completely shocked when the husband filed for divorce. The baby hadn't even been born.'

'It happens – if not during, then sometimes afterwards, we know that. Sometimes the process of finding a baby is what keeps them going, and once they actually have one, they have to look into each other's faces again and . . . *chalo*, game over.'

'They left that baby in a hospital for three months. The first vulnerable twelve weeks of its life in an institutional cot, waiting for its status to be rubber-stamped somewhere. It's inhuman.'

'You sound like you're batting for the other side now!' laughed

Vinod, pausing to gulp down something fizzy, judging by the gentle belches he was now trying to disguise. 'This is virgin territory for humanity, no? Where there are no precedents, things will go wrong – or take time to sort out. But it was sorted out, wasn't it?'

'Sorted out?' Dr Passi laughed dryly, giving up on her hair and twisting it expertly into a loose bun with one hand. 'The last I heard, they finally allowed the baby to go home with its Japanese grandmother on a one-year humanitarian visa. That is not a solution, Vinod, that's a stopgap. Once the year is over, what happens?'

'Well, the new regulations should cheer you up then. If they pass this bill, surrogacy will only be open to heterosexual couples married for two years minimum and only those from countries where surrogacy is legal, and surrogate children will be given automatic citizenship.'

'I read the email, thank you, Master-ji.'

'So be happy, *bhain-ji*! You and I will lose half our business, but as long as they keep out the living-in-sin dirty types, the sad singletons too ugly to find a partner and the queers, it's all worth it, no?'

Vinod paused for dramatic effect; when he used to practise at the bar, this was always his favourite technique – to ask the killer rhetorical question and let it hang in the air whilst the chump in the witness box had to work out whether they should bother answering it. The kind of when-did-you-stop-beating-your-wife? quip which sounded good in John Grisham novels but didn't always translate well in court. The one time he had put this very question to a man up for domestic assault, the man had spat at him, saying, 'Ey, bastard! Why don't you start beating yours? Might help you grow some balls.' And he still had the cheek to plead not guilty.

Vinod had ducked out of criminal work soon after that. He found it too depressing defending the indefensible, prosecuting the pathetic and the dispossessed. Drawing up contracts and dealing with embassies may have seemed a come-down after the drama of a courtroom, but at least there were more happy endings. As he got older, he realized it wasn't multi-vitamins or pounding the treadmill that kept him going, it was what pulsed out of every prospective parent he welcomed into his office: hope.

'Renu? Maybe now's a good time to just help as many people as we can. While we can. Tell some of them we may be their last chance at these prices. No?'

'Let's talk later.' Dr Passi sighed and hung up.

Shyama sat upright on a sofa in the hotel lobby feeling slightly nauseous, caused by a combination of the over-zealous air conditioning, which was raising goosebumps on her bare arms, and the anxious churning in her stomach. God, it felt like some sort of surreal job interview. Will they like us? Will we like her, this as-yet-unknown woman who might be carrying our child? She had to keep reminding herself that she and Toby were the paying customers, the discerning clients, not desperate refugees who had travelled five thousand miles in search of an unfulfilled dream. Ironic, she mused, that she was making the same optimistic pilgrimage in reverse that had taken her own parents to Britain fifty years ago. For them, until recently, India had remained Back Home, the very reason they had invested in the flat: it was the place to which they would return to warm their old bones until the day when their ashes would be scattered on the Ganges, joining all their ancestors before them, reunited in the river that reputedly sprang from Lord Shiva's flowing hair. But having seen her parents spend the prime years of their retirement locked in this endless property battle, Shyama wondered if they would ever repossess that piece of land that represented their final homecoming. And if they failed, how would they cope with the bitter disappointment of all that wasted time? If she and Toby didn't leave India with the promise of a baby, they would have to ask themselves the very same question.

Shyama checked her watch: the clinic's courtesy minibus should have been here ten minutes ago. They had rushed down, both still damp-haired from the shower, Shyama blaming Toby for leaping on her and worried they had missed their lift.

'Ah, come on!' he joshed. 'We're on holiday! Spontaneous holiday tumbles are why anyone bothers to go abroad.'

'Is that how you feel about . . . this? Does it feel like a holiday to you?' she said, surprised.

'Well, I mean . . . let's try and think of it that way. That's all I'm saying. Might be our last one without a kid in tow, eh?'

Toby sauntered over to the concierge's desk and within a minute was deep in conversation with a pretty young receptionist, the air conditioning teasing the ends of her hair, the taut muscles in Toby's arms flexing, then relaxing as he went through some apparently hilarious mime. For someone who had never been abroad before, he seemed entirely at ease. True, he still looked like a turnip transplanted to a hothouse, squatly solid amongst the fine-boned North Indians attending to him, but he wasn't wilting under the shock of the new. He actually seemed to be thriving in this exotic climate, enjoying his role as the stranger in a strange land. The receptionist laughed again, throwing her shoulders back to reveal a smooth unlined neck. She's flirting with him, Shyama realized with a shock, and what's more, he's flirting back. Toby had that lazy smile on his face, legs apart, fingers now looped into his belt hooks, all thrust and grin. It never ceased to amaze her how easily men succumbed to such obvious flattery. What had Priya said? Tell them they're wonderful a couple of times a day, even if you don't mean it, and they're putty in your hands.

Shyama's old marital battle scars wouldn't let her do that. After so many years of begging for affection, she found it hard to lavish excessive praise on anyone else. An uncomfortable shadow of her last conversation with Lydia flitted across her consciousness; they hadn't spoken properly for ages, not since that testy exchange in Lydia's kitchen, although she knew that Tara and Lydia were still in contact. There had been an awkward *bon voyage* kind of supper arranged at Priya's insistence, where the three of them had gone through the motions of being comfortable old friends, with Priya pushing them together insistently like an overbearing mother on a doomed playdate. Something had broken between the two of them, something to do with Lydia's opinion of Shyama as a mother – specifically, as Tara's mother. Well, Tara and Toby knew that she loved them. She shouldn't have to spell it out with bells, whistles and cheerleader pom-poms. And if Toby wanted to dimple his way across New Delhi, her tickling his tummy, then chucking him a biscuit wasn't going to make much difference.

Toby finally turned round and saw her watching him. He waved cheerily, not a trace of guilt on his face, the same eager, happy-to-see-her Toby, wagging his invisible tail. Yeah, he loves me, was her first thought. And her second, which she erased in a nanosecond: he and the willowy receptionist look more like a couple than we do.

'Ready to board the baby bus?' Toby called out, bounding over and indicating the people-carrier with darkened windows waiting on the hotel forecourt. He offered his arm with a mock-gallant bow and Shyama grabbed it gratefully, allowing him to lead her from the chilly interior into the close humidity outside.

Ahead of them, two women were settling themselves on the back seats. Shyama threw them a small smile as she and Toby sat down opposite them, and the car pulled out into the three-lane carriageway outside the hotel. Shyama was grateful that the air conditioning was off and the driver seemed to be happy to rely on the good old-fashioned virtues of open windows and a pleasant breeze.

The traffic was how Shyama remembered it: a cheerful free-for-all of car horns and near misses. The main difference was the number of luxury cars zooming past them – BMWs aplenty, a Lexus or two, a couple of pimped-up Porsches and several Mercedes – all seemingly driven by their owners, busy-looking suited men barking into their mobiles, and stylish women in crisp cotton tops, their oversized sunglasses making them look like shiny-lipsticked beetles. Overhead the sun was a pale golden disc, a bindi nestling between the wide eyes of the cloudless sky.

The noise of the streets assaulted them through the open windows, swallowing them up like a soundscape: traffic, voices, music, around them, inside them. Shyama was amazed by the number of purpose-built shopping malls that seemed to have sprung up on every other block, dotted with branches of familiar chains: Pizza Hut, McDonald's, and the more enticing *desi* fast-food joints serving in five minutes the kind of snacks her mother would spend an hour preparing. Each illuminated window offered a glimpse into a world of glamorous possibilities: Western designer brands of sunglasses, sportswear and shoes vying with the equally expensive homegrown labels, exquisite, intricate jewellery featuring that rose-hued Indian gold whose purity made it almost pliable, homeware and lifestyle boutiques mixing the traditional with the contemporary – linen bedding featuring rustic prints, reclaimed peasant saris fashioned into pouffe covers and table-mats, coffee tables refashioned from the pearl-inlaid wooden doors that once guarded a fallen dynasty's palace courtyard.

As they paused at traffic lights, Shyama was drawn to a window featuring a spotlit mannequin, one hand on hip, a handbag dangling from the other as if she'd just been caught on her way to some exclusive party. But she was not like the shop dummies Shyama remembered from her last trip – busty, beehived ladies with enigmatic painted smiles, generously filling their figure-hugging blouses or shalwar kameezes, the kind of women who would never turn down pudding and would pinch your cheeks as a conversation opener. Here was the next generation's model: pert-chested, smooth-stomached, lean-legged, hips meant for skinny jeans and G-strings rather than sitting on sofas and bearing children. Shyama knew that the price tags hanging from the clothes would be sky-high. 'Ethnic chic' seemed too insulting a term for it. This was aspirational, envy-inducing glamour: around these islands of exclusivity the people-carrier still dipped over endless potholes, the open drains still stank, temple bells and muezzins still called out to their daily worshippers, street hustlers still limped their ragged way along the queue of waiting cars, offering out-of-date magazines and twisted cones of charcoal-cooked peanuts. The old clichés of ancient, modern, rich and poor were intertwined like long-suffering, mismatched lovers.

But something felt different. The shame had gone, realized Shyama, the weight of the colonial yoke, the embarrassment at the dust on your feet and the things that don't work or break down or just look second-best, eyes always raised towards Eng-er-land, the West, those who got it right and had it all. The mannequin seemed to regard her with blank superior eyes, telling her, You can't fob us off any more with your bargain-basement lipsticks bought for your aunties and your Marks and Spencer socks for your uncles, expecting us to ooh-aah at your exotic foreign gifts. Now you are coming to us, nah?

The people-carrier lurched forward, getting a head start on a clump of impatient moped riders, throwing Shyama and Toby forward in their seats. The two other passengers just managed to catch themselves too. The awkward silence broken, they smiled at each other.

'Can't believe how expensive everything has got since I last visited,' Shyama began.

'Yeah, well, luckily some things are still dirt cheap, or we wouldn't be here!' laughed a cheerful American voice. The woman extended her hand. 'Gill. How you doing?' Her eyes were ice-blue chips in a lean, healthy face, she had cropped hair, and surprisingly rough calluses briefly scraped the skin on Shyama's palm. 'And my partner, Debs.'

Toby nodded and offered his hand to the woman next to Gill, immediately confronted by his own prejudices: this one was way too feminine-looking to be a lesbian. You're a clod, he berated himself. They don't all wear dungarees and have moustaches. Debs's handshake was firm and warm. She had long brown hair loosely tied back in a plait, and a sheen of perspiration on her upper lip, which topped a generous mouth. Hellos were murmured all round. A hint of conspiratorial discomfort hung between them for a moment before Gill broke the silence.

'Your first time here? At the clinic, I mean.'

Shyama nodded, unsure how much she ought to say.

Toby thankfully jumped in. 'Yep. And my first time in India.' He grinned. 'Really like it so far.'

'Oh yeah, me and Debs did our fair share of backpacking in our younger days. Never thought we'd be back for a family, but we've been really satisfied with the service here. Haven't we, Debs?'

'Oh, sure. Dr Passi's a true visionary. What's she's done for us . . .'

Debs's voice had an Antipodean upturned lilt, every statement a question, always opening the door, expecting a response. Gill's answer was to produce her smartphone and quickly tap up a series of pictures featuring her and Debs in various poses with a moon-faced, happy toddler, behind them a blue-gold wash of beach and sea.

'She's gorgeous.' Toby nodded towards Gill. 'Has your eyes.'

'And not my nose, thank God!' Gill laughed. 'Our donor daddy's a handsome beast, but we're hoping our son will have some of Debs's lush face. It's her turn next.'

'Yup.' Deb grinned. 'My eggs this time. You're using yours, or . . . ?'

Shyama flinched. She felt as if someone had just reached over, pulled down her trousers and started poking her with a monkey stick. But there was no malice in the two friendly countenances opposite her. She had left behind the pinched faces and empty eyes of the women with whom she had shared those endless private waiting rooms; her new compatriots exuded vitality and good fortune, discussing eggs and sperm as if they were ordering off a menu. Get a grip, woman, she scolded herself. You've come too far to get embarrassed any more.

'No, I . . . we'll be using donor eggs and Toby's . . . my husband's . . .'

'Cool. Well, Renu . . . Dr Passi's got great contacts. She gets eggs in from a load of European countries as well as here. I guess you guys could go native? Indian eggs, I mean, if you want the baby to look like you?'

'Gill, honey!' Debs laid a hand on her knee, leaning forward mock apologetically to Shyama and Toby. 'In Adelaide, she's considered subtle. She pissed off everyone we knew in LA so that's how we ended up in San Diego . . . Remember how nervous we were first time? Give them a break, honey.'

Shyama was now holding the phone and scrolling through an endless parade of the mummies and their baby. 'So, you had your baby here – how long ago?'

'Nadia,' Gill said proudly. 'She's twenty-three months old, so we were last here . . . ?'

'Two years next week, it will be. We came weeks too early, sort of had a holiday while keeping an eye on Kamini, our baby momma.' Debs took the phone and stroked the screen with a finger, looking up at Toby briefly. 'It's so hard being here without Nadia, though. My mum's holding the fort. We're just hoping her brother comes along before her birthday – we so wanted to be back for that, but—'

'Well,' offered Gill, 'we could always ask Dr Passi to bring forward Kamini's Caesarian if she goes over our deadline.'

Debs threw Gill a brief questioning look.

'What, Debs? Renu suggested it, it happens a lot. Babies don't just turn up on schedule, right? And we'll need a couple of weeks to sort out the paperwork afterwards.'

'Oh God, don't get me started on the paperwork,' sighed Debs, rolling her eyes at Shyama. 'You're both British citizens, right?'

Toby nodded. 'Yeah, so . . . ?'

'So you shouldn't have a problem getting the baby home. Just make sure you get in quick with Vinod, Renu's lawyer, as soon as your surrogate's sorted. He's not cheap, but you can't take any chances with the—'

'Don't scare them, Debs,' interrupted Gill. 'Look at their faces. It's going to be fine!'

Shyama's face felt tight with smiling. Toby's left foot drummed a jittery beat on the floor of the moving vehicle.

'Look,' Gill said kindly. 'We're here again. Can't get a better recommendation than that. And some of the crap we've heard goes on . . .'

The rest of the journey passed in a haze of horror-filled anecdotes – of couples presented with the wrong babies due to embryo mix-ups; babies born with incurable diseases and left behind; illiterate surrogates virtually pimped out by their male relatives – stories that would later give Shyama vivid nightmares. She and Toby being handed a screaming bundle, which was then revealed to be a squalling baby with a monkey's face and too-human tortured eyes. Shyama in a toilet cubicle, desperately trying to stuff a gurgling infant into a leather holdall, hiding the child under layers of application forms, while Toby waited outside, holding their passports as the last plane ever to leave for London prepared to depart. Shyama and Toby, older, but clichéd old, as if arranged by a slapdash make-up artist – over-greyed floury hair, pencilled-in wrinkles, sitting in slippers before a fire and raising their faces as they heard, 'Bye, Mum! Bye, Dad! Don't wait up!' Their eyes resting on their son, five foot two, pebble glasses, flaming-red hair. That one at least made her laugh out loud as it woke her, heart slamming against her chest, sheets coiling round her in a damp tangle. This despite the fact that Gill and Debs had ended every tale of doom with the reassurance that 'It would never happen under Renu's watch. She's the best.'

Shyama and Toby drew up outside the clinic at around the same time that Prem and Sita found themselves once again climbing the dusty stairs to L & L Associates' reception. The office was tucked away in a shopping complex which had remained reassuringly unchanged over the last twenty years, one of the low-roofed, whitewashed buildings that were once the commercial heart of the apartment complexes of the nineties building boom. Sita remembered how proudly their estate agent had gestured towards the Chambeli Centre as he drove them towards their almost completed flat just a couple of blocks away.

'You see, everything very convenient for you. Pharmacy, grocery, foot doctor, suitings and shirtings boutique. No need even to leave the complex. Perfect for your restful retirement, *hena*, Madam?'

Fifteen years ago, she and Prem were still healthy working people, confident that they would carry their enthusiasm for life and fully functioning limbs into retirement. They made their plans over their kitchen table as the British winter sank its sneaky fangs into their bones: April to September in London, summer holidays with Shyama and Tara, doing all the touristy things they never seemed to have time for while they worked and lived in the capital – Madame Tussauds, tea at the Ritz. Then October onwards, back to Delhi, catching up with family, until the December damp and pollution set off their chesty complaints, and so off to South India – almost another exotic country to North Indians like themselves: coconut fish curry in Kerala, maybe even a peek at the saucy cave statues. Enjoy their free time and the money they had been working all their lives to amass, the golden carrot after the immigrant's donkey work, munching finally on the future together.

Sita paused for breath on the landing. Fifteen years ago she could have run up these stairs. Ten years of fighting for the flat they had never spent a night in had aged them both prematurely. She could feel it, see it in Prem's face beside her. He wore the same expression he always did when it came to anything to do with this dispute, whether it was one of the many international phone calls conducted at unsociable hours, or scanning and emailing duplicates of complex legal documents, or simply listening to one of their friends tentatively enquiring if there had been 'any good news . . . ?' 'Long-suffering' was too bland a term for what she saw in the eyes of this gentle, generous man with whom she had shared her life for over fifty years. This was not about the loss of money; it was about the betrayal of a brother whom he had trusted. What price could you put on a man's loss of faith? Prem's brother, Yogesh, could answer that: such a bargain he'd got for the sale of a sibling bond.

Sita reached for Prem's arm and they laughed at each other's wheezy *hai-hais* as they negotiated the final few steps.

'So, the good news is that we are listed number three for Friday's hearings.' Ravi Luthra beamed at them from behind his gold-rimmed spectacles. Ravi didn't actually need to wear glasses at all, but he hoped they would lend him some sorely needed gravitas and so had purchased a pair from a young man in the mall with a stupid haircut. This self-consciously cool-dude type had assured him that many young executives were choosing intellectual eyewear to enhance their chances of promotion. Promotion wasn't an issue for Ravi. His father, Luthra Senior, had had to virtually threaten his son with physical violence to make him study law at college so he could begin the process of taking over the family firm. The promise of a hard slap from the back of his hand was undoubtedly exacerbated by Ravi's announcement towards the end of his law studies that he wanted to pursue an acting career. This then set off a chain reaction amongst the entire extended family, fuelled by months of nervous fainting fits and fundamentalist-level prayer sessions led by his heaving-bosomed mother. His father had gone into total meltdown at the news, infuriated that nothing seemed to sway Ravi from his embarrassingly clichéd Bollywood fantasy. Unfortunately, his son had enjoyed some minor success in the uni drama soc, listening to too many hangers-on telling him that he had that certain star quality and he should most definitely give it a go, *yaar*, why not?

'It's not all escapist-fantasy, shake-your-asses-at-the-masses movies nowadays,' Ravi had argued with him. 'The independent film sector is doing some really political ground-breaking stuff. All the major US studios are pouring money into bases over here . . . and with all the cable channels coming in, we're considered cool now. I mean, actually in fashion. Indian actors are winning Emmy awards over in America! This is the new India, Pops!'

Luthra Senior wished he could explain how many times he had heard that very same line of B-movie dialogue over the last thirty years. 'Everything has changed and nothing has changed, my son,' Luthra Senior had told him. 'And besides, take a good look in the mirror. You are skinny, with an unfortunate nose and a squeaky voice, and you will receive not a rupee from me unless you take the gift I and God are offering you. Furthermore,' he threw down his paternal trump card, 'look at the filmi folk – most of the stars are simply the kids of famous stars themselves. All they are doing is following in the family business, because that is how business works. So why isn't that good enough for you, hah?'

This observation, more than any of his mother's fainting fits, had made Ravi pause for thought. And the longer he paused, the further his thespian dreams had receded, until he had found himself sitting in the chair once occupied by his father (who had retreated to a more comfortable office upstairs), playing with a pair of spectacles he didn't really need.

'Number three!' he repeated cheerily. 'So we will definitely get before the judge this time.'

'*Definitely?*' Sita repeated. 'Because that's what you said last time, and—'

'*Hahn-ji*, I know, but this is a very complex case. Jarndyce *versus* Jarndyce, that is the legal system over here. *Bleak House* is, in my opinion, Dickens's masterpiece. A friend of mine did a one-man condensed version of it in Bengali. With some elements of Kathakali dance also. It was a total hit. You have read it, no?'

'No, but I have read every bit of paperwork a hundred times over and I can tell you, there is not one mistake in there. Not this time. And not last time.' Sita fixed him with a steely stare. 'So can you explain why our forms were returned as "incorrect" when we both know they were completely correct? After ten years, we have had a lot of practice in filling them in, *hena*?'

Ravi paused. He felt for these very sweet people, he really did. God knows he had dealt with some very difficult NRI clients over the last few years, all of them choking with fury over some stolen land here, some poached property there, banging their fists on his executive desk and demanding justice. Those who remembered living here got it much more quickly than their kids did, the real foreigners with their English accents and their imported bottled water. The second-generation sahibs and memsahibs would look appalled when their parents handed over paper bags full of money for the various bribes that had to be paid; the

142

bags would include a substantial portion of his own fee (perfectly reasonable in any dual economy, the black and the white side by side), then they would be dipped into by his clerk, then handed over to the court clerks, passed on to their peons, the bailiff and his assistants or whatever *goondas* might be needed to remove the squatters, maybe a locksmith; most certainly some would find its way to the judge (discreetly disguised as necessary administrative costs), and if the police had to get involved, well, then get out the second emergency bag, because there would be a lot of them and you wouldn't want to get into any kind of argument with them, or you might find yourself sitting in jail on some made-up charge, waiting for your traumatized kids to scrabble round for their inheritance funds to get you out in time for your flight home. It wasn't a case of like it or not, it was just how it was.

Of course, he himself would have loved to see all bribery and corruption banished in the new India. He would love to be able to hand in a form and know it would reach its destination simply because people did their jobs properly without the need for a not-so-voluntary donation, to be able to get his daughter into a good school, have his wi-fi connected, call the police when in danger – if he could do all these things without recourse to the paper bag, how simple and clean life would be. But if everyone else was doing it, what kind of a fool would he be to say no and be shoved to the back of the queue? Just as these two people sitting before him had been.

'Sita-ji.' Ravi cleared his throat gently. 'As I have explained to you many times, there is a way of resolving this matter much more quickly . . .'

'No.' Prem finally spoke, staring Ravi down. 'We have already made enough . . . concessions.' Prem nodded his head towards

Ravi's briefcase, where he had just hidden a fat bundle of money wrapped up in a copy of the *Sunday Telegraph*.

Even getting these people to pay cash for a third of Ravi's fee had been a struggle, until he had explained that they were welcome to shop around, but every other solicitor he knew would be asking for at least half in undeclared paisa. But Ravi had felt an instinctive pang of pity for this particular couple when his father had handed over their case to him some eight years ago. They were now officially his most long-standing clients, and although it was entirely in his interest to keep this case going for as long as possible, even Ravi could see that time was not on their side and something had to give.

'*Theklo-ji*,' Ravi continued. 'Compared to what you have already spent on this case, further necessary . . . funding will be minimal. It just means—'

'I know what it means,' Prem snapped. 'I lived here till I was twenty-two, *baccha*, my memory's not gone yet.'

'But *jaan*, just listen to him. All he's saying—' Sita began.

'No. I can't . . . '

Prem sighed deeply. He suddenly felt bone-tired and desperately thirsty. He wondered if Sita had given him all his correct medication that morning. They had left in such a rush, worrying they would be late. Late! How English they had become. Normally Sita had each of his nine daily pills lined up in separate named compartments in his little blue dispenser so there could be no mistake. They had one each, his and hers, a phrase that used to apply only to towels and toothbrushes, pillows and passports. Now it was drugs. Low blood pressure for her, high blood pressure for him, diabetic meds, heart tablets, her osteoporosis, his angina, musical-sounding diseases joining them in their long duet. He didn't care how many pills he had to pour down his throat, as long as they kept him alive long enough to see this resolved, but on his terms. In all his life, he had never borrowed money from anyone, although he had handed a fair amount out, never left a bill unpaid, never drawn government benefit, never bought anything he couldn't pay for upfront (except his houses, and even then he paid each mortgage off before they sold again). He had never been malicious or mendacious in any of his business dealings or on his tax returns, had never had a dispute with his many friends and neighbours. He had never been to Nepal (he had always dreamed of seeing the Himalayas), never stayed in a five-star hotel, never been on a cruise (despite the fact that so many of their retired contemporaries seemed to spend half their lives seeing ten countries in eight days without ever getting off the boat). He had never played poker in a smoky nightclub, something he had dreamed of doing in the brief period when he had passed through Soho, walking from Swiss Cottage to make his early shift at an office in Charing Cross, dodging groups of bleary-eyed punters swaying out of various side-street dives, smelling of cigarettes, stale whisky and male camaraderie. Prem thought it was the most exciting, decadent scent he had ever encountered. He had never bought a diamond ring for his wife, the only thing she had ever expressed a yearning for, and then only because she had been exclaiming over the newspaper pictures of Burton and Taylor's second marriage to each other. 'Of course it's an Indian diamond,' she had sighed. 'Look at the size of it!'

In short, Prem had lived his life believing in the goodness of humanity and the natural justice of the universe, believing that those who worked hard and played fair would be rewarded in kind. That every sacrifice he made, every benefit of the doubt he accorded others, would surely return to him. Not because of karma or fate, the usual suspects, but because people were innately decent. And family, well, they were the best kind of people, because blood ties were the purest and strongest of all.

So when things had first started to go downhill with the flat, when his repeated and kindly requests for Sheetal and her family to move out, as they had promised, had been ignored, naturally Prem turned to his little brother to sort things out. After all, it had been Yogesh's request to allow his daughter and son-in-law to move in, just for a while. Therefore Yogesh would now have to be bad cop to Prem's gently apologetic good cop. Yogesh could let his daughter move into one of the three properties he owned, and Prem and Sita could finally begin their retirement plans. So it was a total shock when Yogesh washed his hands of the situation, when he turned to Prem with that lopsided grin, fingers splayed in resignation, and said, 'What can I do, *bhaiya*? I can't throw them out myself, can I?'

Prem would always remember that moment, the slow, chilling realization that everything he had believed in was broken. Even now, the recollection made him dizzy with nausea. To have thought so well of the world with a wide-open heart, only to have it ripped out by your own brother. It was shortly after this that he had his first angina attack. So how could he explain to this puppy-lawyer, with his designer pens and unconvincing spectacles, that without some shred of honour to cling to he would be swept away on a murky existential tide. That his refusal to grease every outstretched palm was the only way he could survive this journey. That he must try to believe that justice could and would be done, or what was the point of continuing? Otherwise the whole of his life would have been a terrible waste. He wanted to be able to stand in front of a judge with what was left of his soul intact.

At this point, all he could muster as an answer was, 'It's not acceptable to me. Once the courts hear our case, they will see the truth. We must do things the right way.'

Whose right way? Ravi thought with a hot flash of irritation, before smiling and pretending to make some notes, mainly so he would not have to look at Sita's pained, deflated face. He wished that Prem was not in the room, so he could inform her that he was sure this family they were trying to evict had been busily paying their own bribes left, right and centre in order to scupper the case. Misplaced papers, last-minute schedule changes, incorrectly filled-in forms – all of these 'mistakes' arranged and paid for by the other side. The clerk who had performed these sleights of hand would not have felt bad about doing so either. Had Prem and Sita offered more money, they would be sitting in that damned apartment right now, watching soap operas and having a foot massage.

Before he left that afternoon, as he passed the bundled case papers on to his peon, Ravi removed a roll of cash from his brief-case and told his boy to make sure the court clerk received it, with instructions to place their hearing at the top of the day's schedule. At least he could open the first door for Prem and Sita: after that, it really was out of his hands and straight into God's.

Tara shivered at her open window. The start of spring was still a couple of weeks away and mist hung over the distant park-land, grey breath over dull green. No sign of the parakeets today. She tapped on her keyboard, the Skype dial-up tone connecting this time, and waited until Sita's alarmed face appeared on screen.

'Hello, Nanima?'

'Hellooo? Tara, *beti*? Can you see me?'

'Yes, I can see you. And hear you, so you don't need to shout.'

'Hellooo? But why can't I see you then? Can you see me? Hellooo?'

'Nanima . . . stop shouting a moment. Have you pressed the video-activate icon?'

'The what?'

'It's a little icon . . . a button with a picture of a video camera on it.'

'Where is that? I can't see anything. Darling? Prem, *janoo*! Can you get me my glasses?'

'Wait. Nanima? Nanima! Can you get Bitoo to help? Or anyone there under seventy-five? I'll stay logged in, OK?'

Tara sighed, angling the laptop away from her as she stubbed out her roll-up cigarette on the window-sill and threw it into the empty beer can at her feet. She could hear a cacophony of Punjabi squawks off-screen in what she assumed was the sitting room in her uncle's house in Delhi. Despite having given her grand-parents several lessons in how to use Skype before they had left for India, every time they attempted to hook up online, it was the same old shouty pantomime of confusion and chaos.

Shyama had explained to her that in the dark days before computers, the only way of reaching anyone quickly in India was the landline phone, when it worked. Sometimes it wasn't even a phone in their relatives' own house but one of their luck-ier neighbours would act as an informal emergency service for the whole street. So you'd call up sobbing to ask if Auntie X or Uncle Y really had died, and find yourself having a bellowed conversation with a complete stranger, who would then have to send a small child/servant/dog with a note pinned to its collar to your family house for news, while you waited and wept.

'That's why they still shout, even on Skype. Now everyone's got a computer and a mobile, no one bothers with landline phones any more. Shame, really, I used to quite enjoy the drama of it all.'

Typical of my mother, thought Tara. Anything to make life just that bit more complicated.

'Tara, *didi*?'

Tara started as her cousin Bitoo's buck-toothed grin filled her screen.

'Now I think we can see you – you can still see us here?'

'Hi, Bitoo! Yes, finally, it's all working. How are you?'

'Fine, *didi*, very fine.'

Bitoo grinned again, his startlingly large Adam's apple bobbing up and down nervously as he cleared his throat. He had never been one for much conversation. Nearest in age to Tara out of all the cousins, they had been thrown together on the two occasions when Tara had visited India, when they were both primary-school age. Bitoo was, of course, his family nickname. Most Punjabi families had a Bitoo, or a Kaka or a Goody or a Cuckoo – generic affectionate monikers for the cutie-pie younger children. Not so cute, Tara mused, when you're an unconfident teenager hoping to impress the lay-deez. Bitoo adjusted the screen, revealing behind him the usual display of garlanded photos of ancestors who had passed on to their next lives: Tara's great-grandparents and a couple of younger family members who had been taken too early, all wearing the same glum expressions, as if reluctant to be included in this morbid gallery of the long-gone. It had been years since Tara had visited the house, but she found it comforting to see the same familiar faces on the whitewashed wall.

'So, *didi*, why did you not come also with your parents? It would have been good, the whole family here.'

'Oh, I really wanted to, Bitoo, but college work, you know?'

Bitoo nodded gravely. The Indian lot all understood that

149

nothing interrupted Studies. Although in truth, Tara could have easily gone: she had completed all her assignments for the term and being there with her grandparents would have been wonderful. They could have put the right names to all the photos in the dead relatives' gallery, shown her around their childhood haunts, been her translators when her own limited Punjabi dried up and rendered her a smiling, grinning idiot. As she was now, faced with Bitoo's wavering, wide-eyed face. The miles between them and the years apart made Tara feel she was on some weird speed-dating site, searching for a conversation opener that would get them through until the wine arrived. With a shock, she realized this was how she would feel all the time once her grandparents had gone. They were her strongest link to India, speaking history books, their old, gentle bones the creaky bridge between her and her sepia-washed ancestors on the wall.

'You are doing exams right now, yes?'

'Um no, there aren't many exams on my course, Bitoo.' She could see the growing consternation on his face. 'I get assessed continually though,' she added hurriedly. 'I've just made my first small film, my end-of-term project.'

'You're doing movies?' Bitoo's excitement subsided as he remembered, 'Oh yah, right, you are doing some media-style degree, isn't it?'

'Media-style. That about sums it up, yep.' The sarcasm went unnoticed.

'I am also studying hard, *didi*. Right now I am making applications to universities. I have a good chance of getting a scholarship to study abroad. So then I will also be talking to everyone on Skype like you!'

'Oh congratulations, that sounds amazing. You hoping to come to London?'

'No, no, *didi*! America. Everyone wants America only right now.'

Of course they did. She understood then how he saw her: the oddball relative living in a swampy backwater, doing an irrelevant subject in an increasingly irrelevant country. Tara felt a headache begin thrumming at her temples.

'So where's Nanima . . . um, I mean Thayee-ji?' She used the correct title that Bitoo would understand for 'elder uncle's wife'.

Bitoo swallowed again. It looked like a small animal was trying to burrow out of his throat. 'Um, they have gone up-stairs . . . to their bedroom . . .'

Bitoo darted nervy glances towards the door, where raised voices of welcome were now filtering through. A figure appeared behind him fleetingly. Tara recognized the voice and now understood why her grandparents had made themselves scarce. It was Yogesh. He did a comedic double-take at the screen, so cheesy it almost made Tara laugh out loud. It was disconcert-ing – wrong, somehow – how much he looked like his brother, Prem. He cleared his throat noisily and looked down into the camera.

'Hello, Tara, *beti*! How are you?'

This is all your fault, Tara realized. You are the reason we stopped coming over. You broke that thread of continuity, dropped us like a bad stitch, unravelled our shared history with your greedy hands.

'Hi, Uncle. Have you given my grandparents their flat back yet?' Tara asked loudly.

Yogesh's smile flickered for just a moment. 'Very bad connection, hah? See you soon!'

Yogesh left the room quickly.

Bitoo got up clumsily from his chair, sending it clattering to the floor. 'I'll just see if they are coming now, OK, *didi*?' he croaked, and fled to safety.

Tara felt better after seeing Prem and Sita. Bitoo had taken the laptop to them in their bedroom. Yogesh must have still been lurking around downstairs, but her grandparents did not seem perturbed if he was. Tara enjoyed their delight at being able to finally see her clearly.

'*Theklo*, Prem, it's like she is just next door! *Kamaal hai, hena?*'

Her grandmother's favourite phrase, *kamaal hai* – how extraordinary is the world, how often it shocks and delights us, how small we are.

She had looked well, was optimistic about the imminent hearing, even hoping they might get an eviction date within six weeks, before their tickets ran out. Prem, however, had seemed less chipper. He looked as if he'd aged since he'd left. He had sat quietly whilst Sita shouted their news at Tara, but her eyes were on her grandfather. She could have helped them. What they needed were some Western bad manners and bovva-boy bravado, someone who didn't give a toss about all the family niceties. It shocked Tara that her grandparents still stayed in Prem's eldest brother's house, which Yogesh would call into regularly, unchallenged. No one had the balls to say out loud what he'd done, just as no one would allow Prem and Sita to stay in a hotel, not when they could be fed and watered by their kin. Everyone's doing it, she thought. Faking it, like me.

'You're OK, *beti*?' Sita shouted. 'Eating OK? Doing your school work?'

School work. She would always be a child to them, even when grey-haired herself, battling her own dodgy knees and acid reflux.

They wouldn't be around to see her age, maybe would never see their great-grandchildren. The thought made her well up, loneliness flooding her throat so she could only nod her good-byes. However clear the picture, they weren't in the next room; she couldn't smell them, hold them, enjoy silence with them. Life through a glass screen, antiseptic and untouched.

Tara ended the Skype call just as the doorbell rang downstairs. Cursing, she covered the two flights of stairs in ten seconds and opened the door to the same group of friends who had been round virtually every night since her family had left.

'Hey,' Tara panted as they trooped through, Ben, Felix, Lucy, Polly, another Lucy, Jem, all bearing alcohol, party snacks and carrier bags full of must-see movies on DVD. They all knew their way around by now, filing noisily into the kitchen and living room, discarding their wind-chilled coats. Tara was enjoying the fantasy of playing hostess in her own house, feeding people from her own kitchen, playing music as loudly as their neigh-bours would tolerate. Anything was better than being alone. She was about to shut the door behind the last straggler when an unexpected couple brought up the rear.

'Hey Tara, you said turn up if we were free – well, here we are. Hope that's OK?'

'Tamsin! Course . . . yes . . . come in.'

Tamsin laughed her breathy girl-child laugh, revealing small white dolphin teeth, and held aloft two bottles of Prosecco. 'And Margherita with extra jalapeno! Ta-da!' She waved at her lanky, woolly-hatted companion, who was standing behind her juggling an armful of pizza boxes. 'They're still hot, I think. Char-lie, find some plates.'

Charlie barely looked at Tara as he struggled after Tamsin. She threw her coat over the bannisters, revealing her usual uniform of embroidered ethnic-print top, skin-tight jeans and biker boots. Her hair fell in a complimentary curtain halfway down her back.

'Gorgeous place, by the way,' she said as she followed the sound of voices to the kitchen. 'My dad says these houses are gonna be worth a million when the new Tube line's finished.'

Tamsin's father did something in banking. She kept the details hazy – they probably wouldn't sit well with her image as a radical eco-warrior. She was considered one of those in Tara's year who would do well when they left their academic bubble behind. Her weekly blog, Boudicca Babe, was gathering quite a following, once described in the *Sunday Times* style section's online picks as 'Caitlin Moran meets the Jolly Green Giantess'. She was beautiful in that ethereal, willowy way that made men want to protect her and made other women want to swear loudly and chug pints, in order to avoid a direct comparison which they knew they would lose. Tamsin loved all things Indian – the vegetarian food, the primal prints, the bindis, the androgynous blue-skinned gods – and this was the main reason, Tara suspected, that she had turned up tonight. Tamsin also happened to be going out with Charlie, with whom Tara had spent much of the last week arguing furiously.

The issue over which they had clashed had been resurrected in the kitchen – everyone was discussing their recently completed assignment. They had all had to direct and shoot a five-minute film, their only brief being the title 'Now What?' and that they should limit their shoot to a maximum of two actors and one set. The challenge had thrown up the predictable re-hashing of childhood traumas and relationship car crashes: Jem re-created the moment his bi-polar father had been found wandering on a dual carriageway and subsequently sectioned; Tamsin shared her first sexual encounter in a barn in France. Tara's film featured a mother and daughter arguing over a coffin, each blaming the other for the demise of the soon-to-be-cremated corpse. Heavy silences gave way to lots of shouting; the students she had co-opted from the college drama department seemed to enjoy the shouting a bit too much, in Tara's opinion. Still, her tutor had commended her film's 'sensitive honesty', and her friends had been eager to know if it was based on her own life. They became less interested when she said that it wasn't.

Tara entered the kitchen as Charlie was loudly holding court, feet up on the table as if he lived there. He had framed himself perfectly: the deep red of a feature wall behind him, spotlit from above so his killer cheekbones flashed like knives.

'. . . switched off after thirty seconds, all those soapy close-ups . . . bit misery memoir-ish for me,' he declaimed, pausing as he caught sight of Tara.

The temperature in the room shifted, the laughter slowly dribbling away.

Tamsin jumped in, her voice bright and loud. 'Shall I crack open the Prosecco, peeps?'

'Talking about my film, were you, Charlie?' Tara said evenly.

'That description fits all our films, don't you think?' Charlie grinned at her. 'They may as well have asked us all to have a communal wank.'

'No doubt you'd have come top of the form then,' Tara flipped back at him, unable to pass him until he slowly removed his feet from her kitchen table.

'Oh, my *cri de coeur* not to your taste?'

Charlie's offering had been five minutes of a young man – himself – staring in the mirror, deciding which side he should

155

part his hair for a first date, posting continual pictures of himself to an army of online friends throughout. Tara had fumed all the way through it, enraged that he thought a couple of fancy camera angles and some amateur gurning constituted a cohesive piece of work.

'I might have enjoyed it more if you hadn't been in it.' Tara didn't look at him as she grabbed mugs from a cupboard above his head. A 'Whooo!' and scattered applause came from the others, who were enjoying the sparks of one of Charlie and Tara's usual spats.

'Well, I couldn't trust any of those scenery-chewing Drama lot to do my work justice.' Charlie picked at his front teeth with a finger. 'Though luckily it was to Robbo's taste.'

Robert Keen was the feared head of their course, a hard man to please.

'What? You've got your mark already?' Tamsin coughed through a mouthful of crisps.

'Happened to bump into him as I left today. In fact,' Charlie continued, not taking his eyes away from Tara, 'he described my little film as "a brilliant deconstruction of the obsessive narcissism of certain forms of social media". And then gave me a first.'

Tara poured herself a mug of something nearby and took a long gulp, the alcohol searing her throat as it went down. God, she hated him.

She slipped out of the kitchen and headed into the sitting room as the Prosecco cork finally popped to a chorus of cheers. She began rearranging the embroidered cushions on the sofa, punching the soft velvet with unnecessary force. She knew Charlie's type – all thrust and gob – only too well. The same brand of casual machismo that reminded her of her father and which she had loved when she was a little girl. Daddy would decide everything – where they were going, when they would eat, what kind of fun they would have together. It had made her feel like the centre of this powerful man's world, and as though anyone who messed with her would surely come to grief. This paternal protectiveness became more pronounced when her parents finally split up, her father thrillingly purchasing a studio flat in the Docklands where Tara would spend alternate weekends. She felt as if she had flown to Manhattan for a mini-break, sitting on his tiny balcony with hot chocolate and a blanket, the sleek, steely monoliths of city skyscrapers winking at them from across the Thames. Those weekends didn't feel like real life at all; time was pliable as plasticine, stretching to accommodate last-minute theatre trips, spontaneous market rambles, outdoor music festivals, lunches in remote eateries or visits to random friends of her father's, where she would be presented to other strange kids and told to play nicely. Often she would find herself being driven up the motorway on an unexpected business trip, and she would find herself perched in some far-flung office with a pile of sweets and magazines whilst her father sat at several computers talking in a language she never understood. In fact, she still didn't know exactly what he did, other than that it involved designing security software. He got paid 'shitloads of money for very old rope', according to Shyama. During that rose-tinted period, she and her father became giggly conspirators against her mother, who was cast as the moany one, the one who would insist she did her homework or wore something warmer/cleaner, or complained because Tara had been brought home way past her bedtime. Her father would roll his eyes, grinning at Tara, making a secret yak-yak sign with his hands – *there she goes again!* Tara would roll her eyes back at him, bursting with pride that he had chosen her as his ally, fuelled all evening with burning righteous resentment at the sucking-a-lemon-faced nag who spoiled all their fun.

And then, inevitably, Tara began to grow up. She asked questions, she voiced opinions, she had other plans occasionally that didn't fit in with her father's. They began to argue. He accused her of disrespect and a shallow disregard for his feelings, of preferring her mother to him, despite the fact that Tara wasn't asking to spend more time with her, she just wanted some time to herself. He punished her by ignoring her calls or sending texts summoning her to see him now or not at all, a test to see how far she would bend. She bent and wept and raged, turning up to meet him already angry, but mostly grief-stricken at why he didn't seem to like her older and bigger, why he only seemed to have loved her when she was little and cute and didn't answer back. It was only when he introduced his girlfriend to her that she began to understand why she had fallen out of favour. This woman was less than a decade older than Tara, but mentally she seemed a lot younger. She was surprisingly pretty, doll-like, East European –'From Macedonia, actually,' she trilled, throwing adoring glances towards Tara's father. Ah, there it was, that look of unquestioning devotion, puppy-dog eyes and cute pet-me whimper. I used to look at him like that, realized Tara, and now that I don't, he's found it somewhere else. Silly me. For a while, this softened Tara's attitude towards Shyama. She began to have an inkling of what it was that had pushed her parents apart, how her mother must have also bent as far as she could before something finally broke. It was the reason behind her film, which she had been all ready to show Shyama, to begin the dialogue that had evaded them for years. A mother and daughter having a brutally honest conversation over the corpse of someone they loved – surely she would get the hint. But then the whole baby thing had blown up and the moment had passed.

'Wow! I totally looo-ve this room!' Tamsin wandered in with a slice of pizza and a glass of fizz, which she waved at Tara. 'Hope you don't mind, I found a flute. Just can't drink bubbly out of china . . . No way – is that you at the Taj Mahal?'

Tamsin held up the framed photo that always took pride of place on the mantelpiece, the only one featuring Tara's father that Shyama didn't seem to mind having on general display. Tara was about nine, on her last trip to India and the last as a family – her parents parted months later. Her memories of the actual building were hazy: hot white stone beneath her feet, the constant click of cameras, elbows in her face, a spectacularly large wasps' nest hanging like a furry bloated chrysalis beneath one of the massive carved doors leading to the inner shrine. What she remembered most was the tension between her parents. She could smell it, sour and sad, feel it in the way they would both hold on to her too long and hard, as they were doing in this photo. Smiling into the sun, they clasped each other in a desperate embrace, the monument to eternal love squat and silent behind them.

'Is it as amazing as everyone says? How long were you there? Have you got loads of family over there?'

Tamsin curled into a corner of the sofa, waiting for enlightenment. Tara knew how this ought to go now. Oh, she could talk a good talk about her mother culture. She had done it often enough. She could regale her fellow students with her memories of eating mangoes in a monsoon storm (true, she had the photos to prove it), or concoct hilarious tales of her huge extended family (partly true, but heavily embroidered for maximum comic effect), enjoying their rapt and envious expressions. But often she felt like a poor actress in a sketchily written role, all broad brush strokes,

159

no fine detail or emotional depth, a parody of what she ought to be. The truth was, most of the time Tara felt like a fraud, studying a course that led to nothing in particular, eating food for which she had no appetite, engaging in brittle battles of wit which left her bitter and light-headed afterwards, living in a family in which she felt she was an unwanted and temporary lodger. Only with her grandparents did she feel remotely grounded. She missed their familiar ballast. She should have gone with them.

Tara made for the door. 'You know what? How about we get a film on? I'll get the others.'

Some hours later, Tara was trying to stuff a pile of pizza boxes into a bin bag when Charlie walked into the kitchen. The others were lolling around the sitting room watching some high-concept zombie movie, Tamsin's self-consciously dramatic yelps of fear punctuating the ongoing group commentary.

'Why don't you try breaking up the boxes first, like a normal person would?'

Tara ignored him and redoubled her efforts to cram the cardboard into the flimsy plastic, only to tear a side of the bag, spilling old food and empty cans on to the kitchen floor. A viscous pool of barbecue-smelling goo slowly spread across the tiles, a flotilla of cigarette butts scurfing its surface.

Charlie snorted happily and began a sarcastic round of applause. 'Brilliant. Your face . . . like a puppy tied up outside a newsagent's . . . stay exactly as you are.'

He whipped out his phone, preparing to capture the moment. Then he paused, jolted by the sight of the tears beginning to trickle down her cheeks. She was too defeated to move, her shoulders hunched against whatever was coming next. Her head drooped slowly, revealing the mad nest of parted hair and there, the curve of her neck, smooth as a cello.

Tamsin appeared in the doorway, lolling against the jamb with a roll-up in one hand and waving an empty beer bottle in the other. Tara quickly turned away, diving into a cabinet and rustling about in its depths. Charlie grabbed a couple of pizza cartons and began tearing them up vigorously. Voices called from the hallway, the front door opened and a wash of night traffic and cool air rolled in.

'Wow, is Charlie actually clearing up? You've got him well trained, girlfriend. What did you do, rub his nose in it?' Tamsin's giggling at her own feeble joke was interrupted by catcalls behind her. 'OK, people, hang on! We're out of tobacco and toffee cider and . . . oh, loads of stuff actually, so we're off to Tesco – you OK here, lovely homemakers?'

'Bring us back a Snickers?' Charlie shouted at Tamsin's retreating back. She waved an acknowledgement, the door shut and calm descended.

They had left the film running; muted dialogue filtered from next door. Tara stared at Charlie, a tear dripping off the end of her nose, a roll of bin-liners in her hand. She dropped them into the congealing pond near her feet as Charlie pulled her to him, his hands in her hair. After months of having no appetite, no hunger for anything, his kisses felt like food, the bruised apples of her lips hungry beneath his, the gnawing emptiness in her gut sated for a few moments. He pushed her against the kitchen counter, his knee scissoring her legs apart. She felt cool air on her skin where layers were being unpeeled. Maybe he would keep pulling off each papery layer and find nothing inside, except her onion soul.

She tried to free her mouth, her breath smelt of him, his hands

161

were everywhere – he seemed to have grown a couple of extra pairs. She couldn't keep track of them, tried to grab a wrist, untangle searching fingers from places they shouldn't be. He began kissing her again; now there was no air for her to speak, no opportunity to tell him this was a grope too far, further than she had ever been with anyone in her whole young life. She'd never mentioned it before, because her friends would never have believed her – not her, the gobby, grumpy smart-arse. Everyone knew the nice virgins were the ones doing medicine and possibly law, the good girls from the professional, religious, unfragmented families who joined the India Soc – even though Tara knew for a fact that some of them shagged like rabbits behind closed doors. But in public, as always, reputation was all.

Maybe she had absorbed some of her mother's defiant honesty in the wake of the divorce. Shyama's refusal to be pitied or dismissed, the way she had introduced Toby to family and friends, forcing him on them, had been her badge of defiance. But her mother had had something to kick against, a whole set of ancient expectations that she had refused to burden her daughter with. At times, Tara wished that her mother had laid down an unreasonable curfew, argued for her to drop Media Studies and pursue Pharmacy instead, dropped heavy hints about suitable marriage candidates coming round for a viewing, dressed her in a sari and made her hand out home-cooked samosas – anything that would have given Tara permission to reject and rage at her mother. Be a bitch, she'd wanted to yell at her, so I don't have to be! But no, her mother had a boyfriend, her mother was going to have a baby – life stages that Tara had yet to reach, leaving her to watch Shyama leapfrogging her way ahead of her.

She turned her face away to draw breath, to speak, but Charlie grabbed it and locked lips again, harder. Her legs were beginning to give way under her, the sharp counter edge digging into bare flesh. She struggled against him. Charlie grunted in response and held both her hands to her side, pinning her down. Suddenly she realized: he thinks I want this. An image of her Facebook page flashed across her closed lids, indistinguishable from those of all her female friends: happy party faces, a continual relentless celebration of how much fun they were all having, how amazingly popular they all were, how revealingly photogenic they all were, how, with all the choices open to them, their first priority was apparently to look pretty and available. Isn't this what independent young women did, were supposed to do? As good as any man, better than most – my body, my choice; if you want it then you should have put a ring on it. So many sound bites, so little time . . .

Tara managed to release an elbow and jabbed it hard into Charlie's ribs. His eyes widened as he unpuckered himself, flushed and panting. Smiling at her. He was on familiar territory now, this was how they always were, quip for quip, slap for slap. His eyes lit up with the thrill of the chase to come.

A wave of unspeakable sadness engulfed Tara as she opened her mouth to say the word she knew might be too late to save her, the 'No' reaching no further than Charlie's mouth.

# CHAPTER EIGHT

O NLY WHEN RAM made Mala do the photograph did she know it was going to happen. He had borrowed a cell phone from Pogle sahib's son and made her stand outside their house with Seema's children under each arm, their little chicken faces staring out from under her wings. Seema's husband kept telling them to smile, promising them laddoos if they looked snappy-happy, but they just burrowed deeper into Mala's side, nestling under her hot armpits. Then he began shouting at them for spoiling the photo and wasting the battery, which just made it worse. Mala fumed. Now the *bacche* have started snivelling, asking for their real mama, who is refusing to watch our filmi-star shoot, just hiding herself away as if she is the guilty one. Maybe she is. If it wasn't for her, would we all be standing here under the lid of the sun, cooking and crumbling like *mah ki daal*?

So then Mala took charge – someone had to. She pushed a finger into the soft dough covering his ribs – obvious where most of the baby money had gone, straight on to his gut – and told him, '*Theklo*, if you want these kids to look like they belong to me, stop making them piss their pants with fear. They will know something is wrong. Then they will chirrup it to someone else and *bas*, the whole business is everybody else's business and you don't get your commission, *hena*?'

That shut his mouth all right. Then he opened it, then shut it again, a bullfrog with too many flies to handle. He didn't know that Ram had told Mala everything. She had teased the whole plan out of him, pinch by pinch, nibbling at his sleepy ear, so when he was properly awake and saw on her face what she knew, he got scared. Mala smiled inside as she caught him checking her feet to see if they pointed backwards, as if she was one of the demon women who are supposed to haunt the hills. How else could she have sucked out all his secrets? *Mittee* first, *mitta* after: honey works better, dirt comes later. So she held the children gently, did nice auntie chat about their favourite lessons at school (drawing and sums), their favourite snacks in Papa's big new fridge (*rasmalai* and sweet curd), told them the story of Babloo the pan-wallah's accident, how he cycled into a wasps' nest, how the wasps followed him bottom-first, stingers-out for half a mile before he threw himself into a pond and was too scared to come out until dark. When he limped back to the village, covered from head to foot in black sticky mud, the only way his wife could recognize him was by the glow of his red paan-stained teeth. That made them laugh. Mala looked over to Seema's husband, tilted her head for him to press the button, heard the metal eye of the camera-phone wink back at her, click, done.

Mala did not see the actual photo until she and Ram were on the train to Delhi. She did not know who had paid their fare – she guessed Seema's husband again. Who else did they know with money to give away? And the *chor* couldn't even pay for them to go first class. So they sat squashed up against each other, every jolt of the train throwing them together in a sweaty embrace.

Three other families were cooped up with them in the airless carriage. An elderly couple who passed little paper-wrapped cones between themselves, nibbling at roasted peanuts and griddled corn kernels like two whiskery grey mice. A worn-out mother with three children, barely months between them; she must have popped them out like winter peas, thought Mala. Of course, the whole carriage knew why: the eldest two were girls, who sat quietly and round-eyed, knife-straight partings in their plaited hair. They were obviously the rehearsal for the third child, a boy, visibly plumper than his sisters, his skin gleaming with coconut oil and with kohl around his eyes to ward off the evil-thinkers, nestling in his mama's lap, prince of them all. The third couple sat by the window, young, not long married by the way they looked at each other. But God must have been using up his leftovers when he made those two, *hena*? Him all bulgy eyes and no-chin fat neck, her more horse than woman, long-faced, lips stretched over her large teeth; both too dark to be anything but ignored. But they looked at each other like they were the luckiest people in the world. Their hands joined over their shared secret, resting on the tight drum of the woman's belly pushing out the pleats of her bright-green sari. Mala took in the woman's stick-thin arms and legs; her delicate ankles in dusty chappals resting on her husband's crossed legs contrasted with the obscenely ripe dome of her abdomen, as if the baby inside was happily sucking the life from her. Mala's hand flew instinctively to her own flat stomach in memory of those early days of her own failed pregnancy, breast-heavy and nauseous but with that sense of a gradual unfolding within her, new and inevitable all at once.

Then Ram showed her the photograph. He explained how he had got it printed from the cell phone, or rather Pogle sahib's son had – they'd had to go to the town especially, they took out some chip from the phone and put it into a machine. Mala stopped listening, intrigued by the image she held in her hand: she is standing there in mid-story, her face round and sparkling with scandal, Seema's children looking up at her with big wide grins, holding on to her sari and her hands, their eyes enchanted pools of love. *Bacche*, they love anyone who can make them laugh. And I look like a mother, their mother, thank God.

The doctor woman hadn't seemed convinced at first. She had held the photograph for a long time, looking from it to Mala and back again. She had asked Mala how old she was – twenty-four, Mala had lied. They had worked it out, so she could have been seventeen when she gave birth to Seema's eldest. Ram was more nervous than her, his leg jiggling beneath the desk. Mala kicked him, catching his ankle. God, *chalo*, be a man and stare straight back at her, what can she prove? Everyone knows we don't have paperwork where we come from and she needs us to make money for her, understand?

Ram had started getting jumpy the moment they had arrived at the clinic, seeing all the expensive cars parked outside, the silent sliding glass doors, the vases of flowers that he thought must have been plastic until a lazy bumblebee heaved itself out of one of the petal cups, heavy with its dusting of bright-yellow pollen. Then when Mala had approached the receptionist and spoken to her in English, the look he gave her made her want to burst out laughing. If they had been at home, he would have got angry at such a betrayal, showing him up in this hushed hotel place. But here, twanging with tension, ashamed of his scuffed shoes and travel-creased pyjamas, he said nothing, looking at his wife with something like admiration. *Theklo*, she stared back, there is a lot you do not know about me, husband.

*

Seated in the foyer on low leather sofas were the foreigners, pale and perspiring in their new cotton outfits. But the cotton didn't fool Mala, she could see the wealth in their watches, their bags, their sunglasses, even the way they sat together comfortably, like they were at home in this place that made her and Ram feel clumsy and shabby. Some were *desi* couples, homegrown she could tell, because to them she was totally invisible. Some of the *firenge* glanced up briefly as they passed: there wasn't much time to have a good look, maybe to see the ones who might choose her. A blond couple, their hair a silver-white that Mala had only seen before on the very old; but they were young, their skin already bright pink with protest at the oppressive heat. Two women sitting together, too different to be sisters, but holding hands, whispering quietly. One of them was very pretty. Mala willed her to stop talking and catch her eye, but she didn't. And one other pair. The young white man looked strong, moved like a labourer as he stood up to search in his knapsack for something. He found a bottle of water, unscrewed it and handed it to the woman next to him. Indian, but NRI-type Indian – non-resident, like they called them on the news. Mala couldn't tell her age from where she stood – sometimes it was hard to tell with the foreign women, even close up. Some of their faces stretched like wet saris on a rock, their eyebrows arched in surprise that somehow never reached their eyes. But when this woman took the water bottle from the young man, their fingers brushed in a way that told Mala everything she needed to know. What caught Mala's eye, pricked her curiosity, were the red streaks in the woman's hair, little flames glowing around her crown. She likes to be different, wears her fire on the outside; I like that, Mala thought, before an unsmiling nurse came to whisk them away.

*

'You do know that to be a surrogate, you have to have had two healthy children?' Dr Passi said slowly and loudly – but in English, Mala noted proudly.

She pointed to the photograph still in the doctor's hands by way of answer.

Dr Passi held Mala's gaze a little too long and then said briskly, 'OK, I need to examine you,' and fired off an explanation in Hindi to Ram, who sat there nodding silently as she assured him they would just be next door.

Mala lay stiffly on the examination couch, watching anxiously as the doctor woman picked up thin latex gloves, flexing her fingers in preperation. Then she understood those fingers would be going inside her, tapping, pushing, probing. Would it feel as bad as being on the crowded bus to town? The last time Mala had undergone that journey, to buy some *barfi* for Pogle sahib's newborn grandson, she had been shocked by the level of violation. Not just above her clothing but under it, pincer fingers pinching her nipples, fingers so determined and angry they pushed up inside her, dragging her trouser material with them, sending hot darts of pain through her trembling legs. She had screamed out and looked around, at the circle of men around her. None of them would meet her eye, all knowing what was happening, all becoming the same man with many eyes and hands. The men further away just looked bored. Stupid woman, coming on this bus at this time, what does she expect? Then Mala realized that the only other women on the bus were elderly and seated, and understood why Seema would only go to town with her husband or by taxi, now she had the money. In the airless vice of strange shifting bodies, Mala had silently called out for Kali to come down, many-armed, black-toothed, enemy-slicing demoness. Now I know why she screams so wide and loud, now I could rip off a head with my bare hands, if only I could free them.

She did not tell Ram afterwards. Why give him an excuse to forbid her from going out again? When she mentioned it to Seema, saying maybe she should have gone to the police, Seema had laughed at her, spluttering cake crumbs over her second-best plates.

'*Shabaash*, good idea, then they could have had a good feel as well, before slapping you around and sending you home. Solution simple: don't go on the bus any more.'

Later on, Mala had read about this happening in other places. Delhi was especially bad, according to Pogle sahib's discarded newspapers. They had called in lady policewomen to patrol the buses, to stop the 'menace of Eve teasing'. *Lai!* Who was this Eve and what stupid *bakwaas* could call this shameful finger-rape 'teasing'? Even so, she had been relieved when the bus they had boarded after they got off the train had been half-empty, and she sat close to Ram all the way to the clinic.

In the end Dr Passi did not even examine her properly. A phone call came, she took it in the one ungloved hand, left the room and never returned. Eventually a nurse came in and just told Mala to dress herself again. Mala briefly wondered if she should mention that the doctor hadn't done anything except put on one glove, but the moment passed and then there were more tests: weighing, measuring, doing *pashaab* in a bottle, two big injections where Mala watched, fascinated, as her own blood was drawn out of her, so red and thick, the colour of the uncut rubies in Pogle sahib's wife's wedding necklace. The nurse asked if Mala needed water, a biscuit – she was used to some women crying *hai-hai* and fainting away when the blood tests were done. Mala took the biscuit anyway, still munching as she got up to rejoin Ram. And then the paperwork, so much of it, form after form in small-small writing which the doctor woman explained quickly in Hindi only, this time – for speed, Mala assumed, she looked a very busy woman. But they knew it all anyway, Seema had talked them through all the rules several times. Yes, Ram agreed to this; no, they had no claim on the child once born; yes, Mala agreed she would stay at the clinic hostel for the whole pregnancy. When Ram understood what this meant, he halted proceedings, gripping the pen in his hand.

'She will be here the whole time?'

Mala laid a gentle hand on his forearm, felt his sinews below, straining for release. Nodded *hah hah* as the lady doctor explained to him it was the only way to keep Mala well, with good food, vitamins, rest and relaxation, so the baby could be as healthy as possible, but of course he could visit any time on the weekends. All of this is paid for by the couple, understand?

Mala saw Ram doing complex calculations in his head: so now you're thinking how many meals you will have to find on your own, how many evenings you will have to sit and *gup-shup* with your boring mother, how many nights you will have to lie alone with nothing for company but your own twisting desire, just like I had to. Mala saw herself reclining on a soft bed, leafing through a filmi magazine and eating cake off a china plate, just like Seema's, balanced on her proudly pregnant belly. To be paid to rest and eat well, it would be her first-ever holiday – and in Delhi itself. Maybe she could even slip away to do some shopping, maybe they could give her some of the fee in advance? Wait until she met the couple, who knows what they would do for her? Mala held tightly on to her growing excitement, reining it in, whispering quietly to it like a skittery animal – *bas*, we are so close now, just wait. And aware, underneath the anticipation, of a bittersweet tang: if she had been

171

treated this well during her own pregnancy, maybe her own baby would be sitting on her lap right now.

Ram signed the form, throwing the pen down afterwards and abruptly rising from his seat. Dr Passi held up her hand, motioning for him to wait. She told them she had some good news, that this was very unusual, but actually, she thought she had already found a suitable match for them. Of course, they would only sign a contract once Mala's tests had all come back normal, but as they had travelled all this way, why not meet the intended parents right now?

In the few minutes she left them alone to decide, Mala stroked Ram's head, whispering to him about all the things they could afford by the end of the year if it all went OK, coaxing him from the present of this cool, anonymous office to a time when they could buy and plan, not plod from day to day like oxen at a wheel. How strange to think it had been Ram whose idea this was, Ram who had had to whisper the same things to Mala all those weeks ago, and now it was his wife leading him by his clenched fist into the next room to meet their future.

Mala's first reaction was, she is older than I thought, too old for him. The red flames in her hair cover up the grey, and when she smiles I see worries around her eyes. But at least she smiles.

Neither of the men say much at all. Ram nods at different times, his eyes mostly on the floor, sometimes looking up at the blond man, trying to banish from his head the image of the meaty-muscled *gora* thrusting his seed into his wife. Oh, he knows it is all done with tubes and instruments, but still, he wishes he had not had to meet the man in person. A photo would have been fine. The women cannot stop looking at each other, two sides of the see-saw but perfectly balanced, knowing each has something the other wants very badly.

172

She is looking at me like Ram looks at livestock before he buys, Mala thinks. How she lingers on my face, my hips. Maybe I should walk over to her and open my mouth so she can count my teeth.

Shyama is struck by how unexpectedly beautiful this woman is: not just the achingly perfect bloom of youth she wears so blithely, but the wide intelligent eyes, the long proud nose winking with a tiny jewel, the full, almost sulky mouth. The colour of her – brown too dull a word for the dark-golden skin, and that hair, oiled and twisted into a thick plait, blue-black like a raven's wing, the hair of a well-behaved woman. Her English, though heavily accented, is surprisingly good. It's certainly no worse than Shyama's atrocious Hindi, which she attempts in greeting, making Mala cock her head first in polite anticipation and then let out a throaty laugh. Her husband digs her in the ribs, a swift possessive gesture which bothers Shyama, but she lets it go, joins in with Mala's giggling, encourages it with more badly pronounced pleasantries until the two women are locked in conspiratorial smiles and further stop-start chatter.

Toby, already feeling like a pale-skinned spare part, attempts an encouraging smile at Ram. He has to wait a while before Ram looks up from the floor, expecting suspicion, hostility, but instead seeing a keen curiosity in Toby's eyes, a man-to-man look that asks, how did we get here?

Ram looks over at his wife suddenly, hearing Shyama ask about their other children. Will they mind their mother spending so long away from them? Will they see her regularly? Mala answers smoothly in a mixture of Hindi and English, explaining that her mother-in-law and her friend Seema will both help Ram out, and that he will, of course, come every weekend if he can.

Toby takes his first good look at Mala, the economy of her

hand movements at odds with the vitality of her presence. There is something ripening about her: the about-to-turn ear of wheat, the almost-bursting bud. She reminds him of late spring, when the land and shrubs seem to vibrate with suppressed sap, life waiting to be unleashed. She catches his eye and it pierces him somewhere deep. He looks away, embarrassed and slightly afraid.

'No problem for us,' Mala says carefully to Shyama, her head tilting from side to side in that maybe-yes, maybe-no, who-knows universal Indian punctuation, and then more quietly, 'We like to help you.'

This simple sentence almost undoes Shyama, but she clears her throat and reminds herself there is much still to discuss. But they get through the remaining practicalities surprisingly swiftly, and agree that once Mala's tests confirm she is healthy, she will start undergoing hormone treatment straight away. It will take a month or so to prepare her body for implantation of the embryo, created by a donor egg from the clinic's bank and Toby's sperm.

'So you are choosing gestational surrogacy, meaning there will be no genetic link between the surrogate and the baby, which is what most people prefer?' asks Dr Passi.

Shyama and Toby confirm this is indeed their choice. Toby's contribution, when needed, will be much quicker and more private, in a back room with some outdated magazines. Dr Passi shakes hands with all of them and smiles.

'If all goes well, this young lady could be pregnant within the next two months!'

Later that evening, Shyama and Toby sat on their balcony with their celebratory cocktails, the night crickets competing with the distant car horns. Below them the small hotel swimming pool was as still as a mirror, its underwater lights bright and unblinking as lizards' eyes. Behind the glass doors leading to the pool, a wedding reception seemed to be in full swing.

'Look – down there.' She nudged Toby.

Below them the bride and groom, garlanded with marigolds, were greeting their guests beside a chocolate fountain bubbling away like a mini Vesuvius.

Shyama thought back ruefully to her own extravagant nuptials over twenty years ago, held in a five-star hotel just off the A1. Her parents must have nearly bankrupted themselves to lay on an all-day affair for six hundred guests, most of whom Shyama didn't know and never saw again. She knew the drill, she was the only child and a daughter to boot, and even though she had threatened to call the whole thing off if anyone suggested giving Shiv any kind of dowry, the expectation that her parents would foot the entire bill could not be argued with or avoided. Shyama's anti-dowry stance could not be allowed to tip over into full-scale rebellion and possibly scare Shiv's parents into retreat. Furthermore, Prem and Sita had to invite everyone who had invited them to their kids' weddings over the last few decades, for fear of offence, and the same applied to Shiv's parents. That added up to an awful lot of people. But this kind of obligatory bulk invitation just made the day itself feel like a corporate team-building exercise with loud Bhangra dancing at the end. Shyama had worn a traditional red-and-gold sari bought in five minutes flat in Southall, a garment so heavily embroidered that it had left her covered in little red welts afterwards, as if a squadron of mosquitoes had enjoyed their own all-day buffet. She remembered actually feeling grateful that Shiv had waived any dowry gifts, proof that she had married a modern, compassionate man. Yet despite earning well himself, there had never been any offer to pay for one penny of the wedding. All this she found out later, which made the collapse of her marriage even more ironically pathetic.

The couple through the glass looked relaxed, easy with each other. Even their clothes reflected a new comfortable twist on tradition – her sophisticated *lengha* in pale gold, his designer-cut Nehru jacket. They were drinking champagne, for God's sake, not having to take sneaky swigs in a locked toilet with a brides-maid on Auntie-alert outside. Shyama's wedding now seemed from a different era.

'You didn't like Mala?' she murmured, taking an over-enthusiastic sip of her passion-fruit-and-vodka cooler, feeling it burn as it went down.

'No, she was . . . It's just that . . . Well, we didn't meet anyone else, so . . . ' Toby hazarded, already knowing it was too late to change their minds.

'Oh, you think we should have shopped around?' teased Shyama. 'Gone for the friskiest filly with the childbearing hips?'

Toby reckoned Mala was frisky enough for all their needs, but he saw Shyama's point, understood their shared discomfort at the place they found themselves in, picking their brood mare of choice. Somehow making a quick decision based on human compatibility took some of the starkness away. As a dispassion-ate observer, but with his farming background, Toby would have chosen Mala too. The ones with the fighting spirit always came out top. Nice manners and a daft smile usually got you eaten first.

'No, listen, she . . . they both seemed like decent people.'

'And she's . . . open, you know? Some of the women don't have any contact with the intended parents, but she seemed keen to stay in touch once she's . . . you know, a lady-in-waiting at the clinic. Dr Passi says a few of the other surrogates Skype, so there should be no problem teaching her. She seems really bright. That's if you're OK with it? With her?'

Toby kissed her briefly by way of a reply. But later, in bed, he took ages to fall asleep. There was a brief moment when their companionable spooning could have tipped into something more energetic, but eventually both of them decided to pat each other reassuringly and turn away, ready for sleep, which in Toby's case hadn't yet come.

He and Shyama had talked for some time in the darkness, both tipsy on those unbelievably potent cocktails and their shared wonder that they had found someone so quickly, that they might even be back at home in England when, five thousand miles away, their child was being created. Created – was that the right word? Manufactured. Magicked. Whilst Shyama turned to poetry, imagining a plump-faced baby curled up on itself, a beatific smile on its face, Toby could only picture a single cell dividing and subdividing in a bland white Petri dish. He tried not to see a flotilla of tadpoles, each bearing his facial features, swimming aggressively towards a soft spongy egg. He had never resented Shyama for being the one with the problem, even today when, as part of his Intended Parent health check, he'd gone through the whole 'making a donation' ritual again. The only difference being that, this time, he hadn't needed any visual aids. He'd simply imagined a woman, dark-skinned, faintly spiced, slowly unhooking her sari blouse, her eyes dark and calm as a night ocean.

Dr Passi saw them both the next day in her office to discuss the results of the various tests. The whole room was decorated in gradations of beige: creamy-brown flooring and blinds, abstract prints on the wall chosen for their shade rather than content, a tan leather swivel chair behind an old-fashioned wooden writing desk at odds with the large wafer-thin computer screen which took up most of its surface. The only splashes of individuality came from the large metal natraj mounted on one wall – Shyama had a smaller version back home, the Hindu god Shiva with one foot raised in joyful dance – and on the wall behind the desk, Dr Passi's gallery of success: a noticeboard covered with photographs of tearful, beaming parents holding aloft their newly born babies. From a distance they all looked remarkably similar. Maybe this was the official clinic portrait taken after every birth, the tiny mouths making Os of astonishment or protest, the small fists clenched against the shock of arrival, the two ecstatic adults cradling their future. And almost all of them, Shyama noted with interest, were European.

Beside her, Toby sat ramrod-straight in his wingback chair, feeling slightly seasick – the combination of lack of sleep, a slight hangover and embarrassment at having to discuss his bodily fluids with this woman, just a day after being left in a cubicle with his sample jar and soothing piped music. As Dr Passi rummaged around under her desk making clucking sounds of irritation, he thought for one awful moment that she was going to produce the container and use it as a visual aid. Instead she brought out a single sheet of A4 and quickly scanned it before confirming that Toby's sperm was 'not only A1 but your motility is tip-top' and she didn't foresee any problems.

'So we are in a good situation, Mr and Mrs Shaw. Healthy sperm, healthy surrogate. Now all you have to do is choose who will provide your donor egg. Obviously this is a very important decision, as whoever you select will be providing half your child's genetic make-up. We have a comprehensive database here online.'

Dr Passi clicked her mouse and paused a moment before

swinging the computer screen round to face them. 'It's very straightforward, as you can see.' She smiled, navigating the menu with practised ease. 'So you put in your requirements – ethnicity, age . . . and as you make each choice the options narrow down your wish list, and then you go into Profile, for example . . . '

She clicked on the name 'KAMALA' and her details revealed themselves: height, weight, religion, skin tone, education, the briefest of family backgrounds: 'Housewife, married to labourer, three healthy children.'

'Is that all we will know?' Shyama asked eventually, realizing how meeting Mala in person, being able to watch her animated face, hear the curiosity and warmth in her voice, had made a difficult choice so easy.

'Well, for obvious reasons, we cannot show pictures of our donors . . . ' Dr Passi was still smiling patiently. 'But I can assure you, we screen them thoroughly, medically, psychologically. Many of the Indian ones I have met myself, and by the way, most of them are very educated, more graduates than housewives, and I can tell you more about them should you wish. Naturally we have more Indian donors here . . . you did say that you wanted . . . ?'

'Yes, yes, we did, it's in our—' Shyama began.

'Ah yes, I have your details up now. Of course, it makes sense. To match the child as closely as possible to your own . . . ' and here Dr Passi searched for the appropriate word, 'family.'

She then stood up abruptly, her cell phone beeping in her hand.

'I do apologize, I'm being paged . . . please feel free to stay here and keep browsing. I won't be long.'

Only after the door swung smoothly shut behind her did Toby dare to speak, his voice scratchy in his throat.

'Did she really say "browse"? Like we're going shopping?'

'Yup.' Shyama sighed, already surfing the Indian Donor section and wondering if ticking the Graduate Only option made her a fascist or a realist.

'It's a bit bloody clinical, this bit . . .' mumbled Toby.

'Well, we are in a clinic, not entwined under the stars hoping for a baby made of love,' Shyama muttered back. She felt Toby go quiet behind her. She turned round. He was looking at her strangely, arms folded across his chest. Behind him a water cooler gurgled impolitely.

'What do you mean? What does that . . . mean?'

'Nothing. I . . . I'm sorry. It's just . . . this bit should have been my job, shouldn't it?'

Toby came over then and sat next to her, his arm resting on her shoulder. They stayed like that for some time until they made their decision together: 'Sonia – Hindu Punjabi, 25, five feet three, 112 pounds, fair to wheatish complexion, Arts graduate, two children.'

After they had informed Dr Passi of their choice, of which she heartily approved – 'I know her very well, a lovely warm woman, very bright, very decent family' – she reiterated that there was no need for them to stay on. With Toby's sample safely frozen and the donor eggs chosen, she herself would oversee the fertilization of the embryo, and once Mala was at the optimum stage in her cycle, she would undergo implantation. And then, 'We cross our fingers, chant, pray, whatever is your chosen method, and wait for the good news that I am confident Science will provide.'

Shyama and Toby reiterated that they would stay on for the duration of their six weeks' leave, regardless. This was their first trip to India together – why not pretend it was a holiday too?

They had vague discussions about flying down to Kerala and booking a houseboat, or staying in the famous ayurvedic hotel that offered yoga sessions and detoxifying massages, or maybe going west to Rajasthan, having a couple of nights at the Lake Palace Hotel, camel rides in the desert, buying one of those hand-painted Jaipuri cabinets Shyama had always wanted. But despite the box of treasures now open to them, they felt unable to leave Delhi yet, just in case some news or complication called them back to the clinic.

So they spent the next week or so rambling around the city, often hooking up with Prem and Sita for some sightseeing, some of the venues doubling as a wander down memory lane for Shyama's parents. They showed Shyama and Toby the derelict single-storey building that had been their first home together, tucked away in a gulley in one of the most expensive areas of the city, surrounded by huge colonial bungalows and fortified palatial embassies on wide, tree-fringed avenues.

'Back then these were government-owned quarters,' Prem told them, taking in the lush foliage bursting out of the eyeless sockets of the window frames, the group of wild boar that skittered in and out of the surrounding woods. Toby did a double-take when he saw their hairy muzzles snuffling suspiciously at them from the edge of the bushes, continually delighted by how in this country Nature was aggressively, proudly ever-present, even in the centre of the capital. Wild, whipped-looking dogs roamed the streets; noisy birds flew unmolested in and out of the malls themselves; monkeys sat on walls, spitting out fruit seeds as if waiting for a bus; white humped cows chewed thoughtfully in the middle of dual carriageways. He had even seen a rheumy-eyed elephant swaying down a main road, on his back his mahout on a cell phone whilst he gently poked his gigantic steed with a forked steel stick. The animals here had attitude, he liked that. Prem had explained that all true Hindus were vegetarian, 'As the theory is, all life forms are respected equally,' after which Sita let out what sounded like a derisory snort.

They visited Karol Bagh to eat in a dhaba on a noisy bazaar thoroughfare whose *chole* and *paranthe* were considered the best in town. Shyama and Sita left to browse the bustling market. Toby knew Shyama would come back bearing armfuls of glass bangles which she would never wear, and stacks of bindis which looked no different to the ones she could buy in the shop next door to her salon back home.

Over piping-hot masala chai, Toby enquired how the court case was going. Prem's eyes clouded slightly as he muttered, 'Good, good, thank you,' and asked Toby how it had all gone at the clinic. Toby muttered something equally anodyne in reply and they lapsed into awkward silence, both relieved when the women returned with their armfuls of bags, in high spirits and complaining loudly about the price of everything nowadays.

Sita pointed out the two-hundred-year-old Sikh Gurudwara temple tucked away in a backstreet now overshadowed by a twelve-storey office block, its orange pennants bearing the Sikh symbol of the Teg Deg Fateh, defiantly jaunty against the dark brick and steel of its giant neighbour. They swung by the college where she and Prem had first exchanged stolen glances across its red-brick dusty courtyard, where a small group of students now stood outside, shouting slogans and giving out leaflets.

Shyama took one: it featured a stern, bespectacled man with the graffiti 'MOLESTER!' printed in red over his face. It seemed the head of the Economics department had been exacting favours for grades for some years, yet despite the number of female students now brave enough to come forward and expose him, he was still teaching. Shyama noticed how many men were also demonstrating, their voices providing a bass counterpoint to the young women's rhythmic chanting. They seemed relaxed in each other's company in a way she could not recall from her own youthful college days, when she either ran away from men (English boys, too keen and too much hassle) or tried to reel them in (the competition for the handful of eligible Indian boys who weren't Neanderthal or needy was fierce and occasionally bloody).

Sita glanced over Shyama's shoulder, skimmed the leaflet and shrugged dismissively. 'Nothing new. It was happening when I was here, it will always happen. Only now they're talking about it.'

'But at least they're talking about it,' replied Shyama. 'That's half the battle, isn't it?'

'The next battle is how many of those girls who spoke out will be gossiped about. How many of them won't make a good marriage.'

'If it was my daughter, I'd give her a medal,' Toby said firmly. 'And go round later and beat the perv up,' he muttered to Shyama.

'If only it were that easy, *beta*,' smiled Sita faintly and patted him on the arm.

'And any bloke who judged her wouldn't be allowed anywhere near her,' Toby added, emboldened by this gesture of physical affection from Sita.

'You will find that children have to make their own mistakes.' Sita was now carefully avoiding Shyama's eye. 'Sometimes it's like watching a traffic accident in slow motion. You can see it coming. You can shout out to be careful or get out of the way. But in the end, the best you will be able to do is pick up the pieces.'

'And not say I told you so,' Shyama added.

'Hah, exactly.' Sita lifted her eyes to Shyama for a moment and then said lightly, 'When did you last talk to Tara?'

'Oh, a few days ago, maybe? Well, I left a message on her phone . . . the Skype connection's really dodgy at the hotel.' Shyama could hear herself gabbling under her mother's watchful gaze.

'Then maybe try again today, yes? Our Skype connection is fine, isn't it, darling?' Sita took Prem's arm and continued walking, leaving Shyama fuming behind her.

'God, I hate it when she does that,' she muttered to Toby, stumbling as they picked their way over the potholes on their way to the car.

'What?'

'She should just come out and say it, rather than this whole passive-aggressive shit.'

'She was just asking you to keep in touch with your daughter. You're too sensitive sometimes, Shyams.'

'Yes, OK, just because you got brownie points for your white-knight-on-his-charger speech. Theoretical daughters are always perfect.'

'I don't expect perfect,' Toby said sharply, stopping in his tracks. 'Do you remember what that bloke said to us on our first ever scan?'

Shyama's stomach contracted at the memory, long buried. Both of them in one of the basement ultrasound rooms in Dr Lalani's clinic a couple of lifetimes ago, mesmerized by the fuzzy image of the first and only child they had ever managed to conceive, a floating blue planet suspended in a universe of possibilities, its tiny heart flickering like a distant star.

'He said . . .' Toby paused. The words were hard to utter, even after all this time. 'He said, everything looks absolutely average.

184

He said, for most parents, this is the only point when average will do just fine.'

Shyama didn't want to hear any more. She pulled away from Toby, but he gripped her arm fiercely, those thick stubborn fingers used to hard work now too hard on her flesh.

'I never expect perfect,' he said. 'Not from anyone.'

Their final stop that morning, at Prem's insistence, was at the halwa seller on the Pusa road, whose rickety stall had been replaced by a gleaming, glass-fronted superstore where you could still buy the best milk *barfi* in Delhi. For the sake of the tourists, the curious and those old enough to remember the halwa seller's grandfather, the present incarnation of this family business still supervised his vast bubbling pans in the open-plan kitchen, looking like a portly pyjamaed wizard, chucking in rose-water and beakers of nuts and sugar like incantations. They came away with three boxes and Shyama and Toby ate almost a whole one in the taxi on the way back to their hotel. It tasted like vanilla fudge, but crumblier, still warm on the tongue. That was when she told Toby that her Indian relatives had been asking to meet them, but especially him.

'They've been on about it since we arrived, guilt-tripping Mum and Dad. "Oh, the shame, we haven't met them since they got married!" Yes, they think we're married, and no, they don't know why we're here. They think we've come for a delayed honeymoon.'

'I don't mind.' Toby licked each fingertip, trying to prolong the fading *barfi* flavours.

'But I do,' snapped Shyama. She could still feel the tender place on her arm where those fingers had been. 'Thaya-ji's just been sitting on the fence over this entire stolen-flat business. Yogesh still wanders in and out whenever he likes, so Mum and Dad have to go and hide upstairs. It's hypocritical crap, all of it.'

'You sound exactly like Tara when you go off on one,' Toby grinned.

Shyama paused, remembering that Tara had said almost exactly the same words to her all those years ago – how she'd counselled caution, respect for her elders and their way of doing things, staying quiet. She parried another stab of guilt, missing her daughter – her head had been so full of the child to come.

'Anyway . . . I've told you now. So it's up to you. But I won't be going. Just as long as you know.'

'But your parents . . . '

'They understand. I've told them how I feel. Look, if Yogesh turns up, I won't be responsible for my actions.'

'What, you'll just take a swing at your evil uncle, will you? Come on, Shyama, if your folks can handle it, so can we.'

'I don't have to handle it, that's the point, Toby. You don't know how deep this goes . . . it's primal, you know, the whole land thing.'

'So you've forgotten I'm from a family of farmers? I get the "land thing", I've lived it.'

'No, not in the same way. You and your brother share your heritage, you're in the same country. It would be the equivalent of Matt letting Linda's family squat on your land and then sub-letting it . . . and then laughing in your face every time you asked for it back.'

Toby shook his head, sweeping the last of the glistening crumbs off his lap on to the taxi floor. 'You don't think white people shit on each other too? When it comes to land, we're all cavemen swinging clubs at each other. Matt got two-thirds of the farm because he's the eldest, even though I would have run it better. And my dad knew it.'

'It's not the same.'

'Why isn't it?'

Shyama swallowed and stared out of the window, catching a glimpse of what looked like another demonstration outside a gated building, the car moving too fast for her to register any of the home-drawn placards. Most of the demonstrators seemed to be women this time; TV cameras and photographers flashed past as the car gathered speed. Two in one day. This seemed a country far too busy for revolution, although she did remember coming out of a West End cinema in London years ago and realizing there had been a full-scale riot whilst she had been sitting inside eating popcorn. Shiv had been with her; they had picked their way over the debris of shattered shop frontages, dodged lines of fluorescent-jacketed police, held hands as they darted along side streets with sirens wailing around them, trying to find the nearest working Tube station so they could get back to his place and celebrate escaping the uprising in bed. How young she'd been, more thrilled than dismayed by the social unrest that had happened yards from where she sat in the dark, eating, laughing, oblivious.

'It's not the same,' she continued, 'because you still have something. Some land, some respect. My dad's bankrolled the whole family all his life and this – It's like a bereavement. It's the death of so many things – see, you don't understand. You never will.'

'Whoa. I've bent over backwards to understand, the whole time we've been together. Have I ever . . . ?'

'Ever what?'

'I've always made an effort to . . . fit in. I mean, I virtually live with your parents. And they're great. But when did you last see my family?'

'When did they last invite me, Toby?'

187

'They run a farm. They never entertain, but they have an open door. Every time I've suggested we drive over . . .'

'Oh please!' interrupted Shyama. 'I've seen the looks they give me. It's not quite flaming pitchforks and yokels shouting, "Kill the witch!" but if they could get away with it . . .'

This used to be the point where Toby would laugh, despite himself. But now he turned on her, his face reddening with frustration. 'That's bollocks!'

And this used to be the point where Shyama would know to back off, divert him, pretend to check her watch and allow the silence to cover up the moment, let it pass. Instead she said, 'It's humiliating, being stared at in this day and age, when you dare to venture out into the pretty bits of England. OK, maybe they don't want to burn any crosses, maybe it's just curiosity. The result's the same, though. You're reminded you don't belong. Don't tell me you will ever know what that feels like.'

'I know what it feels like right now!' countered Toby. 'And it doesn't bother me. In fact, it makes me feel . . . free. And . . .' he ploughed on, seeing the growing incredulity on Shyama's face, 'you know you've hardly spent any time with Matt and Linda. God, they have no idea we are even doing . . . this. How could I tell them? They don't know you well enough to think it's anywhere near a good idea.'

'Well, at least they must know I'm not after your money,' hissed Shyama, aware that their taxi driver had turned down the blaring radio, either to facilitate their conversation or to listen in to it. Ears everywhere, as usual. Quiet, eyes down, what will people think? She was sick of it.

They sat in miserable silence for a while, Toby still smarting from Shyama's thinly veiled insult. He rolled down the window, the handle slipping under his sweaty palm, letting the mingled scents of petrol, braziers and – always, somewhere – incense assault his nostrils, enjoying how it awoke all his senses. He liked this country, he liked being here. He didn't see the flaws and the frustrations and the million hidden agendas and rewritten histories, how could he, and why would he want to anyway? How could anyone move forward if all they wanted to do was find fault and harp on about the past? There was an ebullient, child-like energy about this place; Toby felt he was being continually propelled forwards, onwards, surrounded by a population in constant motion. No beggars, what beggars? Everyone seemed to have a job and was busy doing it, at the roadside, in parks, in offices. No benefit handouts, so you got on with it. Even the places of worship were humming with the prayers of the drop-in devotees; the entrepreneurial ones set up their own makeshift shrines in tree trunks, alcoves, collecting coins from people on their way to work who tucked their briefcases under their arms to free their hands for a namaste and a mantra. But they stopped to make room for a blessing – that was what struck him. It wasn't a Sunday thing like back at home. He had memories of itchy collars in damp Methodist churches, dirge-like hymns and the drone of the wheezy vicar, tubes as congested as the crumbling organ. It was like Shyama had told him once: the gods were everywhere, but were also part of everything. Just one more stop in the relent-less, joyful flow that made women like Dr Passi say anything was achievable, that had enabled them to be here when every other possibility had been erased.

Suddenly they were stopping in front of a three-storey white-washed house. It was separated from its similar neighbours by a narrow alleyway, across which lines of washing hung. Opposite it was a small park where schoolboys in pristine white school uniforms were engaged in a noisy cricket match.

Shyama reached over Toby and flung open the door. 'You want to meet the family, go ahead. Mum and Dad will be delighted.'

Toby had barely got out and closed the door before Shyama shouted at the driver like a Punjabi fishwife and they screeched away. Toby told himself it must be all the hormones sending her loopy; he recalled similar weepy tantrums during their unending rounds of IVF. And then he remembered, she wasn't the one taking the hormones this time. He thought about the other woman, wondered if she was retching into a bowl or lying in a darkened room with a wet flannel over her eyes, or throwing cutlery at her confused husband before bursting into tears and needing to be held. He had put up with all that and more. He doubted if the other woman's husband would even be around to comfort her – or maybe, because she was so much younger, she just wouldn't suffer as much. He hoped so. The thought of Mala suffering while she carried his child – their child – filled him with unsettling guilt.

He stamped the dust off his shoes, mindful that he might have to remove them as he entered the house, then swung open the steel gate, knocked and waited as excited foreign voices rose and gathered to welcome him in.

Shyama couldn't remember how she had ended up at the clinic. She must have given the taxi driver the address – one of the few she knew off by heart here. It was busy today, with medical staff in scrubs, administrators with clipboards, delivery men being redirected away from the front entrance, all of them a whirlwind of activity around the stoic couples who approached the glass doors hand-in-hand, all of this fuss for them.

Shyama hesitated at the end of the short drive. She didn't have an appointment and even though Dr Passi had said they were welcome to call in any time during this strange waiting period, she didn't want to look like some neurotic control freak, hovering around for a morsel of news. She jumped at a sharp horn blast behind her and stumbled on to the grass verge as a car screeched up the drive, throwing up puffs of yellow dust.

A small crowd was gathering at the clinic entrance, there were flowers being exchanged, balloons bobbing, and a brief burst of applause as two women emerged, one of them carrying an impossibly small bundle swaddled in layers of white cotton. One of the women – and by now Shyama knew it was Gill – loped over to the waiting car and pulled open the back door. She seemed to be checking the baby seat, tugging on the straps to test them, whilst Debs continued receiving shouted blessings and smiled her goodbyes. Dr Passi moved in for a hug, turning to direct Debs towards the photographer who was busy recording the farewell.

After a few moments Debs called out to someone – Shyama couldn't see who, but her gestures became more insistent. Dr Passi disappeared inside for a few seconds and brought back with her a small Indian woman holding the end of her sari over her face. She walked slowly, haltingly, to take her place besides Debs, who held the baby between them as they posed for the photographer. There was a brief embrace between them and more waved goodbyes, before Debs handed the baby to Gill to strap into the car seat and they pulled away. Shyama half raised her hand as they passed in case they recognized her, wanting to be ready to offer some gesture of congratulation. But neither of them looked away from the newborn, a dimpled depression in layers of blanket. The Indian woman stood motionless in front of the glass doors, watching the car until it disappeared. She flinched as a nurse came up behind her and offered an arm. The woman shook her head and walked away from the clinic alone, stepping carefully. Even from this distance, Shyama could hear the faint irregular *chum-chum* of her silver anklets. Maybe it was her gait, the weary, cautious walk of a woman who has recently given birth, that drew Shyama to follow her.

She found herself slowly keeping pace behind the woman, following her along the side of the clinic until the paved road became a narrower dusty track only wide enough for a single car. On her left, Shyama passed what she assumed were the delivery suites at the back of the clinic, newly built brick walls with black-tinted windows and air vents noisily churning out antiseptic-smelling vapours. To her right was a patch of waste-ground between this building and the next, with the usual collection of makeshift dwellings constructed out of tarpaulins and metal sheeting. A mother poured water over an unprotesting naked infant, who stood on top of a plastic barrel like a solemn cherub on a grubby plinth. Old newspapers and discarded food wrappers, caught on the wire fencing which separated Shyama from the pair, flapped like surrender flags. There was something timeless and tender about the scene, she felt. In the midst of a wasteland a mother was washing her child, trying to create order and cleanliness out of chaos.

The silver anklets jangled a little louder as the woman abruptly turned a corner, disappearing out of sight. Shyama quickened her pace and rounded the corner to find herself facing a double-storey whitewashed building, festooned with a tangle of wires which stretched from the adjoining clinic to the flat roof like an umbilical cord. Clothes hung drying from the small balconies outside each window in the jewel-bright shades of the village: unapologetic oranges and brassy blues. The wide shalwar trousers, unfastened and spread out, hung limply like the underclothes of a fat, bow-legged clown, complemented by unfeasibly large brassieres festooned over the iron fretwork, gently steaming as they dried. Competing Hindi film tunes warbled from various open windows, the woman's voice always a winsome fluting soprano, the man's smooth and cheesy as a Lothario at a bar. Shyama wondered why the style of singing had never changed since her own childhood. For the same reason, probably, that there had never been any Indian punk-rock bands – or none that she knew of, anyway. Too angry, too disrespectful. Green hair? Safety pins in your nipples? Hai, the shame . . .

Standing outside this building was like seeing the female world in miniature, a living dolls' house. Shyama could imagine swinging open the whole frontage like a door and discovering all the women inside, incubating in the heat. The songs made sense – the filmi heroines only ever sang the song of caged birds; the sound that came out of their mouths was that of the ideal woman, seductively modest, respectfully flirtatious, high and sweet as a passive girl-child waiting to be plucked.

The woman with anklets entered a side door on the shaded side of the building and was gone.

Shyama stood for a while longer, listening to the shouts of greeting and gossip rebounding within, not sure why she was here, except that it felt comforting. She was about to leave when a figure appeared at one of the balconies and watched her for a few moments, the light catching the small gem at the side of her nose. It was Mala. Shyama waved at her, a half-mast apologetic gesture, and Mala seemed to nod – she wasn't sure, it was the smallest of movements – and then went back inside.

Shyama had almost given up waiting when Mala appeared at the side of the building, beckoning her forward into the shaded doorway. She propped open the side entrance with one leg. Behind her a stout, surly-mouthed woman in an orderly's uniform sat at a modest desk. A whiteboard on the wall listed a dozen first names – Kamala, Firoza, Puja, with scribbled figures and acronyms besides each one. The orderly assessed Shyama in one quick glance and her expression softened slightly. Be nice to the foreigners, even if they are foreign Indians.

'Mala says she is your surrogate, Madam?' she said in a quiet, smiley voice that belied the bulldog in her eyes.

'Yes . . .' Shyama's voice was husky from heat and dust. She cleared it noisily. 'Sorry, yes. Do you need to see . . . ?' She fumbled in her bag.

The orderly shook her head and asked for Shyama's name instead, taking some time to bring up her details on her computer. All the while, Mala stared at the floor, hands demurely clasped in front of her.

'All fine, Madam, but usually our ladies do not go out on visits without permission.'

'Visits?'

'Mala says you want to take her out for a few hours?'

Mala still did not look at Shyama, but her hands tightened around each other, her knuckles whitening. She seemed to give off a low-level hum of energy like a tuning fork, blank and still as metal.

'Yes, that's right,' Shyama replied. 'As Mala is not . . . she hasn't started any procedure yet, I'm sure it will be fine. I wanted to have an opportunity to talk with her.' She remembered her Auntie Neelum's tone with shopkeepers, drivers, low-level officials – act high-status and that's how you will be treated. The orderly's expression had changed; she was looking at Shyama expectantly, waiting for something.

Shyama held her gaze, her smile tightening. 'Why don't you get Dr Passi on the phone then? I'm sure—'

'Oh no, Madam, no need to trouble her.' The orderly let the

sentence hang in the air, a disappointed downturn pulling at her mouth.

Shyama felt a soft tug on her sleeve and swung round to face Mala, who raised her eyebrows slightly and nodded towards the handbag hooked over Shyama's arm. Of course, how English of her not to realize. Shyama fumbled for her purse – she had no idea how much to offer. She turned her back on the orderly, shielding the cash, flushed with shame as if she had been caught with her dress tucked into her pants. Before she could decide, Mala expertly plucked out two notes and placed them in Shyama's hand, closing her palm over them, then went and stood by the door. Shyama held her hand out as if offering a handshake and then stopped halfway. In the end she just dropped the money on the desk and hurried out, the orderly calling after her, 'OK, Madam, no problem. I will arrange.'

It wasn't until the two women were sitting on the back seat of the hire car that they finally spoke. *Vichare*, thought Mala, she is more nervous than I am. And that business with the *rishwat*, like a clumsy child caught with her hands in the butter jar. How can a woman reach this age and not know how the world works? At least she kept her mouth shut in front of that *kuthee*. Mala hoped fervently that she would not be made to pay for her escape later, knowing that that particular orderly had a reputation for meanness and for stealing the home-made snacks left by families for their gestating wives and daughters. For now, she just wanted to make the most of these sweet stolen hours, and she knew exactly where she wanted to go.

'Madam?'

'Please don't call me that!' Shyama exhaled, relieved the silence had been broken. 'Shyama is fine.'

195

'You don't mind?' Mala nodded at the car, aware that the driver had given her the filthiest of looks when Shyama had beckoned her on to the back seat. Her obvious poverty lowered the tone of his vehicle; now he, too, had slipped a few rungs down the complicated social hierarchy of those who served. Her dark face and no-class sari had demoted the seething Raju from luxury chauffeur service to a mere cabbie.

'No, no, of course not. I . . . it's good, we can get to know each other. I mean, if everything goes to plan . . . Where would you like to go?'

'Ronak Mall.'

'A mall?' Shyama had been hoping for something a little more intimate and . . . yes, authentic – the iced coffee and *paneer pakore* of her childhood treats here. But maybe this was the new authentic. And there was no doubting the hope on Mala's face, held in, braced for disappointment. Like ten-year-old Tara, asking for her first sleepover, all moony-eyed.

'Raju, do you know where this mall is?'

Raju shook his head sorrowfully. 'Haha, Madam, but it is too far.'

'How far?'

'Gurgaon . . . outside Delhi itself.'

'A mere twenty minutes on the new NH8 highway and only fifteen kilometres from the airport.'

Even Raju forgot himself and stared open-mouthed at the junglee woman on the back seat, who at least had the decency to flush with shame under Shyama's amused gaze.

'Sorry, Madam, I remember this from a magazine.'

'And so precisely. I'm impressed.' Shyama laughed. 'And the airport's not far at all from here. I don't suppose either of us have to hurry home, so . . . why not? And not "Madam". Shyama.'

Raju pulled away more quickly than necessary, almost colliding with an entire family who were balancing on a small moped with a large quilt strapped to the back. Mala caught his eye in the rear-view mirror and would not look away until he gave in and dragged his gaze back to the road ahead, but not before she saw something very like grudging admiration on his face.

Ronak Mall was all Mala had expected, and more. Even before they had reached the turn-off from the eight-lane highway snaking out of the centre, when the soaring skyscapers and glittering obelisks of Gurgaon's commercial district rose into view, she had let out a small *hai* of wonder which made Raju wrinkle his nose in derision. You sniff your bad smell, *sala*, she thought. You see this view all the time. How would *he* know what it was like to wake up day after day in the village and be confronted by nothing but flat-flat all around, so many shades of green and all of them boring. Open fields stretching for miles, so, even far away, someone, anyone, could spot you with your water pot or your washing, and know what your business was and if it was acceptable business. Nowhere to hide yourself, to lose yourself, like here. Anthills, Mala decided – just the same as the towering stacks of red dust pitted with holes, except they were full of people and shone shamelessly

Once they had entered the cool recycled air of the mall, no one gave them – her – a second glance, not even the shark-eyed security guards at the entrance when she passed them, pulling her sari over her head. Maybe they think that I am her ayah, that she has brought me along to carry the bags of kids' clothes we will buy without even checking the price. *She* will buy. Every floor one kilometre long, plus kids' Fun Zone, Relaxation and Meditation Spa, and ten-screen 3-D cinema with reclining leather seats. Even Shyama Madam seemed impressed.

Shyama spent the first ten minutes trying to absorb the scale of the place. The mall, and Gurgaon itself, made her think of those post-apocalyptic disaster films where the earth's population end up having to resettle underground or in space, entire cities re-created, reconceived, with the chance to do things better, bigger, cleaner than before. Gurgaon had been mentioned by her parents' friends many times over the last few years as the place to buy. Even Priya had turned up one day bearing armfuls of glossy brochures featuring luxury purpose-built apartments within grassy, gated complexes, clearly targeted at the NRI population hoping to buy their little piece of the Motherland.

'Compared to London it's dirt cheap, of course,' Priya had remarked. 'Especially if you buy off-plan. The local government is offering incredible tax incentives to build here, that's why it's expanding so rapidly. Loads of the Fortune 500 industries are rushing in now, though I reckon the major players will be IT and outsourcing and offshoring hubs. The nice man who answers your call to the bank, who says he's called Geoff and loves pie and mash, despite his suspiciously Punjabi accent, he probably works in Gurgaon . . . Blimey, they've even got built-in servants' quarters in this duplex . . . I mean, it would make you go more often if you had a home there, wouldn't it? Might even force the kids to actually learn some bloody Hindi.'

Shyama had reminded Priya that her parents^ desire to go home more often had resulted in the unmitigated disaster that was their stolen apartment, but Priya had replied, 'Well, exactly, that's the attraction of this kind of investment. No family involved, twenty-four-hour security to stop the squatters, leisure complex, all that shopping . . . Come on! We could go in together. What do you say?'

198

Shyama had said nothing, and days later, Priya had declared it to be a terrible idea. She'd done her research and apparently half the complexes had regular power cuts because the infrastructure was so weak. ('They even close the malls on Tuesdays to save energy. Why Tuesdays? Random . . . ') And there'd been loads of cases of NRIs turning up to find their apartments had been occupied or rented out during their inevitable long absences. 'Security guards taking bribes . . . builders moving their families in . . . you can splash out for private security – lots of people have, anyway, since the Mumbai bombings – but that's another expense which we could just blow on an amazing hotel whenever we visit, no?'

Nevertheless, at least two couples that Prem and Sita knew had bought in Gurgaon and regularly extolled the virtues of the ever-expanding satellite city.

'*Theklo*, Prem, we can spend all day without going further than the mall, everything is on your doorstep – food, fun – all air-conditioned. And so many of our neighbours are from England also. We have even started our own cards group with some very nice people from Watford.'

Meeting other Brits over indoor fast food wasn't Shyama's idea of fun, but then she had never been a mall fan, even though Tara and her friends had indeed used them as holiday homes in their early teens, spending what seemed like entire weekends there, all their needs under one roof, their main need being not to be anywhere near their parents.

True to tradition, there were gangs of young people in Ronak Mall, but not the feral, hooded kind that Shyama remembered from her youth, who would occupy the top balconies to gob on passers-by below. The Ronak Mall posse looked like perky Disney-style teenagers, fresh-faced and fashionably dressed and often with other family members in tow. In fact, everyone looked happy and successful. Maybe they piped something into the air ducts. And whilst it felt like progress, to Shyama it didn't feel like India.

For Mala this was exactly how India should feel: rich and fast and as good as – no, better than – all those places she'd seen on the cable channels on Seema's now-connected super-deluxe TV: Beverly Hills, Knightsbridge, Park Avenue. She wasn't stupid, she knew she would never be able to afford nearly everything behind each shopfront. In her head she had already spent every rupee the baby might bring them, and very little of it was for her. It was for the other children, the ones waiting to be reincarnated, her own – so they could look as fat and content as all the kids around her now. But, *chalo*, today let me be like one of those drunken dusk moths who are almost too heavy to fly, dusty wings heaving them up towards the one street lamp outside Pogle sahib's house. Let me just bump my head against all these windows, just to see inside, just to remember for later.

Shyama asked her, 'Is there anywhere special you want to go?'

Mala shook her head, so they just walked past shop after shop – Shyama pulled towards the few brand names she didn't recognize, Indian designers, homeware, music; Mala more interested in Marks and Spencer and Next – until they passed a place called Miracles in Beauty. Shyama perused the treatments on offer, surprised that the prices here were not so very different from hers, impressed by the subtly lit interior and the range of organic ayurvedic products.

'Do you mind if we go in here quickly?'

*

200

Mala stood to one side for a while as Shyama started chit-chatting with the girl at the desk. She wished she could sit for a moment; she felt nauseous. She had got used to the daily injections but the accompanying cocktail of drugs she was taking made her feel light-headed, remote from her own body. Still, she was already making extra money for the suffering. Doctor sahib had asked her if she wanted to give away some of her eggs before she was made ready to host Shyama Madam's baby. Not give away, she then corrected herself – give and get paid for them. This sounded like a better idea. Mala did not understand all of the medical terms, but as far as she could remember, she must have one type of medicine to let her eggs be taken, and then another to stop her making eggs so the made-up baby could be planted inside her. So many eggs. No wonder she felt as fat and confined as a chicken. It meant she would spend an extra month at the clinic, but who would be waiting for her to come home anyway?

Another manager-type lady came to greet Shyama, with surprised high eyebrows and hair almost as long as Mala's, but so shiny, like it had been poured out of a tube. Only then did Mala dare to sit down on the soft sofa with the piles of magazines, many titles she had never heard of, all of them in English. But she could easily translate most of the titles and headlines; all those stolen hours poring over Pugle sahib's discarded newspapers had not been a waste. But she only pretended to read, her ears trained on the two women talking. Shyama Madam was some kind of businesswoman – a good one, judging by the way she talked, confident and in control, asking lots of questions about products and supply and overheads and export duty. Mala watched how she talked, how she occupied her space, filling it, pushing it out with her earthy voice and expressive hand gestures so that it expanded with her energy. When she smiled it filled her eyes, when she laughed it came from her belly, not the polite hand-over-teeth titter that some of the high-class women affected in imitation of their favourite movie heroines. Now she began to see what the handsome blond man saw in Shyama; she herself saw it in the older women in the village, whose children were grown and husbands slowing down. They didn't have to pretend and they didn't care what people thought of them, because an old woman is almost invisible anyway, *hena*?

Then Shyama Madam was calling her over excitedly, saying something about a treatment she wanted to try out and wouldn't it be fun for both of them, and before Mala knew it, she was lying on a long squeaky chair having her face scrubbed and rubbed with something that smelt like summer roses, and then something else which didn't smell as good and dried on her skin like the top of boiled milk and then was peeled off in one whole piece, as if they had removed her face and replaced it with a similar one but softer, shinier, newborn.

'Wow,' breathed the girl as she wiped Mala's cheeks clean with a warm scented flannel. 'Her skin is totally flawless. I mean totally, nah? Like there's not one open pore anywhere.'

'I use *dehi*. Gram flour. *Haldi* sometimes,' Mala said without thinking.

The three women swivelled their heads to stare at her.

'Yoghurt? And turmeric? Yes, we know all about traditional village remedies.' The tube-hair lady smiled at her reassuringly. 'Most of our treatments are done in consultation with—'

'Lime juice and sugar for leg hair. *Chaaval* and *channa* for face.'

'Chickpeas and rice? For massage . . . like a scrub?' Tube-hair lady was looking very interested now.

Mala nodded, rubbed her fingers together as if she was making crumbs. 'But small-small . . . also with coconut oil.'

'Don't give away all your secrets!' Shyama said, half-jokingly.

Mala prickled at the sideways look she gave her, the look she sometimes got at the riverbank from some of the other women when she laughed too loud or made fun of one of their husbands. But then Shyama Madam started coo-cooing over the jars and bottles that were brought out for her to smell and rub their contents between her fingers. They obviously made some deal, tapping details on to their matching cell phones before Shyama was given a bag of samples to take away. Before they left, Shyama asked if she could use the computer at the reception, and she and the tube-hair woman spent some time looking at the screen, deep in serious talk. Then Shyama beckoned Mala over, pointing at an image of a room not unlike the one they stood in, with leather chairs, walls of mirrors, pretty Indian women in white coats.

'This is my salon, back in London.'

'Yours? You are manager?'

'I own it, Mala. It's all mine.'

Mala looked at the picture and wanted to dive into it, take her place next to the smiling smart woman with the tiny yellow sun emblazoned on her coat pocket.

'*Surya.*' Mala pointed upwards, despite the fact that they were inside, miles away from a real sky. 'The sun, you know?'

Shyama nodded. 'I know. A beautiful name for a girl, don't you think?'

As they were leaving, Mala grabbed some leaflets from the reception desk. Even if she wasn't able to make sense of most of the words now, she was sure she could learn enough over the next few months, and wondered fleetingly if Shyama Madam could be persuaded to buy her a dictionary.

\*

In another part of the mall, seemingly miles away from where they had started, they sat in front of a tumbling fountain of unnaturally blue water, eating cones of hot buttered corn kernels, shiny snail-trails running down their chins. In a bag at Mala's feet sat the small Hindi–English phrase book that she had lingered over for a good fifteen minutes until Shyama had finally taken the hint. She thought this was such a good idea that she had also bought one for herself, declaring, 'If we both do our homework properly, soon you will be able to chat to me in English and I will answer back in Hindi.'

Mala had to ask, it had been playing on her mind ever since they had left the beauty salon.

'Madam . . . Shyama . . . you wouldn't mind? If you have a girl?'

Shyama stopped mid-chew, swallowed carefully and wiped her chin with the heel of her hand. 'Why would I mind? I already have one lovely daughter.'

'Oh!'

'From my first husband. She's nineteen now.'

'Oh . . . he is dead? Your first husband?'

'Ha! He may as well be, I hardly see him . . . But no, we're divorced.'

'Oh.'

'I hope that doesn't shock you, Mala.'

Mala half laughed, wishing she had the language to express how ridiculous that question was. Wasn't every other soap opera nowadays about some independent woman battling with her husband or even leaving him after he had shouted at her, drunk too much, sided with his mother against her, even hit her (though only when drunk and always he was very sorry afterwards). It was meant to make everyone feel better, Mala supposed, that despite their big houses and expensive clothes these people were also unhappy with their lives, still wanted more. She and Seema would sit munching snacks for hours in front of these *bahu-sus* stories, as they were known – daughter-in-law versus mother-in-law sagas – because apparently it was always the women who created trouble for each other to start with. These firework stories had been exploding for real in the villages since Mala could remember, but dirtier, messier, darker. Men half-blind on moonshine kicking their wives and kids till they bled into the dust; men killing each other for land, or killing themselves when their land failed, forced to use fertilizers that strangled the soil or crippled with debt after a crop failure. Lying side by side with the corpses of the brutalized baby girls were the fathers too poor to afford them, leaving behind widows too unprotected to survive for long. Divorce was there in all but name, too. It was obvious to everyone that Pogle sahib couldn't stand his wife and nor she him, but they still roly-polyed about the village with their competing stomachs, hands raised like great gurus dispensing blessings, never mind that the sound of their screams and smashing plates regularly set off the stray dogs howling into the night. But to actually leave? For what? Where to? The soapy-women characters, they had money, an education. Half the time the teachers in the local school didn't bother to turn up if they had more pressing engagements elsewhere. In Mala's birth village, she had been the star pupil, but her dreams of college had died with her father. What was more shocking, to get divorced or to have never had the choice in the first place?

'There is a movie,' Mala began haltingly. 'Sushma Bajaj is the heroine. She has divorce and her husband steals her children. First-class songs also.'

'Wow, I'm so behind with my Hindi movies,' Shyama laughed. 'I think the last one I saw was *Kabhi Kushi Kabhi Gham*.'

'Very good movie. But very old.'

'Right. So this Sushma film . . . ?'

'Is out now.'

Three hours later, the two women were sitting in the cool, darkened cinema hall at the top of the mall, reclining in the top-price luxury seats, chomping on popcorn (mixed for Shyama, salty for Mala) and cheering on Sushmita as she delivered her final tear-soaked rallying speech to a mesmerized courtroom, calling upon society, the judicial system and God to recognize the right of the modern woman to be single, respectable, and a good mother to boot.

It was dark when Shyama finally dropped Mala back at the clinic. They walked down the untarmacked side road wordlessly, Mala clutching the sheaf of magazines that Shyama had insisted on buying her, noticing her hungry gaze as they passed the magazine stand, with the beauty-salon literature tucked inside a copy of Indian *OK!* No need to declare her interest, not yet anyway. The wasteground slum houses looked less desolate in the dark: oil lamps flickered here and there, cooking odours and a smoky haze from dozens of bubbling pots hovered over the battered roofs, stork-legged, bare-footed children scampered in and out of the narrow gullies between the dwellings, shouting to each other in bold, hoarse ululations.

Shyama drew her shawl around her, facing Mala. 'I hope you won't be in trouble for getting back so late? Should I come in with you?'

Mala shook her head. She knew the other women would

already be gossiping about her disappearance, she didn't want to fan their smouldering curiosity by turning up with her employer in tow. Even within this small group of women, there was already an unspoken hierarchy: at the top those whose second or third surrogacy this was – they got the top spots in the dorms, the quiet side of the building away from the slum, the coolest spots shaded by the trees. The Hindu/Muslim divide wasn't so much of an issue here, though the women tended to dorm with others of the same religion, if only to make the daily pujas or *namaaz* less of an inconvenience to their neighbours. More significant was the presence of a couple of Dalit women – untouchables, as they weren't allowed to be called any more, but everyone knew what was in a name; after all, it changed nothing. Some of the other Hindu ladies refused to use the same toilet as them or eat anywhere near them, and privately wondered if the poor *firengi* couples realized their expensive offspring were being grown inside an impure vessel. What would they all think if they could have seen her today, strolling along like Shyama Madam's best girlfriend, eating, having beauty treatments, movie watching with knees touching. Say what you liked about the Western Indians – and everyone had plenty to say, especially the Shiv Sena types with their Hindustan for the Hindustanis and attacking young people who held hands in the street and trying to ban Valentine's Day – would any of those crazy fundy types have bought Mala popcorn? She realized, being a first-timer in the lodgings and so young, that she would be ignored, as she was of no interest to anyone, and that's the way she wanted to keep it. Even though she was queen of the riverbank back home, here she knew it was best to be like a stray animal in another's territory and stay silent, downwind of trouble.

'I'm so glad we spent some time together, Mala. And I hope

207

. . . well, you know what I hope. Some good news soon, *hena*?'

'*Hahn-ji*. Good news.'

They were distracted by the sounds of a heated argument coming from the wasteground: two men were yelling at each other, both in the labourers' uniform of worn vests, lungis and checkered scarves tied around their heads. To the side stood the young woman Shyama recognized from earlier, the same toddler clinging to her hip like a koala. One of the men threw down his bidi and took a swing at the other, losing his footing and slumping to the ground, where he lay, mumbling obscenities to himself. The other man, swaying on unsteady feet, flicked the young woman on the shoulder and handed her some notes. Wearily, she unpeeled the baby from her side and handed it to a young girl in a tattered frilly frock who appeared beside her, then gestured for the man to enter the hut in front of them. As she held open the strip of plastic sheeting, the lamplight inside momentarily caught her face, impassive as the statue of the nameless goddess watching from a shelf behind the woman's bowed head.

Shyama and Mala caught each other's eyes, a moment of understanding passing between them, beyond language. Shyama found herself pulling Mala into a brief embrace, sniffing coconut oil and the faint lingering scent of the rosewater face mask, glad that she was here and doing this and hoping it would change Mala's life for the better. Mala submitted to Shyama's strong arms and soft chest; it had been some months since she had seen her own mother, whose farewell embraces were always hesitant, doom-laden at yet another goodbye. And as she held her breath, she kept looking over Shyama's shoulder to the woman's small hut with its plastic curtain, and thought, we are not so different, *bhain-ji*, we have to sell the only thing we almost own.

*

Toby was disappointed to find Shyama fast asleep when he climbed carefully into the hotel bed beside her. Had she always snored? Maybe he'd only just noticed. He had a whole evening's worth of anecdotes from her family, many of them featuring her own childhood scrapes and embarrassing teenage incidents, which he would have liked to share. He had been treated like a demi-god, lavished with attention and an unending cornucopia of delicious home-cooked food, whilst Prem's eldest brother and his wife, whose house it was, kept reiterating what an honour it was to have received their new son-in-law into their home. Numerous other relatives had called in on their way back from work, having jumped into rickshaws especially to meet him. He had found it overwhelming, how kind and interested everyone was in him, how disappointed they were that Shyama herself hadn't been there to enjoy the first family meal as a new bride. Prem and Sita's gaze had flickered only momentarily every time marriage was mentioned. They were keeping the secret and so would he, and what did it matter anyway, that flimsy piece of paper? He had never felt so much part of any family, including his own, as this one, with its noise and warmth and open arms.

He had wanted to apologize to Shyama for their stupid row earlier, but, more importantly, he wanted to make her understand how bloody lucky she was to have these people. The rogue uncle was an aberration – every family had a black sheep and hopefully the courts would punish him for what he'd put Prem and Sita through. And luckily, tonight Yogesh had stayed away. But one selfish git wasn't enough to break the bonds he had seen and felt tonight. They've got it right, this lot, he told himself as he snuggled into Shyama's back – family first. And our child is going to be part of this. How lucky are we?

*

When Dr Passi had first discussed her database of egg doners with Shyama and Toby, she said they could try to find as near a physical match to Shyama as possible, Shyama had joked, 'Couldn't we find a nearer physical match to Angelina Jolie?' And then, 'Or Mala. I wouldn't mind if the baby came out looking like her.'

It was a flippant remark, but one that had stayed with both Toby and Dr Passi. The doctor noted that this couple would have no problem if the baby emerged on the darker side of 'wheatish', unlike most of her local couples, who were quite open about their preference for a fair-as-possible child. As one bullish father put it, 'As we are having a baby to order like this, why not order what you like?'

This logical extension of the principles of her life's work had occasionally put Dr Passi in a difficult position. It was relatively easy to abort a damaged foetus at an early stage as frequent scans revealed any problems early enough to take preventative action. No one chose to have a disabled baby, why would they? She had seen the way many disabled children were treated once they were born – a life of being shut away in shame or abandoned to an institution – and it brought into stark relief the difference between life and quality of life. That was the whole point of selective conception, as far as she could see: to identify and remove all those defective genes, some of which could be passed on through the generations, to stop the cycle of misery and only bring forth healthy useful citizens of the world.

But when people got choosy, that's when Dr Passi began to feel a little uncomfortable: the skin tone was one such issue, although understandable, given their centuries of conditioning about the superiority of fairer skin. She had presided over some nasty cases of poisoning and irreparable skin damage during her training, hundreds of women seduced or shamed into using over-the-counter skin-whitening creams. What the European models on the packaging hadn't revealed were the long-term effects of such concoctions, which used mercury and hydroquinone. Symptoms would range from skin thinning, raised capillaries, tell-tale blue-grey patches and rampaging acne to liver and kidney failure and skin cancer. (Dr Passi herself had been considered a little on the dusky side, her childhood punctuated by regular and vigorous massages with oily gram flour and turmeric by her ayah, her mother watching anxiously to check whether this traditional cure would scrub away the darkness, leaving her daughter with glowing, paler skin. Dr Passi doubted that it worked, though one happy side effect was that she hardly ever had to wax or shave; the years of grainy exfoliation had killed off most of her body hair.) Sex selection was also understandable, at least in her clinic. If a family already had girls or boys and wanted a balance, no problem. Most of her local couples usually asked for boys first, and the way Dr Passi saw it, if she was preventing another ignorant family from aborting an unwanted girl, it was better to acquiesce than to argue. One of the reasons why she had abandoned her hospital work was the number of female foetuses she had found herself terminating, the daily scrape and sluice of healthy little girls into overflowing buckets, too many needless endings. Eventually she had left that post; she needed to be somewhere creative, literally, as her training had prepared her to be.

She was immediately encouraged by the discovery that the foreign couples in her new clinic hardly ever expressed a preference for a boy or girl. This felt like progress. But then as time went on, the demands and requirements became more specific, the boundaries of what could be done more elastic. She recalled two sets of couples whom she suspected were perfectly able to

211

have children, but preferred having a child made to order with minimal disruption to both their careers, one lot from America, the other from France. In both cases, the women were high-flying professionals, whip-thin and efficient, their partners similarly worldly and handsome in that groomed magazine-cover kind of way. The French couple had dropped out fairly quickly when they had realized the legal complications of taking the baby back home. She had directed them towards a nearby orphanage, not expecting they would ever get there. The Americans, however, were more persistent, until it came to discussing why they could not have children of their own. That's when she knew: not just because their explanations were minimal and vague, but because every other couple who had been through the trauma of years of futile baby-making attempts wanted to talk about it in precise, emotional detail. For most of them, Dr Passi was their last hope, and they needed not only to share the suffering that had brought them to her door, but to grieve for all the ghost babies that haunted their journey. Dr Passi directed the American couple to a rival clinic, unable to condone their intention to use a surrogate as another convenient labour-saving device. Mummy-as-microwave: it calls us with a ping when it's ready and we can take it home.

That was in her early idealistic days; since then she had got used to parents being very specific about how their child-to-be should be: tall, with handsome regular features and a high IQ. They even sought assurances that only the eggs or sperm from MENSA-registered donors should be used. It was at times like these that Dr Passi would use her discretion, telling her clients what they wanted to hear, but mostly using the stock she already had, so her conscience was relatively clear. She was aware that consultants like herself were often criticized for playing God, but whose? Her reference points were the amoral deities of her Hindu upbringing, blue-hued and smiling, constantly reminding humanity to accept and endure joy and pain equally, as both are temporary, and neither can be ordered or controlled. As Lord Krishna counselled his kinsman, the archer Arjuna, before they launched into battle with their own cousins, you cannot control where your arrow lands, but fire it you must. Or words to that effect. Take action without presuming to know or predict the outcome, because to take no action, to remain static and undecided, was the worst sin of all. In her lab, under the bright lights and with a microscope to her eye, Dr Passi often recalled this verse in the *Bhagavad Gita*. Pipette in hand, piercing the filmy wall of a human egg to place a wriggling sperm inside, she knew this was one deliberate action with profound life-long consequences. She took this so seriously that her actions also extended to curbing the excessive demands of some of her clients: she knew what they needed and maybe even what they deserved.

It was a collision of circumstances that pushed Dr Passi into the decision she made that day, the day when Mala lay unconscious on the operating table waiting for her eggs to be harvested for the clinic's ever-dwindling stocks. Her British couple had no idea this was happening, that it would delay the creation and implantation of their embryo, but in Dr Passi's opinion, they seemed relaxed enough to wait another month. However, that morning, several other couples would also have their hopes delayed: a whole batch of embryos had defrosted unsuccessfully, five implantations cancelled at the last minute. It happened, but time was money, and also, as so many of Dr Passi's clients knew too well, money could not buy time.

The ultrasound the previous day had confirmed that the drugs had not over-stimulated Mala's ovaries but had done their job well: she had produced a pleasing number of healthy eggs, glistening like unwashed pearls on the grainy monitor, ripe, unused. Hadn't Shyama herself said she would be happy if their child looked like this handsome village woman? And how long would it be before the stringent new rules became law and Dr Passi would lose perhaps half her clientele, bowing before a power greater than her own ambition, desire and conscience? In this moment, she could become goddess of her own small universe, unleash her bow and accept the outcome, however it might fall.

So it was that harvest and planting defied Nature's rules and occurred on the same day, the seasons collapsed into each other within the glass walls of a small test tube, the hand of fate holding steady the pipette, the universe contained within the eye of a microscope. Five days later, Mala was called back to receive the embryo that would settle and burrow and feed and become the child that would be half hers, half Toby's, all of Dr Passi's creation.

Her other eggs would go on to bring forth an architect, a naval engineer, two teachers, a professional saxophonist and a beautiful manic depressive who would kill herself on the eve of her twenty-seventh birthday. Her parents, in their grief, wondered about Mala then, though they did not know her real name, and what she may have passed on in her DNA that brought years of torment to a child so beloved, so wanted. But by that time, the clinic no longer existed, and what difference would any answer have made?

Less than ten miles away, Sita walked out of court number four, Patiala House, wrestling with her own arrows of outrageous fortune. It had started so well, they had been called up first on the list – a good sign, as this had never happened before. Ravi had spoken eloquently and with less drama this time, thank God, emphasizing the length of time this case had been dragging on, indicating the 'respectable and elderly couple who have been cheated, like so many others, out of their legitimately bought home'. The fact that they had paid for the flat in clean, declared cash seemed to impress the judge, and this time, Yogesh's son-in-law Sunil had not even bothered to turn up for the hearing. His lawyer was there, a moustachioed, middle-aged man with the typical Punjabi barrel-shaped belly and spindly chicken legs, who sat bored throughout Ravi's address, picking food from between his teeth with the edge of a business card. He has given up, Sita thought, hope flaring in her breast. Even his lawyer is hardly bothering to put up a fight. It turned out that he knew there was no battle worth getting out of his seat for: after hearing all the evidence and perusing the entirely correct paperwork, the judge declared that the case could not proceed further without form 'ABCD' from the local police and thus would have to be adjourned until this final legal requirement was produced.

Ravi stood up, shouting in indignation, 'What form is this, your Honour? No one has mentioned such a form before? Your Honour?'

But the judge was already on his feet, declaring a break, officials scraping their chairs as they stood too, papers being shifted and shuffled, cheery conversations begun. But Sita saw it, so did Prem and Ravi: the slightest of nods passing between the judge and Sunil's laywer as they both turned to leave.

Outside the court, Prem was saying his usual thank-yous to Ravi, a well-rehearsed speech he had delivered so many times it had the formality and familiarity of a mantra. Sita feared that if she opened her mouth, the fury she was trying to suppress would spew out of her, dragging her intestines with it. She found herself walking rapidly away from Prem and Ravi, avoiding them, until she looked over and saw Ravi with his arm around Prem's shoulders, concern etched on his face. Sita hurried back over.

'What's wrong? Darling?'

'He's just feeling a little dizzy, Auntie,' Ravi reassured her, leading Prem over to a shaded bench, jerking his head at the two young clerks who sat there sharing a cigarette, who got up sulkily to vacate their place of rest.

'I'm fine. Stop fussing, all of you.' Prem attempted a weak smile, but his face looked ashen and his hands shook slightly as they rested on his knees.

'It's his blood sugar,' Sita said briskly, grabbing the emergency banana from her shopping bag and feeding Prem small morsels until his colour started to return. She handed Ravi the remains of the banana to hold as she scrabbled around in her bag and found the small polythene bag, its neck tied with a bit of old ribbon, containing a few handfuls of roasted cashews and almonds. She offered them in her cupped palm. Prem took a couple, smiling his thanks. Sita pushed the remaining nuts into his hand, then got up, indicating Ravi should follow her.

'You finish that, *jaan*, I will just get you some sweet tea, OK?'

Sita marched towards a chai-wallah who had set up his portable stall under the shade of a banyan tree on the far side of the square. Dwarfed by the twisting trunk, he looked like a long-legged insect trapped in a web of meandering bark.

Sita didn't look at Ravi as she walked briskly.

'How much?'

'Sorry, Auntie?'

'Just drop the auntie business, OK? You know what I'm saying. To bribe the clerk, the judge, buy some *goonda*s to get them out. Just tell me how much.'

Ravi did some rapid calculations in his head. He knew people who could get it done, as they had for so many others, and not be traceable back to him; he added on only a small commission for himself, because this was almost a favour. He quoted a figure which left Sita both elated and depressed. Elated because she had enough in her teachers' pension fund to pay it without Prem knowing anything about it; depressed because they could have paid it years ago. It was a fraction of what they had already wasted on legal fees, air travel, medicines . . .

'You will arrange everything if I give the money straight to you?'

Ravi nodded, marvelling at the change in her. This sweet old lady had suddenly turned into some Mafia boss, all hard-faced and talking out of the side of her mouth. On one level he felt relieved – at least they now had a fighting chance of getting those bastards out. But on another level, he felt a stab of regret as he watched this auntie-ji's face contorted with bitter resignation. Ah, how often had he seen that expression, even worn it himself. This old couple's innocence, their childish belief in the goodness of the world and the triumph of justice, had somehow become a little beacon of hope for Ravi Luthra over the last eight years. Only now, confronted with its loss, did he realize its significance. Rather like his own aborted acting career, it was having the promise, the possibility of some kind of change that made life bearable. Looking around the square, everyone, everything around him was busy with the business of living: the besuited lawyers, carrying files containing the detritus of lives gone wrong; the snippy-snappy career women in their heels, laughing with each other, stumbling over potholes as they tried to keep hold of their takeaway lattes; the wiry rickshaw-wallahs with their cell phones wedged under woolly hats, weaving in and out of the honking, impatient cars; the day-tripper families with their new cameras and monkey-chattering children, unwrapping their *malai kulfi* which gave off icy clouds like smoke; the sweepers and rubbish-sifters in their bandanas and vibrant saris, clearing and sorting refuse that would be back again tomorrow; the scarlet mouths of the bougainvillea bushes; the pulsing green throats of the parakeets in the banyan tree; this country of his in all its greedy, galloping glory, going two steps forward and one step back. Everything changes, everything stays almost the same.

'I will bring the cash to you myself, no need to mention it to my husband, OK? And you get a new court date as soon as possible. Any longer than a month and the deal's off.'

Sita gave him a hard cold look, handed him a steaming earthenware tumbler of tea and walked, with the other held out carefully in front of her, towards her waiting husband.

# CHAPTER NINE

FROM A DISTANCE, they looked like any other family group out for the evening, enjoying each other's company, perhaps marking a birthday, an anniversary, tucked into the corner of the hotel dining room. Only on closer inspection did the oddities become apparent: the older woman with her white companion, trying to fill the long silences with loud, over-polite chatter; the dark thin couple with their hands on their knees, staring at the starched tablecloth; the elderly couple with their fixed, glassy smiles. And unlike all the other diners, with not one child at the table.

Dr Passi had told Shyama that she did not think this was a good idea. 'I understand your wish to celebrate the good news. But we don't encourage this . . . level of socialization. And, of course, Mala is at a very delicate stage. We encourage as much rest as possible during the first few weeks of a pregnancy.'

'I'm not planning to get her drunk and take her clubbing,' Shyama replied, not looking up as she was about to tap her card pin number into the machine on Dr Passi's desk. 'But we are leaving tomorrow and we just wanted to . . . say thank you. I mean, we probably won't meet again until the birth, will we?'

'I don't envisage that, no. And while I think this a very thoughtful gesture . . . oh sorry, is this a credit or debit card?

There's a ten per cent surcharge on all credit-card transactions.'

'Ten per cent?' Shyama paused with her fingers hovering above the keypad. 'I do have a debit card, but it's back at the hotel.'

'Here,' Toby intervened, fumbling with his wallet, his face reddening as he struggled to pincer out the slim plastic rectangle and handed it to Shyama. She raised her eyebrows at him, didn't want to say it out loud, but they both knew what she was asking. Is this OK? Can you afford this? It was a delicate area, the fact that she had been paying for him throughout their relationship, and the not-so-casual remark about their unequal finances during their row in the car still lingered between them. Toby was surprised by the knot of tension twisting his gut, the twitch in his fingers, as if he wanted to smash something. Instead he flashed Shyama what he hoped was a manly, reassuring sort of nod whilst doing quick calculations in his head, almost sure the funds he had borrowed from his brother would cover this first instalment. He hated the whole money aspect of this – it made him feel squeamish, shady. Maybe because the nameless surrogate now had a name, a face, a character. That should have made him feel better, getting to know the woman who would nurture their baby. And yet he privately agreed with Dr Passi: a cosy farewell meal somehow did not feel right.

His unease was confirmed as he sat at the table across from Mala and her catatonic husband, who did not look up from the glossy menu he gripped between his hands like a shield. Shyama was wittering on about various dishes, trying to include them both in the conversation, but fairly soon gave up on Ram and focused on Mala, who responded to her enthusiastic questioning with short whispered answers, which gradually expanded into longer, more animated ones, punctuated with pauses in which she searched for a word in English, followed by a quick, shy glance at her husband. Prem and Sita sent Ram and Mala the occasional beam, but otherwise whispered excitedly between themselves, no doubt buoyed up by their recent good news in court. They had secured a surprisingly swift hearing in front of the same judge who had dismissed them previously, who had suddenly ruled that their claim was indeed lawful and proper, and had fixed an eviction date for the end of the year, around the same time that their second grandchild was due. The bewildering speed of both these longed-for events added a frisson of anticipation to the atmosphere, Shyama's voice a little too bright and sharp, Prem and Sita's smiles a shade too effusive. Ram's defences were primed and quivering, his ears pricked as if tuned to the higher-than-normal frequency of the festivities. The more Mala talked, smiled, responded to Shyama's questions, the smaller he seemed to become, hunching his shoulders until they almost touched his ears. At one point Toby whispered to Prem, 'Can't you speak Hindi to him? I'm not sure he's keeping up with the conversation.'

Prem dutifully fired off a couple of questions, which Ram answered in monosyllables. Everyone was grateful when the food finally arrived.

The steaming platters of daal, saag, chicken and rice were laid out with serving spoons. Prem picked one up and offered it to Ram, who looked so nervous that Sita briskly took over, ladling a portion of each dish on to everyone's plate and encouraging them all to eat before it got cold.

'Extra portions for you then,' joked Shyama, offering a buttered naan to Mala, who took it with an uncertain smile, until Shyama added, 'You must eat lots. For the baby.'

The mention of the B word made everyone pause for a millisecond, hands halfway to mouths, then continue as if nothing had been said, a pebble thrown into a pool causing a rippling tension which they covered with vigorous chewing and compliments to the chef.

As Mala broke into the yeasty clouds of warm flatbread, she felt another sharp dig at her side. Her evening had been punctuated with warnings from her husband's feet and arms – a tap to the ankle here, an elbow press to her ribs there. For every answer she slowly constructed in English, for each smile she reciprocated, Ram jabbed and poked and squeezed his wife, conducting their own silent marital exchange under the table. Like ducks on water, Mala thought fleetingly, all beaky smiles up top and all kicking below. She knew what Ram was trying to do – he had made it clear before they had entered the restaurant, during a hurried conversation in the hallway of the hostel when he had come to collect her.

'You don't get too friendly with these people, *acha*?'

'Why not? The more they like us, the more they will give us, *hena*?'

'Everyone here knows.' Ram lowered his voice, leading Mala out of the door and out into the warm night air.

The sun was setting over the glass towers of the luxury hotels, its fiery trails like scratch marks on the curved cheek of the sky. Mala felt the familiar heavy pull in her belly: only a few weeks in and already nausea and tender fullness were affecting her body.

'Knows what?' She took a gulp of air, tasting cooking smoke and metal. Over on the wasteground, oil lamps were being lit. She looked for the woman with the small child on her hip, but her hut was dark.

'I heard them.' Ram cocked his head, indicating she should keep up as they walked. 'Saying you are thinking you are a madam yourself, acting like you're special.'

'Let them. Bored, fat chickens all of them, pecking for any

bit of dirt. That place becomes a prison, once you are pregnant. Nothing to do except sit, eat, get bigger, like they are fattening you up for a festival killing. They are only jealous. Most of them can't even write their name.'

'Why should you? You want them to notice you even more?' Ram strode along the path parallel to the clinic's outbuildings, their industrial air vents whirring like the beating wings of some huge iron bird. '*Theklo*, think, woman. If anyone finds out we said we had two kids . . . If they want to make trouble for you . . . Maybe we can end up in jail, hah?'

Ram had continued berating her until he noticed he was talking to air. He stopped and looked behind. Mala was leaning against the wall, supporting herself on one arm as she tried to draw breath. Out of the corner of her eye, she noticed him sauntering back towards her. Bastard can't even run to me, she thought, and wheezed even harder, coughing up a little bile which she spat out, only narrowly missing his chappaled feet. Hah, now you're sorry, she noted as the annoyance drained out of his face, replaced by an anxious curiosity. He placed a tentative hand on her forehead, the back of her neck, so gentle it made her want to weep.

'You're not sick?'

'I'm carrying a baby, idiot. What do you think?'

My husband is offering me his arm, noted Mala with wonder, walking me like a memsahib, making his voice low and sweet like a river. Now he is telling me not to worry, he will take care of everything as long as I am well, we are safe. For a few minutes Mala wasn't walking along a litter-strewn pathway smelling of fried food and disinfectant, she was the wet sari in the fountain, the wind-swept dancer on the hillside, the garlanded goddess on a plinth. Until she realized that what he was worshipping wasn't

223

her, but inside her, what he longed to protect wasn't his wife, but his investment. Otherwise, why hadn't he thrown flowers under her feet the first time she was carrying a baby? *Their* baby?

By the time they reached the restaurant, Mala had made up her mind. You want me to look at the floor and *chup* like a half-wit? Watch me.

No one saw it coming. One minute Mala was chatting away to Shyama, expanding on the face scrub she had invented that every woman in her village now used. 'Only yellow *channa*, not black . . . small-small pieces,' then suddenly Ram was on his feet, yanking Mala up by her wrist and overturning his Vimto in his haste to escape the table.

'Thank you . . . sorry . . . thank you,' he muttered as he pulled her towards the exit, Mala banging her leg against the edge of a chair and letting out a small involuntary *hai* of pain. Shyama and Toby were both on their feet, Toby blocking Ram's path, Shyama scooting around the other side to pull the table out a little, trying to reach Mala. Sita was busy applying serviettes to the fizzy brown stain invading the tablecloth.

'Hey hey, steady now,' Toby said somewhat foolishly, using the tone and words he employed to herd the cows towards the milking shed.

'You OK?' Shyama took hold of Mala's hand. Now she and Ram were on either side of her, pulling at an arm each like a party cracker.

Mala glanced from one to the other, Ram sending her a death stare, daring her to break rank.

'Tell them you're tired,' he whispered to her in Hindi, forget-ting that Prem and Sita were sitting opposite, Prem's hand still hovering above his plate, dripping spinach.

'You are tired, Mala?' Sita asked gently, and then in Hindi to Ram, 'If she's tired, of course you must go.'

'*Hahn-ji* . . . tired,' Ram repeated and tried to tug Mala with him, but found himself eye to eye with Toby. Even though Toby was the broader and stronger of the two, as he faced Ram he saw the eyes of something wild, cornered, with fangs bared. He lifted up his hands, an old gesture, like the namaste, assuring him he held no concealed weapon.

'Is everything OK, Ram? Um . . . *thoom teek-hay*?'

Hearing Hindi come out of the *gora*'s mouth was almost enough to make Ram laugh and let go, but he had gone too far now, in front of all of them. Shaking his head, he managed to yank Mala away from the big-mouth woman with the stupid red hair and stride for the door. Shyama made to go after them, but even though Toby held out a restraining arm, it was Prem's voice that halted her.

'Leave them!'

Shyama couldn't remember the last time she had heard her father raise his voice. He hated conflict, she could hear it in the tremor of his tone, the careful way he wiped his buttery fingers with his napkin, turmeric-yellow fingerprints on clean white linen.

'They have taken your charity. Now leave them with some dignity.'

'This was perhaps a mistake, Shyama,' Sita added. 'I know you meant well, but things are done differently here.'

'What? I shouldn't try and be nice to the woman who's going to change our lives?' Shyama tried to control her breathing, aware of curious eyes on them from different corners of the restaurant. She looked at Toby for support, but he was carefully avoiding her gaze.

'Darling, it's just a job to them,' said Sita.

'*Them?*'

'Please don't do this. Don't do your flag-waving thing at me,' Sita snapped back. 'You think we don't think they are human? Two bad harvests and we would have been in their shoes all those years back! But you made them feel . . . awkward, bringing them here. How could they ever return the hospitality, open their home and pockets to us?'

'I wasn't expecting—' Shyama began.

'You don't expect because you don't know.'

'I know when a woman is being bullied by her husband. Or is that another local custom I'm supposed to respect?'

'Shyama! Don't—'

But Shyama was already on her way out. Toby didn't need to see Sita's frantic gestures, he was already behind her.

In the hotel courtyard, Mala pulled free from Ram, heading for some greenery in the side lobby, away from the imperious moustachioed doormen in their mock-maharajah outfits who had given them both fearsome looks when they had arrived earlier. She felt dizzy, either with nerves or speed-eating. The food had been so rich and abundant, she wondered how she had managed to talk as much as she had. But she had managed some-how. Good. She stood facing Ram, who clenched and unclenched his fingers slowly, knuckles cracking. *Chalo*, she thought, here we go now. Will he hit me finally, this husband of mine? Nostrils flared, ready to buffalo-charge me. Look at him.

And as she looked, she saw something she did not expect: not anger, not violence, but a fearful sorrow. A man burnt by the sun and thinned by hard labour, staring at his wife, knowing he would never understand her and could not control her, so what else remained? How could that peasant mouth ever express the complex poetry in his eyes? Mala saw his soul then, flickering behind his barred pain, and understood he was as trapped as she was. And would keep her trapped too, because even with the money to come, he knew no other way.

'You . . .' He reached for each word. 'You . . . disobeyed me.'

'Yes,' said Mala softly.

'Why?' Ram's hands kept on opening, closing. 'Why so quickly?'

'Quickly?'

'You . . . already pregnant. With me it took you months. Why?'

Mala shrugged. 'Maybe because the doctor did it.'

'How do I know? I wasn't here, was I?'

*Acha*, so this is it. Mala almost relaxed into her relief. Now we get to it. Even though all this *tamasha* was his idea – his *sus-sus* whisperings in her ear day and night for weeks, the way he looked at her as if working out which limb would pay for his extra acre of land – now apparently she was the whore. Condemned for a sin she had not even been awake for.

'What? You think I danced to his hotel room, sang him a song and opened my legs?'

Ram balled his fingers into fists and took a step towards her. From the corner of her eye she became aware of Shyama and Toby arriving on the other side of the glass. 'You shut your mouth right now,' he hissed, 'Or—'

'Or what? What will you do? What can they do? Rip my child from my belly and ask for their money back?'

'*Your* child?' Ram shook his head, trying to dislodge the words from his ears.

'My body. His child. But if he had asked me, husband,' Mala

whispered, positioning herself so her back faced the hotel window, 'I might have said yes.'

Ram never meant to hit her. In fact, he still wasn't sure that he actually had. All he did was swing his arm back – usually that was enough to shut someone up, the threat of the raised sandal his own mother used to discipline him with. Most of the time she would not even have to take her shoe off; just seeing her wagging finger creep down towards her foot was enough to send Ram and his siblings scurrying into the corner begging for forgiveness. Even afterwards he did not know what had happened. One minute his hand was in the air, the next Mala was lying curled up on the floor, clutching herself and screaming loudly enough for not just red-hair woman and her blond *chamcha* to come running, but also the two guards who threw him away so hard he had bruises for days afterwards.

He had tried to tell them, in a Hindi these stupid *firenge* could not even understand, I have never struck her, not once. It was like she ran into my fist. Towards it. I don't even remember feeling flesh on flesh. But too quickly Mala was bundled away, back into the hotel. People were around her, lying her on the squashy sofa, letting her put her feet up, passing her water. All the while Red Hair was at her side, talking, stroking, holding the cup to her lips, both women's hands on Mala's belly, which was now, Ram understood, the centre of the whole universe. He had tried to explain to Blondie that there had been some misunderstanding, but the *haramzada* had just looked at him like he had just crawled out of a dung heap, and that just made Ram get angrier and shout louder, forgetting that not one word would be understood.

'Just calm down, OK? Back off, fella . . . I'm warning you!'

Toby knew he sounded like an inefficient bouncer, but he had to keep talking to hold the man before him at bay, and to stop

228

himself from flying at him and ripping his head off. It wasn't just that he had attacked a pregnant woman, that the baby she was carrying was his, for Christ's sake, but the woman herself. Mala – small, crumpled, bewildered – aroused the most primeval protective instincts in him. His fury tasted like acid, he burned with a violence that made him feel righteous and invincible and, worse still, he was enjoying the feeling. We are just cavemen swinging our clubs, he thought to himself. We are both only doing what we are programmed to do, somewhere deep down. We are, in fact, fighting over the same woman. And who has the bigger claim on her now? This made Toby feel both hugely important and deeply insignificant, as if he was representing the whole of mankind in some messy after-hours pub brawl. They finally lapsed into silence, both circling each other, panting. Then Ram spat on the floor and loped off into the night.

Shyama was shaking more than Mala; it was Mala who ended up patting her arm, smiling her reassurance that all was OK.

'I knew this would happen,' Shyama muttered. 'I could see it coming.'

In her head, she was scrolling through the pages of small print in the contract she and Toby had signed in the lawyer's office just days ago. Vinod Aggarwal seemed to have a clause to cover every unforeseen circumstance, but she couldn't remember one which advised what their options were when the surrogate's husband beat her up. What protection could the clinic offer if he kept turning up, threatening trouble? Mala wouldn't be the only one he would upset. She had read enough articles on the effects of stress on the unborn child and pregnant mother to know that Dr Passi would be as worried as she was. She felt a squeeze on her hand.

'Madam, I am better. It is late, nah? They will be worrying.' Mala let the question hang in the air.

Shyama shook her head. 'He knows where you are. You're not going back tonight.'

Back at their hotel, it wasn't difficult to book an adjoining room now the various wedding parties had gone; they even had a connecting door. Shyama had dispatched Toby to the clinic hostel to explain to the night nurse what had happened, and she had left a long message on Dr Passi's answerphone suggesting they have an emergency meeting the next day. Sita and Prem had hurried back to Prem's elder brother's place, already knowing that Shyama and Toby would not make their flight home the next day. There were cancellation and rebooking fees to consider and arrange, none of it convenient but all of it unavoidable.

'We can't just leave her in this state . . .' Shyama hadn't needed to convince Toby, they both knew what was at stake. Their packed cases sat accusingly in the corner of the bedroom. Next door they could hear the faint sound of water running, the toilet flushing; Mala's proximity was making them whisper, even though they were separated by a thick wall and a double-bolted door.

'I can't believe he actually punched her.' Shyama was still wired on adrenalin, sitting up in bed in the dark.

'I couldn't see . . . just saw her fall, that was bad enough.' Toby patted Shyama's bare shoulder. 'Let it go. She's safe.'

'For now,' Shyama muttered, easing herself down and settling on to Toby's chest. 'How can we protect her when we're not here?'

'I dunno . . . we could ask Dr Passi . . .' Toby hesitated. 'Pay Dr Passi to put her up somewhere else, or—'

'But then what about all the medical checks? The monitoring . . .'

'Maybe they have another clinic somewhere else, somewhere he won't find—'

'They don't. I already checked, this is their only one. She's just expanded the site rather than open other branches. Wants to stay hands-on. I mean that's what we're paying for, this level of attention and care.'

They both paused, registering the unmistakable gurgling coming from next door.

'Is she . . . she's running a bath,' Shyama breathed.

'Bit late,' Toby said, suddenly uncomfortable at the vivid image of Mala unwinding her sari in clouds of scented steam.

'Probably the first time she's stayed in a hotel.'

They listened to the sound of the rising water, the emptying cistern, the faint strains of a girlish humming, tuneless and unselfconscious as a child's. As Shyama's breathing slowed and steadied, Toby's gradually increased. Then the sound of running water stopped. In the silence he thought he could hear the rustle of clothing removed and shed like a silk skin, feel the weight of her as she entered the water, smell the perfumed bubbles, foamy white against the dark hollows of her body. He turned to Shyama, running his hands over her legs, her thighs, trying to ground himself in the familiar feel of her, wanting to open her up so he could lose himself inside her. But she was fast asleep.

On the other side of the wall, Mala was enjoying the curious sensation of floating almost weightless in the deep enamel tub, only her knees and toes visible through the meringue whips of bubble bath, all four complimentary bottles thrown in together. The deepest she had ever ventured into the river was waist high, and then only nervously; like every other woman in the village, she had never learned to swim. This is how the *baccha* must feel, she realized, a small boat bobbing in Mama's sea, every noise sounding like fishtails flapping in waves, faraway music pulsing to the swoosh of my blood. Ram must be sitting outside the hostel now, on his haunches like a faithful dog, waiting to bark at me.

The thought of him waiting all night, watching the dawn rise over the slums, made Mala sad, then defiant. Whatever happened, she was not going back, she knew that now. They would use the money to find a home here in Delhi. It would be a small place, no land to work, but Ram could line up on the roadside like all the other newly arrived refugee farmers and make twice as much on the building sites, if he was picked. She had been listening carefully to the other women in the hostel and their boasts about their husbands – where they worked, how they found work – though they all knew that if their husbands were at all successful, none of them would be sitting on their low beds with heat rash itching under their distended bellies. Now that Shyama Madam and Toby sahib had seen what could happen, they would do anything to keep it from happening again. Maybe there would be another fight between the two men outside the hostel, then the idea of putting Mala in a flat somewhere close by, with her own bedroom and bathroom, like this. Maybe even in this hotel. Then Ram would understand and eventually come round to her way of thinking. Someone had to do the thinking, long term, not just hand-to-mouth with no time to stop and smell the samosas.

The heat of the bath was now making Mala uncomfortable; her cheeks felt flushed. How could they enjoy this, sitting in the scum of the day? She stood up carefully, swaying a little, careful careful now. How stupid it would be to slip and break her head after all that had happened this evening.

232

What Mala didn't know, would not know till days later, was that Ram was not outside the hostel, but asleep on a bench in the district coach station, waiting for the first bus back to the village.

The house, Tara thought, had never looked cleaner or tidier. Since she had stopped socializing so much, she had found the best way to spend the long evenings was to scrub, polish, dust, de-clutter. She had started with the sitting room, initially to remove any evidence of that night. The zombie movie was still in the DVD player, surrounded by empty bottles, cans, pizza cartons, skanky ashtrays. Everything went into bin bags – sod the recycling, she just wanted to see clear surfaces. Then she had begun to notice other things: the dust on top of the picture rails, the frayed edges of the cushions, the random groupings of the books on the shelves, not alphabetical, not even by any kind of genre. It had taken her three evenings, but the room looked new, or at least redecorated. She'd decided to bin some of the garish knick-knacks and old candles that cluttered various crannies, had looked online for how to remove wax stains from wood and goat smells from old throws. The purging continued through every room in the house, bar her mother's bedroom, because God knows what she might find in there.

After a week of nightly clear-outs, she disabled her Facebook and Twitter accounts – no point getting anxious about the gossip and get-togethers she was missing. True, there were a few withdrawal symptoms and some separation anxiety – she'd often have to ring her smartphone from the landline to locate it somewhere under a dishcloth or a pile of soon-to-be-recycled newspapers. But within a fortnight, she didn't bother calling her phone when it went missing. One day she turned up at lectures without it. This only confirmed to her friends that Tara was indeed becoming a bit unfriendly, if not downright weird, eschewing all their social invitations, and now going offline like it was something to be proud of.

Only Charlie expressed anything like admiration. 'Going old-school, eh? Samuel Beckett could only write with the view of a blank wall.'

But she barely acknowledged him. Even eye contact would have been too risky for her. No one knew what had happened: by the time Tamsin and the others had returned that night, drunker and on their second wind, it was all over. Any illusions she might have had about Charlie wanting to explain himself, apologize, had melted like candlewax by the time they had all finally left, around four in the morning. All the tea lights she had placed around the sitting room were long since dead, blackened wicks in crumpled metal; there was something so sad and stark about light that had eaten itself, the end of the celebrations, the guests departing; a door slammed shut inside her. She knew that what had happened was wrong. She also knew how thin the line was between consent and coercion, no matter how many successful date-rape convictions were reported in the news. No means no, even if you're so pissed you can't remember. But she knew that for every conviction there were a dozen that failed, either at the police station or in court, where the skimpiness of her under-wear and the apparent enthusiasm of her foreplay would be up for public scrutiny. Imagining her grandparents sitting in the court gallery or reading a newspaper headline made her feel physically sick. As for her mother, well, if she found out, she would be the one marching her down to the local nick, scream-ing for justice, no matter who knew and how messy it got for Tara. It would be a point of principle to nail the bastard who had nailed her little girl, despite the whispers, the online judgements and jury, the fractured friendships. Just the thought of it made her feel exhausted, on top of the weary lassitude she now battled every day. She woke up tired, despite being in bed most evenings by ten p.m., windows open just for the pleasure of hearing the chatter of the wild parakeets in the morning as they swooped across the grassy flats, cackling their freedom. She would put on one of the twenty-four-hour news channels before she tried to sleep; a lullaby of the world's wrongs somehow felt comforting.

For weeks the headlines had been full of male public figures, often pensioners now, who had been outed as sexual predators, their crimes committed decades ago, and finally brought to book. Most of the women who came forward preferred to remain anonymous, but some came out fighting. Maybe that was the wrong word. It disturbed Tara to see these middle-aged women, most of them mothers of grown-up kids themselves, revert to the bewildered, ambushed children they once were as they recounted their experiences in a shaky monotone. Maybe that will be me one day, thought Tara, prematurely grey from sitting on a festering secret in a house with a sideboard groaning with photos, too old to care any more what anyone thinks; Charlie, balding in bi-focals, probably wouldn't even remember what had happened. Or rather, he would remember it completely differently. As she'd been taught, the story was in the editing.

When she went to her mother's salon to get her hair cut some days later, she recalled Charlie's short film, his narcissistic admiration of his own reflection, as she now faced hers in the mirror, Geeta standing nervously behind her with her scissors and comb ready. The embroidered sun on her breast pocket seemed to wink back at Tara, daring her on.

'How much off? Hope your mother does not kill me when she gets back . . .'

Tara indicated again, her fingers skimming the back of her neck.

As Geeta began to snip, the carefully constructed edifice of spray and backcombing was demolished by the snickering blades. Tara watched the wasted locks pile up at her feet. She was being re-edited; images that could never be seen or repeated now lay abandoned on the cutting-room floor.

Sita was amazed at the change in the house, the change in her granddaughter. She went from room to room, exclaiming at the spanking brightness of everything: the old stuff that now looked new, the sparkling windows, the OCD-neat cupboards, Tara herself with her cropped hair.

'Oh it looks so . . . neat!' Sita laughed, and then, 'But you will let it grow a bit longer than this, no?'

The news that her mother and Toby weren't going to be back for a while due to 'unforeseen circumstances' didn't bother Tara much. If anything, she was relieved, it meant she had her grand-parents all to herself. She preferred eating with them over at their place, or even better, sleeping there, curled up on their pull-out sofa bed in front of the television. Sita was at first gratified by this display of devotion, then puzzled by her granddaughter's camp-ing out in their sitting room.

'Not that we don't love having you here, *beti*, but wouldn't you be more comfortable in your own bed?'

On the contrary, Tara slept better in the over-soft chintzy box than she did on her own queen-size sprung mattress, comforted by the pneumatic snores that drifted from her grandparents' room in distant stereo. She found herself becoming addicted to the evening programmes on the Asian cable TV channels.

Sita and Prem would pretend to scoff at the soap operas. 'Look at the size of the houses! Who lives like that? How much make-up has that mother-in-law got on? That bindi is the size of a spaceship. She looks like a clown . . . Ooof, how bad is the acting? Why does everyone shout or cry all the time? *Chalo*, they even go to bed in their jewellery . . . terrible. Such rubbish.'

Yet they couldn't tear themselves away from the screen, every show a repeat of the same family drama: fathers were either cold tyrants or well-meaning bumblers confused by their wives'/ kids' demands. Mothers were matriarchal martyrs or scheming witches, especially towards their daughters-in-law, who were either long-suffering sweethearts or selfish-bitch modern types, depending on what the mother-in-law was like. There was no point having two nice women on screen at the same time, where was the drama in that? The younger men were either firm-jawed, decent heroes, terribly stressed at the office but never too busy to pat the kids on the head or touch their elders' feet, or else they were scheming Lotharios, trying to get their hands on someone else's woman/business/house/land. The teenagers wore ironed jeans and talked like American high-school dudes; the little kids were always precocious and beyond cute, giving the adults a run on the over-acting front, and strangely, there was always a fat one for maximum comic effect. And everyone seemed to live in a mansion, cavernous, ballroom-sized dwellings with rooms large enough to contain three generations in one wide shot.

'Not exactly *EastEnders*, is it?' Tara remarked. 'Don't they ever do any dramas about poor people?'

Prem would lose interest fairly rapidly, check the cricket scores and yawn his departure, leaving Sita and Tara bonding over cups of hot tea and the delicious dilemmas of their distant contemporaries. Once Sita had turned in for the night, Tara would switch to the Indian news channels, most of which were conveniently in English, although she would dip into the Hindi-speaking stations, too. She was beginning to understand more words, sometimes entire sentences. It took longer to familiarize herself with the political landscape. The issues seemed epic to her: angry demonstrations against positive-discrimination legislation for lower castes; swathes of villages ruined by the construction of a huge controversial dam; another fall in the tiny tiger population; hundreds killed in seasonal flooding; yet more killed in an unprecedented heatwave elsewhere; an epidemic of farmer suicides; every financial graph rising upwards, pushed by a growing assertive middle class, a new generation all out-earning their parents; Bandra the nightclub hub of the entire country, Bangalore the best place to bag a potential IT-trained millionaire husband; a group called The Love Squad providing safe houses for eloping couples determined to marry without parental consent; the ever-growing success of a debt-collection firm who only employed sari-clad eunuchs, 'Because everyone is too frightened to say no to a *hijra*.'

The chat shows were more illuminating, with confident, articulate twenty-somethings locked in furious debate with middle-aged conservatives about corruption, choice in marriage, domestic violence, dowry. Never had the generation gap seemed so wide, it was as if the two groups came from different species, not just different age groups, especially when some village head honcho or religious elder was brought in to balance the debate. Tara occasionally felt sorry for them, these old men with loud voices who were used to having a room hush at the raise of a digit, their eyes darting in confusion as decades of assumptions were snatched from them and shredded like used tissues, the young high on their own self-belief and the rotting smell of dogma way past its sell-by date. It excited her, the approaching tide of change, the rushing inevitability of it, too fast to escape, hold your breath, dive in. The women who often presented these programmes were a world away from the dimply simpering movie-heroine types she'd carried round in her head for years. These chicks had hair as short and sharp as hers and lethal tongues to match, cutting a swathe through the experts yelling over each other, unafraid to look – well, it had to be said, a bit butch. Never was the anger greater than when the subject of women came up, as it often did, from the role of the modern housewife to the rape of five-year-old girls. There was the tearful interviewee recounting her tale of horror, her scars – both visible and invisible – eliciting gasps and tears from the viewers; nods of recognition punctuated the tales of the man on the train who had used his fingers, the husband who had used his fists, the mother-in-law who held the kerosene can, the jilted admirer who flung the acid, the men in the audience who proudly declared their devotion and respect for their mothers/daughters/sisters/wives, the social workers and campaigners with their sprinkle of success stories, their dark and beautiful anger, their bloody and unbowed hope. Some days, it seemed it was everywhere, on every channel in every language: the story of yet another abducted or battered girl or woman. Tara would lie in the dark and try to steady her breathing. It's always been here, she would tell herself, it's just that now it is reported more, which is a good thing, isn't it?

Despite her insomnia, now that her grandparents were back Tara had settled into some kind of routine, one which involved spending as little time as possible out of the house. Sleep, eat, study, hang out with the old people: it suited her.

Suddenly, the news came that Shyama and Toby were on their way home with an unexpected companion. It sent her spinning off her precarious axis. She re-read Shyama's hurriedly sent email, grabbed a bottle of wine from the kitchen counter and left for Lydia's house.

'Hello, stranger!' Lydia greeted her warmly, not questioning her unannounced arrival. 'I'm just finishing off with someone. Hang out in the kitchen and I'll be with you in ten.'

Tara sat at the kitchen counter in her usual place, next to the radiator, beside the cork noticeboard with its various flyers of local takeaways, a timetable of classes at Lydia's gym and Keith's cricket fixtures, and photos showcasing some of their frequent exotic holidays. Next to it lay a small green-glass bowl containing Lydia's collection of old badges. Tara ran her fingers over the lovingly worn metal discs, finding her favourites, which Lydia had described as 'medals from the frontline of my youth'. The slogans were certainly unequivocal: 'ALL MEN ARE RAPISTS!', 'MAN FUCKS WOMAN: SUBJECT, VERB, OBJECT' and 'MEN ARE AFRAID THAT WOMEN WILL LAUGH AT THEM: WOMEN ARE AFRAID THAT MEN WILL KILL THEM'. Shyama had once drily observed that she had spent her youth trying to be a good wife and mother and no one had given her a badge for that. That had been their connection, Shyama and Lydia's – the seasoned feminist and the newly hatched divorcee, Shyama having lived through the trials that Lydia had marched about but had never undergone herself. Shyama had embraced the messages on the badges with the zeal of the enlightened during long,wine-soaked evenings when she, Priya and Lydia would laugh and unburden themselves, sometimes forgetting that Tara was there too, in her Princess Jasmine pyjamas, ears flapping, appalled and fascinated by the Stuff That Happens to Women. It was supposed to be her blooding, she saw that now, like the newbie at the end of their first fox hunt smeared with the sticky victory of the kill. She knew her mother must have hoped that being around all this female frankness at a tender age would ensure she grew into a confident, assertive young woman. She at least knew how to do a great impression of one.

The door leading from Lydia's consulting room to the passage alongside the house banged shut and Tara glimpsed a client passing the window and exiting the front gate. Lydia bustled into the kitchen a moment later and, before she had even sat down, Tara spat it out.

'Mum's arriving back on Saturday and she's bringing her with her.'

'Sorry, what . . . who's "her"?'

'The Baby Mother. Rent-a-Womb. Whatever you want to call her.'

Lydia was too shocked to say anything immediately and instead opened the wine, carefully pouring out just the one glassful and handing it to Tara. The smell of it hit the back of her throat as she passed it over and she salivated as if anticipating a kiss, but no, she had promised Keith. A spectacular fall off the wagon at a dinner party two weeks ago had resulted in a screaming match with her host, projectile vomiting in the cab home and sitting under a cold shower for half an hour whilst her husband slumped on the loo seat and wept like a baby. That, in fact, was the only bit of the evening she could accurately recall.

'I had an email from her.' Tara gulped a mouthful of wine, wincing slightly. It had been weeks since she'd had a drink. She took another gulp, forcing it down like medicine, which it was – anaesthetic.

'But how . . . Is she allowed to do that?' Lydia reached automatically for her herbal cigarettes, then remembered that her last blood-pressure reading hadn't been too good. She couldn't

241

even have a bloody biscuit. With growing irritation she peeled an over-ripe satsuma, needing to keep her hands occupied, her mouth busy.

'I dunno, you know Mum, she must have found a way. Nanima said they have some old college friend in the visa department who arranged it.'

'But how's this going to work? So she'll be looked after here, give birth here?'

'All Mum said was there had been a "change of plan". I don't know the details.'

Tara ran a few of the badges from the bowl over her fingers idly, comforting as prayer beads.

'I bet I know who does,' smiled Lydia faintly.

A quick phone call and twenty minutes later, Priya flew into the kitchen, her head wrapped in a towel.

'She never told me a bloody thing! Pour me a glass . . . Ooh, your hair!' She air-kissed Tara and flopped on to a chair. 'Very Parisian, suits you. Have you lost weight? You're looking a bit pale . . . You're not on drugs, are you?'

'Like I'd tell you,' Tara deadpanned. 'So desperate for gossip you jumped out of the shower then?'

'It's my monthly henna-and-indigo treatment. I'm boiling now.'

Priya removed the towel, revealing her head wrapped in layers of clingfilm. Without her usual glamorous mane she looked older, her skin drawn tightly across her cheekbones. She poured herself a generous slug of wine, gave the merest flicker of a glance at Lydia's glass of water and sighed deeply. 'Now tell me exactly what your mad mother said.'

*

Two hours, one more bottle and three cheese toasties later, no one was any the wiser. The facts were that they were all due to arrive in two days' time, the spare room was to be aired in readiness and the official story to anyone outside the family was that this woman was a family acquaintance who had come to stay.

'Must have cost them to bring her over,' Priya murmured. 'With all the new restrictions on visitors' visas from outside the EU, they ask for a huge deposit before you land. I'm not sure she will be eligible for any NHS treatment either. Shyama must have put herself up as guarantor or sponsor or something . . . don't you think, Lyd?'

'I'm the last person she'd tell,' Lydia said. 'I suppose all we can do is just what we've always done . . . be there if she needs us.'

'How very noble,' Tara muttered.

Priya snaked an arm around her shoulder. 'Come on, sweetie, you know how much this means to your mum . . . how long she's been waiting . . .'

Tara shoved Priya's arm away and stood up. 'This was your idea, wasn't it? This whole weird lab-rat thing.'

'Lab rat? Darling, if it's good enough for Sarah Jessica Parker and co . . . and quite a few of the Bollywood folk are starting to do it now.'

'Baby as accessory. Too busy to breed . . . I knew Mum could be shallow occasionally, but if that's the reason . . .'

'You know it isn't!'

'Maybe she doesn't,' Lydia interjected. She turned to Tara. 'She was trying a long time with Toby, the miscarriage really took it out of her . . .'

'Miscarriage?'

'Quite late, thirteen weeks, I think . . .'

'She never told me. But then she wouldn't, would she?'

'She didn't want you to worry, sweetie.'

Priya edged carefully towards Tara – like I'm some care-in-the-community case raving on a bench, Tara thought. She was trying to recall any memory she might have of her mother being sick, absent, depressed. No, there Shyama stood in her mind's eye, as combative and unbreakable as she'd always been. But all the while she'd been on this campaign, this mission of blood and pain. There was a flicker of sympathy somewhere, but too deeply buried to bother her much now.

Priya was next to her; every time she raised her eyebrows, the clingfilm around her head squeaked softly. 'Listen, in India this . . . process has been going on for centuries, family members having kids for each other.'

'She's not family, is she? Or maybe she is now, God knows . . . I'm sure we will have some lovely cosy chats across the breakfast table for the next few months. I mean, didn't either of you ever once say to my mum – who is nearly fifty, by the way – that this just may be the most stupid thing she's ever done?'

Priya's gaze swivelled to Lydia, who spread her hands in resignation.

'And that's why she's gone all huffy with you?' Tara finally understood why her mother had apparently dumped one of her oldest friends. 'Unbelievable.'

'I probably could have handled it better,' Lydia offered, following Tara as she stomped towards the door. 'And anyway, it's done now. Tara?'

'What?'

Tara knew she was behaving like a bratty seven-year-old, she knew that's what they both saw now, Lydia and Priya, these women who had watched her grow up. Maybe that was the problem, that in their eyes she would only ever be Shyama's little girl. And yet what she had wanted this evening was some time alone with Lydia, to tell her about what had happened with Charlie. She hadn't thought through what she would say, how she would introduce the subject: 'Hey, you'll never guess what happened to me the other week!' or 'Hey, should I be reporting this somewhere?' or 'Hey, do I just write this off as part of becoming a woman?' How was it possible to feel so raw and helpless and yet so very old? Priya's arrival had ended any hope she'd had of asking these questions, and she simmered with frustrated disappointment.

'Tara,' Lydia repeated gently, 'I know this is going to be really challenging for you . . .'

'Save it for your patients,' Tara snapped, and left.

The two old friends continued chatting for a while, Lydia providing a stream of cups of fresh mint tea which she threw back like shots. She knew she would be pissing like a Trojan for most of the night, but at least the monster inside her had stopped snapping its jaws. The hunger for a drink had gone and she was becalmed, floppy as a beached seal. They discussed their concerns about Tara, about Shyama and Toby, their empathy tempered by the shameful thrill they both felt at the unfolding saga.

'You know, whatever happens,' Priya said, 'at the end of the day, there is going to be a new baby arriving. Generally when that happens, everyone calms down a bit. You can't go round screaming at each other when there's this cute little thing needing your protection. I swear I wanted to strangle my mother-in-law right up until she walked into the delivery room, and then—'

'You made up?'

'God no, but I didn't want to kill her any more. I hadn't got the energy, frankly. And she's been a bloody life-saver when I've been working away. You rally round when it comes to the kids, that's all I'm saying.'

'I hope so. I just hope Shyama remembers she's got another child.'

Priya sipped her tea and briefly checked her mobile phone.

'I didn't think she'd go through with this, you know. I mean when I found the clinic I thought she'd have a sniff at it, think through what it meant, starting all over again at our age with a baby, and then . . . just give up.'

'When have you ever known Shyama to give up without a fight?'

'I couldn't do it again.' Priya suppressed a small shudder. 'The sleepless nights, the inane baby talk.'

'Then why did you—?' Lydia began.

'Because she was in pain and I'm her friend. And maybe it's not up to us, or anyone, to tell someone when it's the right time to stop chasing a dream.'

'That's quite sensitive, for you.' Lydia smiled.

'Well, I remember how I felt when we were trying and it didn't happen for months . . . that blind panic and desperation. It makes you crazy. So now it's happening, we get on board, right?'

Lydia hesitated. 'It's Tara I worry about.'

'Tara's jealous, that's all. When Maya was born, I bought Luka a DS and said it was from his new baby sister. Still didn't stop him trying to tip her out of her Moses basket for a few weeks, but he adores her now.'

'She talks to me. Tara, I mean, she . . .' Lydia hesitated, aware, even with Priya – or maybe especially with her – of the dangers of breaching confidentiality. 'She's troubled. She was before all this, and now . . . it just isn't great timing for her.'

'Look, sweetie, and don't take this the wrong way . . .'

Lydia stiffened. All Priya's sentences that began thus generally did go the wrong way.

'But you don't have kids and so . . .'

'So what?'

'All I meant was, teenagers are incredibly selfish and incredibly dramatic. I know mine aren't there yet, but all my hormonal nieces and nephews are usually round my place moaning about their parents and quite casually breaking their hearts and shredding their nerves at every opportunity. That's what parents are, at this stage, emotional punchbags. I'm going to send both of mine to boarding school the minute I smell a whiff of it, I swear . . .'

'So you're saying I'm not allowed an opinion because I'm not a mother?' Lydia said evenly.

'No, I'm saying sure, you know loads from your work, your patients . . .'

'Clients, and thanks very much for your endorsement.'

'Come on, Lyd . . . I didn't mean—'

'What did you mean, then?' Lydia stood up and took the mugs to the sink, aware that Priya's was still half full. 'Do you realize how many assumptions the world makes about women who don't have children? That we're weird? Selfish? Neurotic? Tragic?'

'Lyd . . . I asked you years ago why you didn't have kids and you said—'

'I said what was acceptable at the time. That Keith and I couldn't. Because at least then we had a modicum of sympathy, as opposed to this patronizing shit you're chucking at me now.'

In the silence, the whirr of the fridge, the hum of the central heating thrummed between them, thickening the air. Priya searched her friend's face for a hint of anguish that would give her a clue to this outburst. Lydia looked as she always had:

groomed, lithely in control. Well, we all have secrets, Priya concluded. Skeletons come tumbling out of every cupboard in my house: Marco in Milan, George in Lisbon, the memorable all-nighter in Paris, although not memorable enough to recall an actual name. True, the early encounters hadn't remained secret from her friends, it had been fun to share them out, to see the shock and, she thought, grudging envy on their faces at the thought that she was someone who really was 'having it all'. It was also the main reason why she had never encouraged cosy get-togethers with either Shyama or Lydia and their partners; she had enough taste not to parade her husband in front of them, compromising their friendship. But lately she hadn't wanted to share so much – and the affairs were less frequent. She had no doubt they would both approve of this, considering it proof that at last she was seeing sense, living a mature and healthy lifestyle uncluttered with corrosive duplicity. The truth was that she didn't get as many offers, sometimes none at all, despite her ferocious grooming. Something had happened in the last year, something beyond the odd tiny wrinkle, the slight slackening of inner-thigh muscle tone. Maybe it was something hormonal: she wasn't giving off the same bedroom smell, the one that allowed her to reel in a man with the merest flick of an eyebrow. It was as if someone had taken a large eraser and was slowly rubbing her out, pore by pore. Why else, when she walked across a hotel lobby, did she not attract a single male glance?

'Lyd, I would never patronize you, you're far too clever. So you chose not to have kids, no big deal, right? Probably means you will be the only sane auntie Shyama's baby's going to have.'

Lydia paced her garden into the early hours. She knew how to handle this one, the insomnia triggered whenever she dwelt on the choice she had made all those years ago. She had made it clear to Keith what and who he was taking on – a woman who might never feel clean enough of her addiction to be responsible for a child. Mostly, she felt it had been the noble and right thing to do. Other times, when she saw slack-faced teenagers shouting at babies in buggies in the supermarket, or listened to wealthy mothers on her couch who felt drained or trapped by their kids, she had doubts about her long-ago sacrifice. She found herself muttering curses like some home-counties harridan – 'People like that shouldn't be allowed'– and had to pinch herself hard and read all her badges again to remind herself who she was when she'd made that decision. Choice. We marched for choices. The hardest time was always when she saw Keith with other people's children. She knew how tender he could be – he would have been the kind of daddy who would wipe up goo and sit up all night with a sick child and cancel long-held plans because he was needed. She knew, because he had done all that for her, and more. And that's what made her sadder than anything else.

It was some time before Priya got into her bed, having had to unwrap her sticky hair from its clingfilm cap, wash and blow-dry it, cream her entire body and pluck a horrifically long hair from her chin. How had that one escaped the bloody laser? Anil barely stirred as she climbed in beside him, his laptop still open on the floor beside him, showing columns and graphs moving in slow projections. He never seemed to notice whether she was moisturized or not, whether her roots were showing or whether she was wearing a new piece of underwear. For years she had assumed that he was doing the usual spouse-taking-wife-for-granted routine. But now she thought that perhaps he didn't say anything because it – she – simply didn't matter enough to him.

When she had told him about the surrogacy clinic before she approached Shyama with the idea, she'd expected some kind of negative reaction, or at least a degree of suspicion. Instead he had shrugged and said, 'Imagine not having our kids . . .' and had looked away. At the time, she had taken that as a vote of approval for suggesting surrogacy to Shyama. Now she wondered if it was a veiled insult, a barbed warning. 'God, yes, imagine if we didn't have kids, then at least I wouldn't have to stay with you . . .'

No, ridiculous. Priya wasn't having any of this. She had a whole morning of meetings and if anything was going to keep her awake, it was worrying about them. She put on her padded sleep mask and spooned into her husband's back, her hand resting on the furry mound of his stomach, too tired to feel the slight flinch of his flesh under her palm.

# CHAPTER TEN

IN AN AGE full of surprises, perhaps the most unexpected
discovery for Mala was how clouds were not what she had
imagined they would be at all. From the swollen riverbank, in
between the waving sugar-cane stalks in the fields, from her
perch on her wobbly stool in her courtyard whilst she watched
chapattis rise into floury discs, clouds were blowsy, corpulent
pillows far above her head, soft yet firm enough to cradle her
weight. Imagine jumping on to one of those, *hena*? Your body
would sink into it, like the Pogles' imported feather sofa, so
springy you would be bounced back on to your feet. In the aeroplane she had braced herself for the impact as they ascended
straight into a bank of dawn-tinted cumuli. Instead the world
went grey, metallic vapour obscured her final view of Delhi, her
old life exhaling its last foggy sigh until suddenly they were
dazzled by bright sunlight again. Now the clouds were below
them, but they looked like nothing that belonged to the sky, more
like an expanse of curdled buttermilk or a heaving, slow-moving
sea, or maybe a shifting desert, all dunes and hollows, forming
and re-forming with indolent ease. Somewhere down there were
her village, her husband, her pots and pans, her trunk. I could
have said no, she thought, so many times; a simple shake of the
head and everything would have stopped, and I would be back

down there, thinking I could bounce on clouds. But instead she kept saying yes: to Shyama Madam's idea of coming away with her; to fleeing the communal dormitory without a backward glance; to every form thrust in front of her, awaiting her careful signature, which she still felt did not belong to her. Yes, yes, yes, because I know, she told her belly, I know there is no home for either of us there any more.

It was the news about Seema that had confirmed everything. Just a lucky chance, listening in to the brood mares sitting on their charpoys *hai hai*-ing about their fat ankles and bulging veins, boredom making them indiscreet. Virtually every woman was there in secret, only their husbands knowing the truth about their confinement. They feared the reaction of their neighbours and friends, village elders and local gossips. Then Mala heard Seema's name mentioned, and the name of her own village. Her ears pricked up whilst she carried on nonchalantly leafing through the pages of her *Elle India*.

'So they had the house built, AC, widescreen TV and all. But someone must have told someone else, you know how it is. They go off shopping, they come back, *bas*. The whole *koti* is burned to the ground.'

Also all that Shyama Madam had done, how she had done it, Mala would never comprehend, but the two of them – she and Toby sahib – were always huddled together doing *sus-sus* whispers and then looking over at her with that fond faraway smile that made Mala feel both special and utterly transparent. As if they looked through me, nah, not at me, as if I was made of smoke, of cloud. Then there was schoolwork – at least, that was how it felt to her. What to say, what not to say, especially to anyone in a uniform or at an airport.

'Not that all of this isn't perfectly legal,' Shyama Madam would

252

say. 'I mean, we have paid enough to make it happen, but . . .'

Mala held up a hand. No need to explain, she conveyed, I live here, I know how some pot belly in khakhi who's had a row with his wife or didn't collect enough *rishwat* that day could decide to make your life more difficult simply because he could. Hadn't she managed to sit with her blank-wall face whilst Dr Passi shouted and banged desks and wagged witchy fingers, and then totally calmed down when Toby sahib told her in that deep soil voice that she would still get paid? Then, Mala sniggered as she recalled, doctor-ji couldn't do enough for the *firenge* parents: hot chai and the special cardamom biscuits and the patting of my hand and telling me how lucky-lucky I was to be so looked after and so special. God knows how I didn't spit biscuit crumbs in her face. But then, Mala told herself as she opened another packet of complimentary cashews, I have had a lot of practice, hiding what is heating me up inside.

There had been one very sticky moment – actually a few days of stickiness – when the question of leaving her children had arisen, the *bacche* in the photograph still pinned to the wall behind her small dormitory bed, smiling as if they loved her and would never let her go.

'But surely,' Shyama Madam said to Toby in front of her when this whole running-away idea had come up, 'this is not going to work. How can Mala leave her two children behind?'

*Hare*, that was the moment when everything could have crumbled like laddoos in milk, for why should you tell the truth when the truth is only going to make you look bad and make them feel like first-class fools?

'Madam . . .' Mala began, keeping her eyes to the floor, 'those children . . . I didn't . . . they are my husband's children . . . you understand?'

Mala had seen the confusion in her face, then the suspicion, and then the thing that disturbed her most, the disappointment.

'You mean they are your stepchildren?' Shyama registered Mala's uncertainty and continued impatiently, 'Your husband had another wife then? They are her children?'

Mala nodded, relieved she did not have to think on her feet and find the correct English translation at the same time.

'So you didn't give birth to these children. This . . .' Shyama continued, a soft gesture towards Mala's abdomen, 'our first baby . . . is your first baby as well?'

Mala nodded again. She felt Toby sahib's eyes on her. Would he be coldly furious, the way he had looked at Ram that night outside the hotel when his boyish features had hardened into something bestial and thrillingly cruel? She had glanced up briefly. Toby had placed a restraining hand on Shyama Madam's arm. She had talked too quickly and loudly for Mala to pick up everything, but she had known it was not good. Something about taking the doctor to court and proper background checks and what would happen if something went wrong 'with her', looking at Mala, pecking at Toby sahib like some heat-crazed, red-feathered bird until he had put his hand up, just like some traffic cop on a highway.

'Nothing will go wrong,' Toby sahib said to her, while looking at Mala, who realized that she should say something, anything to make this OK.

'Madam,' she said softly, 'those children . . . they were mine, but not mine. I loved them, but I can leave them also. Just the same with this one. I can love this baby, but also I can leave this baby when I have to.'

*Vah*, how she had come out with such perfect poetry Mala still did not know, but it had worked and now she was here in an aeroplane, a speck in the sky, a blink of God's eye, about to watch her third movie on her personal television screen. She could not resist one more look at the secret tucked away in the inside zip-up compartment of her new nylon travel bag. She had checked the pocket every fifteen minutes or so since they had boarded the plane, until Shyama Madam had smiled and asked if maybe she wanted to hand it over to her for safekeeping. Mala had shaken her head. She saw the amused pity in the other woman's face, it rolled off her like ghee spitting from a hot griddle. She unzipped the compartment and brought it out again, feeling its weight on her palm, so light; she wanted to press it to her nose and inhale the newness and promise of its leathery smell, the deep-blue cover, the shiny gold stamp. '*Theklo*,' Mala whispered softly to her stomach. 'This is because of you, *baccha*.' Mala rested her hands on her ribs, still clutching the passport, and wondered if the fluttering in her stomach was tremors of fear, joy, or the first tentative flexing of tiny limbs.

It was only when they had pulled away in the taxi and left the endless roundabouts and flyovers of the airport behind that Shyama's pulse rate finally began to slow down.

'My God . . .' she breathed to Toby, 'I thought I was going to throw up at passport control. That bloke kept her there for ages . . . I thought they were going to deport her, chuck us in jail . . . I mean, how do people ever have the guts to smuggle drugs or—'

'We had nothing to worry about,' Toby soothed her. 'She said exactly what's on her visa. She's our domestic, here for six months. The only thing we haven't mentioned is that she's pregnant, and they didn't ask, so we didn't have to lie. She did great.' Then, uncomfortably aware that the subject of their conversation was sitting opposite them, Toby leaned forward and smiled. 'You did great, Mala.'

Mala barely registered Toby's compliment. She sat with her nose pressed to the window, an expression of intense concentration on her face. She had hardly spoken since they had left the airport.

'She's probably shell-shocked right now . . .' Shyama whispered, leaning into Toby, smelling their long journey on him – recycled stale air, antiseptic handwash, lukewarm coffee still on his breath. 'I'd hoped at least it might be sunny . . .'

'Ah, why fill her with false hope, eh?' Toby whispered back, wishing he could get to his fleece, folded away in his hand luggage in the boot. The slap of the freezing rain as they ran for their cab had surprised him too. He had got used to the freedom of flinging on a T-shirt and wandering out into bright light and balmy heat. His childhood was one long sequence of sullen skies and platter-flat fields, punctuated by the occasional exclamation mark of an unexpected, fleeting sunny day. He supposed there must have been more of them, but they had been overpowered by his memories of damp and drizzle. Suffolk lads were meant to tolerate wind and wet, he supposed that was why they all shared a similar wide-legged stance, feet rooted to withstand whatever gales came buffeting them from The Wash with nothing in between to slow or calm them down. And yet here he sat, shivering in the back of a taxi, numbed by the bleakness of the landscape rolling past, every colour bleached to steel, so few people out on the streets, the few that there were hunched miserably against the weather. No street vendors, no car horns, no lone cows or shamefaced stray dogs dodging the traffic, no eye-watering clash of the pinks and greens and reds of saris and painted trucks and awnings. Toby's chest tightened; if he hadn't been born here, he would have called this sinking sensation a kind of homesickness. So what Mala must be feeling, he could not begin to imagine.

Sofa Workshop . . . Storage Solutions . . . M & C Garages . . . Polski Sklep . . . Mala recited each one in her head, like the pupils under the peepul tree at school, repeating every word the lantern-jawed Master-ji pointed at, like eager scrawny parrots. No need to explain the word itself, not to these children who will only end up herding buffalo or scrubbing dishes, so repeat, nah? Shell Petroleum . . . Little Tykes Togs . . . World of Leather. This last one would have made her mother-in-law spit on the ground and fling prayers of forgiveness at the heavens; a whole world of dead flayed cows? And what was she doing now, the toothless, bat-eared *buddee*? No doubt smearing Mala's name with every word of shame she could imagine, telling the wide-eyed villagers that her ungrateful *bahu* had run off with a heroin dealer / was selling her scrawny body to building-site lackeys / had been most unfortunately knocked over and killed by a runaway three-wheeler. Of the three, Mala hoped it was the last one. She prayed fervently that Ram and his mother had decided to take the easiest option and kill her off completely. Then, *chalo*, I will never have to go back to the family village. She felt only a tiny twist of regret when she imagined the news reaching her mother's ears. No, better for her I am dead. How would she survive this, in a place where a disgraced woman is better dead and forgotten than walking around, brazenly and digracefully alive?

She had noticed all the Indians at the airport – so many of them, behind the desks, serving in the shops, sweeping the floors. They looked the same in many ways as the ones she'd left behind, but there was a difference Mala couldn't quite define. Same clothes, same straight partings and carefully placed bindis, same trimmed beards, turbans, hijabs. Maybe the women seemed sharper-elbowed and more straight-staring, occupying their space with no mousey glances from side to side. But then, back home, the only women who did that were the lower castes, the poor ones who would stand aside with eyes lowered when any of the madams needed to walk in their space. Maybe that was it: here, Mala could not tell, just from looking, who did what job, what low-class bazaar or high-class mall their clothes came from, how rich their husbands were from looking at the gold they wore around their wrists and necks, how much of the day they spent on foot by checking the dirt on their shoes; even the shade of their skin gave no clue as to how many hours they'd had to labour outside. The man who had checked her passport was darker than Mala; the woman cleaning the toilet had a glowing milky sheen that would not have disgraced a filmi heroine. A person could get lost here, Mala realized. Me, I could walk along these too-clean streets and be anonymous and free. She could put up with a few drops of rain for that.

As the taxi finally pulled into Shyama's street, she squeezed Toby's hand, which lay limp as a fish in hers. He gave a slight shiver in response.

'Nervous?' she said softly.

'Cold,' Toby replied, and pulled his hand from hers so he could leap out of the car and run round to the other side to open the door for Mala.

Sita had had little to do in preparing the spare room. Tara's recent feverish bout of spring-cleaning had taken care of the elbow-grease jobs. Shyama's instructions, conveyed via Skype, were to transform what had been her study back into the bedroom it used to be. Prem took the laptop to Shyama's bedroom, the sofa was opened out into a sofa-bed and *bas*, it was pretty much ready. Sita had asked Tara a few times to put out fresh towels and a few basic toiletries – shampoo, soap, toothpaste – and ensure there were hangers in the small oak wardrobe which had been doubling as a makeshift stationery and DVD store – but somehow Tara kept forgetting. Too much time in her room probably, on that stupid computer, thought Sita, though thank God those loud locust friends had stopped visiting so much. Actually they had not been round at all recently. So Sita arranged the toiletries in what she hoped was a welcoming pattern on the chest of drawers, the top now clear of old photographs and the drawers empty of spare linen, and as a final and, she thought, generous gesture, added a bunch of tulips in a vase she had found tucked away under the kitchen sink. One more strange gesture in these strangest of times. She was putting out flowers for a woman carrying her daughter's baby. The idea of a newborn in this house was disconcerting enough, the fact that her daughter had chosen this path too much to digest right now. Sita only hoped she would not be roped in for babysitting, she was way too old and tired for that – something she wished Shyama had paused to consider for herself. The tulips bowed their crimson crowns to her, a pop of colour in the stark room. This will seem like luxury to that village girl, Sita thought not unkindly.

She had no objection to the girl giving birth over here – it made sense, given the behaviour of her low-life husband that evening. But she had her own personal and bitter experience of what happens when generosity is mistaken for stupidity, sacrifice for spinelessness. True, they had an eviction date now, but she knew only too well that it could still come to nothing, thanks to lost papers, incorrect data, courtesy of Sunil making the rounds of the clerks' offices with his oily moustache and greasy palms. The money she had paid out in bribes meant nothing to her – how much of their income had been sent back to Prem's relatives over the years without her approval? But there had been a bigger price to pay: for the first time in her fifty-year marriage, she had lied to her husband. It sat like a furball in her throat, choking her every time Prem remarked on how strangely fortuitous it had been to get this date, and so quickly after the judge's refusal! Didn't it prove his point all along, that good would eventually prevail, that Gandhi-ji's theory was right, and passive honourable resistance would erode all obstacles like trickling water on rock? And Sita would swallow and avoid his eyes and nod her miserable yes. All this, because some people had got too comfortable with the good fortune which had landed in their laps. Of course, Sunil and Sheetal were never going to quit voluntarily, it was always going to end this way. And the woman carrying Sita's next grandchild – once the baby was out and her job was over, with no husband or village to return to – well, what then?

Tara heard the doorbell from up in her room, the hearty greetings as her grandparents welcomed everyone in, the heaving and grunting as cases were set down, the clink of crockery as tea and snacks were put out, a constant hum of chatter pierced by Shyama's shout up the stairs, 'Tara? We're back! You coming down?'

Tara checked her reflection in her dressing-table mirror; it had been a bog-standard pine dressing-table with a swivel mirror set on top until she had dropped a bottle of nail-varnish remover on it a couple of weeks back. The resulting stain had looked a little like undivided India, which she had always thought resembled a diagram of a womb, with Pakistan and Bangladesh the ovaries on either side. So she had stuck a picture of an Amul butter baby she'd downloaded from a vintage-Indian-ads site in the middle of the V. The perfect *desi* infant, fair, fat, ladling cholesterol into his smiling mouth. Soon she was adding more images, until the whole surface was covered with beehived Air India hostesses, Brylcreemed men in flares lounging over motorbikes, beatific housewives smiling adoringly at their families as they proffered plates of steaming rice, men in vests pointing at objects in the far distance, carrying briefcases and clipboards to show they were studious professionals and not just lazy layabouts hanging out in their underwear, pigtailed schoolchildren with white uniforms and smiles, touching their grandparents' feet, and everywhere brides and bridegrooms, newlyweds still in their traditional outfits extolling toothpaste, starch, hair oil, everything except the one product they might actually need in bulk: condoms. Marriage and Family, they could make you buy anything. Tara wasn't sure why she found all these retro images so comforting, but they made her smile and feel nostalgic for something she had never had or known. She had been so pleased with the result that she had broken her unspoken vow never to return to social media and had logged on again, just to post a picture of her pimped-up dressing-table. There was a frenzy of responses, ranging from the predictable 'Are you still alive then??' to a huge number of likes and comments, including a gushing reply from Tamsin: 'WOW!! So freaking cool! Cd sell that down Camden for a bomb!! Make me one girlfriend??'

Tara had been on the point of replying when she had spotted the post from Charlie: 'Nice to know u got an alternative career lined up . . .' plus a sinister-looking winky face.

She logged off again and stayed there. Even seeing his name in type brought back the evening she was trying so hard to forget: it came to her unbidden in sharp, flashing images – a dripping pizza box, a candle flame flickering in rhythm to Charlie's laboured breathing, the corner of a kitchen unit pressing into her back, her view of the kitchen door obscured now and then by his head, wishing it would open, dreading that it would. At least now she looked different enough to pretend that person wasn't her anymore: her hair had grown back a bit since the drastic chop but it was still short enough to reveal her newly sculpted cheekbones. Ten pounds had dropped off her in a month – some of the girls wanted to know her secret, those who were still making an effort at conversation. Tara had muttered something about healthy eating and Pilates, which fooled nobody. The only reason anyone ever lost weight was either prolonged drug use, an eating disorder or lots of sex with a new partner, everyone knew that. And as Tara seemed still resolutely single, rumours began to circulate about her eating habits and her newly acquired drug habit, which also conveniently explained why she was so freaking boring all the time.

Tara changed out of her floppy jumper into a skinny-ribbed top, relishing the novelty of having a waist, of feeling her hip bones press against her jeans. She then double-lined her large eyes with kohl and gelled the front of her hair.

At that moment, Toby knocked on the door. 'Tara? Did you hear your mum calling?'

'Coming,' Tara called, starting as Toby pushed open the door.

'Oh sorry, I thought you said come in . . .' Toby trailed off. He hardly recognized this huge-eyed, spider-legged creature in front of him, all spiky limbs and malevolent stare.

'No,' replied Tara, enjoying the shock on Toby's face, 'I said I am coming. See you down there.' She turned away pointedly.

Toby remained where he was, his goosebumps gradually replaced by a growing flush of irritation. 'So, no hello? How was it? See any holy cows?' He attempted to smoothe the edge in his voice.

'I thought we were about to do that over cuppatea,' Tara said over her shoulder, attending to a panda ring of black under one eye. 'Is she here then?'

'By she you mean Mala?'

No reply.

'Yes, she is. I'm sure she'd like to meet you.'

Tara laughed. It was a hard, ugly sound, not one Toby had heard before. 'Why would she want to meet me, Toby?' She turned to face him, her eyes glittering. 'Does Mum want me to buddy up to my . . . well, what is she exactly?'

'She's just arrived, she's confused and probably a bit scared. I can't make you give a shit, but as far as your mum's concerned, and for the health of our baby . . .' and Toby saw the flinch of Tara's shoulders as he said it. 'How about pretending, for now?'

Shyama heard the slam of Tara's door from the kitchen and one set of heavy footsteps stomping down the stairs. Swallowing her disappointment, she turned to see Mala sitting before her untouched mug of tea, her side plate empty of snacks.

Sita proffered up a plate of freshly made bhajis. 'And you must try the chutney. Made from mint from the garden!'

Mala shook her head, her eyes lowered.

Sita pulled Shyama to the sink, covering her whispers by rinsing out some mugs. 'She won't speak, she won't eat . . .'

'She's settling in, Ma. Give her time,' Shyama muttered, turning to raise her eyebrows at Toby, who shook his head slightly and sat down next to Mala.

'Bhajis! My favourite!' he said jovially. 'And you have to try the chutney, Mala. It's made from mint.'

'I don't think she's hungry, Toby. Maybe I can make you a fresh roti, Mala? What do you enjoy eating at home?'

Sita repeated the sentence in Hindi, but it made little difference. Mala smiled faintly and shook her head again. Shyama and Toby eyeballed each other over her bent head, their eyes darting towards the door as Tara's usual pony trot sounded down the stairs.

Toby cleared his throat. 'Shyams, when you see Tara, well, she's . . .'

'What?'

Shyama hadn't meant to emit an actual yelp of horror when she saw her daughter enter the kitchen. But she couldn't take it all in – the hair, the clothes, the make-up, and where had her boobs gone? Was this what happened with kids, even at her age, if you turned your back for a mere few weeks? How could you ever really let go?

'Hi, Ma.' Tara kissed her perfunctorily and then swivelled to face Mala. She put her hands together in an exaggerated namaste, bowed low and intoned, '*Namaste, Mala-ji. Thum teek hai? Mera naam Tara hain, aur mein Shyama hum kevalee bacchee.*'

Sita clapped her hands and Prem threw out a congratulatory *vavah!*

Mala looked up from her lap and stared Tara in the eye, a faint smile tugging at her lips.

'You see how good her Hindi is becoming, Shyama?' Sita teased. 'She could teach you a few things now, isn't it?'

'I'm sure there's a lot Tara knows that I don't,' Shyama muttered, aware that Mala and Tara were still fixated on each other. 'So, Tara, enlighten your poor old mother, what did you just say?'

'She told me her name is Tara. She asks me how am I,' Mala replied in a clear, steady voice. 'And she says she is your one child.'

'Only child,' Tara interrupted. 'Some things do get lost in translation, don't they? Oh great, Nani's bhajis. Only made on very special occasions. I expect everyone's told you about the chutney already.'

Tara barely paused for breath as she loaded a plate with food, poured an exaggerated amount of chutney on top and waltzed out with a cheery wave.

Shyama sat down, suddenly feeling exhausted. If she had been alone, she would have put her head in the crook of her arm and cried. Instead, looking around at the expectant faces trained on her, the enormity of her decision punched her in the gut. She was the still eye of this vortex of responsibility; everyone around this table and the renegade upstairs wanted something from her, depended on her for something: food, shelter, care, entertainment, sex, boundaries, money. And she knew she encouraged it: from insisting that her parents move next door, to encouraging her daughter to stay at home, to inviting Toby to move in, to starting her own business and refusing any financial settlement from Shiv. And now the woman with the jewel in her nose and the enigmatic smile was in her home, finally helping herself to chutney. She always seemed to choose the long hard way, always wanting to prove that the world was only as heavy as the strongest woman's back. And then she watched other women like Priya, who despite her slinky femininity was actually a bareknuckled street-fighter, who somehow managed to get people to do things for her with a twitch of a manicured finger.

'The curse of the strong woman,' Lydia had once told her. 'The whole sod-you-I-don't-need-anyone's-help attitude becomes the very thing that stops anyone ever asking. Why offer and get your head bitten off when you can ask the giggly woman with the grateful eyes who will make you feel needed?'

'I don't do giggly or grateful,' Shyama had deadpanned back.

'Which is why Priya will always have someone to carry her bags, and why you will always be expected to carry your own and everyone else's.'

'So you're saying I should bat my eyelashes and play dumb just to get a bit of help now and again?'

'No,' sighed Lydia. 'I'm saying it doesn't make you weak to ask for help. It makes you human, Shyama.'

'We are going now, *beti*.' Prem was standing over her, concern in his eyes. 'You will be OK? Maybe you all need to rest now.'

'Yes, fine, Papa. Talk later.'

Toby, as always, elected to walk them through the back garden to their gate. Shyama rose heavily, automatically reaching for the dirty crockery destined for the sink.

A hand clasped her wrist, surprisingly strong. 'Shyama Madam? Leave it, nah?' Mala rose smoothly and began gathering up the mugs and plates.

'Mala, you shouldn't be doing that,' Shyama protested.

'Why? I do at home every day.' Mala placed the crockery in the sink, pausing a moment whilst she studied the swivel tap. The same as in the hotel, no problem. She mixed the water to the right temperature and picked up a dishcloth.

'No,' Shyama said, rising and joining her. 'That's for cleaning the surfaces. We use this one. But please, I would rather you rest.'

'Shyama Madam,' Mala turned to face her, 'I don't want to sit.

Do nothing. You are so kind to bring me. I must help you. You do too much, yes?'

In the end, they cleared the kitchen together in silence, working to the familiar domestic rhythms of washing, rinsing, wiping, Mala asking with a raise of an eyebrow where this plate went, that spoon, until she had opened each cupboard and drawer and apparently memorized their contents. On finding a mouldering potato sitting in the concealed vegetable rack in one cupboard, she wrinkled her nose and extracted it with a nimble hand.

Shyama felt hotly embarrassed. 'Our cleaner left just before we came away . . . her visa ran out, so . . . anyway Tara's been tidying up . . . she must have missed that one,' she said lamely.

Mala deposited the fuzzy mess in the bin and began wiping down the table as Shyama fussed around moving placemats and scooping up crumbs.

'Your *beti*. Tara. Very pretty. But too thin.'

'Yes . . . she wasn't when we left.'

'She missing you too much, maybe.'

'I doubt that.'

'Sorry? Don't understand.'

'Tara . . .' Shyama paused. She wasn't sure how much she should tell this woman, a stranger bound to her by biology, who was cleaning her kitchen. 'She is not . . . she is still getting used to this whole . . . baby thing. I'm sorry, I'm not putting this very well . . .'

'She does not like me. I know this.'

'No, no, no,' protested Shyama weakly. 'It's not you, it's . . .' She instinctively gestured towards Mala's stomach. 'It is still strange for her. She will love the baby when he or she is here, I'm sure of that.'

But not me, thought Mala silently, squeezing out the small

sponge which magically inflated back into shape. I know that look your *beti* gave me, the same one as those witches on the riverbank, the same one Master-ji gave me when I answered too many questions at school, the same one my husband punished me with time and time again – you say too much, Mala, you take up too much space. But what she found confusing was that this girl Tara and her mother were the same kind of women as her. The ones who could not just say *hahn-ji* and *nahin-ji* and look at their feet. This woman standing next to her with crumbs in her palm and the red fire in her hair had produced a child simmering with the same embers, so why was she so scared by her? For the first time, Mala wondered about the child she was carrying. Half of Toby sahib, and half of who else? What would Mala see in that newborn face? Nothing of herself. If the child wanted an easy life, maybe that was a good thing. If it was a boy, with Toby sahib's kind ways and gentle strength, that would be best. Another burning girl in this house of dry wood would be a dangerous thing.

Toby entered the kitchen and stopped in surprise at the sight of the two women at the sink.

'She's not got you doing housework, has she?' he joshed a little too loudly, throwing a questioning look at Shyama.

'No, I—' Shyama began.

'No problem, Toby sahib. I can help,' Mala said, leaving it unclear whether she had been corralled into cleaning up.

Toby picked up Mala's shawl from where it had been left draped over a chair and smiled. 'You haven't even seen your room yet. I've put your case up there, so . . .'

'Want me to take her up?' Shyama asked.

'No probs,' Toby replied, already holding the door open.

Mala obediently walked through, pausing to let Toby overtake her and lead her upstairs.

*

The room could have been a suite at the Savoy, going by Mala's delighted reaction to it. She said nothing but walked around touching everything, tracing the embroidery on the bedspread, pressing the plumply folded towel, stroking the petals of the tulips to see if they were real. Toby ran through all the storage space, taking care to speak slowly and enunciate clearly, though he had the strangest feeling that everything he said amused her. He showed her the workings of the shower in the family bathroom along the landing, warning her about the slightly sticky lock and how you had to push the door in to release it.

'We all share the one bathroom, I'm afraid. Couldn't afford the planned en-suite with all the . . .' he trailed off, she didn't need to know that they had forgone their longed-for wet room for the longed-for baby, but Mala simply nodded her head and there it was again, that secretive twitch playing on her lips.

'Did I say something funny?' Toby asked.

'Oh no, Toby sahib. I understand all. Now I can sleep, yes?'

'Oh sorry, you must be . . . Yes, of course. And, Mala?'

Mala paused in the doorway of the bedroom – her bedroom.

'Please . . . no more Toby sahib. Just Toby.'

'Yes, Toby sahib.'

Mala's throaty giggle followed her into the room and Toby could still hear it fading as he made his way back to the kitchen.

Toby lay on the bed, showered and restless, his body craving sleep, his brain throbbing against his skull. Above him he could hear Shyama talking to Tara, her bass tones an undertow to Tara's staccato bursts of energy. It was a familiar tune; he'd often lain on the bed listening to the dialogue become a screaming match until eventually the desire for peace dragged him upstairs, where he would referee them apart, careful not to take sides, astonished that the next day the two of them would be laughing conspiratorially at the breakfast table and treating him as the interloper. It wasn't going to happen this time. The voices reached their climax, halted by a slamming door and Shyama's angry steps down the stairs and into their room, where she threw herself next to Toby, her face flushed.

'Home sweet home, eh?' she said flatly. 'I've never . . . it's like she's not there. Nothing gets through. I thought, with us being away so long, she might have . . .'

'Grown up?'

'Come back to herself. You didn't know her as a little girl, Tobes, I wish you had.' The memory of that plump, cheerful child, her sticky hand in hers, exclaiming at the newness of the world, brought an ache to Shyama's throat. 'She was always so . . . kind. She would make a bee-line for anything small, fluffy or injured. Not that she was ever a pushover, but she saw vulnerability and wanted to protect it. She got into fights defending the weak kids from the bullies, and I never told her off. I was proud of her, her need to make things fair. I thought it was the one thing I'd got right with her.'

Normally Toby would have jumped in on cue, reassured her she was doing a great job, had done the best anyone could have done in difficult circumstances, et cetera, but he was lost in his own fantasy, one where he'd met Shyama years ago when Tara was a pliable toddler, when he could have been the only father she'd have remembered. He could have helped shape her, discipline her, guide her, all the stages he had missed out on. Without that history to draw on, he would never have the nostalgic reminders that could soften his judgement now and give him the authority to intervene rather than having to bite

270

back continually what he really thought. His own upbringing, he now saw, had been a process of benevolent neglect, both his parents too busy with the backbreaking daily grind of farmwork to worry about how their sons felt about anything. As long as they were fed, healthy and productive, that was enough. Then when his father had dropped dead of a heart attack in his early fifties and his mother had died of cancer just two years later, leaving Toby an orphan in his late twenties, it had been too late to record all the memories they must have had of him, his birth, his childhood. There were plenty of photos of Matt, the first-born, messy birthday parties with gap-toothed kids around the kitchen table, school reports, even a baby book, not quite complete but with a few milestones recorded in his mother's slapdash italics: *'Matty's first lock of hair!'*, *'Matty's first Step!!'*. But for Toby, just a handful of snapshots, no baby book, a lone report from his first year at school, in which his teacher described him as 'still settling in but very good with his hands'. Shyama, on the other hand, had a filing cabinet full of Tara's achievements, every school concert and sports day logged and preserved, her gym and swimming badges, articles for the school magazine, school reports running into pages. ('I should bloody well hope so after the fees I paid.') It seemed as if there hadn't been a moment when Tara hadn't been monitored, assessed and prepared for success. Still doesn't stop the little buggers breaking your heart, Toby thought grimly, so what was the point of all that expensive grooming? If you give them everything they ask for, how can they cope when it all goes tits up, as it one day inevitably will? Much as he wanted to be understanding, he felt Tara's behaviour was mostly because Shyama had spoiled her rotten, and now, when her nose had been put out of joint by a foetus, for Christ's sake, she was kicking off like a prize brat. There. He'd said it. Not out loud. Yet.

271

And then, a pinprick of fear. What if this was going to happen all over again? He and Shyama had never actually discussed how they were going to raise this baby, not in any detail, but if he had a choice between his parents' approach, the feed-and-wipe-clean-and-leave-to-their-own-devices method, and Shyama's military hothousing, he knew which he would choose.

'Did you hear what I said?'

'Sorry?' Toby shifted on to an elbow.

Shyama's eyes glistened at him. 'I said, do you think she's . . . *on* something?'

'Be surprised if she wasn't. Everyone at college was trying all sorts, but it doesn't mean—'

'It's different now!' Shyama sat up, furiously rubbing at her eyes. 'It's not just a bit of spliff and a bottle of cheap cider round the back of the bus shelter . . . They've got this skunk stuff that causes schizophrenia, they've got kids dying from alcohol poisoning because of dares on social media . . . that's apart from all the other pills and horse tranquillizer and chicken-fattening tablets and all kinds of shitty crap that we couldn't even make up.'

'Chicken-fattening what?' Now Toby was interested, sitting up to join her.

'There are these tablets,' Shyama continued in a shuddery voice, 'that farmers use to fatten up their chickens, and women – girls – have been taking them to give themselves bigger bottoms. Not here – in Jamaica, I think . . . or in the places where men actually like big bottoms, which is a good thing, obviously, but not like this, and once again vulnerable young women are killing themselves just because of this intense pressure they're under to be . . . and she . . .'

'I think we can safely say that Tara is not on the fat-chicken tablets, because the one thing she does not have is a big arse,' Toby said gently as he pulled her to him. She let him, half laughing, half sighing, sinking into him, too tired to cry or to think.

From Mala's room, where she shivered under the unfamiliar duvet, it sounded like the moan of a woman being undressed, caressed, slowly slowly, and trying to be quiet. Mala lifted her pillow, punched it with cold fists and buried her head beneath it, waiting for sleep.

The next few weeks passed in a merry-go-round of doctor's appointments, more form-filling, endless trips in Shyama's battered Golf to supermarkets, clothes shops, health-food shops, each visit seemingly for Mala's benefit only; they bought a whole new wardrobe of warmer clothes (though Mala had to be reminded that most of what she wanted would soon not fit her, so she ended up with a variety of smocks and elasticated-waistband trousers). Shyama pushed a trolley up and down endless aisles, exhorting Mala to pick what she liked to eat. In the health-food shop it seemed anything was allowed, judging by the number of pills and potions that Shyama heaved into her basket (although Mala did not fancy any of the 'treats' on offer here – the biscuits looked like cardboard and none of the nuts had chilli or lemon on them).

It was only in the doctor's clinic that Mala felt she could relax, that there was nothing she could say or choose that would be wrong. Lying on the examination couch, scratchy paper crackling beneath her, she could finally let down her guard. This is one thing I can do and she cannot, she would console herself, taking pleasure in the wonder flooding Shyama's face when her baby appeared on the sonographer's screen. The view of the baby itself was strangely disappointing at first: a small shrivelled frog in a bag, amphibian limbs and hooded alien eyes. Mala had seen this shape before, in the bloody debris she had left in a sticky pool on the riverbank, oh so long ago. But then her eyes were drawn to the centre of the screen, towards the strobing light, flashing on and off, on and off, throbbing like an electrical pulse cradled by the fishy limbs. Then when the woman in the white coat put a cold trumpet to her belly, she heard the galloping of wild horses' hooves, relentless, unstoppable, the woman's finger pointing to its source.

'That's your baby's heartbeat,' the sonographer smiled.

'So loud!' Mala breathed, and felt a hand on hers. Shyama Madam, eyes brimming, squeezing her hand in rhythm with the tiny pumping that held both their gazes.

'Everything looks normal, there's nothing to worry about,' the woman said.

Mala barely heard her. *Theklo*, this must be the machine they use to see if you have a boy or girl inside you, she was thinking. They could look inside you and tell your fortune, better than the sandalwood-smelling *buddee* back in the village who would read your palm for a few paisa and some leftover food.

'It is a boy?' Mala asked, seeing the swift glance passing between Shyama Madam and the white-coat woman.

Shyama shifted uncomfortably in her seat.

The sonographer answered for them both. 'It's far too early to tell that,' she said, busying herself with paper towels, handing a few sheets to Mala, who began wiping herself down.

'We don't care . . . I mean, we don't mind, do we, Mala?'

Mala heard the warning note in Shyama's voice. Good job there's no machine like this that can look inside my head, she thought, before widening her smile and answering, 'No.'

\*

274

Shyama had been ignoring Priya's emails and increasingly demanding phone messages. Now she was back, what was going on? She could hear the hunger in her recorded voice, desperate for a first look at the new arrival. But Shyama was afraid to leave this domestic cocoon into which they had retreated since their return, with a routine that had finally settled into something approaching normality. They would breakfast together before Toby left for work; Tara would usually grab something on the go, always polite, never staying. Her parents would call in at some point during their usual round of shops, doctor, card games with neighbours. Then Mala and she would go on their daily jaunts. There was always some little thing to buy or look at. Mala's curiosity at everything she saw encouraged Shyama to organize mini-sightseeing tours around the city. First they drove around the landmarks — Buckingham Palace, St Paul's Cathedral, the Tower of London, following the course of the Thames from St Katharine's docks all the way along the Embankment, veering off and rejoining it later on towards Richmond, one day going as far as Hampton Court. Shyama had parked up and offered to buy tickets for a guided tour – 'This was home to Henry the Eighth, it's one of our historic royal palaces.' Mala had declined the offer. She had seen more interesting buildings on a day trip to Chandigarh, and what was this depressing red-brick house compared to the Taj Mahal? Not that she had ever seen the Taj itself, but any fool could see even from pictures that the white marble dome to a dead queen was always going to come out top. Instead she had chosen to walk around the maze, Shyama trotting behind her, clutching a guidebook and a cardboard cup of that dirty-smelling coffee she always seemed to have on the go. As Mala enjoyed the sensation of losing herself amongst the sweet-smelling leafy walls, she remembered snippets of the Taj

Mahal story from school: how the great emperor Shah Jahan had built it in honour of his departed wife, Mumtaz, who died having their fourteenth child. But wasn't it true that, for rich and poor, your children were your investment for the future? For the rich, it was to pass on kingdoms; for the poor, to have another pair of hands to forage and plough, to have extras because disease and hunger would carry so many of them away. And this one, still hidden beneath her second-best sari, just a taut pot of a secret, this child would have Shyama Madam and Toby sahib to shower it with every best thing they could afford, and just one sister, much older, hardly there and never to play with. A lonely emperor or queen. *Chalo*, it wasn't her business what happened afterwards. What she should be concentrating on was what palace she could buy for herself when she returned home. The word 'home' sent a tingle of . . . what was it? Something . . . along her exposed spine. Maybe it was the same feeling Shah Jahan had suffered when he lay sweating with fever in the Agra Fort across the Jumna river from his beloved Taj, imprisoned by his own son, knowing the palace of love he could only now see in blurred glimpses had always been a tomb and would soon be his.

'Mala! Where were you?' Shyama Madam had come after her, her face angry and flushed as if she had been running. Yes, she had, there were beads of moisture pinpricking her forehead, and her guidebook was crumpled in her hand.

She had told her off like a little girl, a two-minute finger-wagging – I couldn't see you, you were lost, something could have happened – which drew curious looks from some of the other people wandering around, trying to find their way out. Mala's first instinct was to look at the floor and wait for the wind to pass, but then curiosity lifted her head to Shyama's face, and what she saw was not anger but fear. The more fear she saw, the taller Mala felt, the weightier she became as Shyama Madam started to fade and shimmer like insubstantial air. As I climb, she is falling, Mala realized. It made her feel powerful and also sad, the same melancholy she used to feel standing at the fields' cropped edges, hearing the peacocks' sobbing sighs which heralded the approaching rain; they were wailing that cloud bursts were coming, bringing thunder and relief.

Shyama wasn't surprised when she opened the door to Priya, who swept past her, kicking off her heels and dumping her various briefcases in a corner of the hallway.

'Don't even bother apologizing,' Priya said airily, throwing off her coat with a sigh and briefly checking her reflection in the hall mirror.

'I wasn't going to,' Shyama replied, automatically picking up Priya's coat and draping it over the bannister.

'You've been back nearly two months! I wouldn't have known you were back at all if I hadn't bumped into Tara at Westfield . . . she looks a-maa-zing, by the way, very French. She was giving out leaflets for something or other. I didn't have time to chat, but . . . anyway, come on, this is ridiculous . . . what's going on? Is everything OK?' Priya stopped mid-flow, her eyes widening as she stared over Shyama's shoulder.

Mala stood in the kitchen doorway, a damp tea towel in her hand. 'You want tea?' she asked Priya, who for once was lost for words.

'I think that's a very good idea, Mala.' Shyama smiled, nudging Priya into the kitchen and whispering, 'I'd close your mouth, very unforgiving double chin on show . . .'

Priya couldn't take her eyes off her. It wasn't just her obvious beauty – OK, she was a little dark, but those cheekbones, those eyes, that figure that you only usually saw on the prow of old ships or adorning temple walls in impossibly athletic sexual positions – it was the way she seemed to glide around Shyama's kitchen as if she lived there. Of course, she did for now, but it was as if the two women were unconsciously attuned to each other. They moved effortlessly around the space in each other's wake, with none of the awkward gridlock that always ensued whenever Priya's mother-in-law presumed to help herself to a cup of tea.

She had been expecting some scrawny timid refugee type, a woman thinned and cowed by poverty, because why else would anyone do this for such a measly sum of money? But this one, she looked you straight in the eye. She wanted to talk in English, asking Shyama for help if she got stuck or bringing out a small dictionary she kept tucked away in her sari pleats, confident that everyone would wait a few moments for the right word to be found. The woman could even cook. She brought to the table the best pav bhaji that Priya had ever tasted. As she ladled another helping of the spicy vegetable mix on to a hot buttered roll, she told Mala, 'The last time I ate this was on the street in Mumbai . . . it was supposed to be the most famous pav bhaji stall in the city, but yours is better. You have to give me the recipe.'

'Oh, I've asked her, but she always cooks when I'm not around so I still don't know the secret!' Shyama smiled, then said, more reflectively, 'It's going to be really strange going back to work next week. I hope you won't be lonely, Mala?'

Mala shrugged, licking the tips of her fingers thoughtfully. Priya was struck by how sensual the gesture was, filing it away for future use. Maybe she should try it at the dinner table later, though she knew her husband was likely to wrinkle his nose and pass her a tissue.

278

After Mala had excused herself and gone upstairs, Priya took a proper look at Shyama, who seemed lost in thought as she put away the last of the dishes.

'Doesn't she do that?' Priya broke into her reverie.

'It's not her job!' Shyama said a little too quickly, and then, 'But she does, all the time. And the cleaning. I can't stop her. Toby thinks I'm forcing her to pay for her keep or something. She says she likes to keep busy. She's devoured all the magazines I've given her, and is just starting on the bookshelf. She reads a lot. I don't expect her to do much else. Anyway, I'm looking round for a replacement cleaner for when . . . well, as soon as possible.'

'I'm sure Marta would like to earn a few more quid, if you want me to ask her?' Priya paused. 'Shyama?'

'Sorry . . . sorry.' Shyama sighed and dropped into a chair with a grunt. 'It's the whole going-back-to-work thing . . . It's weird . . . I don't want to leave her.'

'No, I wouldn't want to leave her with my husband either!' Priya chuckled.

'What? What do you mean?'

'Oh, come on.'

'No, what?'

Priya saw the ice in Shyama's eyes and, for once, swallowed what was on the tip of her tongue. Mainly the name, Corazon – the Spanish au pair she had employed the first year the children were both finally at school full time. Priya had specifically avoided the French or Swedish variety, following advice from other mothers who swore their husbands found just the idea of a girl from either region forbidden and exciting. And, of course, the accents didn't help, far too seductive. Spanish girls, now they were more like Indians – they lived in extended families, and came from a culture where religion and respect for elders

279

were still part of the fabric of society. And in Priya's vast experience, most Asian men still got their erotic thrills from the idea of bedding a blonde, pale-skinned beauty, the kind of girl they would never have had a chance with as tumescent youths, the ultimate forbidden fruit and as far away as possible from the kind of women they would end up marrying. Got that one wrong, Priya recalled, remembering the number of times she had come across Anil and Corazon casually chatting in the kitchen, or how often Anil would volunteer for the morning school run, where he would help bundle the kids into the car and have Corazon sitting beside him up front, always revving the car a little too enthusiastically as they pulled out of the drive, and how he'd blushed like a teenager when the Iberian minx had told him over morning porridge that her name meant 'Heart'. The children had wailed in protest when Priya had sacked her; she'd told Anil she thought they should find someone French after all, as the children would soon be learning it. He, of course, said nothing, but he went into a major sulk for about a month, going out of his way to be as formal and distant as possible with Céleste, the next au pair, who had the voice of Brigitte Bardot and the face of a trucker sucking a lemon. Priya had managed to stop an accident before it happened; Anil, of course, had no idea she was such an expert in these matters, adept at sensing the swell and promise of a budding affair. One day he would thank her. And she knew absolutely that Shyama wouldn't.

'She's like our daughter,' Shyama snapped.

'Right, of course,' Priya replied.

'Actually,' Shyama's face softened, 'it's only just occurred to me, but we've been doing a bit of sightseeing, and . . . actually it did feel like when Tara was little again. How we'd just take off in the car and have adventures and she was just so fascinated by everything, even a trip to the car wash or a dash round the super-market. I'd forgotten how much fun that was.'

'Good practice for when the real thing arrives . . . Sorry, didn't mean to call your unborn child a thing, but you know what I mean,' Priya added quickly.

Shyama laughed, and Priya breathed a sigh of relief.

'I'm used to translating your foot-in-mouth language into English,' Shyama said. 'I'm sorry if I'm . . . I didn't mean to shut you out for so long, but . . . this takes a bit of getting used to . . . But I'm beginning to feel it's going to be OK. It is, isn't it?'

Priya took her oldest friend in her arms. 'You're going to have a beautiful baby at the end of this. That's what you wanted, isn't it?'

'Oh, so much.'

'When's the due date?'

'December – mid December.'

'A baby's for life, not just for Christmas, eh? Then relax. The hardest part's out of the way. It's going to be fine.'

Mala's pav bhaji was an unqualified success with the rest of the family. Sita even took a Tupperware of leftovers when she and Prem made their way across the back garden later, a fresh bundle of legal papers under their arms which Toby had spent an hour download-ing and printing off as soon as he'd got in from work. Now he was sitting back in his chair, a cold beer in his hand, with that slightly vacant look of fatigue that often descended at this hour.

Shyama watched as Mala moved around him, clearing up silently. The only time she looked anything like the cliché of the demure Indian housewife was when she was around Toby. He, in turn, never once looked at her. At one point their hands brushed accidentally whilst they both reached for a discarded mug and he stiffened awkwardly.

Shyama felt less guilty now about snapping at Priya earlier. She adored her, but it was no wonder Priya saw intrigue in every shadow – how long had she been playing away? Although, thinking about it now, it had been some time since Priya had regaled them with any fruity foreign anecdotes. Maybe she'd finally grown up.

Watching Mala expertly wipe down the draining board, Shyama imagined her standing at her own sink or cutting vegetables in her own kitchen. How hard this woman must have worked throughout her entire young life, for only experienced hands performed domestic tasks so quickly and capably. Shyama remembered what she had first sensed in Mala during that initial meeting in the clinic – her intelligence, her hunger to engage and learn (she found it touching, the way Mala carried that Hindi–English dictionary with her everywhere, its cover already stained with turmeric and smelling faintly of garlic) – and she remembered how, back then, Mala's surly, silent husband had seemed to drag on her life force like an anchor against an impatient tide. She reminded herself how much Mala had given up and left behind to be standing here in her home. She couldn't let her wipe sinks for another five months, cooped up like a battery hen, confirming everyone's prejudices about women like Shyama herself – women who bought a womb as unthinkingly as renting a car for a package holiday.

'Tobes?' Shyama ruffled the hair at the back of his neck, the baby curls hidden at his hairline.

'Mmm?'

'Need to talk to you about something.'

As if on cue, Mala dried her hands on her sari and asked brightly, 'It is OK I have bath?'

Shyama waited until they heard the bathroom door slam

shut upstairs. 'She loves her baths, doesn't she? Twice a day, a minimum of an hour each time . . . we're spending a fortune on bubble bath.'

'Still cheaper than the medical bills.' Toby grimaced as he shifted in his chair and discovered an aching muscle he didn't know he had.

'She can't go to the NHS, Tobes, not for antenatal . . . if it was an emergency . . .'

'I know. It's fine.'

'We're lucky Mum and Dad know so many private doctors, we're still getting a bit of a discount and—'

'Shyama, honestly, I'm not counting pennies when we've come this far. If she's happy, the baby's happy. And it's not for ever.'

'On that note . . .' Shyama paused. 'You know I'm back at work next week, and I was thinking I should take Mala with me.'

'Why?'

'Well, I think she's bored and she will be home alone all day.'

'We could do her a Mala flap . . . like a cat flap, only bigger.'

'Are you listening to me?'

'Well, you do make her sound like a pet . . .'

'Yes, that's the point!' Shyama twisted round to face Toby, who to her surprise wasn't smiling. 'She's clever and she wants to learn, and I want her to take back something that might be useful . . . She's going to be a single woman and that's not going to be easy back in the village.'

'*If* she goes back.'

'Sorry?'

'To the village,' Toby corrected himself. At least he seemed to be listening now.

Shyama ploughed on. 'She seems to know a lot about skincare – just basic home-remedy stuff really – and when we visited that salon in Gurgaon she seemed to have some good ideas. I was thinking, why not let her just muck in and see what happens?'

Toby rubbed his eyes slowly, adopting his man-in-deep-thought pose. It used to charm Shyama, how he'd tune out and ponder her bigger suggestions, never wanting to be pushed into anything too quickly. It had taken a good month of conversation to get him to take the whole surrogacy idea on board. But now, she wondered why on earth she needed his permission for this. He was at work all day, why should it bother him?

'I suppose at least you will be able to keep an eye on her,' he said finally.

Shyama squeezed his hand, felt the calluses on his palms, all her irritation melting away. How could she forget it was this man, her love for this man, that had brought them here? She wanted to see those work-worn hands cradle their baby's head, watch his slow smile as he took in their toddler's first steps, the first time he or she rode a bike, read a sentence, broke their hearts with worry or pride. It was all to come, and she would be the first person he would ever have those experiences with, and hopefully the last. She'd only recently realized that rather than mourning not being able to carry this child herself, she was secretly relieved to be avoiding the nine-month journey from nausea and rusty-mouth to stretch marks, heartburn and piles. Her pregnancy with Tara had been uncomfortable and seemingly never-ending: whilst the other mothers in the local NCT classes had paraded around looking like flowers in slow joyful bloom, Shyama always looked like she'd been sleeping rough on a greasy bench. Her hair went lank and started to fall out, her skin dulled to the texture of parchment, and she cried at anything and everything – toilet-roll adverts, old people at bus stops, passers-by who dared to do a double-take as she waddled past with tissues in one hand and a bag of jalapeño-flavoured tortillas in the other. True, the sensation of her daughter growing inside her had been fantastic and freaky in equal measure, but although she was glad she had done it, she didn't yearn to do it again. Maybe that was why Toby was so distant with Mala – he was angry at missing out on that intense initial bonding where the doting daddy lays his hands on his wife and feels his progeny tumble to the sound of his voice.

'Tobes?'

A sigh. 'Yes?'

'Are you sad? That she's not me?'

'What?' Toby's sharp tone made her blink.

'I mean . . . I know you're missing out on the whole look-at-my-fat-fecund-wife,-I-did-that stage.' She managed to raise a wry grin. 'You know, singing to my tummy, feeling the kicks . . .'

'Going out at midnight to get you pickles and pineapples          '

'Rubbing wheatgerm oil into my skin . . . and other places . . .'

'Now, that's beginning to sound like fun,' Toby smirked.

'Not what you think. One of the dads – the kind that suggest all the expectant fathers ought to wear fake pregnancy bellies so they can really feel what their partners are going through—'

'I hate him already.'

'He spent weeks massaging his wife's perineum with the very same wheatgerm oil, so she would stretch nicely and avoid tearing during the birth. I'll never forget when he boasted one week that he'd managed to get a whole fist in. I thought Shiv was going to throw up.'

'You got your ex to actually attend birthing classes?'

'Just the one. I used to go on my own.'

'Well then,' Toby filled the growing silence, 'seems like you missed out, too. So we're quits. Make you feel better?'

285

'I'd feel better if you were . . . nicer to Mala. I mean, if you stopped being so weird with her. I know this is all weird anyway, but . . .'

'I wasn't aware I wasn't being nice.'

'Then why didn't you come to the scan?'

'You were there, you didn't need me too.'

'It's our baby, Tobes. Yours and mine. You shouldn't let your awkwardness with Mala stop you sharing the important stuff with me. Tobes?'

The telephone rang in the corner of the kitchen. They both looked up. It was so rare that anyone ever called them on anything other than their smartphones.

Toby got there first. 'Oh, hi Lydia!' he answered with genuine warmth.

Shyama stiffened at her name, feeling increasingly uneasy as she caught the tone of Toby's exchange with her. 'OK . . . When? . . . Where? . . . She's here, do you want to . . . OK, I will.'

He replaced the receiver.

'Get your coat. Tara's been arrested.'


There was a disappointing lack of graffiti in the police station cell, Tara decided. She'd seen enough gritty crime series to expect the windowless, white-walled room with a smelly toilet in a corner and the wire-framed bed with a wisp of a mattress. But there had been nothing much to read during the hours she had already been left there: mainly the names of people wanting to let whoever came after them know that they had been there too, scratched randomly into the flaking walls: Kash, Maz and, more surprisingly, Otto. Another nice middle-class kid who had got in with the wrong crowd, sending his parents into a tailspin of panic and soul-searching. Except that Tara hadn't rung either of her parents with the single phone call she had been allowed. Lydia had been her first port of call, maybe because she was worried about one of her grandparents picking up the phone if she called home. It would have been like one of their Skype calls to India, loud hysterical shouting with the juiciest snippets repeated for maximum effect. 'Prison! Yes, she's in prison! No . . . pris-on! Jail! With pimps and murderers! Don't tell Thaya-ji! The shock will kill him!' Trying to explain to her bewildered grandparents that she had been arrested for obstruction on a demonstration against female genital mutilation would have been way out of their comfort zone. She wondered where her fellow protesters had been taken. She'd assumed they would all be shoved together in some sort of holding pen, but maybe that only happened in American prisons. Only in the movies did one of the featured support cast turn up with a wry smile and cash for bail.

Her wrists still ached from the handcuffs, her neck from where she had been wrestled from the human chain she had formed with the other women from the group and dragged along the ground. It was a familiar story: a peaceful demo outside an embassy, coordinated by a network of women's organizations, had soon swelled in size as other uninvited supporters turned up, ostensibly to show their solidarity but clearly using the opportunity to promote their own causes. The spirited chanting of the placard-holders was soon drowned out by the mega-phones of the professional demonstrators, mostly male and young, fiery with passion and hostile to the police, burning with indignation for all the other global injustices that continued around them. There were so many, once you started counting them – that's when sleep and hope began to leave you. Tara knew this already. She had spent weeks struggling with an over-load of nightmare-inducing imagery and statistics. All around the globe, women and girls were burned, bartered, battered, bestialized. The obsessive pull of the internet provided all that information at one click, opening windows into parallel worlds of suffering you never knew existed, and once seen, there was no going back, no forgetting them. What had started as an attempt to understand and contextualize what had happened to her in her mother's kitchen that night had led her initially to a couple of feminist groups based in her university, but they had seemed too small, too earnest, too close to her own department, which she only visited for the odd lecture and to check the post in her pigeon hole. It was on the net that she really found her tribe, other young women reeling from the everyday war on their sex being waged around them, wondering why they seemed to be the only ones who could see the bombs going off, why others around them weren't as scared and exhausted as they were by the scale of this insidious campaign, so common it was almost banal. From those initial discoveries of fellow travellers, Tara was soon linked up to other regional, national and international campaigns: there was a sisterhood out there, not as visible and vocal and fêted as the one Lydia and her own mother had been a part of decades ago, but better connected. They talked to each other across oceans on flickering screens, spurring each other on with a constant dialogue and the sharing of images and ideas. She read blogs and posts from women in Afghanistan setting up secret beauty parlours, schoolgirls in Pakistan defending their right to attend school, mothers in Argentina holding placards for their disappeared children, Indian Dalit women fighting daily abuse by landowners, survivors of domestic cruelty in Chicago. In every country, the scars of ongoing battles lessened her own, eased the prickling of healing skin which gradually hardened into close-fitting armour. Strange how the same machine that had always made Tara feel like an outsider, like the frump in the corner of the party always missing out on something, was now her guide and companion, her portal and her balm, all her loneliness soothed away by its benevolent blue light.

Tara began idly chipping away at a corner of the peeling wall with her thumbnail, hearing raised voices and slamming doors somewhere far along the corridor. She wondered if anyone had turned up to claim her. Lydia had advised her during their brief exchange not to answer any questions until she had a lawyer in attendance. She'd promised to call a couple of solicitors she knew and find out who might be able to come out at this late hour. Tara knew saying 'No comment' to their questions wouldn't help much; in the end it was her word against the police. She'd followed the usual drill that was drummed into the group before every demo: be like Gandhi-ji and resist peacefully through non-cooperation. Their tactics might have worked if it hadn't been for a breakaway gang of young men – who knew where they were from – their faces obscured by scarves and hoods, who decided to snatch the embassy flag from its pole, breaking down railings in their quest. Someone thought it would be a fun idea to urinate on a nearby statue of some colonial official. Stones from the embassy's rockery became makeshift missiles, cars swerving to avoid the flying debris, ploughing into demonstrators and officers.

'Stupid macho tossers!' one of the women had spat out during their journey in the police van. 'Why does it always become about them waving their dicks about?'

There had been other men on the demo, good men whose wives, daughters and sisters had all suffered forced mutilation, but Tara thought it best just to nod and agree, given where she was. She knew she could easily slide into despising all men – oh, it was so easy after everything she had seen. But somehow the face of her grandfather always popped into her head. He was from a generation of men whom you would expect to be possessive patriarchs, and yet all she ever felt when she thought of him was the unflinching certainty that she was respected and loved.

She needed to pee. One look into the cell toilet convinced her to hold on as long as she could. It was getting colder; how long had she been here? No watch, no phone. They'd even confiscated the Mars bar she'd kept for an emergency snack. Would her name hit the papers? Surely they wouldn't throw her off her course – wasn't it a kind of badge of honour amongst students, getting arrested on a demonstration? Bloody well ought to be. She almost smiled, imagining the reaction of her fellow undergrads when they heard. Pictures of her struggling in a uniformed headlock were probably already online somewhere. Inevitably, the departmental whispers about drug addiction had been replaced by the absolute certainty that Tara was now a fully fledged dyke. She'd been ensconced in a booth in the student union cafeteria when she'd heard a familiar drone coming from the next table.

'She's probably been too scared to come out of the closet because of her religion or something,' Tamsin was speculating over the clatter of trays being unloaded and discarded. 'But Tara's definitely hanging out with the lesbos. I mean, it all makes sense now . . .'

Tara had begun quietly gathering her things, ready to make an unseen exit, when the next voice she heard froze her in her tracks.

'What does?' She could hear the faint sneer in Charlie's lazy drawl. Her heartbeat quickened. She didn't want to see him. She had been doing so well. She couldn't see him now.

'Oh come on, Charlie. The way she was always so aggressive towards you, for a start,' Tamsin purred back. 'At first I thought she fancied you . . . now I can see it was a totally alpha-male-bashing thing. Besides the fact that you can be a complete and utter arse.'

Catcalls and cheers around the table. Charlie had joined in, but his laughter sounded hollow. Tamsin was taking very public revenge on her own private humiliation: the fact was – and by the way, it had never happened to him before – he just couldn't get it up with her any more. She was as winsomely gorgeous as ever, he knew half the lads in the department would be queue-ing up for a shot at Tammers, if this got out. But he'd managed to convince himself that his recent un-manning was entirely her fault, and fortunately, she had taken the hint and was dump-ing him in the same way that all his other girlfriends had: with slow-burning, passive-aggressive hostility. He wondered why he'd ever found Tamsin's ethereal flakiness attractive: more and more often recently he had found himself longing for the barbed honesty of the verbal jousting he'd enjoyed with Tara. He missed it in the painfully addictive way you miss rubbing a mouth ulcer with your tongue or picking at a scab. But, as usual, he'd ruined a perfectly good working relationship by having sex with her. And no wonder she hadn't spoken to him since, if she'd been a lesbian all along. She should have said something. It definitely wasn't his fault. It had occurred to him after the act that she might have been a virgin, and it occurred to him again now the whole sapphic theory was being mooted. But if so, why hadn't she said anything? No woman with that amount of gob on her could have possibly been untouched. Why then, he wondered, did he feel a creeping sense of dread every time he thought of her, of that last evening they had seen each other? Why, every time he reached for Tamsin, undressed her, laboured above her, was it Tara's face he kept seeing?

Tara had stood up, placing herself deliberately in view of their table until the laughs and chatter had dribbled away into embarrassed silence. Charlie looked as if he'd seen a ghost. The memory of her had just become flesh before his uncomprehending eyes – how could she have known? Of course, he managed to collect himself; he had an audience.

'Oh hi, Tara,' he had said smoothly, enjoying the hands over mouths around him. 'How come you're avoiding us? Something we said?'

'No, Charlie,' she had replied in a clear, calm voice. 'Something you did.'

Tara had stared straight at Charlie; she had not blinked, not looked away. She had wanted him to gaze right into her soul and see the damage he had left behind.

Everyone around the table had seen something else, something wholly unexpected: the slipping of Charlie's mask, his constructed cool collapsing like melting wax, the sneer sliding into a slack-jawed stare.

Tara had felt herself rise like fire, like air. She had almost laughed out loud. She had been staring at the monster through the wrong end of a telescope. How small he was, after all. She had turned on her heel and walked – no, floated – out of the cafeteria, and she had been floating ever since. That had been way back in July. It had been a summer of protest, painful growth and self-reclamation. It had brought her here, to this cell. It cushioned her now as she followed her solicitor through the dividing doors and into the foyer of the police station, where her mother and Lydia were waiting.

*

'Are you OK? What happened?' Shyama flung her arms around her daughter, shocked at how little of her there was to hold: no cushioned hips, no rounded belly, even her breasts felt sharp and confrontational.

Tara winced, pulling away from her mother's embrace.

'What's wrong? Are you hurt? She's got bruises . . . we have to take a picture.'

Shyama fumbled for her phone.

'We've already done that, don't worry.' The sharp-suited woman with blue-black skin and killer heels was holding out her hand to Shyama. 'Gina Trotter. Duty solicitor – and Lydia's friend.'

Lydia was standing a few paces away, watching. She and Shyama had barely spoken during their vigil at the station.

'Thank you so much for coming out,' Shyama began.

'No problem. Tara's free to leave, she hasn't been charged with anything yet, but she gave a very good statement.'

'Yet?' Shyama interrupted. She turned to Tara. 'What did you do?' She knew the moment it came out of her mouth that it sounded wrong.

Tara looked up at her wearily, then at Lydia, rolling her eyes. A small gesture that stabbed Shyama somewhere soft and hidden.

'She was arrested on a demonstration,' Gina filled in quickly. 'They did the usual mass round-up, but there's a lot of footage confirming the troublemakers and the ones who just got in the way. Thank God for mobile phones.'

'But will she . . . she won't go to court?'

Gina indicated that Shyama should accompany her out to her car, to talk her through the various legal processes that might follow.

Lydia joined Tara and held out a plastic bag. 'Got your stuff back. Are you hungry?'

'No, but I need a rollie . . .'

Tara fumbled for her papers and tobacco and, despite trembling fingers, expertly rolled a thin cigarette. She had never smoked in front of her mother before. She had always told herself it was a mark of respect, which made this smoke, she thought as she exhaled gratefully, somewhat symbolic.

'What did Mum say to you?' Tara asked as she removed a shred of tobacco from her tongue tip.

'Hardly anything.' Lydia shrugged. 'Obviously she was upset that you had called me first, and then when I told her you'd asked me to stay . . .'

'I'm glad you did, Auntie Lydia.'

Hearing her moniker from Tara's childhood brought a lump to Lydia's throat. She had always had a soft spot for this kid, firework-bright and pugnaciously curious, the kind of daughter she would have been proud to raise. She loved her mother, too, often reaching to call Shyama's number, especially since she had heard that she had returned with a surrogate in tow. But there had been so little contact between them since that spat in her kitchen that she wondered if she would still be welcome. Ridiculous, this was infants' school stuff – she's not my best friend any more, boo hoo. But Lydia understood all too well the complexity of women's friendships from the lives of those on her consulting couch; unconsciously, most women expected to be disappointed by a man at some stage of their lives, but when the betrayal came from another woman, it brought with it disbelief, outrage, a sour aftertaste. All this distance, because Lydia had been trying to straddle the impossible fence between a mother and a daughter, understanding how Tara felt, knowing that Shyama had no idea, not wishing to betray either of them. Now she realized she should have just treated them as she would any other clients: sat them opposite each other in a neutral space and encouraged them to talk. Fat chance of that happening now the baby mama was here. Lydia had her own theories as to why Shyama had wanted this baby so badly, because she had seen this kind of behaviour before – the desperate yearning of an older woman for a child and the obsessive lengths to which she will go to acquire one, both emotionally and financially. She'd seen it all: the older woman/younger man see-I'm-fertile-too baby; the last-chance-saloon baby when peri-menopause suddenly arrives; the empty-nest, don't-leave-me-on-my-own-with-my-husband baby; the classic glue baby when a long relationship begins hitting those old rocks of boredom and habit; the baby for the single professional woman who's fed up with waiting for Mr Right and wants one right now; and the always upsetting cases of those women who have put their bodies through years of medical torture, hoping for a miracle that doesn't arrive. Lydia's sympathies were always with the last group; with the others, she looked beyond the wished-for baby to what it actually symbolized – a barren marriage, a fear of abandonment, a refusal to face ageing and death. And it could take weeks, months, to break through this ovarian fever; you had to tread so delicately, picking your way through a minefield of unexploded ancient bombs, for there was nothing more primal, more personal, than the desire to carry a child. Lydia was glad to be free of it; she had laid her ghost babies to rest some time ago. But she had seen how it could change a woman. Watching Shyama now, deep in conversation with Gina, she missed her fiercely and wondered if she'd ever truly get her back.

'You need to tell your mum what's going on, Tara,' Lydia said quietly, enjoying the waft of tobacco smoke across her face.

'I've tried. There's never enough time to get beyond the shouting stage,' Tara murmured. 'She's got Mala now.'

'What's she like?' Lydia couldn't help but ask.

'As you'd expect. Young, poor, dependent. Perfect breeding stock.'

'Your mum went to a lot of trouble to bring her here, care for her. That must make the whole thing less . . .'

'Exploitative?' Tara threw her stub to the ground, extinguishing it with a grind of her heel. 'Come on, we both know this is fundamentally wrong. This is no different to the old crones who cut off girls' labia in the name of tradition, or the mothers who insist their daughters have their feet bound or marry their fat old cousins or stay in violent marriages, because if they had to suffer, why shouldn't all the others who come after them?'

'No, I don't think it's the same. . .' Lydia began.

'It's women once again exploiting other women!' Tara hissed back. 'Mainly because they want to keep some man happy. Mum's not doing this because she wants another kid, she's doing it so Toby won't leave her for somebody younger. You knew it, you tried to say it, and she's dropped you like she drops anyone who doesn't agree with her . . .' She was wiping away furious tears now.

Lydia extended a hand, which Tara batted away.

'Priya's met Mala . . . did you know?' Lydia asked quietly.

Tara shook her head.

'And she says she's smart and seems . . . content. Said she didn't strike her as a victim. No one forced her to be a surrogate.'

'Maybe no one did,' Tara said, wishing she could stem the tears that kept flowing like a warm river down her cheeks. 'But her poverty did. Her lack of choices. She has no idea that she's going to be paid a tenth of what any white woman in the West would be paid for the same thing, with laws and regulations to protect her. Why couldn't my mum just be happy with what she had?'

'Why can't any of us?' Lydia smiled sadly. She recognized

every word, every angry tear – she had been there at the same age, though never as eloquent as Tara, when the world lost its wonder and all you could see was what was wrong, what needed putting right. How she envied her, with all that righteous energy, the unshakeable belief that with enough marching and shouting and protesting the young could start to repair the mess they had inherited from the old and the cynical. Then one day, you woke up and you were old and cynical too, and you shared your bed with compromise and resignation and someone you loved not passionately but enough, whose snoring could bring down barricades. Tara would not understand why Shyama had done this, not whilst she lived in a world of black and white, right and wrong, not until she understood how much of life was, in actuality, shades of ever-shifting grey.

'Can I come home with you?' Tara asked finally.

Lydia glanced over at Shyama, who seemed to be finishing off with Gina, nodding earnestly whilst tapping notes into her phone.

'I don't think that's a great idea, sweetheart,' Lydia began.

Tara looked at Lydia, all her anger gone, her face drained by the queasy yellow of the neon street lights. Something jangled at the back of Lydia's head, the same sensation she would get when listening to a client telling one story when they actually wanted to scream another.

'Tara? Is there something else?' Concern made her blurt it out. 'Has anything happened? I mean, is there anything else you need to tell me?'

Tara dropped her gaze and zipped up her jacket, shivering slightly. When she looked back at Lydia, she seemed ten years older.

'Not now,' she said simply and walked off to join her mother.

*

297

Toby had resigned himself to not sleeping until they returned. On a whim, he had spent an hour browsing the internet for farmhouses in Suffolk, stunned by how much his parents' smallholding must now be worth. A million quid wouldn't get you more than forty acres plus a few outbuildings, though there was one property for sale he kept returning to, a substantial former rectory with its own small dairy and livery stables, with two converted barns which could be rented out to holiday-makers as the coast was a mere three miles away. He imagined himself running full-time stables and a riding school, with holiday accommodation offered on site. He'd checked out how much city folk would pay to stay on a real-life working farm – they apparently even wanted to muck in for free, all part of the authentic rural experience. Plus he could produce the sort of crumbly rustic cheeses that he saw sold for eye-watering prices at the local farmers' market every Sunday. There was just enough land to keep some pigs as well, so there were your organic sausages sorted. Once he'd got his share of his inheritance, even after repaying his debts, and chucking in the money they would get for the sale of this house, he could just about do it. It was a possibility, though he hadn't discussed it with Shyama yet. He knew how she felt about the countryside in general, but this was different, they would be running their own business. With her financial brain and his farming experience they could make a success of this, and she would never be bored – they would have visitors from all over, stopping them from feeling like inbred hicks cut off from civilization. And most importantly, their child would grow up like he had done, breathing clean air, eating fresh food, running around outside instead of being slumped over a screen all the time, like he was now.

The more he dwelled on this line of thought, the more excited he got. It might even be good for Tara, like a sort of detox haven, far away from the people and stresses that had landed her in the nick this evening. There was the more pressing issue of Sita and Prem, of course, but there would be plenty of room for them to come and stay for long stretches, and once their flat was finally sorted, they would probably be moving back to India anyway.

Toby wasn't used to ideas catching him unawares; he felt restless, his pulse racing with possibilities. It all made sense now. It wasn't farming he hated, it was the idea of working for his brother that had driven him away. And it was the reality of impending fatherhood that was now pulling him back.

Toby started at a gentle knock at the bedroom door.

'Toby sahib?'

He opened the door to Mala, who had a shawl thrown over her night-time shalwar kameez. His eyes were drawn to the obvious swelling of her belly, straining against the cotton material.

'Sorry to disturb . . . I heard Shyama Madam go out, long time ago. No problem?'

Her English was so fluid now. That jewel in her nose, he had always assumed she removed it at night, but there it was, catching the light reflected off the computer screen.

'No Mala, no problem. She's . . . gone to collect Tara from somewhere . . .'

Mala's gaze fastened on the computer, her eyes lighting up. 'Apple Mac, yes?'

Toby nodded dumbly.

'Shyama Madam says I should practise. Because they have same one in the salon. You know I am working there soon?'

Toby could hardly refuse this bare-faced request. Awkwardly, he stood to one side as Mala pushed her way past. She stood silently for a while, then pointed to the Suffolk property still on the screen. 'Very beautiful. You want to buy?'

Toby nodded again. He felt trapped, not just physically but also by his promise to Shyama. *Be nice.*

'It's just an idea at the moment . . . I grew up on a farm not too far from this house.'

'I also.' Mala smiled, her eyes never leaving the screen. 'Green everywhere around . . . corn, vegetables. I milk, um . . . *bainse*?'

Mala patted her body, her hand snaking into her top. Toby watched her small hands move beneath the cloth, glimpsed the dark shadow of her cleavage. He looked away, at his hands, his feet, anywhere.

'My dictionary . . .' Mala said. 'Downstairs. I don't know the word for . . .' She broke off, mimed a pair of horns above her head and emitted a bellowing sound so comically loud it shocked Toby into laughter.

'What was that?' he chortled. 'Don't tell me you milk elephants.'

'Elephants?' Mala was genuinely affronted until she realized. 'You are joking!'

'Sorry, but it sounded like something huge and in pain . . . too big to be a cow, obviously.'

'Not cow . . . *bainse* . . . I know this . . .' Mala was shaking her head, half amused, half annoyed with herself.

'Buffalo, maybe?'

Mala's face flooded with relief. 'Yes, buffalo! I milk buffalo. Very hard. They have bad temper. Like husbands.'

Toby laughed again. It was OK. It was working. This wasn't awkward at all.

Mala never meant to talk so much, but she was hijacked by so many memories of her childhood which she had never shared before. What was the point, with Ram? He had seen the same trees, the same wheat, stepped over the same piles of dung that she would have to collect and dry in the sun for fuel and to cover the walls in winter. She had been as free as any boy until her chum arrived. That was Mumbai speak – she had heard it on a chat show about women's health problems. Chum, a stupid word for the curse, which meant her ramblings around the village stopped overnight, as if the smell of her blood would bring all the menfolk slavering on their bellies to her feet. Why was it her fault if they couldn't control themselves, why couldn't they stay indoors instead? When she had asked her mother this very thing, she had got a hard tight slap.

But Toby sahib seemed to find everything she said fascinating. And *chalo*, maybe it was – his face lit up like a firefly as she described the journey of the warm milk straight from a teat to the earthenware pots, where it would be mixed with a few spoonfuls of old yoghurt and left overnight, wrapped in faded cloths, to form new yoghurt, clotting and creaming all by itself. And the rest of the milk was for the churn, which she would turn and turn, her arms burning like smouldering ropes, until finally it separated into two layers. On top – and her mouth watered at the memory – was that double-thick layer of white creamy curd which would be pat-patted into pure milky butter. Not like here, *hena*, she cautioned Toby – your butter is too yellow, too heavy in the gut. Ours is the lightest, on a hot roti it melts away to nothing, but you taste everything – even the grass the buffalo ate that morning. And underneath this crust is the water, tangy and full of clouds. You call it way? Oh, w-h-e-y. Not that way, this whey, yes? Hang it in a cloth, a very fine and light cloth . . . Muslim? Oh, mus-lin. Yes, only water can go through it. You hang it up with a bowl underneath. The next morning, in the cloth is cheese to make paneer – you know what that is, you have it here in your shops, but not like ours, not spongey-fresh, and in the bowl is a first-class health drink, see, nothing wasted! You just mix with salt and pepper and keep it cold as possible, no fridge, no ice, just somewhere dark inside. My father drank it every lunchtime, *gut-gut* in one go, and then he would pat his thin belly and say, 'Drink of kings!'

And here Mala paused, remembering her father, with his hard wiry arms and soft eyes and his smell, fresh sweat and soil and Brylcreem, how he used to look at her, as if she was something, as if she would be something. No one else had looked at her that way until now. There had not been a single man who had talked to her like this, as an equal, as if what she said was interesting and important. She knew these men existed. Obviously they were there in the movies and on TV, making cow eyes at their wives and lovers, breaking into song whenever their feelings of devotion got too much to bear, those moments when only a song and dance would do. But everyone knew they were only words: a script written on a page, lyrics that had to be learned, dance routines you had to practise until you could do every thrust and *balle!* with a smile. Everyone knew those men weren't real. But there were others, real-life good men, she had seen glimpses of them, like a woman in purdah through a trellis screen. Her papa. The couple she had seen on the train so long ago now, on her way to the clinic. After the husband had rubbed his wife's swollen feet, they shared a packet of peanuts. She fed him. They had a pretend argument – she wouldn't allow the hands that had touched her feet to touch the peanuts, so she placed each chillied salted nut on the tip of his tongue, he opening his mouth like a baby bird. They had talked in whispers and smiled together, whilst Mala had sat in tense silence with Ram. And then there was her sister's husband. Her own baby sister, whose marriage had been arranged just as hastily as hers had been, when she reached sixteen in turn. He was the son of a farm labourer; they worked less land than her family but were willing to accept less dowry from her mama, the unfortunate widow with two daughters burdening her. Her sister met the boy on the day of the marriage ceremony – their first view of each other was when they lifted the tinsel strands off his turban, which had been covering his face, and she raised her eyes from the floor. They had stared at each other with growing delight, like children given an unexpected present. They were children, after all. All the horrors they must have imagined about what kind of face the unveiling might reveal: frog-faced, squinty, toothless, half-witted, cruel. So they liked what they saw; good. But it was no guarantee, that's what Mala had thought grimly. Mr Filmi Face may have a nice moustache, but wait till you see it flecked with spittle when he's shouting at you, or drenched in sweat when he's grunting on top of you. Not so handsome then, *henu*?

But six months later, when the sisters met up again on a rare visit to see their ailing mother, Mala had seen it again. The same delight in each other, but this time shamelessly in front of everyone. All the neighbours noticed it, how the not-so-newlyweds would talk to each other as if no one else was in the room waiting to be respected, how they would swap little looks and smiles behind their elders' backs. Mala even caught them trying to sneak an embrace in the courtyard when her sister should have been serving tea. And her brother-in-law did not even have the decency to look ashamed, he thought it was funny! They giggled as he scuttled away, her eyes still on the space he had left, whilst Mala tried to shake some sense into her.

'Hasn't the novelty worn off yet, *oolloo*?' Mala had snapped, eighteen months into her own marriage and still feeling she was joined to a stranger who shared her bed.

'Oh, *didi*,' her sister had sighed. 'You never told me a husband can be like a friend. Like my best friend, he wants to talk about everything. And he asks me, *didi*, he wants to know what I think. He even tells his mother: God and you chose me the best wife ever. He's clever, you see? That way she feels special also, and then she is *sooo* nice to me. And he respects me sooo much . . . except at night, when I don't want him to!'

Mala had not been able to join in with the dirty talk that was allowed since they had become proper married *bwotis*. Who could laugh and do nudge-nudge when all she felt was jealousy, acid green and thorny, constricting her throat? *Chalo*, maybe I am cursed, she had thought on her way back in the overcrowded bus, or perhaps my sister is just blessed.

But now, talking with Toby sahib felt like some kind of blessing. Or a door opening, and beyond it, another land which she knew had been there all along but hadn't known how to reach. He asked her about the crops she had seen grow, the ploughs, the fertilizers. She told him how many farmer suicides there had been, those poor men offered money to use imported chemicals which brought bumper crops one year but killed the land off the next; no one had explained to them that, once poisoned, the soil would never return. So they poisoned or hanged themselves, knowing that their families might get some compensation for their early deaths. Toby sahib said the same thing was happening here, but much less, more hidden, no compensation. Living off the land was the hardest thing, they both agreed. She told him her ideas for Shyama Madam's salon, all the beauty treatments from the village if she could re-create them. Toby sahib told her you could find anything nowadays with a computer, and then showed her so many things on it. Then suddenly, they both heard the key in the lock downstairs. How late was it? Mala hauled herself to her feet, almost toppling in her haste to leave the room. Toby caught her by the wrist. Hai, his grip was strong.

'Mala,' he whispered, and downstairs they could both hear Shyama and Tara switching on the lights in the kitchen. 'This whole thing about the house . . . in the country . . . the one I showed you?'

Mala nodded, not daring to speak. She did not want to be found in here, but she did not want to leave either.

'Don't say anything to Shyama yet . . . it's a secret. Yes?'

'A secret,' Mala repeated. And then Toby sahib did something so surprising that she had no time to even stop him. He held her fast with one hand and placed his other, gently-gently, on her stomach. Mala could barely breathe; she felt her skin ripple beneath his touch, responding to its heat.

They both felt it at the same time, a fish tumble of a kick.

'*Theklo.* Your child knows you, Toby sahib.'

She couldn't help but say it. She had been repaying the kindness he had shown her, and it was true. Even when she lay in bed later, willing the baby to move again and it didn't, she was still convinced she had done the right thing. Now they had two secrets. And she would guard them as tightly as the child itself.

Her window was open, as it was most nights; she felt claustrophobic not being able to hear the night sounds, so different here, before she slept. At times the wailing of sirens could almost be mistaken for the ululations of distant peacocks, the gruff catcalls of beery youths on the pavement below were not so different from the drunken singing of the village men weaving their way back across the fields from their illicit moonshine hideouts. Hai, the moon! I don't miss much, Mala sighed to herself, but how could I ever have taken that for granted? No need even to put the lamps on when *chanda mama* was full and ripe, her light so thick it was like wading through silver water which drenched every pore. And then when she hid her face all the stars came out to play, the sparks in the eyes of the gods, and us below looking back up, always reminded that everything is connected.

That's what is broken here, Mala realized – the embrace between Nature and God and a person. My face looks the same as it did back home, maybe plumper, maybe a bit lighter, both good things, *hena*? But I know the connection is slowly going, I know what I will become soon. Don't I see it every day in the faces of the *desis* who shop in the Pakistani supermarket around the corner? All the people who come to a place where they are allowed to pinch and prod their vegetables, who look like me, until I ask how much is this aubergine, where is the channa daal kept? The look in their eyes, like a blank wall or a locked door or sometimes, yes, pity – poor freshie off the boat, feeling the cold and getting lost all the time, that was me once, long ago. Then the shutters come back down, closed for business, come again soon. But they have good clothes, nice houses, their children will do and see things they will never do. I understand, I'm not stupid – this is the price you pay for a better life. You forget the moon and you eat.

Even so, Mala remembered to place some sunflower seeds on her window-sill before she finally turned off her light. She thought she had seen a flock of green parrots swooping across the nearby park. Probably her imagination, but just the possibility had made her almost weep with longing. She wept a little more often these days, but always alone, and it passed quickly. *Chalo*, she had thought as she scattered a handful of stripy kernels across the ledge, if they are real, they will come.

# CHAPTER ELEVEN

I T WAS SURPRISING how quickly Mala settled into the routine at
Surya Beauty Salon. Shyama was glad to be back at work,
even more grateful that no one seemed to question the new
employee she had recruited from India whose job was to do light
assistant duties on the shop floor and work with Gita on testing
out some natural ayurvedic treatments. She was lying about the
ayurvedic bit but she knew it impressed the clients – better than
telling them they were going to chuck some leftovers together
from a village pantry and hope some of them worked.

Walking back into the buzz of the salon, a balmy September sun
turning every window to beaten gold, Shyama felt that familiar
tingle of pride. The place was still busy, still filled with multi-
lingual chatter and the ever-present background soundtrack of
the local Asian radio station, with its mash-up of old classics,
new rap-fusion hits and truly terrible ads for nearby businesses,
all voiced by the same hammy actor, who clearly wished he was
doing blockbuster-movie trailers but had to make do with extolling the merits of the Lahore Carpet Emporium and Beena's
Astrological Consultations: 'All marital, financial and exam trou-
bles welcome!'

None of her staff knew anything about the surrogacy situation
and Shyama wanted to keep it that way. Mala had already been

primed about what her back story was – 'Just say you are the daughter of one of my uncle's employees, if anyone asks' – and other than ensure that she was kept away from any heavy lifting or exposure to chemical fumes, Shyama left them to work out the rest of the routine together.

By the end of the first week, Mala had produced her first batches of facial scrub and body lotion. They had sent the staff off with samples and tested some themselves at home, much to Toby's amusement. Even Shyama's parents had joined in. There they all were, sitting at the table, Shyama and Sita's faces covered in bright-yellow paste, Prem dabbing uncertain fingers into the lotion like a man confronted with an alien artefact, and Toby taking photos on his phone, when Tara walked in. There was an intake of breath in the room. Why was it they all seemed to be scared of her lately? The ice was broken by Mala coming forward and dabbing a smear of turmeric goo on Tara's nose. Tara said nothing. She dabbed a finger across the paste and licked it. 'Needs more salt,' she said.

Mala pulled Tara on to a chair, her excitement so infectious that soon Tara was giving her detailed feedback, which Mala scribbled down in her new executive-style notebook, muttering to herself, repeating the new words in English, paraphrasing the meaning in Hindi. Shyama had more or less said everything Tara was saying now, but she didn't dare break this moment of connection between them.

'It really works, my skin feels amazing, but no one's going to buy anything that smells like mould . . . The lotion needs more oil, it's not being absorbed . . . See here, it's left a crust . . . See this thing on my skin?' Tara offered her arm up for Mala to inspect.

'OK, so . . . I think maybe rose oil? Good smell?'

'I hate roses,' Tara said dismissively. 'Too . . . girlie, you know? You want to go for something more unisex.'

'Uni-sex? More . . . naughty?'

Tara grinned. Oh, it was good to see her smile again.

'No, something that both men and women would like. Something more . . . woody? Lots of perfumes are for both now. More profits, right? You understand profit, I'm guessing . . .'

'Oh yes. I understand profit.' Mala nodded back at her.

Shyama realized Mala must be humouring Tara, bringing her in gently, trying to build bridges. She was doing a better job with her than Shyama had managed. Ever since Tara's arrest, they were no longer arguing, because her daughter met each attempt at conversation with polite formality. Shyama preferred the spats, missed them – at least there had been an emotional exchange. This polite indifference reminded her painfully of the last months of her marriage to Tara's father, when his infidelity had been confessed and validated. Yes, he loved the other woman; no, he wouldn't change his mind; no, of course he wouldn't fight for custody, what kind of a man did she think he was? One who didn't want a little girl getting in the way of his testosterone-fuelled shag-fest – that kind. Being polite was the only way Shyama could restrain herself from attacking him with a fork. But with Tara, it felt like a sudden bereavement, the withdrawal of barb and banter. No matter how much she kept trying, taking up cups of tea and snacks and hanging around the landing when she thought Tara might be at home, her daughter dismissed her with the same pleasant poker face. It didn't help that they were still waiting to see if the police were going to bring charges. Until then they lived in this limbo, waiting, as they were waiting for the baby to appear in a few months' time, both situations now out of their control. Nature and the law – both had their own rhythms and mysterious workings, unpredictable and inevitable.

And now, a mere month after Mala had tried out her first experimental batches on the family, it seemed that Shyama had a profitable sideline on her hands. At first the samples of scrub, lotion, hair-removing sugary peel, shampoo and conditioner had been offered as a complimentary gift to any woman who came into the salon. Shyama had sourced some pretty containers from one of her cash-and-carry contacts and Toby had painstakingly printed up labels listing all the natural ingredients, with some mystic descriptions extolling the virtues of products handed down through generations of village women and now available here, freshly made. Then women began coming in especially for the free samples, which quickly became non-free but were still vastly cheaper than any similar organic products. Then women came in wanting to have treatments incorporating the products – facials, body scrubs, massages – and ended up spending more time and money. Why not make a day of it and have the hair done also, Madam?

It was Priya's endorsement that really set the ball rolling. Shyama arrived at the salon one day to be greeted by her friend almost floating out of a consultation room, smelling of sandalwood, her hair still wrapped in a leopard-skin turban.

'Oh my God,' she breathed, 'I don't know what she's put in that facial, but my skin feels like a baby's arse . . . a few more of these and I can stop the Botox. And that lotion! Feel my arm, it's like I've drunk the blood of a virgin. I've got virgin-girl glow everywhere!'

Shyama, struggling with several boxes of gram flour and organic honey, declined the offer, managing to place the boxes on the counter before groaning as she stretched out her back.

'Oooh, you need Surya Spa Ginger and Pepper Massage Oil

rubbed into that, preferably by that hunky farmhand of yours,' purred Priya.

'Hunky farmhand has, I think, got a bad case of Couvade syndrome. He thinks he's pregnant,' winced Shyama, beckoning Priya into her small office at the back.

'Is he getting a sympathy pot belly and piles?' asked Priya, flumping into Shyama's chair. She always took Shyama's chair.

'Kind of. It seems to be more of a general hormonal grumpiness with Toby,' sighed Shyama. 'I wouldn't mind, but I'm not even the pregnant one.'

'Oh, he's probably getting the whole cold-feet-I'm-gonna-be-a-daddy shivers. Women worry about the pain, men get all weird about the responsibility. Am I going to be a good enough role model, provider, that sort of stuff. It's a good sign, though, shows he's really invested in the baby, no?'

Shyama didn't answer for a while. She wanted to tell Priya more, but she couldn't put it into words, this heavy sense of unease that had been seeping into her over the past few weeks. It wasn't just the lack of action in the bedroom – these things went in phases, she knew that, and in any case most nights she collapsed into bed wanting nothing more than to be held while she tried to breathe away the worries cobwebbing the far corners of her mind. If anything, she should be feeling lighter, more reassured. Mala was settled, in fine health, busy and happy with her new hobby. Toby seemed to be getting over his initial stiffness with Mala, and at least Tara was civil towards her now. After a long time, she could see that they could be a family, an oh-so-modern, blended, rainbow-hued, outsourced, chucked-together temporary family, but one nevertheless, who could just get on with life together. So why did she feel so tired all the time? Why did the sight of her parents, silver-haired, walking up the garden hand-in-hand, bring a lump to her throat? Why did the discovery of a bundle of Tara's baby photos in the back of a drawer make her weep so much that she had to lock herself in the bathroom and sob into a towel? Maybe she was having a sympathy pregnancy too, although the one person she really felt sorry for was, bizarrely, herself.

'You have to get this stuff out there . . .' Priya was talking and probably had been for some time as she took a selfie and began tapping buttons on her phone.

'Right, I've just tweeted about Mala's stuff to a couple of journalists I know, they'll come sniffing round . . . What does she put in there? Can't just be what it says on the bottles . . .'

'It is, I think . . . I mean, I buy all the stuff, it's all natural . . . I suppose it's the way she puts it together, I'm not sure,' Shyama replied, distracted by the now constant buzzing of Priya's phone.

'Aha, wants to keep the magic to herself, eh? Wise woman. Which, of course, is just another name for a witch . . .'

And that was that. After Priya's social-media campaign, everything seemed to happen at breakneck speed. Shyama quickly had to train up a couple of extra girls to handle the swell of clientele for the new Surya Spa range and suddenly they had a waiting list on a daily basis for Mala's cottage industry. She also had to employ someone full time on the reception desk and get used to having her kitchen taken over every night by Mala, supervising her bowls, mortars and jars of unmarked liquids and granules like a corpulent conjuror, muttering incantations to herself.

Shyama was worried that all the extra work would put a strain on Mala's ever-advancing pregnancy, but if anything, she seemed to be thriving on the pressure and bustle of activity. Now Shyama understood why it was called the bloom of motherhood;

Mala's face, her whole body, gave off a warm sensuality, open and inviting as unfolded petals. Heads turned, like sunflowers following the light, when she walked down the street or through the salon with that Indian-woman wiggle that Shyama had never been able to perfect. 'They will always know that you are a foreigner,' her mother had told her in India when Shyama's attempt to haggle down a trader had been laughingly dismissed. 'Your hips give you away, you walk like you only walk on concrete.' Shyama had wanted to say that she had seen plenty of hard-stepping women on the streets of Delhi, striding their way to their offices, that only women who had nothing much to do or laboured in sweltering heat ambled with that somnolent sway, but that would have shattered the myth of how all dusky maidens balance the *Kama Sutra* between their thighs.

Mala was young, that was most of her appeal, and the joy of gaining her independence and having the best of care would make any woman happy. And if Shyama occasionally suspected Mala of playing to the crowd somewhat, tossing her now unbound and styled hair so it tumbled around her shoulders like a shampoo ad, embroidering her ever-evolving village anecdotes with more scandal so the girls in the salon gasped and covered their mouths in wonder, stretching her back whilst she held court so her stomach rose proudly before the world to take centre stage, undeniable proof of the life force surging within her, well, all was forgiven. Whilst she carried her child – their child – Shyama had no choice but to smile and let it go.

Her tolerance levels, however, had been severely tested at their last scan. Their obstetrician had called Mala in at thirty weeks, wanting to keep a check on the baby's weight. Nothing to worry about, he had assured them, but given they were private patients, why not pay to stop the worry? So this time Toby had eagerly accompanied the women and he and Shyama had walked in hand-in-hand like a proud couple, Toby offering his arm for Mala to lean on as she lowered herself on to the sonographer's couch. Even for a man like him, used to the mundane stages of animal procreation, it seemed to be overwhelming. He stared at the neon-blue screen for some time, his jaw working steadily to keep control. For Shyama, it was a shock, seeing how much the baby now looked like a little person – the toes, the eyelashes, the softly sucking mouth.

'He's amazing,' Toby said finally, and then, 'Sorry, didn't mean to say "he". It just came out . . .'

'Anyway, it doesn't matter,' Shyama murmured. 'We don't really want to know. We're just grateful that—'

'He *is* a boy,' Mala interrupted. 'You don't have to tell me. I know.'

Shyama stared at Mala, who smiled back at her, innocence itself. She wavered under Shyama's questioning gaze, looked at Toby for reassurance.

'Sorry, Shyama Madam, should I not say . . . ?'

'No, it's fine, Mala,' Toby soothed her. 'You'd know better than us, that's for sure. Is she right, by the way?'

Shyama stiffened, glancing at the sonographer, who looked from her to Toby to Mala, assessing what must have been an unusual situation for her. She must know, she must realize that Shyama and Toby were the ones who counted here.

'She is spot on,' the sonographer beamed back at Toby. 'It's a boy.'

Toby would never admit it, but this was the moment that he fell in love. Not the hearts-and-flowers kind, the dizzying rush that had flung him headlong into Shyama's arms six years ago, but the kind of love that enables a parent to lift a car off a child or rush into a burning building. Neither would he admit that the primal surge he felt flooding his veins had anything to do with the fact that he was going to be the father of a boy-child. But it was there, the thrill pulsing through him every time he said to himself, 'That's my son. My son.'

Shyama didn't have the expected altercation with Toby when they returned home, somehow the fight had gone out of her, and his delight was so tangible it brought them together. They made love, they talked into the night, old times buoyed up by new news. Good news – a boy meant Tara would still be the only daughter, her place intact. Still, they both decided not to share the information with her or Shyama's parents, not yet.

'Won't they gucoo when we paint the nursery blue?' Shyama teased Toby, running her hands over his stubble, so fair you would only know it was there by touch.

'The nursery?' Toby asked.

'Well, once Mala's gone, that's the obvious room for our boy.' She listened to Toby breathing in the silence.

'Well, that makes it sound very . . . stark,' he said eventually.

'Stark? She's only got ten weeks until she has the baby, and then—'

'What, we just shove her back on a plane?'

'Well . . . obviously she'll need to recover first . . . but her visa's only for six months, and anyway, if we'd stayed in India . . .'

'But we're not in India, are we?'

'No, but if we were, she would have just handed him over and *we* would have got on a plane. Would that have made it any worse?'

'Not for us, Shyama, no.'

Disorientated for a moment, Shyama disentangled herself. She could hear Tara talking loudly in Hindi up in her room – she must be on Skype again. She was getting good. The conversation sounded intense; once Tara was on a roll, she was unstoppable. Shyama wished she was down here now, next to her, on her side. Though she wasn't sure when the sides had actually appeared.

'I think you're forgetting whose idea it was to bring Mala over here,' she cautioned Toby.

'No I'm not, I'm just—'

'Who set her up in a job? Which she's making a success of, by the way.'

'Actually, I wanted to talk to you about that, Shyams . . .'

Shyama sat up and switched on the bedside lamp. Toby blinked in the unexpected glare, his eyes briefly dropping to her naked, exposed body before he turned away, reaching for a glass of water. But not before Shyama had seen something on his face. What? Disappointment? Embarrassment? She'd stopped going to Pilates ages ago, had let her gym membership lapse last month. There was so much to do and she'd thought all the running around heaving boxes and managing the rush at the salon would keep her fitness levels up. But she'd noticed it herself, the slackening of her muscle tone, especially on her upper arms. She had wings, but not ones that would fly her anywhere nice. She'd even neglected her red highlights, despite the fact that Gita kept trying to push her into a chair every time she passed, to redo them. Now they had all but grown out, just the ends of her hair were tipped with colour like the last embers of a slowly dying fire. And with Mala's delicious curries on offer every night or lurking in the fridge, she hadn't been surprised by the extra roll of flesh on her stomach. She quite liked the feel of it, squidging against her waistband – it felt like protection. During her marriage to Tara's father she had been numb from the neck down for most of the time. With Toby, spring had invaded her every pore, the rebirth spectacular after a long winter. And now this: reaching self-consciously for the sheet before he turned around again, an adolescent covering-up for a woman of her age. The absurdity of it. Surely they weren't going to sink into that tired cliché: young man wearies of old flesh. She knew him better than that. And he must know that if she sniffed any scent of that on him, she would fight it with every ageing tooth and nail.

'I hope you're not going to tell Mala to give it up.'

'Quite the opposite.' Toby drained his glass. 'I'm assuming her products are good for business.'

'Amazing,' Shyama admitted. 'We've never done better, not over such a short period . . .'

'So you will be giving her a share of the profits, obviously?'

It should have been obvious but it hadn't crossed her mind. Shyama had been too focused on the practicalities to think about long-term division of the spoils.

'I haven't discussed it with Mala yet . . .' she began.

'Of course she wouldn't have asked, she doesn't think that way,' Toby interrupted. 'But it's only fair – it will set her up for the future. So sending her back won't feel like we're just . . . you know – thanks for your womb, see you later . . .'

'Of course not, no. I mean, yes, that's fair.'

She wasn't sure if she found it stupid or just touchingly naïve that Toby assumed Mala would not already be thinking that way. Poverty had brought her into their lives – she was an economic migrant, not a charity-giver. Of course she would have asked about her share of the profits eventually. Of course, eventually, Shyama would have offered. To engage in any kind of prolonged discussion with Toby now, she knew, would make her seem mean, exploitative even. They swiftly agreed that once

317

their costs were covered, Mala should get three-quarters of any profits made, Shyama keeping the rest for backing and housing the project, and hopefully continuing it in some form after Mala returned to India. It wasn't what happened on *Dragons' Den* – the entrepreneurs who took on some beginner's bright idea often took at least half of the profits – but as Toby pointed out, Mala was their fairy godmother too. Without her, their son would still be a beautiful idea waiting to happen.

With the increase in orders, Shyama offered to help Mala with the nightly preparations, but she refused, in the sweetest manner possible.

'Thank you, Shyama Madam, but I can do it fine. I like to be alone. It is good relaxing for me, *hena*?'

And yet often Shyama would come downstairs and find Toby – and, more often, Tara – sitting in the kitchen with Mala, helping to bottle and jar up the freshly made cosmetics or taking them to the extra fridge they had bought for storage which now sat in the garden shed. Whilst she was always welcomed in, she felt like a gatecrasher. They seemed to have more fun without her. When she mentioned this to Toby, he looked genuinely puzzled.

'It's your kitchen, Shyams. You can come in any time you want. I mean, she never asks us to help, we just end up hanging out.'

Shyama tried it one evening, just sitting with them all at the table. The usual cooking smells of garlic and frying onions had been replaced by heady wafts of jasmine and citrus, mingling with the warmth of the gently heating pans. Fragrant steam filled the space. It felt cosy, female.

Toby sat filling in paperwork, a chunk of maleness in the corner, lifting his head every so often to listen or throw in a sentence. He reminded her of a full-bellied daddy lion lolling

318

amongst his pride. Shyama's attempts at conversation were soon edged out by Tara and Mala's constant stream of chatter, Mala speaking in English, Tara usually responding in Hindi, each of them correcting the other. No wonder they were both getting so proficient, this was their classroom and they were both teacher and pupil. Shyama felt envious and a little redundant. Why hadn't she paid more attention when Sita had tried to encourage her to speak Punjabi, Hindi? Anything would have been better than the very little she had acquired. How ironic that her daughter would end up practically fluent while she could only speak a halting schoolyard mother tongue.

But something wonderful had also happened: Tara seemed to be coming back to them, slowly slowly. She was shedding whatever shrivelled and mysterious cocoon she had been wrapped in for months and was emerging scale by scale, feeling her way forward in her sensitive new skin. The dark bags under her eyes had disappeared and she had filled out a little – hadn't they all? Her hair was still short but less severe now, and her smile reached her eyes, which looked at her mother more often now, shyly, sideways.

Mala declared she had done enough for this evening; massaging her lower back with one hand, she watched benignly as Toby and Tara cleared away the used utensils and packaging. It seemed to be a well-rehearsed drill. After heating herself a cup of warm milk – she didn't need to ask permission now, the kitchen was her domain – Toby offered his arm to escort her to bed.

'Someone's got to help the fat lady up the stairs,' he joked.

Shyama tried to ignore the darts of envy jabbing at her ribs. It wasn't Mala – it was the baby. She must be more exhausted than she thought. She probably just needed a good night's sleep.

And then she was alone in the kitchen with Tara, who was offering her a cup of something herbal.

'It's ginger and cardamom, one of Mala's concoctions. In about half an hour, you will do the best burps you've ever done in your life . . .'

As Shyama took it, she could feel tears welling up again. Good God, maybe this was the menopause or something, she had to get a grip. And yet this small gesture cracked something inside her, opening a fissure in the wall of the dam, and behind it she could glimpse the ocean waiting to rush through. How long had she been waiting for this? All of this? This life in this kitchen with a man and a grown-up child and another child waiting to be born . . . now it was all so close, and she had to hold on just a little longer.

'So, it's good news, isn't it?' Tara looked up expectantly from her steaming cup. Seeing Shyama's puzzled face, she said, 'Gina did call you, didn't she?'

'I haven't checked my phone . . . so they . . .'

'They've decided not to press charges. I thought they wouldn't. Not with all the footage we had. Good job the crew had my back . . .'

Tara didn't get much else out. Shyama had her arms around her, both their mugs splashing hot liquid.

'Mum!' Tara said, half annoyed, half laughing, managing to grab the mugs and get them to the table.

'Oh thank God . . . thank God . . .' was all Shyama could manage, muffled against Tara's neck.

'Thank Gina and social media, actually,' Tara said chirpily, gently extricating herself, thrown by Shyama's stricken face. 'Were you really worried then?'

'What do you think? You could have ended up in prison.'

'Very unlikely, on this charge. First offence and all that.'

'Well, at least you could have ended up with a criminal record,

320

Tara! That would have followed you round all your life! Every time you applied for a job or a visa, or—'

'Mum, if convicted paedophiles and terrorists and celebs with drug convictions can get about as easily as they do, I think I would have been all right, don't you?'

'No, I don't! I think . . .' Shyama took a deep breath. Tara was here, talking to her, being happy. Don't spoil it again. 'I'm just relieved for you, baby girl. That's all.'

'Baby girl . . .' Tara repeated with a gentle laugh. Her face softened, something flitted across it that made another crack in Shyama's wall, and then it was gone again. 'Talking of babies . . . not long until my little brother arrives then?'

'You . . . how did you . . . did *she* tell you?'

'Mala?' Tara blew on her tea, took a small sip. 'I made her. It was obvious she knew . . . she made me swear not to tell you that she'd told me. You can see why that was getting complicated, so here we are, sharing in the kitchen. Just like on *Jeremy Kyle*, except no one has to take a DNA test this time, I hope . . . I guess you did all that back at the clinic in India, right?' Tara looked up when Shyama made no reply. 'You're not annoyed, are you?'

'No, no . . . It's just . . . We were going to wait until—'

'Until what? I assumed I'd be one of the first people you would want to tell. I'm fine about it now, anyway.'

'Are you? Really?'

Tara put her mug down again, warming her hands on it. She had written something on the back of her left hand. The ink had faded slightly, but Shyama could make out a few random letters and the word Shakti, or maybe Shanti?

'Mala's . . . something else. I was a bit of a shit to her before, I know that was just that old thing we do, taking it out on a sister when we can't see the bigger picture of . . .

321

patriarchy and exploitation . . . and then there's the whole legacy of colonialism and the infrastructure of the caste system. I mean, it's complicated . . .'

The words sounded a little rehearsed to Shyama, but she didn't dare interrupt.

'Anyway, it's been . . . it's been amazing . . . and humbling, and really hard, hearing about her life back in India . . . everything she's been through. God, we have it so easy here, don't we?'

Shyama could have said that 'easy' was a relative term – her life didn't feel especially easy at the moment – but she recognized that feeling a bit lost and weepy wasn't a fair comparison with being hungry and dispossessed, so she wisely held her tongue again.

'I'm still not sure it's right, what you're doing . . . but I can see it's going to change Mala's life so much and she says anything is better than what she had before . . .'

'Well, I . . .' Shyama felt safe to talk now, but Tara held up a hand.

'No, this is the important bit. What you've done for her now – bringing her over, helping her do her beauty stuff, the money you're going to give her – that makes it better. You've done the decent thing, Mum. That's how everyone should live, isn't it?'

Sita had been observing the developments in the new family unit with some misgivings, but she had her own urgent preoccupations to deal with – namely that the eviction date for their illegally occupied flat had been brought forward to 1 November, and suddenly they were going through the familiar routine of booking the cheapest air tickets they could find and dragging out the suitcases from under their bed. But this time it was different, this time they would be going with fire in their bellies and an end in sight to this whole *tamasha* – no, that was too easy a word, it was not just a fuss or complication. She could not think of a word in Punjabi or English that could possibly sum up what the last twelve years had been like for them, had done to them. It had been a slow-acting toxin, poisoning every good memory they had cherished of place and family. The final chapter of a long story, with no happy ending for anyone. Relations would be broken off for ever with that branch of the family – throwing their own flesh and blood out on to the street, how could they? She could foresee the wailing from Yogesh and Neelum, how they would claim they would have got their children to move if there had been somewhere suitable for them to go (never mind the two other properties they owned), and now this – the rich relatives who had so much, acting like the Empire itself, marching in and evicting the Indians from their own soil! See if I care, Sita muttered fiercely to herself as she carefully listed and packed all the medications they had to take along with them for every trip. In the old days, Prem's status as second-eldest brother who had bankrolled all his siblings' weddings from abroad would have counted for something. Now what were they? The idiot NRIs who had handed over their keys, never suspecting that the door would be shut in their face.

Prem rode this unexpected turn of events with his usual good-natured stoicism. 'The sooner the better, *nahin*, Sita? We could move in and have our first Diwali in the flat.'

Sita made vague noises of agreement. Diwali was just two weeks away. Who knew what would happen, whether they would set fire to the place out of spite before leaving – she had heard of such things. When it came to kin fighting kin, all common sense and decency got trampled underfoot; all those weasly namastes and tearful touching of the elders' feet were all for show. When it came down to defending and claiming land and home, everyone became an unknown savage. Sita hoped this would be their last legal battle, the last time they had to pack their bulging files of paperwork amongst their underwear and towels. Prem was slowing down, she could see it. So was she, probably, but you never noticed it happening to yourself. As in everything else, they were each other's changing reflection. The halting walk, the thinning hair, the shaky hands, the dimming eyes – she noticed it all in her husband, so he must be seeing it in her. Now she understood why they called it the sands of time: their youth together had been a long unspoilt beach stretching before them; they had grabbed handfuls of it and thrown it to the wind. Now she felt she could count every golden speck left to them as it slipped grain by grain through their entwined hands.

'But Mama, you will be back in time, won't you?' Shyama had fretted. She had called her Mama. She must be worried.

'In time for . . .' Sita trailed off. How could she have forgotten? 'Of course, we will be back before the baby comes. We have an eviction date; we just have to appear in court to confirm we agree, *bas*. Also we can't afford to stay much longer than a month, not this time . . .'

Prem had thought it wise to forgo staying with his elder brother on this visit. They didn't want any of the extended family to have any hint of why they were back again. Even though Sheetal and Sunil would have been served an eviction notice (which of course they would ignore), they would have no idea whether or when it would be enforced. Ravi Luthra, their lawyer, had advised them that surprise was the key, literally.

'You see, Sita-ji, if the miscreants suspect their removal is imminent, they could change the locks, barricade the doors and we are stuck. The bailiffs are not allowed to break and enter the property, understand? They have to be allowed inside. But once they get in, then we are hitting a six right out of the park, slam dunk, or back of the net as you say in England, isn't it?'

Sita couldn't remember ever saying such a stupid thing, but nevertheless, Prem had booked them a room in a modest hotel equidistant from Ravi's office and the flat. Yet more money they should not have to be spending, fumed Sita, but after this, they could finally close their wallets. Of course, she did not mention to Prem the large wad of sterling that she had secreted between her two best saris for the bribes she knew would have to be handed over on the actual day, but she intended to give that job to Ravi himself. They had come too far to go all shy and English now.

Shyama had once seen a sad-faced stuffed monkey tied to the front of a refuse truck as it roared its way down her narrow street. That's how she felt now: lashed to a juggernaut that was hurtling its way towards Mala's due date of 14 December, and towards the Christmas build-up when she knew business at the salon would reach manic levels. And on top of that, she had begun to panic about having nothing ready for this unnamed, unborn boy. She had forgotten everything she must have known when she gave birth to Tara nearly twenty years ago. She could just about remember how to change a nappy, but how often did you actually feed a baby when you weren't breastfeeding on demand, as she had done before? Would Mala insist on feeding him? Or would they get her to express milk so she and Toby could have that shared experience? Would Mala mind being milked like a prize cow? Should she even care that Mala might mind, because if they'd been in India, she would have had no say in the matter.

A quick dash around the local department store's baby section left her breathless and baffled; there were so many gadgets now.

Luckily, a smiling sales assistant seemed to be following her around. Eventually Shyama turned to face her.

'Anything I can help you with today?'

'Er, I'm just . . . I need a start-up package really,' said Shyama.

'How long before baby's due?' the assistant enquired.

'Um, about seven weeks, I think . . .'

'Oh you've got time. Pretty much everything here is in stock and the longest wait on ordered items is three weeks. So is it a grandchild you're waiting for?'

'Pardon?' stammered Shyama.

The woman's expression barely rippled. 'Or maybe a niece or nephew? We have a lovely range of Gifts from Grandma, Auntie or Godmother, all very personal . . . if you'd like to follow me?'

Shyama would have liked to buy the Peppa Pig baby thermometer and stuff it into one of the assistant's orifices, but instead told her she had been very helpful and that she would come back later with Grandpa. On the way home, she put Priya on speakerphone and regaled her with the whole story and they both laughed so much that she almost missed her turning home.

'Cheeky mare! Although, fair dues, you could have been a child bride, because "They do that in your culture, don't they?"' Priya snorted.

'And I thought Mala's face masks were actually doing some good! Maybe she's given me the reject batch, the ones that age you instead.'

'Does this all feel incredibly weird now?' Priya asked, sounding like she was at the end of a wind tunnel.

'Oh, I think we've redefined weird, don't you?' Shyama replied. She noticed that a couple of the pound shops already had tinsel edging their windows. One window display featured a gaggle of ugly dancing reindeer. December the fourteenth. D-Day. Due date. By the time every one of those Rudolphs had been unwrapped and broken, she would be holding her son.

'Thanks for listening to me bleat on. I needed to laugh. And now I need to wee.'

'Welcome to the golden years,' Priya deadpanned. 'I'm booking you in for the first weekend in December. We will go to John Lewis and kit you out with anything we can't borrow or beg from mates and contacts. Don't worry about being ready. Who's ever ready for a baby? And at least you won't be worrying about cracked nipples and stitches when yours arrives. You will be looking rested and lovely, and yes, very very young. There's got to be some advantages to doing it this way, right?'

She was only a few streets from home when she got a call from Tara.

'Mum, are you free? Can you come and meet me?'

'What, now?'

'It's . . . sort of urgent.'

Shyama didn't need to be asked again. It was a rare enough call, and for Tara to reach out to her with something urgent . . .

She had been through every possible scenario by the time she reached the Bluebird Café, tucked away in an alleyway between two trendily reclaimed warehouses not far from Tara's college: an STD, nervous breakdown, drugs, being thrown off her course, a broken heart. As far as she knew, Tara had never had a boyfriend. Or girlfriend, for that matter. She couldn't have guessed what was coming in a million years.

'Sorry, say that again?'

Shyama's elderflower fizz remained halfway to her lips. She

was surrounded by students tapping constantly on their laptops and tablets; leaflets for yoga classes and upcycling requests were stuck on the noticeboard behind Tara's head.

'I'm not dropping out, it's an assignment. For my second-year dissertation. Did you know I'm on a steady first in all my modules?'

Shyama swallowed. She could still feel bubbles bursting at the back of her nose and throat.

'I'll only be gone three months maximum. It was all they'd allow me and even then I had to plead for a special dispensation. You've always wanted me to spend some time in India, Mum, and with Nanima and Nana being there, it seemed the perfect time to go.'

Except they both knew it meant Tara would not be at home for the birth.

'So what exactly will you be doing there? Where will you stay? How will you pay for this—'

'Assignment,' Tara finished her sentence. She was beginning to sound impatient. It didn't seem there was any room for negotiation here. She wasn't asking her mother, she was informing her.

'OK. I'm going to be shadowing an organization called Shakti, a women's activist group based in South Delhi, and filming their work, which I will present as a finished documentary for my dissertation. Secondly, I'm going to be staying at Nanima's hotel to start off with, and then hopefully I'll find somewhere through the women I'm going to be working with . . .'

'Sweetheart,' Shyama interrupted, 'it's not like London. Most women your age still live at home—'

'I still live at home, Mum.'

'You know what I mean. A woman living alone out there . . . it's a different mindset. You need family, not colleagues.'

'I've got family there if I need them. Thaya-ji's not far. I won't be alone. I'll find a flat-share or a hostel if I have to. I could even live in Nana's flat once it's empty . . .'

'And Nanima and Nana suggested that, did they?'

'They said they'd pay for wherever I end up. As long as it's safe.'

Shyama blinked. They had arranged this whole thing without even consulting her. And then another thought wormed its way to the surface.

'Did you talk to Mala about this? Was it her idea?'

Tara shifted in her seat. Of course she had discussed this with Mala. It was partly all her stories about her village, her husband, the fate of so many other women she knew that had inspired Tara to go out there, to do something practical instead of sitting in her room raging at her computer. But she knew her mother wouldn't understand any of this; all she would feel was betrayal, when for Tara, this trip was some kind of absolution. She needed to purify herself and the only way to do that was to give something pure back, balance the abusive act she had endured by fighting abuse elsewhere. If her mother had been younger, if she could remember how it felt to be almost twenty, a half-formed woman finding her way in the world, she would have given her blessing. But she was looking older nowadays. The pale autumnal sunlight filtering through the steamed-up windows picked out fine lines around her eyes and on her forehead, a slight tugging at the corners of her mouth giving her face a melancholy air that hadn't been there before all this surrogacy malarkey. It came to Tara then, a dull realization that this was the price they both had to pay: her mother had chosen to start all over again with a new baby, nappies and nurseries and playdates and homework and music lessons and sports days and exams and only being able to book holidays in the most expensive season, her whole life shifting on its axis to revolve around the sun, the son. All Tara's other friends had mothers who were planning travels with their grown-up daughters, spa breaks and walking holidays and theatre trips. Hers would be far too busy. It wasn't Mala who had pushed her out of the nest, it was her own mother. And, Tara suspected, maybe this was the only way that she would truly learn how to fly.

'This has nothing to do with Mala, Mum. It's what I need to do. Anyway, you'll be too busy with . . . With everything else going on, you won't even notice I'm gone.'

Tara had been given strict instructions to leave her luggage in the hallway the night before they were to fly to Delhi. It was an early start. Toby knew everything would take twice as long with Shyama's parents in tow so he'd asked them to do the same.

Tara set her single canvas holdall down next to her grand-parents' battered suitcases. She wondered if they were the same ones they'd arrived with fifty years back, with their dodgy brass locks and the bright scrap of scarf that Nanima always insisted on tying to the handles, 'So they don't get mixed up with anyone else's.' No one else would risk transporting their belongings in these creaky old bags, but Prem and Sita held on to everything – clothes, kettles, ironing boards – until they literally died of old age, fusing the house or splintering beneath their touch.

Shyama had been shocked at how little Tara was taking, but she'd explained that she wanted to be able to move around unencumbered by too much stuff.

'Shakti have a lot of rural outreach work going on, I may end up on the road quite a bit . . .'

That ensured Shyama packed a couple of extra packets of

diarrhoea tablets for her; if travelling with the contents of a pharmacy made her mother feel a bit better, Tara would do it. She could afford to be magnanimous, she was leaving.

She didn't want to switch on any lights. All was quiet and dark downstairs, and there was no sound from her mother's room. The street lamps outside were bright enough. As she turned to go back up to her room, she heard the faint creak of a floorboard behind her.

'Tara?'

Mala stood beside her, her finger already on her lips, gesturing towards the open door of her bedroom. Only when they were inside and the door was firmly shut did she flick on the bedside lamp. Tara hadn't been in this room since Mala had moved in. It didn't look as if anyone actually stayed here, it was so neat and clean, with the feel of a recently serviced hotel room. There was a new cork board hanging on the wall near the bed. Toby must have put that up. Pinned to it were treatments lists from the salon, articles cut out from magazines on various beauty products, and the faces of assorted female celebrities marked with Mala's spidery writing, with arrows pointing to their eyebrows, lips, mouths. And, more surprisingly, estate agent details for a number of properties – some local flats, others grand detached houses way out of any normal person's price range, and most definitely Mala's. What struck Tara was that amongst all the information, there was not one article even vaguely related to pregnancy or babies.

'Sorry to disturb, Tara . . . you will mind taking these to India for me?' Mala handed her a couple of letters, both unstamped. 'I have no Indian stamps . . . I give you money for them?'

'No, that's fine, Mala, I can cough up for a couple of stamps.'

'Cough up?' Mala cocked her head to one side.

331

She's like a little sponge, thought Tara, greedy to absorb every-thing. There was a hunger emanating from her so palpable it seemed to fill the room. You could get sucked down into those eyes.

'It means I can pay, no problem.' Tara took the letters from her. They were thin, one sheet maximum.

'My mother. And my sister. They maybe think I am dead.' Mala shrugged. 'But I don't say about the baby. I say I have a job here.'

'And did you tell them when you're going back?'

Mala looked at her steadily. A noise at the open window made Tara look round, and she let out an involuntary gasp. Perched on the window-sill, its wings fluttering for balance, was a bright-green parrot with a scarlet gash of a beak. Spooked by Tara's exhalation, it flew off again in a whirr of feathers, a solitary mournful shriek fading into the night.

'I'd given up seeing one up close,' breathed Tara. 'Been trying for months to get one to visit my ledge. What's your secret?'

'Sunflower seeds. Or maybe he wants to talk. He finds some-one else far away from home.'

The night before the eviction, Sita couldn't sleep. She sat on the small balcony of their hotel – maybe guest-house was a more accurate description as there was no fancy lobby or communal restaurant, but the rooms were clean and airy and theirs over-looked a small park, where she counted the poor and homeless slipping through a gap in the railings to find a corner to sleep for the night. Scrawny men and women holding sleeping children and their thin rolls of bedding, as silent as ghosts flitting through the semi-darkness, seeking a hidden spot where the night-watchmen or some passing policeman wouldn't spot them. It was a nightly ritual. In the few days she and Prem had been in India, Sita had seen the same family groups infiltrate the park.

She was getting to recognize them: the toothless man with hair dyed bright orange from an over-enthusiastic application of henna, with his limping wife and three small children who followed them in a blank-eyed raggle-taggle through the railings. The young couple, she heavily pregnant, whose clothes always seemed clean and pressed, her hand always holding her sari end over her face as if the shame of sleeping rough compelled her to hide her identity. And occasionally, a courting couple would dare to scamper under the low hanging branches and exchange fevered kisses, desperately pulling themselves into each other's bodies and mouths. Sita felt sorry for them. *Vichare*, they probably both lived at home, where else could they go? In her day, you waited until you had taken your seven steps around the holy fire before you even dared to hold hands; maybe that's why parents tried to get their children married so quickly. They knew Nature would not wait. The young would always sniff each other out, find the secret places on the street, in each other.

Inside the room, Sita could hear Prem's usual symphony of irregular snores. He was exhausted. They had spent the whole day with Ravi Luthra, going over last-minute plans which he seemed to have arranged with impressive precision: meet at eight a.m. two streets away from their flat, where ten hired labourers, the bailiff and his two assistants and two police officers would all be joining them, hopefully.

'Only we are not sure about the policemen. If some emergency comes up, well, they cannot stop chasing criminals to come to a routine eviction.'

Sita knew this meant they wanted more money. So be it, she had it, all in rupees now, rolled up in a sponge bag. Prem had the official fees in his wallet: let him feel he was in charge, that he was doing the right thing, after all.

Ravi continued reading from his notes, looking up at them for occasional emphasis. 'There are certain rules we must follow, otherwise the whole thing could be abandoned on legal grounds. Firstly, we can only gain access if we are allowed in without breaking and entering. This means they cannot prevent us from entering once the door is opened. But if they lock themselves in, we will need another application for forcible entry – that is much harder to get. Secondly, when we get in, each of you must occupy a room to prevent them locking any doors. If they lock any room, we cannot legally gain access to it. You will have to remain in each room until all their possessions have been safely removed on to the street. Thirdly, there must be no physical contact that they could claim was violence. If you touch them roughly, for example, they can then claim they were manhandled into leaving . . .'

'May I just ask something?' Prem interrupted. He was looking pale; this list of instructions had left him shaken. It was all so . . . matter-of-fact. 'Won't they say they need time to shift everything? They have been there for so long, how can they be moved so quickly?'

'Listen, Prem-ji, they have been served with three eviction orders and have been given time to respond. The man just rips them up and laughs in your face. He will have been told this procedure is happening – if not the actual day then certainly the month. They have had plenty of notice.'

'What if they attack us?' Sita interrupted. 'What rights do we have?'

'This is why we have so many men with us. And I hope even they would think twice before striking two respected elders of their family.'

You don't know them, thought Sita grimly. And yet her kind-hearted, sweet fool of a husband was worried about upsetting them, even now.

'This is why,' Ravi spread his hands helplessly, 'it would be better if we had a police presence. Then we are protected, and we can say we followed all procedures in the proper manner expected by the law.'

'The proper manner?' Sita laughed bitterly. 'You talk about the law? How much money has been passed around in paper bags so the law can be followed properly? How many times have our papers been lost or mislaid or altered by some peon in some office so he can follow the law? What is it like, Ravi *beta*, to wake up every day and come to your office and open your files and wonder who the law is going to be kind to today? Because you don't know. Unless we were super-rich or knew a government minister or had been to school with the judge, our fate is decided by the size of our cheque book and our prayers, if anyone is listening.'

Ravi sat back in his chair. He seemed winded. For a horrible moment, Sita thought he might be about to cry. He shuffled a few papers and sniffed loudly.

'This is not the profession I thought I would follow, Sita-ji, but my father . . . Never mind . . .'

Prem laid a restraining hand on Sita's arm as she opened her mouth to reply.

'You try your best, Ravi,' Prem said quietly. 'We understand.'

'Not always, Prem-ji,' Ravi admitted, looking at his desk. 'Some days I can see there is no hope for justice. It kills a person inside, you know? You wonder what is the point of trying to be . . . good. But then people like you come along and I remember why I keep trying.'

No one said anything. For a moment the sounds of the street

overtook the room: the staccato urgency of car horns, the gentle response of bicycle bells, labourers and hawkers with their guttural shouts across gulleys and traffic, children playing somewhere, their sweet high voices overlaying the soundscape like faraway flutes. This was as familiar to Sita and Prem as an old lullaby, a song bone-deep that they would never forget and would always respond to with visceral memories, an ache where a severed limb used to be.

How I love this country, despite everything, Sita thought, and how it has hurt us. After we get the flat back – if we do – what then? How will we manage now, with our illnesses and infirmities? Fifteen years ago they had been healthy and active enough to manage living here, but the long struggle had taken its toll on them. Now they needed to be near their daughter, their doctor, their grandchildren. Many of their old friends had moved out of Delhi or were dead already. They were fighting now for a principle, not a home. But nothing could bring those years back to them. It was too late for that.

'There was one more thing I needed to say . . . point five, I believe?' Ravi had snapped back into his usual brisk manner, and began collecting the paperwork on his desk. 'I must warn you, this will not be pleasant. In these circumstances, people naturally get very upset, very angry. They will try anything to stop you. Threats, begging, they will parade their kids in front of you, they will show you their operation scars. If they can get you out of the door, they know they have won. And in this case, as with so many others, these people are not strangers, they are your family.'

Sita answered for both of them, trying not to look at Prem's sombre face. 'Don't worry. We are ready.'

*

336

Tara had offered to accompany her grandparents the following day, but they were both vehement about her staying away.

'We have so many officials to help, *beti*,' Prem had told her. 'It is a delicate situation. If you come, we will just be worrying about you on top of everything else.'

Tara was worried about him. She knew how much strain they were both under, but her grandfather was not taking it well. She had packed away her bedding from the pull-out sofa and entered the bathroom to find him standing over the sink, pouring water over his head from the toothbrush glass.

'Nana-ji?'

'Oh . . . my head . . . it feels very hot, that's all,' he had said, grabbing a towel and rubbing fiercely at his dripping hair. It was only seven in the morning and already it felt humid and close.

'You know how to use the mobile, don't you?' Tara had checked before she left the hotel. They had both bought mobile phones at a local shop and Tara had carefully logged in her number and put it on speed dial for them.

'Yes, yes, now go, don't be late,' Sita had fussed, stuffing papers into her handbag. 'And take a taxi, not a scooter, OK?'

'Call me when there's any news . . . or if you need help, or—'

Sita was bundling her out of the door 'We will. Love you . . .'

'Love you too!' Tara called back. Her grandfather didn't seem to have heard her. He was standing quite still, his silver hair poking up in irregular tufts, giving him the startled look of a baby bird, staring at the towel in his hand as if he wasn't sure what it was.

When she entered the Shakti offices for the first time, Tara had felt nervous, sweating from the climb up three flights of pitted marble stairs. From the outside the building looked Dickensian:

a crumbling brownstone edifice garlanded by electrical wires which looped in and around the disused ironwork balconies, advertisement hoardings for local businesses stuck on its face like grubby plasters on old scars.

It had taken her almost an hour to find the place on that first day. South Extension, lying off one of the major ring roads in South Delhi, was famed as a popular shopping destination. With its designer malls interspersed with funky street markets, it didn't seem a likely area for a feminist activist group to be based. And yet when Tara had finally located the office in a quiet cul de sac, she had felt the familiar time-shift sensation she associated with being in India, wandering from the twenty-first-century steel-and-chrome malls into a hidden alleyway populated by stray dogs, washing lines and parked-up old Ambassador cars.

Today, she had come to work early because she wanted to get some exterior shots. She planned to make herself a cup of coffee, charge her camera battery and get a head start. To her surprise, the office was already busy. Rohney, one of the workers, was already in the small kitchenette, making coffee. Her long hair was scraped back in a ponytail today, although she was in the usual office uniform of kurta top and jeans. Her small round eyes widened in pleasure when Tara entered.

'Tara! Were you called for the meeting?'

'Er, what meeting?'

Tara automatically looked across the open-plan office towards the glass enclosure at the end, where some kind of discussion was in full flow. She recognized almost everyone in there. Except the woman who seemed to be doing most of the talking, a slim woman with cropped hair, swathed in a long cotton dupatta, gesticulating energetically with her hands.

'Oh, OK, you're just on English time then. Early, no?'

'Yes, give me a few more weeks and I will be coming in two hours late like I'm supposed to,' smiled Tara.

'Great. But you will finally meet Kavita. She's off to UP to assist on that Dalit rape case later on, but she might have a few minutes before her train leaves. I will tell her you're here. Coffee's brewed.'

Rohney bustled off. Tara didn't ask which rape case this might be – there were so many, it was hard to keep track. During her preliminary research back in London, she had unwisely mentioned to her grandmother that Delhi, her home city, had the dubious status of being the rape capital of India. Figures suggested that every day six women were assaulted in the capital, possibly due to the number of uneducated labourers flooding in from the neighbouring countryside, used to sexually segregated lives and suddenly finding themselves surrounded by mobile independent women whom they assumed were ripe for picking and abusing. Nanima had almost withdrawn her offer to fund Tara's trip after hearing that; only after Tara had promised never to use public transport or three-wheelers, never to travel alone at night and never to wear revealing clothing did she relent. Tara had wanted to say that this was the whole point of going out there – to challenge the idea that women should have to restrict their lives in order to be safe, and to concentrate on changing centuries-old attitudes and procedures. But it had seemed easier to nod vigorously and pack her bags.

The meeting ended and the office began to fill with movement and chatter. Tara could put names to most of the faces now: the older woman who always wore the most elegant saris and coordinated jewellery was Meenakshi, the legal advisor; Seema and Mamta worked on the girls' education and boys' re-education projects in various schools; and Rohney ran the counselling service. To Tara's surprise, there were also two male volunteers, both in their late twenties: Neel, tall and rangy with perpetual designer stubble, and Dhruv, the stocky and silent type, who occasionally looked up from his computer screen to throw enigmatic looks from behind his John Lennon specs.

This was one of those occasions: he caught Tara's inquisitive glance, raised his eyebrows and cocked his head in mock warning. Tara followed his gaze to see Kavita striding towards her with her hand outstretched.

'Tara, right?' She pumped her hand enthusiastically. Tara felt the force field around her, warm, restless. Her intelligent eyes took in Tara briefly from head to toe; it felt like being scanned at the airport.

'Kavita, project coordinator. Settling in OK, I hope?'

'Oh yes, fantastic. Thanks so much for allowing me to film your work—'

'Don't thank me yet,' Kavita interrupted. 'It depends what you film. You will give us the right to veto anything we don't like? We guard our reputation fiercely here.'

Tara bristled at the word 'veto' and Kavita saw it – she missed nothing.

'This is just a student project, a very personal piece, not for broadcast or anything,' said Tara.

'I should hope not, or we wouldn't have said yes.' Kavita smiled tightly.

'And obviously,' Tara continued, 'I wouldn't want to show anything you were unhappy with—'

'Good,' Kavita interjected, 'because we have enough do-gooders parachuting in from the West trying to save the poor native women from their savage bestial men.'

The office chatter suddenly dipped. Everyone seemed to be

concentrating very intently on their screens, except for Dhruv, who took off his glasses and began to chew one end of them thoughtfully.

'I . . . sorry?' Tara said foolishly. She knew where this was heading; she just couldn't quite believe it was being directed at her, and so publicly.

'No doubt you're going to quote facts like we have 24,000 rape cases waiting to be heard in court, and our conviction rate is currently twenty-four per cent. All true. But I do hope you're smart enough to understand the context: what are the stats in the UK? America? The Congo? Do you think it's so much better elsewhere? Is this just our problem, or is it easier to come somewhere exotic and save us from our colonial sorry selves?'

'God no, I . . . I'm not a misery tourist!' Tara said, a little louder than she expected. 'I've been involved with campaigns back in London. I just . . . this is more my . . . culture?'

She knew it sounded laughable the moment it came out of her mouth. She waited for the tongue-lashing that would follow.

Instead Kavita exhaled, a faint smile tugging at her mouth. 'Tara, God knows what that word means, and I have been born and brought up here. I'm not sure we have a homogenous culture that unites us. We have tribes: the rich, the poor, the Dalits, your caste, your religion, your regional language, your sexuality . . . the miracle is we are still the world's largest democracy, and I would lay down my life for that. But you're here and that's a start. You're a woman and you're of Indian origin. That's even better. It's just we don't need white men saving brown women from brown men. Have a great day.'

Kavita swooped out with Rohney following her, talking loudly in the usual masala mix of English and Hindi as they both clattered down the stairs.

Tara leaned on the counter for a moment, slightly stunned.

'Good time for a coffee?'

Dhruv was next to her. His glasses were now perched on his head, revealing soft, heavily lashed eyes. He looked like an inquisitive giraffe.

Tara nodded, too embarrassed to look him in the face.

'It's a quote, you know,' Dhruv said casually as he poured piping-hot liquid from the cafetiere. 'The white-men-saving-brown-women phrase. Not sure who said it. She uses it a lot. Who wouldn't, it's cool. Here.'

Tara took the mug gratefully. He hadn't added milk, but she wanted it black and bitter. She waited for him to say there there, something patronizing that would smooth the atmosphere and allow her to walk away with some dignity. Instead he said nothing, just sipped his coffee loudly and kept looking at her with that annoying frank curiosity that she usually associated with the many onlookers who would gather every time she got her camera out on the street.

After a couple of minutes she finally said, 'Well, good talking to you, Dhruv,' and made to leave.

'What are you doing today?'

Tara shrugged. 'Whatever seems interesting that is happening round here. I think Meenakshi said there was some meeting later on with a human-rights lawyer who—'

'I'm off to interview some college students who have set up a name-and-shame campaign on their campus. Want to come?'

As Tara scrambled into Dhruv's grubby dented Toyota, the hot fabric shocking her back as he started the car, less than two miles away Sita and Prem stood in a dusty alleyway, pressed to a chalky wall that afforded a small strip of shade. They had been waiting for almost two hours, unable to get within sight of the occupied apartment in case they were spotted. Ravi Luthra stood in the mid-morning heat, talking loudly on his mobile phone, a rim of perspiration already circling his shirt collar. Sita thought it touching that, even today, he had put on a smart suit and a tie featuring a repeat pattern of Gandhi-ji's cotton spinning wheel. Good to be patriotic, no doubt, but she fervently hoped their lawyer was not going to fight fire with yet more form-filling, not today. A small pack of mangy wild dogs limped listlessly from lamp post to spindly tree, half-heartedly piddling over each other's territory markings.

Ravi ended his call and cocked his head at Sita. 'Everyone is in place, Auntie. You are ready for this?'

Sita's heart suddenly began hammering against her ribcage. She turned to Prem, who stood motionless, eyes closed, head bowed as if in contemplation.

'Prem?'

He lifted his head as if the weight of the world lay upon it. 'I am ready.'

Ravi offered each of them an arm as they set off along the main road through the complex. He must have looked like a devoted son taking his elders for their morning constitutional. It was that quiet time of the day when the sun was set to a gentle simmer as the sky closed like a lid; children had long since left for school, parents for work, only the servants occupied the roads and balconies.

Each four-storey building they passed contained sixty or so apartments, all with large balconies overlooking the central gated park where vegetable sellers, knife sharpeners, laundry collectors paused in their various duties to swap gossip, their handcarts and laden bicycles abandoned for a moment, resting their old metal bones. The sellers called out to their friends: maids shaking out clothes and dusters; ayahs singing babies to sleep in gruffly tender monotones; disgruntled boys walking pampered pooches, which panted noisily as they strained against their leashes; handymen tending lushly packed hanging baskets, wiping the dust from the leaves of forests of potted plants. Every balcony flaunted its own eco-system, its own individuality: a child's pink scooter, a painted wooden screen adorned with fairy lights, Hindu deities hanging like wind chimes from a small olive tree.

Sita didn't remember this area being so green, so quiet, so prosperous. When they had first bought here, the park had been nothing more than a patch of orange-earthed wasteground, the road untarmacked and rutted. Now it felt like an oasis of calm in this ever-changing city. Oh yes, they could have been happy here.

As they reached the end of the park, Sita saw them: a group of ten or so wiry men in bush shirts and loose-fitting trousers casually grouped around their building entrance. Two large pick-up trucks were parked up nearby. One of the men – the only one who appeared to be in uniform, a neat, compact sort of fellow with a knife-sharp parting in his Brylcreemed hair – smoothed down the creases in his khaki jacket as he walked towards them, clutching a small clipboard. The others stood to attention behind him, stubbing out bidis and hitching up their trousers.

'Must be the bailiff, no?' Sita whispered to Prem, who raised a finger to his lips as Ravi exchanged a few brief words with the man, who quickly examined some paperwork. Then Ravi indicated that they should follow him and they entered the side stairwell of the block, enjoying a brief moment in the damp coolness of the overhang before pressing on upwards to the second floor, where they faced a quartet of front doors. Sita pointed at the only one that had no personal touches adorning it, no welcome mat or fabric garlands hanging from the lintel – just a thick wooden door with a small eyehole in its centre.

'You wait there, Auntie . . . Uncle,' Ravi whispered, indicating that they should tuck in behind him at the top of the stairs. 'You know what to do once we are inside?'

Sita nodded dumbly. She and Prem had been rehearsing this moment for days, weeks. She held her breath as the bailiff knocked loudly, cleared his throat gently and waited. They all waited. He knocked again. Maybe no one was in. They were too late. Ravi had said, be here at eight in the morning. They had done so, but none of the hired men had turned up – bloody Indian timing, as usual – and now all this, for nothing. They would have to start all over again. And Sita knew that if this did not happen today, it would never happen at all.

All of this she said to Prem wordlessly as they clutched each other's arms, so when the door suddenly swung open, Sita almost groaned aloud in relief. A skinny youth answered the door; he looked around eighteen, with unkempt bushy hair and a single eyebrow stretched across his forehead that gave him an angry, suspicious air, as if he would not think twice about stabbing them with the small vegetable knife he held in one hand.

The bailiff barked at him in rapid Hindi, holding up an official document in front of the boy's face. The boy shifted the knife to his other hand and looked behind him nervously: this was the moment when either Sunil or Sheetal would come screaming at them, tearing the paper in two and slamming the door in their faces. But instead, he shrugged his shoulders, wiped his nose on the scrap of cloth draped over his shoulder and stepped aside.

And suddenly, they were inside. For a moment, Sita found herself in the middle of a bad action movie: all the men seemed to appear out of thin air, rushing up the stairs and into the apartment, all

345

shouting together, with the bailiff and Ravi screaming at her and Prem to get into any room that wasn't locked and stay there. Sita flung herself at the nearest door and found herself in a bedroom, and Prem hurried across the hallway to a door opposite and slammed it behind him. Trembling, Sita realized she was sitting on an unmade bed strewn with rumpled clothing. Without caring whose smells and germs she might now be inhaling, she leaned back on to a bank of pillows and closed her eyes.

Sita awoke with a jerk and swallowed hard, feeling disoriented and thirsty. Her throat felt like sandpaper. Her initial panic subsided and she sat up carefully, trying to ease herself gently into focus. She had no idea how long she had been asleep, how many hours had passed, but it was long enough to feel seriously dehydrated. She wondered how Prem was. Clearly something was happening. The door which she had closed behind her was now open, giving her a view of the hallway and some rooms beyond. The flat was filled with the shouts of the workmen, the crash and clump of furniture being moved, then groans and heaves as they hauled the heavy items away and down the two flights of stairs.

Sita coughed gently, trying to clear her throat, and began to take in her surroundings. She hadn't been inside this apartment for so many years, it was difficult to remember what it had been like before. But Sheetal and Sunil had spent money on it, that was for sure. There was a new kitchen, which she could just glimpse through the half-open door. She was sure hers had been grey and plain; now the units were gleaming white with gold trim. There were air-conditioning units in each room – those definitely hadn't been here way back then. She thought she had caught sight of a breakfast bar of some kind, but in the sitting room, with a large drinks cabinet behind it. None of their original furniture seemed to have remained. Had they just thrown it away? Sold it, more like. This bedroom now had an en-suite bathroom. They must have thought they were staying for ever – that's how insignificant all of Prem and Sita's requests and eventual demands had been to them. The thought made her feel nauseous.

Sita realized she must be sitting in one of the son's bedrooms, maybe the teenage one – the other must be twenty or so by now. Clothes were strewn everywhere, discarded shirts, socks, a pile of expensive trainers. There was a shiny laptop, a large sound system and a widescreen TV – oh yes, they had money – along with school textbooks, two cricket bats, posters of some pouty Bollywood heroine and a Manchester United wall calendar. A boy's life. He had left home this morning as usual, and when he returned, all of this would be in a box on the street. It wasn't his fault that his parents had become upmarket squatters – he probably had no idea when they put in his bathroom or boasted to friends about their new kitchen that they were living rent-free in someone else's longed-for home.

But any sympathy Sita might have been harbouring vanished when Sheetal finally arrived. She heard the shrieks first, hysterical shouting, and such language – the woman swore like a street-walker, *your sister's this, your mother's that* . . . She could hear the bailiff's steady bass replies; he sounded as solid as a mountain, let her try and move him. More shouting followed, and then suddenly Sheetal was in front of Sita, her phone in her hand, her hair in disarray. Sita could barely recognize the young slim woman she remembered. Sheetal had always been a beauty, with her olive skin and hazel eyes. Now it was as if someone much older and fatter had swallowed that girl, who was peeking out from inside her, squeezed into a silk designer suit, gold adorning her ears, neck, wrists. The first thing Sita thought was, she has turned into her mother. The second was, if that is what she wears to go on her morning errands, what does she wear for a wedding?

'Get off my son's bed,' Sheetal spat at her.

Sita looked away. You are invisible, she told herself like a prayer, though she had to sit on her hands to prevent herself from heaving her old bones up from the bed and pulling those earrings straight through Sheetal's thieving pendulous lobes. Sheetal muttered something obscene under her breath and swept out.

That had been hours ago. And still they waited. Sita wondered if the water in the bathroom was safe to drink. She was so thirsty she understood those dogs that ended up drinking from toilet bowls. She and Prem were old-school about pets – so unnecessary, what was the point? Let animals roam free and leave their germs outside. But Neelum, Sheetal's mother, had acquired a yappy Pomeranian some years back, when people used to talk to their pets. It had been the fashion then in Delhi society, so naturally Neelum had had to keep up. She would sit with this appalling animal on the bed with her, stuffing sweets into her mouth and occasionally feeding the dog from her own fingers, her baubles clinking and the bedsprings creaking under her bulk as she laughed at her own jokes. And some of them were very funny. There had been good times, Sita couldn't deny that. And Prem had always had a soft spot for Yogi, his favourite brother. He had missed him, she knew that, over all these years of estrangement. And today he must be suffering. She had to see him.

Sita was about to desert her post when she heard more yelling, this time a male voice, high and indignant. She stood in the doorway, careful to wedge a towel in the hinges so she could not be dragged outside and the door locked behind her, and saw Sunil trying to wrestle a dining chair from one of the labourer's hands. Unlike Sheetal, the years had been kind to him. Other than a few more grey hairs, he was unchanged: he still had the anonymous features of some middle-management clerk, brushed side parting, pencil moustache. Wealth and comfort had no doubt given him the regulation pot belly, but she'd seen bigger.

The bailiff stepped in, had a few stern words with Sunil and waved the stamped document in front of him. Behind them, Sita saw Prem, also standing in a doorway watching the scene. She gestured to him, but his gaze was fixed on Sunil, who was now crying in what Sita thought was a very melodramatic way – no tears, but lots of noise, tugging at the bailiff's arm, pleading with him to give them just one more month, or even a week, to have some pity on his wife and children. The bailiff produced other sheets of paper, pointing out that several letters had been sent asking for a response, that he could even have lodged another appeal, but all had been ignored, although it was hard to hear him over the wailing.

Then suddenly it stopped, as if a needle had suddenly been yanked off a record. Sunil had seen Prem. He threw himself at his feet, holding them, attempting to kiss them. It was more than he had ever done in all the years they had known them.

'Thaya-ji, I beg you . . . as my father-in-law's elder respected brother! Think of Sheetal, your blood niece! Your two nephews, our boys! We will pay you back every rupee we owe! With interest! On my life!'

Sita leaned on the doorframe, weak and dizzy. She could see that Prem was crumbling. He gaped at this man clutching his feet, his hands hovering uselessly at his sides. He wanted to touch him – of course he would, she knew that. Usually he would never allow anyone to get as far as the actual feet – just the gesture of bending to touch them was always enough for Prem.

'*Jaan*,' she tried to call, her pet name, the Urdu word for life itself. This man was her life and his big heart would betray them. But the word died in her throat, swollen by heat and thirst.

And then, just as Prem seemed about to offer his hands to Sunil, to bring him up with his blessing and forgiveness, Sunil got up abruptly and turned to the bailiff, producing a wallet from his pocket. 'How much?' he asked in a calm, cold voice.

The bailiff began muttering something about bribing a government official and obstructing the course of justice, but Sunil merely peeled a few more notes off the rolled bundle in his hand.

'Hah, hah . . .' he mimicked him dismissively. 'Name your price. Look at them . . .' He gestured to Prem and Sita. 'They don't even live here, you know that? They just want to make a quick sale and take the money back to their English mansion. And anyway, how long are they going to live, heh?'

He pushed the notes into the breast pocket of the bailiff's shirt. Where was Ravi, Sita thought wildly. He should be seeing this, he should be taking pictures on his phone or something. She grabbed her handbag and pulled out the sponge bag. She stood in the doorway and waved bundles of cash at the bailiff, shouting at Sunil, even though every word tore at her throat.

'You want us to play this game? Here! How much? Have everything! Doesn't matter what is fair, I have more money than you so I must be right, *hena*?'

Sita threw a roll of notes at the bailiff, who caught it expertly in one hand. A small noise came from somewhere: Prem, looking at her as if she was a stranger. He shook his head slowly, just once, and backed towards the bed, where he sat down heavily, his face in his hands. The bailiff seemed to consider the weight of the cash for a moment, then removed the notes from his breast pocket and returned them to Sunil. At that moment, Sheetal entered, puffing with exertion and fanning herself with her dupatta.

'Well?' was all she said to Sunil. She could see the answer in his twisted face.

Sheetal threw him a look of blazing contempt and briefly checked her phone before saying casually, 'Mummy's got rid of her tenants in the South Ex flat. We can be in there by Friday. No thanks to you . . .'

As they turned to go, the bailiff cleared his throat. 'Your auntie and uncle require some water. We need permission to help ourselves in the kitchen.'

Sheetal didn't even bother to look at Prem and Sita as she walked out.

'You don't touch anything. I don't know these people. Buy your own water.'

And they were gone.

Sita wasn't sure whether to laugh or cry. More than anything, she wanted a drink. She pushed past the bailiff and sat down next to Prem, taking his shaking hand. 'It is finished, *jaan*. Finished.'

Then the bailiff was standing next to her. She hadn't noticed before, but he had a grave sweet face and touchingly sticky-out ears. He could have been any age between twenty and forty, a man-child of indeterminate age, and he was holding out her money in his open palm.

'Take it, Auntie. It would be kind to buy the men some lunch. I will get you water.'

Tara spent the rest of the day feeling constantly wrong-footed, expectations and assumptions peeled from her layer by layer as she talked and walked and listened. The students who greeted her and Dhruv were so different from those she had left behind on her course – not just the obvious external stuff like their clothes (cleaner jeans and T-shirts, not a whiff of grunge or shabby chic), but because of their infectious zeal to reform and challenge, which made her feel quite heady. Oh, they were angry, with the usual spitfire fizz of youth and possibility: they attacked their country's insidious corruption on every level, the growing gap between the poor and the newly minted million-aires, the cancer of the caste system, the sexual war being waged in their cities and villages, the growing number of disaffected men who found themselves jobless, without women, due to the growing imbalance caused by female infanticide. One lone voice stood up and raged against the commercialization of cricket and the over-reliance on foreign imported players. But for every complaint, they offered solutions, suggestions: marches, cam-paigns, social-media action. They talked about spirituality in the same breath as politics. It was as if everything was up for grabs, no sacred cow going unchallenged. It was the surge of hope, the lack of cynicism that made all the old arguments seem real and urgent to Tara. And how comfortable they all seemed in their skin; all of them dated someone – some of them kept it quiet from their families, others didn't. The subject of arranged mar-riage never came up, nor the scourge of the slums or Bollywood. This was a generation just pushing through the pangs of birth, emerging newborn, baring their teeth and eager to run. There was so much to do, but that's where the thrill lay, with what could be.

Afterwards, Dhruv took her to a dhaba café nearby, with Formica tables and framed posters of black-and-white Hindi films on the walls. They ate chicken kebabs, which sizzled on the plate, and dense creamy daal, which they licked off their fingers in the rare pauses in their conversation.

'This looks just like my mum's mate's café back in the East End,' laughed Tara. She was almost full but couldn't stop eating. At some point that day her appetite had come back; her whole body felt hungry.

'Not homesick, are you?' Dhruv asked through a mouthful of naan. He obviously liked his grub – the slight roll of his tummy under his sweatshirt told her that. Tara found it comforting, the sight of someone at ease with their body and their food. You can tell what a man's like in bed by the way he dances and the way he eats – she had read that somewhere. She imagined Dhruv breaking buttons on shirts and ripping seams in his haste to get naked and tuck in.

'OK, do I have pickle on my nose again?' Dhruv asked her, rubbing his face with his sleeve.

She had been staring at him, maybe even drooling. Old deeply buried feelings pushed at her skin, too painful, too messy. She needed to eat some more.

'Homesick?' She bit into a *papard*, which splintered satisfyingly on her tongue. 'Sick of home, more like. Wherever that is now. I love it here, it feels . . . relevant. New. Does that make sense?'

'Totally.' Dhruv nodded. 'You know India is the world's youngest nation, statistically? Almost half our population is under twenty-five, the median citizen is a twenty-nine-year-old city dweller. By 2020, sixty-four per cent of the population will be of working age. It's what economists call a sweet spot. Now, if we can develop our neglected manufacturing sector and pull emphasis away from our over-developed service industries, we could do something about all the jobless bored men who take out their frustration on our newly emancipated working women . . .'

Tara stopped chewing and stared at Dhruv. 'Bloody hell, is that your election speech or does it just come out of your mouth like that?'

'I've thought about it a lot,' Dhruv said reverently, nodding. 'And I'm an unemployed Economics graduate hoping to go into journalism, and those are my best chat-up lines right there.'

'Always does it for me, statistics and flow charts,' Tara shot back. It struck her how impressive it was that he could be witty in several languages. Dhruv had made the students laugh on several occasions with a stream of Hindi, only some of which she had understood. All those impromptu lessons with Mala hadn't helped with comedy banter in the slightest. But then, everyone seemed to be effortlessly bi- if not tri-lingual. Why did the English ever need to acquire other languages when everyone did them the favour of speaking theirs?

'So, you finished college and started volunteering for Shakti? Why?'

Dhruv swallowed down a mouthful and wiped his hands on his paper serviette. He took some time to do this, cleaning around each fingernail thoughtfully.

'My sister,' he said finally. Tara waited. 'Usual story – married to a guy the family knew. The minute she's his wife he turns into some . . . caveman. He had been violent towards her for some time before she finally told us.'

'God . . .' Tara breathed, afraid to say more.

'Of course, the minute we knew, we brought her home. She filed for divorce – and then found out she was pregnant, so . . .'

'She went back?' Tara blurted it out.

Dhruv nodded. 'We told her so many times . . . My parents, they didn't care about what the neighbours would say, they supported her, but Nisha . . . she wanted the child to have a father. And she thought it would change him.'

'Is she . . . I'm sorry, don't say if you—'

'Oh, she's alive,' Dhruv said. 'She told us the beatings stopped. She had a boy – that helped, I suppose. I don't know if he's still actually hitting her. But she's scared of him, you can see it. He doesn't like her visiting us. I've hardly seen my nephew. And this is an educated middle-class woman who was given every chance to just . . . leave. That's what made me want to do something. That's how deep it is, the conditioning, the brainwashing. Physical violence – you can see it, you know what you're dealing with. But this – fear of change, choosing to stay in your prison – that's where the war is. In your head.'

Tara's phone rang. She couldn't answer it for a moment, still with Dhruv, with his sister in a flat somewhere not far from here, holding her son and listening for dreaded footsteps at the door. When she saw it was Nanima's number, she snatched it up. Dhruv saw the colour drain from her face.

'Where are you?' Tara said in a high, scared voice. 'I'll find it. I'm coming.' She stood up, disoriented. 'Where's Batra hospital? Is it far?'

'Not near . . .'

'My grandfather's . . . he's been taken ill. I need a taxi . . . can you—'

'I'll take you.'

Dhruv gathered up Tara's equipment, looped her handbag around his arm and led her away.

He crumpled slowly like a deflating balloon. That's what Ravi Luthra had told her. Walking in the heat of the day to the government offices to ensure the water and electricity in the flat were switched off, then finding the locksmith to change all the locks . . . why did Ravi let an old man do all that when he hadn't eaten or drunk anything?

'I couldn't stop him, Auntie,' Ravi told her, shaking his head. 'He insisted it all must be done today. I told him I would do it, but . . .'

Ravi assured her they were in the best neurological hospital in Delhi – they would know if it was a stroke, they would know what do to afterwards. Thank God they had been sensible enough to keep up their travel insurance. Prem was hooked up to a lot of machines; she had to find his hand carefully under the wires and tubes and not move it too much, because of the drip which had left a vivid purple stain around it. He had always had very delicate skin. Bruised like a soft peach. Sita was very impressed with the hospital, so clean and modern. Didn't Indians always make the best doctors? No joke to her. The nurses called them Uncle and Auntie – that kind of thing made a difference. They had discussed only once where they would like their ashes to be scattered, because that kind of talk upset Prem. They had both expected the other to say, 'In the Ganges, of course. Back to Ganga Mama to join the debris of our ancestors.' But neither of them had said that. Sita liked the idea of Brighton. They had been on several day trips there over the years and she loved the noisy pier and the sound of the waves on the tumbling stony beach. Prem wasn't too specific, but he had insisted it should be somewhere in the mountains. Somewhere high and remote with no other people around, where he could get some peace. It had surprised Sita. It made her wonder, had he not found peace with her? Now she thought about it, in the hospital room with its soundtrack of soft beeps and trills, when had the poor man had any peace? He had fought his way out of poverty, endured the loss and trials of emigration, seen his daughter grow and suffer an unhappy marriage just when they thought she was settled, and now, this new baby. Could she have done more, to cushion him from all the stress of their lives? On the other hand, hadn't they been more fortunate than most?

Of course, Prem couldn't hear any of her thoughts, but if he could, if he had been able to speak to her, he would have told her that for him there was not a moment of regret, not a moment he would not have had again with her.

The sound of the phone ringing had dragged Shyama up from the depths of slumber, reeling her towards a surface she still hadn't found. Everything that happened afterwards felt as if she was still somewhere underwater, each movement clumsy and slow, as if weights were dragging on her feet. She might drown. Tara's voice so far away, she sounded like she was six years old again and it wrung her inside out. Toby's strong arms, his voice on the phone, ringing round for a plane ticket. Throwing a few belongings into a bag. Where was her passport? A hurried scribbled list of instructions for Geeta at the salon, her diary wiped – for how long she wasn't sure. It was only when she stood motionless in the hallway, her single bag at her feet, and looked up to see Mala peering at her from the top of the stairs that it struck her across the face like a slap. Mala. The baby was less than four weeks away. First babies often came before the due date, especially South Asian ones. 'We cook more quickly, sweetie,' Priya had advised her. How could she leave? How could she not go?

'Shyama . . .' It was the first time she had heard Mala use her name without the Madam attached. 'So sorry for your papa. I can do anything? When you are away?'

Shyama shook her head, gathering her thoughts; it was like trying to catch surf, her head pounding rhythmically like an incoming tide. 'Just . . . look after yourself. I will be back before . . . very soon. I don't want to leave you alone—'

There was an end to that sentence, but she couldn't remember what it might be. Toby. He had thrown on the first clothes that came to hand, a rumpled sweatshirt, stained jeans. He still had bed hair and pillow creases across one side of his face. She thought he had never looked as handsome as he did now.

They drove in silence for a while. It was early enough for the usually choked North Circular Road to be fairly empty – they would make good time. Night frost glistened on roofs and lamp posts, made cobwebs into icy doilies on passing hedges and fences. The first flush of a wintry dawn glowed far off on the horizon, pearly grey, the pale moon fading as if being slowly bled dry.

'I wish you weren't going,' Toby said finally. Then corrected himself. 'Sorry, I know you have to . . . I mean, I'm sorry you have to . . . like this. What I meant was, I wish I could come with you.'

They both knew why he couldn't.

Toby's unease felt like a physical pain, his guts twisting with every bend they took. He would have always said he was fond of Prem, comfortable with him. Now the possibility of losing him made him feel weak and lost, ambushed by how much he missed both of those dear old people. But there was something else, a fear that chilled him even with the car heating on full blast; he bit his tongue to stop his teeth chattering. He would be alone with Mala. It felt like staring into the headlights of an oncoming car, messy and inevitable.

'Careful!' Shyama called out sharply. A car horn screamed at them, its banshee wail dying away just as quickly. Toby jerked the wheel quickly, steadying the car.

'I should have got a cab. You're still half asleep, love.' Shyama placed a gentle hand on his thigh. Even through the denim he felt cold. 'You didn't bring a coat,' she said. 'Funny, neither did I.'

Shyama called Toby from Delhi every hour on the first day. By the week's end, Prem was still in a coma but the tests were looking hopeful – no apparent brain damage. There was no obvious reason why he hadn't woken up yet. The prognosis was 'cautiously optimistic', although the doctors stressed they could not tell for sure what damage there might be until he regained consciousness. Sita had joked that it was the only way he could get some rest, after all the chaos of the last couple of months. They were all there, his wife, daughter, granddaughter. All the relatives had wanted to visit, but Sita was the gatekeeper, she only allowed in a favoured few – this wasn't a sideshow, after all – Prem's elder brother, his two sisters. No sign of Yogesh, the former favourite. But then Sita had warned that if he dared to show his face, he might end up in hospital himself. Toby wasn't to worry.

Neither, he replied back, was Shyama. The last scan had reassured them that although smallish, the baby seemed healthy, and that their due date could well be later than they thought. Which was good news given the circumstances.

Sita and Shyama had both made Tara return to work.

'No point sitting here all day, *beti* . . . you come when you can.'

As it happened, Tara came every day, sometimes early in the morning on her way to Shakti, often around six o'clock after work, bringing her Nanima and mother magazines, bags of hot just-fried jalebis, or masala chaat from her favourite stall, still in its flimsy paper tray. And she brought a small CD player and soundtracks from old movies that Prem would remember – *Pakeezah*, *Three Char Sau Bees*, anything with Raj Kapoor in it.

'Just play them to him, Nanima, I know he can hear us,' she urged Sita.

Tara looked just like an Indian girl now, Sita observed proudly. She had grown her hair, thank God, and she must have been putting in coconut oil because it had come back thicker. She wore it in a ponytail or sometimes loose: a plait would have looked nice, but you can't have everything. No more horrible black smears around her eyes, lovely cotton tops and smart jeans, and her face had filled out. Even without a scrap of make-up she looked healthy, even in such terrible circumstances. And all the adventures she was having! Some school project here, some internet project there, some out of Delhi. Those were the only couple of days when Tara didn't visit, although she phoned annoyingly often to make up for it.

One day she arrived and Sita worried for a moment that Tara's old demons had returned, whatever they might have been. She looked pale, her eyes red-rimmed. When she kissed her grand-father's forehead, as she always did, she let her lips linger as if she wanted to warm herself on his skin. She later told Sita that she had been to a special hostel where a charity housed and rehabilitated the victims of acid attacks, all women, all of them disfigured by men they had known – rebuffed suitors, abandoned husbands, jealous boyfriends. The cruelty of the world shook her like the sapling she was. Sita let her sway and grieve. Let her learn it now; there would be much more to see and mourn some day, hopefully still far away.

'I am very impressed with your knowledge of Hindi films,' Sita told her, until she realized where the knowledge must be coming from. The plumpie boy who was so often with her grand-daughter nowadays, sitting in his car in the parking area below, tapping on his phone. She couldn't tell much about him from this high-up window, but she watched them drive away together so often it had become a sort of comforting ritual, along with combing Prem's hair every morning and massaging his feet. Along with the daily scooter ride from Prem's eldest brother's house (they had insisted on pain of torture that she and Shyama should stay with them, so they could be fed and watered and have company around them every evening). She let them spoil her – it made up for the years of feigned deafness and blindness about the stolen flat. They hadn't wanted to get involved. Well, they were now.

Shyama's anguish for her father was renewed every day as she walked into the hospital room and saw him again, unchanged, seemingly asleep. It never left her, a shadow that moved with her when she ate, talked, flicked through endless magazines. But it was tempered by her growing realization of how her daughter was changing before her eyes. Every day that Nana-ji slept on was another day when Tara grew a little more in confidence, poise and knowledge, bringing back morsels from the world outside this room that Shyama fell upon hungrily, always eager for more. Their conversations never seemed to have a beginning or an end: they picked up from where they had left off the day before; they parted with sentences that ended in those three dots that Shyama had always thought denoted irony. Now she knew they meant there were some stories with no clear ending.

Tara had told her mother about Dhruv after the first week, when Shyama had asked why Tara wasn't staying at her uncle's house with them.

'It just feels wrong, you paying out for a hostel, on your own, when we're all here,' Shyama had told her.

Tara shuffled her feet, her old childhood sign that she was hiding something, and pretty unsuccessfully.

'I'm not in the hostel any more, Mama . . .' She called her that now, reverting to her first word. Shyama felt a sharp pang of something like *déjà vu*, except she saw before her not the child Tara had been, but the woman she was becoming. How had those years flown by so quickly? There was a new baby coming soon to fill the void, but Shyama knew now that nothing could replace a child – not even another one. The fact was, from the moment they existed they claimed a piece of you; as they grew, so did that sliver of your heart in their hands, and when they left you, they took it with them without a backward glance.

'I'm staying at a friend's house . . .' Tara shuffled her feet some more.

'The friend who is also your taxi service here and back?' Shyama enquired. She'd clocked the young man sitting like a devoted pet in his car downstairs. She'd half expected to see him stick his head out of the window and let his ears flap in the breeze whilst he waited.

'It's not what you think,' Tara continued.

'You don't know what I think,' replied Shyama, enjoying this.

'He lives at home, with his parents. I'm staying in his sister's room, sharing with her, Devika. She's lovely, she's a first-year Chemical Engineering student, really brainy, and his mum and dad are so sweet. They offered to put me up after they heard about Nana, because they said, why waste all that money on a hostel? They put up loads of Dhruv's friends because they've got this huge house – it's really ancient, falling apart practically. They're not rich, it's an old family home, and there's always

362

a bunch of young people hanging around. They're sort of old hippies really, his parents. I think you'd have a lot in common and they've been asking to meet you, but you've been so upset and—'

'I'd take a breath now before you hyperventilate,' Shyama said.

Tara did so, letting out a shaky sigh. She tucked a strand of hair behind her ear, her wrist jangling with thin silver bracelets.

My girl is so beautiful and young, thought Shyama with a swell of pride and envy. 'Do you like this boy?' she eventually asked. Seeing Tara's sheepish expression, she added quickly, 'You can tell me it's none of my business . . .'

And then they both said, 'But it is . . .'

Tara insisted that Dhruv was just a friend, a good and special friend. Shyama asked for his parents' number; she felt out of her depth as to how awkward a social situation this might be, but they were putting up her daughter and she had to meet them. She had to make contact as soon as she could – she didn't know how much longer she was going to stay, would be able to stay. She called up immediately, had a brief but friendly chat with Dhruv's mother and was invited to supper the following evening.

'Are you worried I'm going to embarrass you?' Shyama asked Tara later.

'Make up for all the times I've done it to you,' her daughter grinned back.

They were walking through the car park. Tara waved at Dhruv, some distance away, who flashed his lights in response. The sun was sinking in the sudden way it did in this sky, a fat yolk swallowed in one gulp by the horizon. Shyama declined to meet him then – she would wait till the next day.

'Unusual name, Dhruv,' she remarked.

'I know. It means North Star,' Tara said with a small smile, before she ran towards him, glowing scarlet in the last rays of the day.

Mala could now name every different bottle of perfume on Shyama's dressing-table. The one with the curved surface that curled in on itself like a wave and smelt of tuberose: Hermès; the fat, satisfied one that looked like a large medicine bottle with its thick amber liquid: Acqua Di Parma; the two thin glass columns with silver lids: Jo Malone; and her favourite, a bottle shaped like a temple goddess, all breasts and hips in shimmering pink: Jean-Paul Gaultier. She said each name like a mantra as she lifted them to polish the dark-brown wood, wiping the glass so they sparkled like soldiers lining up for inspection.

She knew almost every inch of this house now, roaming round it restlessly like a caged animal with a duster in one hand and a can of Pledge in the other. Toby sahib had said it was best she stopped going to the salon, with Shyama not being there to look after her. If something were to happen . . . She understood. *Chalo*, I can't even walk now anyway without puffing like a she-elephant, she grumbled to herself as she waddled around looking for something, anything, to tidy and clean.

She missed the women in the salon – they laughed at her jokes, they stroked her hair, she could have spun them any stupid story about the village and they would have sat there catching flies with their pretty open mouths. Now all her inventions and potions were being used and sold without her. Even though the money was flying through the air and into her bank account with just one press of a computer button, it didn't make up for the loss of her independence.

It had been a revelation for Mala, that you didn't work just for the money, you worked for the freedom work gave you, for the chance to be a stronger, more interesting version of yourself. She had assumed she would simply do the same thing when she got back to India. Why not? She had enough money to open her own place, be total boss herself, impress people with her specialized knowledge all the way from a top-class A-One exclusive London salon. And then she began to realize it would never work that way: here, her humble background meant nothing to the women she met; if anything, they liked her better because she was 'the real thing' – hah, that's me, natural and fresh as newly shat dung. But back in India, what high-class madam was going to let her lay her dark small hands on her expensive fair skin? One look at her and they would know everything. It doesn't matter how far you have come, it is where you have come from that matters, and that she knew she couldn't hide easily. Of course, hah, have your own salon, but not in our mall – try a few miles out of town where you can cater for the ladies that look like you, understand you – cutting hair and removing moustaches. That's what she would end up doing, when where she wanted to be was sitting with the madams without ever having to call anyone Madam again.

Too many thoughts, too much energy and an overwhelming desire to create a nest, which also felt like a prison. None of it made any sense. So she just kept cleaning.

Shyama's clothes were well organized: Mala approved of the colour-coding system, the way she kept her tops and trousers separate but next to each other, the ones that matched. Her shoes were far too big for Mala – all that striding about running a business and owning your life, you needed huge feet for that.

Toby sahib's wardrobe – well, that was as she expected, every-thing crushed together, all his shoes jumbled up, some still with farmyard dirt on them. She enjoyed scraping off the dried mud with an old toothbrush over the sink. When the soil made contact with water, it released a deep loamy smell that made Mala inhale sharply, and then slowly, breathing it in as deeply as her compressed ribs would allow. Hai, the smell of the fields! The smell of a man – better than any perfume. It made the little man inside her wriggle with pleasure.

'Oy! Stop kicking me, little pony!' she laughed at him, and then stopped herself. She kept forgetting: she shouldn't do this. Eat well, rest, think happy thoughts, yes. But not this: not the chit-chat in the nights, because he woke up and wanted to play whenever she lay down. She knew exactly where his body lay: there was his funny foot under her rib, his naughty knee in her side. He did circus tricks, little monkey somersaults and tumbles as she watched her stomach ripple and dip with each move, cheeky show-off. Just because he ate what she ate, pissed with her, laughed with her, missed the smell of ploughed fields with her, made her jump when he got hiccups, made her wince when he turned over, fed on her blood and her breath, that didn't mean he was hers. I am just your safe house until you hatch, little chick, Mala crooned to him. She tried her best not to make it sound like a song.

Toby sahib was taking it badly. He came and went like a ghost – a very rude ghost, as it happens – leaving a room and banging the door only a minute after she entered it. Most nights he would remain in his room, Skyping India or on his computer, the tap tap tap like the parrots pecking up the seeds on her window-sill. Now they knew where to come, they never left her alone.

366

The ledge outside her room was caked in birdshit, and they squabbled in furious feathery clouds. Even the novelty of finding their discarded emerald feathers wore off when she realized that within a day the shimmering green dulled to a flat lifeless brown.

Mala and Toby still ate together – he still wolfed down anything she put in front of him – but it wasn't the same without Prem, Sita, Shyama and Tara all there, chattering away. He reminded her of her husband, the way he ate with his arm around the plate, protecting it as if someone was going to take it away; no conversation, just eat, burp, go.

She knew why. The empty space in the house that was Shyama-shaped was a force field between them, and yet he looked at her all the time when he thought she wasn't watching him. *Chalo,* that was exactly like her husband in those long-ago days when she wondered why he stared and didn't touch. It had meant something then, because she had been his wife. But this time, how could she know what to do when she didn't know what she was to him? She carried his son, not through an act of love, but for money. The child lived in her and yet had nothing of her – half Toby's, half some other woman's. Although she had more claim to the baby than Shyama did – there was nothing of her in the boy. But I am in this kitchen and she isn't here. I am feeding this man and carrying his child, and she isn't here. And he has stopped being kind to me because she isn't here. All these thoughts jumbled through Mala's head as she washed saucepans and rinsed dishes. She dropped the dishcloth on the floor, bent without thinking to retrieve it and gasped as a sharp pain jabbed at her side.

Toby sahib was next to her, quick as a flash. 'Mala?' He sounded panicked.

'It's OK. I will sit . . .'

367

Toby led Mala to a chair, rinsed the dishcloth and began finishing off the clearing-up. 'I'm sorry, you shouldn't be doing this. My mind's been . . . No more housework, OK?' He handed her a glass of water and paused before asking, ' Mala . . . did you tidy up my clothes?'

Mala nodded, enjoying the cool moist glass between her hands. 'It's not OK?'

'Not really.' Toby fidgeted; this was horribly awkward. 'They're my things. Personal, you know?'

'Sorry. I get bored. That is all. No insult meant, Toby sahib.'

Toby immediately felt ashamed. She looked so small, hunched in the chair with that absurdly huge stomach in front of her. I did that, he thought, then shook his head to fling the crass observation away. What was the matter with him? He was either sneakily following her every move, spying on her because he couldn't stop wanting to look at her belly, to touch it, or he was ignoring the poor woman, punishing her for . . . what? He wasn't sure. When Shyama was here, he knew who they all were: the couple and their surrogate, Mummy and Daddy waiting for their employee to safely deliver their son. But since Shyama had gone, all the boundaries and definition had faded to nothing but watermarks. He was lost without one of the women. He was someone else with the other.

'Toby sahib?'

'Mala, for God's sake, how many times . . . how can you call me "sahib" when you're sitting there, looking like that? That's not an extra helping of pudding in there, that's a baby we made together, so please, please, drop the "sahib". OK?'

In the silence that followed, a tap dripped like a pulse. They had both heard the word he had used. Together. They both decided to pretend that they hadn't.

'OK, Toby, mate?'

They laughed in the manic way that everyone laughs when something unspeakable has just happened, over-compensatory guffaws, until Mala clutched her side again and Toby was next to her again. She waved him away, wiping tears from her eyes.

'I must ask you one thing,' she said when they had both recovered enough to share a companionable cup of tea.

'Anything,' Toby said expansively.

'We are not going to buy something for the baby?'

'Such as . . . ?'

'Only a few weeks away and we have nothing. Not for me, you understand, but maybe a bed for him? Some clothes? Just in case, *hena*?'

This floored Toby. That was much too soon. He wasn't ready. Shyama had emailed him the details of the private maternity unit in a large teaching hospital where the labour would take place. He had been there a few times now and had met and liked their obstetrician, Mr O'Connell, the tall Irish consultant with the kindly eyes and worryingly large hands. So he knew where to go if anything started happening, but that was about it. He had been to no antenatal classes, done no breathing exercises to pant along through the labour, had no idea whether she might like her back massaged or what kind of music she might want playing when Junior emerged into the world. The nearest he had come to research was watching a few episodes of a documentary series set in a maternity ward, which he had stumbled across while channel-hopping one evening. Shyama had watched one with him, sharing anecdotes about Tara's birth. 'She's lucky– it took three goes to get my epidural in . . .'

Shyama got misty-eyed every time a baby was born, no matter whose it was. But then she wearied of watching what was effectively the same story over and over again with a different set of women each time. She had been through it, she had a history that Toby could never share with her, reminisce about. And now it was going to happen again, albeit in a slightly different way. He would not be able to stand around with other men, regaling each other with competitive expectant-dad stories: how her waters broke on a bus or in the back of the car as they got caught in traffic; how she swore and nearly broke his hand with every contraction; how long, how bloody long it had gone on for; how his first glimpse of his child had affected him – whether he cried or stared or fainted. It had been agreed ages ago that Shyama would be with Mala during labour – for her to have Toby watching her push and pant was obviously out of the question. They had also agreed that they wouldn't insist on a Caesarian, as so often happened in the surrogacy clinic; they wanted the baby to come when he was ready. And they hoped, if all went well and Mala agreed, that Toby would be called in to cut the cord – something he had done many times with livestock, as he had pointed out to Shyama.

'Yes, but you have also lassoed animals in utero and yanked them out with a rope. Try not to do that with our baby, will you?'

That had made him laugh. Why the hell wasn't she here?

'I wanted to buy all the nursery stuff with Shyama,' he said helplessly.

'I understand. But when is she coming back? Do you know? It is just that . . . babies are not like trains. He can come whenever he wants to now.'

An hour later, Toby and Mala were walking around the same department store that Shyama had visited just a few weeks earlier. This time, the sales assistant – the one who had mistaken

Shyama for a grandmother – handed them the New Parents' Checklist, and beamed.

'Oh, not long for you two, by the look of it! When's your due date?'

'December the fourteenth,' they both said together.

Alarmingly, the store had already started its Christmas season. It was busy, piped carols playing in the background as early-bird shoppers hovered around gift displays with furrowed brows, as if ticking off checklists in their heads. The baby section was an oasis of calm amist the chaos, the one department that did steady business all year round.

At that moment, Priya was heading for the ladies' loos, confident of a shorter queue in the baby section. She had already done her Christmas shopping, naturally: a pleasing blend of fun and educational presents for her children, Maya and Luka, and a surprise romantic four-day trip to Venice for Anil and herself just after New Year. She thought they needed some time away together: she had let things slip, they both had. She had just purchased some new underwear for the occasion, which lay folded in frothy layers in her bag. After spending so many years perfecting the art of seduction, maybe it was time she used some of her techniques on her husband. As she passed the first rails of Babygros and bootees, she wondered if it was time to buy something for Shyama's impending arrival. She had clucked her tongue at Shyama's insistence not to buy anything until the last minute – silly superstitions, she had her kids' nurseries designed and ready two months before their due dates. Anyway, surely it was OK now, and that hat with the baby-bear ears attached was to die for. Her phone rang, buzzing like a trapped bee inside her bag.

'Lydia!' she exclaimed with pleasure. 'Sorry about the other night. I hope I didn't keep you up . . .'

Priya had been busy photocopying and scanning various legal documents, following a call from Toby, whose printer had broken down. The papers all related to registering the baby as a surrogate birth in the UK and making Toby and Shyama the legal parents. It had taken a good hour to complete the task, emailing the papers to Shyama's lawyer and making hard copies for safety. So close to the birth, everything had to be ready: Shyama's panicked calls from India to both Toby and Priya had spurred them into action. As it happened, Lydia had been round at Priya's for supper whilst the rest of the family were at the cinema. They had intended to have a girlie catch-up; instead they spent most of the evening talking about their far-away friend and her complicated life as the printer hummed and regurgitated papers in the background.

'So you haven't seen her at all since she came back with her baby mama?' Priya was astonished.

'Only at the police station. I thought there would be some sort of . . . reunion then, given the circumstances, but . . .' Lydia sipped her cranberry juice.

'Well, thank God that worked out OK. Can you imagine, her daughter in prison with everything else going on? You got her that amazing lawyer, didn't you? She didn't even thank you?'

'She did,' Lydia admitted. 'But since then, nothing.'

Lydia had been more hurt than she'd let on. She was hoping that once the baby arrived, once the worry and waiting were over, she and Shyama would find their way back to each other. Tara's occasional emails told her she was thriving in India. That girl had needed a reinvention, not an intervention, and maybe now her daughter was more at peace, Shyama would forgive Lydia, although she still wasn't sure if there had ever been anything concrete to forgive. It all seemed so long ago.

'Lyd, I'm in Mallinson's baby section . . . want me to pick up something on your behalf for the kid? Can I send you a picture of this adorable hat? . . . Shit.'

On the other end of the phone, Lydia heard heavy breathing; rustles and crackles popped in her ear. 'Priya?'

'Lyd . . . can you hear me?' Priya's voice was a whisper now, she sounded as if she was at the end of a wind tunnel.

'Just about . . . what happened?'

'They're here!'

'Who?'

'Oh my God . . . they're buying a bloody car seat . . . buggy . . . half the bloody shop!'

'What are you—'

'Toby! And her!'

'Mala?'

'Who else? Wandering round like a happy couple. This is *so* not right. I'm going to say something . . .'

'Wait!' Lydia's tone was sharp enough to rein in Priya, who was now hovering behind a display of musical potties. 'What can you say?'

There was a pause. Lydia could hear the faint strains of 'Silent Night' in the background.

'Shyama's not here, they need stuff,' Lydia eventually said.

'I could have gone with Toby. I've had kids!'

'Listen, I know it must look strange, but from what I understand from all those contracts you were printing out, once Mala has this baby she signs a piece of paper and then never has any contact again. Do you begrudge her choosing a couple of romper suits?'

'Romper suits went out in the sixties,' Priya answered. And then, 'I know what you're saying, Lyd, but you can't see them . . . Should I tell Shyama?'

'No. What can she do from out there? Maybe she told them to

go ahead and stock up. They've left it rather late already – maybe she knows.'

Priya would bet her entire designer shoe collection that she didn't.

Toby didn't even bother checking the total when he handed over his credit card. He was feverish with anticipation; every purchase brought his son closer to him: the tiny vests, the downy soft blankets, the pleasingly hi-tech rocker, the basket which sat on its own wooden cradle. Baby in a basket, like Moses. It was real. He was going to be a father and this was how fathers felt: complete, expansive, generous, a provider. Shyama had always outearned him, she probably always would, and whilst he appreciated and accepted her generosity (what choice did he have?) and tried to repay it with his support, practicality and muscle-power (yes, he took out the bins, he mended things, he ran errands for her parents), he also wanted to be the kind of man who could whip out a bit of plastic and buy whatever made his woman happy, without sneaking a horrified look at the receipt afterwards. The few times he had insisted on paying for a meal, a book Shyama had seen and admired or a pair of earrings she'd cooed over in passing, she had thanked him warmly and shown off her gift to her parents after-wards, and yet there had always been a slight awkwardness about the exchange, a sense of charade about it, as if they were play-ing roles in a badly written scene, because they both knew that the house they lived in, the food they ate, much of the life they shared, was only possible due to her, and had very little to do with him. Now Mala's happy face was radiating rapture, lit up like a lamp, eclipsing the decorations, all sparkle and shimmer.

Then his phone rang.

'Toby?' Her voice doused him like a cold shower. He instinc-tively moved away from Mala.

'Shyama . . .'

'Are you out? Where are you?'

'Er . . . bought a few things. For the baby. Didn't even have any nappies . . .' He didn't mention that he wasn't alone. 'Sorry, Shyams, I know you wanted me to wait, but—'

'No, that's fine. You did the right thing. You can show me everything soon.'

'What?' Toby's head felt heavy, he was a lumbering oaf.

'I'll be back soon. Papa's just woken up.'

Prem opened his eyes and, like a newborn, encountered a strange new world. He couldn't put his finger on what exactly had shifted: there was his beautiful granddaughter, his smiling daughter, the woman he assumed was his wife, kissing his hand and smoothing his brow. She obviously adored him and there was something so familiar about her, a sense of a shared history, that he felt almost sure that she was indeed Sita. If it turned out not be her, he would be very cross indeed. He sat up, he ate, he walked around on faltering foal-like legs, he had all kinds of tests involving syringes of blood and scans and lights being shone in his eyes, and everyone around him kept telling him well done and talking about miracles and luck and the grace of the gods. The woman who was his wife even went to the local temple to say puja and to make an offering of thanks – although that wasn't like his Sita at all. But he was sure, once he got home – they said in the next couple of weeks – that all the missing pieces in his jigsaw brain would be found and the picture he saw would be him and Sita, together again.

Shyama didn't book her ticket home straight away.

'I want to wait a couple of days or so, just to make sure Papa's OK to travel. Maybe we can all fly back together.'

'Shouldn't you at least reserve a seat or something?' Tara asked through a mouthful of coconut water. They were strolling through one of the street bazaars near the hospital. Neither of them liked the malls, despite the welcome air conditioning. They were enjoying their shared magpie taste for the goods on display, attracted to the cheap glass bangles and the dupattas embroidered with tiny mirrors which caught the hissing flare of the gas lamps dotted like fireflies amongst the stalls. 'The flights will all start booking up soon . . . you don't want to miss my little brother turning up.'

Shyama's stomach contracted at Tara's words. Brother. They would be almost twenty years apart and have no genetic link, and yet her girl was letting him in finally.

'There's still a month to the day,' Shyama said brightly. 'And actually, I want to spend more time with you before—'

'—you spend your days mopping up poo and sick?'

'Before I sit like a Madonna with the chosen babe, overcome with the wondrousness of birth,' Shyama said in her best hippy voice. 'Seriously though, aren't you coming back with me? Your term's nearly over, isn't it?' she continued, skilfully avoiding a large pothole through which a couple of large crows sifted expertly, delicately picking out discarded morsels of old food. 'Your project must be nearly finished now.'

'Ye-es,' Tara hesitated. 'But I have so much work still to finish, a five-thousand-word essay, and all my research material is here. I mean, I could come . . . for a week, maybe?' she added hastily, seeing Shyama's deflated expression. 'If you need help, or—'

Shyama bit back her disappointment. 'No, it's fine. It would be silly for you to fly back just for a few days.'

This wasn't a surprise. Ever since she had had supper with Dhruv's family, she had suspected that Tara would draw out her

India stay as long as humanly possible. Tara's description of the house and his parents had been spot on. They lived in one of the few remaining family *kotees* in central Delhi, in a shady street near a small park. All of the houses around them were impressive new builds, whilst theirs stood aloof in dignified disarray: peeling shutters, a riotously overgrown front garden bursting with bloom, a defiantly battered Maruti on the drive. Dhruv's mother, Gauri, was a literature professor at a local college; his father, Shekhar, did something in publishing. The house was lined with books, paintings were propped up haphazardly against the walls, student types wandered in and out of the open-plan sitting room with food in their mouths – it was the kind of creative chaos Shyama would have loved to have grown up in. The conversation was easy and erudite; Shekhar chain-smoked tiny bidis that smelt of cloves, dropping trails of ash as he waved his hands to emphasize yet another indisputable fact, which his wife would then demolish with a finely turned phrase. Tara and Dhruv sat together, not touching, a calm connection between them.

Shyama managed to get a moment on her own with Gauri late on in the evening, when they were all flushed with good wine and lazy lingering chatter.

'Gauri . . .' she began.

'Oh, please don't do the big thank-you speech, we adore having Tara here. She's been so good for my daughter – such a focused young woman. You must be very proud of her.'

Shyama could only nod. How proud she was she couldn't express. She always had been. She didn't say it enough.

'It's just . . . how can I put this?' Shyama hesitated. 'I don't want to offend anyone . . . a young single girl living here with your son . . . and you, of course. It would be generous and unusual in London. I don't know how it looks in Delhi . . .'

Gauri shrugged her shoulders. 'I don't think anyone is looking, but if they are, I don't care. Do you?'

'Does it seem . . . proper? Sorry if I sound like an old auntie, but you have to help me out a bit here, Gauri. Nobody in my circles back home would let their daughter do this. I mean my Indian friends . . .' Yep, there was the old auntie speech, jumping right out of her mouth. How did that happen? 'Not that I'm in any way traditional . . . I mean I'm divorced – I don't know if Tara told you. I'm with a younger man, English, we're not even married.'

Gauri was listening intently, her keen eyes showing nothing but understanding. Shyama thought, I could tell this woman almost anything, yet she left out any mention of Mala. She had an uncomfortable feeling that this would be the one thing Gauri would not understand.

'So I'm hardly a model mum. In fact, if I tell you all the things I've done wrong or just messed up, we'd be here all night . . . and Tara's weathered them all. And for some reason, she still seems to quite like me.'

Shyama knew she was gabbling now, but this felt like a confessional, an epiphany. All those years spent trying to mould her daughter into the young woman Shyama thought she ought to be, only for Tara to find her own way without her help – or maybe despite her. After so long trying to bend her daughter's will to hers, it was only now that she saw her child clearly, just when she had to learn to let her go.

'What I mean is . . .' Shyama steadied her voice. 'If she stays with you, I would like to cover any expenses . . . we don't want to take your hospitality for granted. But I need to know she's safe. And welcome. And that she won't get hurt . . .'

'Listen to me,' Gauri said softly. 'I did the proper thing for my older daughter and it left everybody broken – her, us, her son.

The people I was trying to impress, appease – they are the same ones who now whisper behind our backs. Who was it for? All of that . . . properness? I trust my son. I trust your daughter. As long as she's under my roof, she is my daughter too. They're decent kids. If anything changes, they will tell us. Right now, they're testing the world together. It's so much easier with a friend, isn't it? Now I think we need a top-up . . .'

Shyama booked her ticket back for 14 November. On 13 November she sat with Sita and Prem in the hospital gardens at the back of the complex. It was a perfect November day in Delhi, warm enough to lounge comfortably outside without a jacket in the crisp air, which would turn chilly after sunset. In their room in Thaya-ji's house, with no heating or curtains, they would have to sit huddled under thick quilts stuffed with layers of raw cotton, so heavy they trapped you where you lay.

The doctors had advised that Prem should stay at least another month to be fit to travel, which would be the baby's due date, but Sita had insisted she could cope now without Shyama, he was back to his old self and the rest of the family were around, of course Shyama must go home.

At the boundary wall, shaded with deep-green Maulsari trees, two men in white kurtas and pressed slacks, armed with long wooden sticks, were trying to scare away a monkey hiding amongst the dense waxy leaves of the upper branches. They didn't seem committed to the task in hand, poking lazily in the general direction of the animal, which strolled around unconcerned, dropping empty peanut shells on their heads.

'Funny, you don't see so many monkeys on the streets any more,' Sita remarked, passing Prem a handful of just-rinsed grapes before she rose stiffly, brushing herself down with quick, impatient movements. 'Bathroom,' she told Shyama as she hobbled off. 'Make sure he finishes that fruit . . .'

Shyama was remembering the monkey on their hotel balcony when she and Toby had first visited the surrogacy clinic, how Toby had quickly undressed her under the slowly revolving ceiling fan, how she had still been talking when he entered her, how much she had taken that enthusiastic passion for granted.

'Is she coming back?' Prem asked, offering her a grape. She popped it into her mouth, the sweet grainy juice bursting on her tongue.

'She won't be long, Papa.'

'She's . . . nice. But she will never replace her.'

'Sorry? Replace who, Papa?'

Prem sighed, rolling the grapes around his palm like worry beads. 'Your mummy.'

Shyama forced the rest of the fruit down her throat; it had become a rubbery tasteless mass. 'That was Mummy . . . she was just sitting here . . .' She tried to keep the panic out of her voice.

Prem patted her hand, his voice husky with emotion. 'I miss her too . . . but she's not coming back, *beti*.'

Shyama took out her phone and by the time Sita returned, she had cancelled her flight.

Mala found Toby sitting on the stairs, his head in his hands.

'Toby sah— Toby?'

Toby looked up wearily. He didn't seem to see Mala, he was talking to himself.

'I asked her, what's more important? I said, if you're not here then what has all this been about?'

Now he was looking at Mala. Was he asking her a question? She lowered herself clumsily on to the step above his. She wanted to smooth his hair, press his head to her stomach so he could feel what she was feeling: elbows and knees responding to his voice. She had never wanted to do that for her husband. It was true, what her family pandit had told them all those years ago after he had performed the funeral rites for her father. Her mother had been sitting cross-legged in their courtyard, her hair loose and unkempt, small cuts on both her wrists where the glass bangles had smashed into her skin as she broke them against the stone floor, her face as pale and unadorned as her new widow's sari.

'Now you must teach your daughters to be *mittee*.' He had squatted next to her, a sheen of perspiration glistening on his bald head, his sandalwood prayer beads entwined around his long thin fingers. 'Sweet like honey to bring them a good man. They have no father, no brother to protect them. Open their hearts like petals. Like the lotus whose roots are in mud, don't let them be bitter. From the mud of this sorrow let something beautiful grow.'

Mala, holding up her sister, both of them numb with shock, had wanted to laugh at the stupid old goat. All his *pagal* pronouncements about flowers and bees weren't going to stop their neighbours crossing the road to avoid her bad-luck-bringing mother, shaking their heads with pretend sorrow at the skinny dark girls who would never get married now. It had taken these many years to understand what he had meant. When Ram had married her, it was an act of charity which he somehow never let her forget, in his easy ownership of her, in his assumption that she would do whatever he wanted and he never had to thank her, because wasn't she the lucky one? Her sweetness would have been seen as weakness; the more she gave, the more he would have drunk her dry.

But with this man, she was giving him something he could

never have achieved without her. So he offered honey as thanks, and thus she opened just for him. But it was brief, this honeymoon. Soon she would not be needed any more. *Chalo*, let me enjoy this, just for a small while longer.

Toby seemed to see her now. He stood up and offered her his hand. 'I had a trip planned . . . a surprise for Shyama. Now she's not coming . . . would you like to?'

Whenever they passed the signs for Stansted airport, Toby always felt that they had finally left London behind. This time it wasn't Shyama sitting next to him, or driving whilst he fed her wine gums and changed CDs on the car stereo. But the same sense of anticipation was there as before, a quickening in his blood, a gradual unknotting of the muscles around his neck and shoulders. He began to whistle loudly and tunelessly, like a happy-chappie workman. Which is, after all, he thought, what I am.

The landscape scrolled past for a while, like the painted background of a cheap cartoon when the same trees and fields keep reappearing behind the frantic characters caught up in a chase, running fast and going nowhere. Then suddenly there was a shift in tone and shade: the denuded hedgerows were further apart, their bare branches revealing unobscured miles of flatness, so many shades of brown, the land in winter repose as stark as he loved to remember it.

They had just crossed the border from Essex into Suffolk when Mala finally spoke.

'We can stop somewhere? For . . . the latrine?'

The coy quaintness of the word charmed him. He found everything charming today.

They eventually found a roadside café a mile or so off the motorway, and decided to stop for lunch. He had expected plastic chairs and microwaved chips. Instead it was a family-run restaurant with gingham tablecloths and home-made pies, with thick serrated crusts that they broke open with their fingers, releasing herby clouds of steam. Mala ate every meal she encountered in the same way she would eat chapatti and daal: she would fashion a piece of bread, a pie crust or a chip into a scoop to mop up whatever else was on the plate. Toby watched the way she walked to the Ladies, swaying from side to side to balance herself like a fat-sailed schooner setting off from shore. Whilst she was on her third toilet visit since they had arrived, Toby pulled out his dog-eared road map and checked the remainder of the route. The car had a built-in sat-nav but he preferred to calculate his own journeys, enjoying the challenge of finding a secret shortcut and not having to drive with a disembodied posh voice telling him when to turn left and right. By his reckoning, they were only an hour or so away.

The gunmetal sky was beginning to fragment near the horizon, in the direction they were heading. As Toby had hoped, by the time they pulled into the driveway, the sky was a pale midwinter blue.

'*Acha!*' was all Mala said when Toby helped her out of the car. They stood for a moment on the gravelled path, taking in the red-bricked rectory with its casement windows framed by climbing ivy which covered most of the front of the house. Toby could tell from Mala's face that she remembered this place, from that evening when he had shared with her his dream of moving out of London, of running his own smallholding. It was meant to be Shyama standing with him now, listening to the big speech he had been rehearsing for weeks – how this all made sense for their new life together as parents, how happy they would be. But it was Mala who smiled back at him like a co-conspirator, Mala who stood by his side when the local estate agent, a hearty middle-aged man with a wind-reddened face, turned up in a muddy Land Rover and shook their hands in greeting; Mala who wandered round the warren of rooms with him, all fusty and dusty as houses without people are, but they could both see beyond the tired wallpaper and dirty windows, knew what a beautiful home it could be. He naturally offered her his arm for balance as they toured the outbuildings and stables, the estate agent warning them away from the iced-over potholes which pitted the main courtyard. It needed work, he agreed, a lot of work, but the potential was huge and he knew for a fact that the owners would take an offer, as it had been empty for some time and they were keen to sell.

'Sadly, the couple in question have gone their separate ways, so . . .' The estate agent shrugged mock sympathetically, brushing a non-existent speck from his brightly patterned tie. 'Why don't I leave you two alone for a while to have a think? Anything you want to view again . . . just give me a shout, I'll be in the car.'

Toby stood looking out over the paddock, one corner of it given over to a training ring; the four-bar fence around the grey sand was weathered, splintered in places. A few jumps remained, the red-and-white-striped poles lying on the ground beside the rusting steel drums on which they must have once balanced, whilst children wearing hard hats and nervous grins hugged their knees to the warm sides of their ponies and prayed for flight. His boy was going to grow up in the saddle – he'd make sure of that.

Mala joined him and they stood in silence for a while, enjoying the birdsong, the wide-open views. She had buttoned up her coat to her neck – or rather Shyama's coat, as Mala owned nothing warm enough that still fitted her any more. Toby remembered Shyama wearing this one, a smocky-type thing with three large buttons, the kind you might find on a toddler's coat, in a bold

384

blue-and-black print. Shyama had told him it was sixties-style, based on a Mary Quant design. He had told her it made her look 'six months gone'. She'd worn it defiantly for a while after that, enjoying the spark that passed between them every time she emerged from the house wearing it. But once they'd started trying for a baby and it became clear that there were problems, the coat had been consigned to the back of the wardrobe.

'You like it so much, don't you?' Mala finally said.

Toby nodded. 'I think Shyama will like it too, don't you?'

Toby looked at her. Her face was so still she looked as if she had been carved out of polished wood. He couldn't understand how she did not seem to know how beautiful she was.

'Who would not like this place?' Mala shrugged. 'You see, horses here . . . cows in that field, yes? With the gate and the high ground. And in this one,' she indicated a small overgrown meadow, 'I would plant food. Not the same as my village. Here you must plant wheat, barley, sugar beet, carrots.'

'You've just named the major crops grown in East Anglia,' Toby said, impressed.

'I know, I googled it. And in this corner . . . just flowers.'

'Flowers don't feed anyone,' smiled Toby.

'When you are not hungry, then you have time for something beautiful.'

Toby jumped as his mobile buzzed in his pocket. He saw the caller ID and walked rapidly away from Mala, further up the dirt track. She saw the guilty twitch, a veil already filming his eyes as he left her behind.

'Toby?' Shyama said, sounding as clear as if she was standing in the next field. 'Are you out and about?'

'Er . . . yep . . . just a few last-minute odds and sods.' He tried not to pant, slowing down his pace so she wouldn't hear the frosted crusts breaking under his boots. 'How's your dad doing?'

'Oh, Tobes . . .'

He wished the line had been less clear so he wouldn't have known she was crying. Shyama never wept loudly or with any great drama, her tears came from somewhere deep and private, unwillingly shed; she always feared seeming weak, appearing needy. He braced himself for bad news.

'Shyams?'

'Sorry.' She sniffed loudly. 'He's . . . he seems so . . . normal. It may be temporary amnesia just from the stress . . . or it could be the beginning of something else. Mum's not coping well.'

Toby spun around at the sound of a loud horn. He saw the estate agent waving from his car window, miming a telephone receiver with his finger and thumb. Toby nodded back in a similarly clichéd manner, doing a thumbs-up Roger-Roger-understood gesture, wishing to Christ the man would just bugger off as quietly as possible.

'Where are you? Is this a bad time?'

'No, no . . . sorry, the traffic is . . . keep talking.'

She carried on while Toby listened, watching a huge flock of starlings swoop across the fields in wide synchonized arcs, tea leaves swirled by an invisible hand around the blue bowl of the sky. She missed him so much, she said, was being torn apart by her conflicting loyalties, tending he who had given her life, wanting to be with the one yet to take his first breath. But her father's final batch of test results would be discussed the day after tomorrow, so she still hoped she could be on a plane home before the baby's due date.

Toby finished the call and turned back towards the rectory. As he walked around the side of the black-painted barn he saw Mala lying on her side, one leg splayed out awkwardly revealing her pink winter sock, the shoe that had covered it a few inches away. The surface of the pothole was all ice and blood.

'Mala?' he shouted, running now, knowing she would not lift her head to hear him.

After the stillness of the farmyard, there was so much noise. The men's voices shouting, and instructions in her ear so kind and calm, the *wa-wa* wail of a siren like keening women following a funeral and the sounds of a fat man puffing loudly in hissy breaths, tyres on tarmac, then the clanging of doors, cold air on her face, the sensation of being lifted as easily as a child, set down, swept away, then more voices, women this time: 'Mrs Shaw? Can you hear me?'

Through her closed lids flashes of light alternated with darkness as she was wheeled through places where sound echoed and bounced back to her, far away, as if she could hear through a conch shell other lives, other worlds. But only one life existed for her, now lying still in her stomach; they were all satellites around a dead star.

'Mr Shaw?' Dr Pardew led him into a small office and shut the door behind her. She looked risibly young at first glance, hair scraped back into a ponytail, a crumpled blouse under her white coat; the bags under her eyes made her look older – it must have been a long shift. In her hand she held a set of what looked like X-rays, except these were black grainy images printed out on thin white paper, a stark relief map that meant nothing to Toby.

'The baby's not in any danger. There's been a slight bleed, but that's all under control and they're both stable.'

Toby felt as if he had been holding his breath for hours; only now could he let out a long exhale, which took all his energy with it. The doctor briefly consulted the form in front of her, checking with him the date of their last scan, how had the results been?

'All fine, as far as we were told . . .' Toby said cautiously. 'Is anything wrong?'

'We are just a bit concerned that the baby seems a little small for its dates.'

Toby wanted to say *his* dates. It bothered him, the refusal to assign an identity to his son.

'Or that . . . no, we were told he's a bit on the small side, but the doctor said he looked fine . . . We were told South Asian kids are generally smaller . . . you know, they're usually under that average weight line of those charts they show you. And maybe we got the dates wrong . . .'

He was aware fear was making him gabble. He wanted to tell her that he had finally read all the baby books Shyama had had piled up on her bedside table for months. He'd even remembered to say 'South Asian' instead of just 'Asian'.

'OK, well that's good to know. Hopefully we can get hold of your last scan results. Do you happen to know if there were any queries then about the amniotic fluid around the baby?'

'I . . . I don't think so.' Toby tried to recall, but his head felt packed with wet cotton wool.

'And has your wife mentioned that the baby hasn't been moving as much recently?'

Toby hesitated, then confirmed that Mala had said something about that a couple of times the week before. They had assumed that he'd just slowed down, as there was less room in there for the little fella to tumble around. The doctor continued writing in rapid strokes until Toby's question made her look up.

'Is there something wrong with him?' Toby's voice sounded high and strange to his ears.

Dr Pardew closed her file slowly. She knew she wasn't firing on all cylinders today. Her job's ridiculous hours helped her make swift decisions and sharp diagnoses, but occasionally did nothing for her people skills. 'I do apologize, Mr Shaw. There are a couple of things which may need investigating.'

'Things?'

'Well, it's a combination of factors. The baby's weight—'

'I already said—'

'Yes, absolutely . . . but that combined with the slightly unusual amount of amniotic fluid and lack of movement . . . What we would like to do is rule out the slight possibility that there may be any chromosomal abnormalities, sometimes indicated by—'

'What? But no one has ever mentioned— Chromosomal? Abnormal?'

'I don't mean to alarm you.'

'Well, you bloody are!' Toby stood up. 'We've been under the best . . . very expensive doctor. How come this hasn't been picked up before?'

Dr Pardew came out from behind her desk and stood beside Toby. Her eyes felt gritty, she badly needed another coffee. 'I am probably being over-cautious, and when I've seen your previous scans and talked with your own doctor, we can all relax.'

'Relax?' Toby slumped back in his seat.

Dr Pardew perched awkwardly on the desk beside him. 'Would you prefer to be under your own consultant? We can arrange—'

'No,' Toby said calmly. 'First tell me what you think is wrong and what you think we should do.'

Dr Pardew recognized the set jaw of the stoic in this young man and her explanation was swift and frank. The procedures were simple: an amniocentesis and parental blood tests would confirm or dismiss any suspicion of chromosomal issues. The only point at which Toby blanched was when she informed him that the test results would take at least ten days to come back. As his wife was still bleeding, Dr Pardew did not advise moving her until she and the baby were stable, but she could offer a transfer to a London hospital after that. She would of course discuss all of this with their own doctor in the morning. And in the meantime they should try not to worry. It was probably nothing.

Nothing.

Toby had been following everything pretty well until she started talking about translocations. The science of it was blandly comforting.

'. . . if we find the translocation in either you or Mrs Shaw, that's fine. If it's present in both of you, there is a fifteen per cent risk of a genetically inherited flaw, and then we can look at further options . . .'

His mind was on the larger truth of what all these tests would reveal. That Mala was not Mrs Shaw, that she had no genetic connection to this child – only he did. But would they then refuse to treat her? Would they inform the authorities? All those nightmare stories whispered in the back of the clinic's people-carrier returned to him: surrogate children who ended up stateless, left to languish in foster care whilst red tape looped around them, strangling their futures. Shyama would know what to do; she had dealt the most with their lawyer. Maybe the minute they did the tests they would know the truth anyway. As he didn't know what he could and couldn't say at this moment, he simply nodded his head until the doctor was standing up again, clipboard under her arm and furtively checking her watch.

'Mr Shaw? Is there anything else you need to ask me?'

Toby cleared his throat. 'So if we find something . . . anything
. . . I mean he's due next month – so there's nothing we can do
now anyway, is there?'

Dr Pardew sat down again next to Toby with a faint sigh. It
would be hard getting up again. She knew she owed this man
another half an hour. And all the other patients waiting for her,
short-changed again. Never enough time. 'I'm sorry this has all
happened like this. Normally you'd be offered genetic counselling. We don't have anyone here right now, but I can get on to
that first thing tomorrow. And I will say it again at the risk of
sounding repetitive – this may well all be a false alarm, and in
ten days' time all you will have to worry about will be welcoming your healthy baby into the world.'

Even though Shyama had been unsure about going out to eat
that evening, Tara had insisted she needed a break. Prem was
sitting up, chatty, animated; his hand never left Sita's, whom he
seemed to recognize so naturally that he thought it odd when
she carefully asked him once or twice who she was. In fact, he
couldn't remember ever not recognizing her, was shocked by her
tears, saddened by her relief that he had come back to them.

'I haven't been anywhere, *jaan* . . .' He patted her arm and
waved off Tara and Shyama. Half an hour later they found themselves at Koti, the trendy new establishment which had fashioned
itself on a Rajasthani bazaar. You had to pay an entrance fee to
be admitted.

At first, Shyama assumed the ringing phone was not hers but
Tara's, as she had been texting on it every ten minutes, no doubt
providing a running commentary of her evening for Dhruv,
whom she would see in an hour or so and then repeat the whole
story to again.

'Sorry, Toby!' Shyama said breathlessly, finally finding a quieter spot behind a stall selling carved wooden trunks with heavy brass locks. 'I should have called earlier . . . Dad's suddenly turned a corner, he's . . .'

She had to walk further away to hear everything, found herself leaning against the boundary wall, the stone cool against her back, crickets violining their legs somewhere near her hair. She repeated what Toby suggested she had to do: talk to Dr Passi, get the medical records of the egg donor and email them back immediately. Yes, he had done the right thing to say nothing yet; yes, she understood the baby was fine, she wasn't to worry.

'Have you got hold of Mr O'Connell?' she managed to say. 'What hospital are you at? Sorry? What the fuck were you doing in Suffolk?'

Toby, shivering in the hospital car park, spoke without thinking, his mind clouded with worry. He still recalled the easy honesty of their last conversation and hoped that everything he said would reassure her: he'd been hunting down a new home for them, buying clothes and a bed for the baby. Yes, Mala had been with him, but only because Shyama couldn't be, and he had missed her every moment. He offered up the truth as a gift.

All Shyama heard was his assumption that she would sell the house – her house – to fund his pipe dream. All she saw was Toby walking hand-in-hand with Mala, choosing changing bags and tiny knitted hats, wandering around a country place she had known nothing about until now, planning a future in which she was a distant bystander. Flashes of memory spooled into a story, frame by frame: how he had rushed to open the car door for Mala when they first arrived; how he always insisted on escorting her upstairs before her bath; how, many times, she had caught them talking into the night, and their sudden silence when she entered the kitchen; how he had ignored Mala so studiously at first that it was clear he had wanted to look; how, after that, he couldn't stop looking as she glided around making potions, feeding them, the fecund Lady Bountiful doing everything that Shyama did, but better, and so much younger. Shyama had always imagined that she would fight for this relationship if it faltered. Initial worries about losing Toby to a woman his own age had faded when they had embarked on this journey together, a commitment more significant than marriage. Since then she had always assumed that she would be battling different rivals: boredom, wrinkles, the libido-draining sleepless nights that accompanied a small child. But not this. How could she fight the woman who sustained all their hopes of a shared future? Who nourished her lover's child, which she had paid her to carry?

'Are you in love with her?' Shyama asked him calmly.

'What?' Any answer he may have given was drowned by the scream of an ambulance siren as it pulled into its bay. By the time Toby had moved far enough away to ask her to repeat what he thought he had heard, the line was dead.

Toby sat by Mala's side all night, checking his phone every half-hour, willing it to ring, waiting to hear Shyama's voice with all the answers. In the morning, he brought Mala treats from the small but well-stocked on-site supermarket: chocolate, apples, milkshake in a carton, glossy magazines. Of course he loved her, but only because he loved the baby she carried. This was what he told himself as he held her hand and watched the long, almost invisible amniocentesis needle puncturing her protruding stomach. He half expected to hear a loud pop and a rude noise as she deflated, revealing the child on the screen, so unmistakeably a small person now with eyelashes and restless fingers, to be a hologram, a hoax. But his boy slept on soundly; the only sign that he had even registered the intrusion into his silent watery world was a sudden twitch of his small and perfect foot.

He left her for a while to have his own blood test, welcomed the discomfort as a distraction, watching the syringe fill with the ruby liquid that contained all his secrets, the inherited flaws of his past, the possibilities of his cellular legacy. And then back to her bedside in the noisy six-bed ward. She looked almost comical in her blue gown, a tiny head and slim legs and feet bookending the enormous dome of her, a beached whale, a python who had swallowed a giant egg. She looked grave with responsibility and only broke into a wisp of a smile when she waved him farewell. His throat felt thick with emotion. He had another nine days of this.

In the car park, he checked his phone again. Shyama had not called, but she had left a short text. 'Dr Passi out of the country. Told no one else available to give more detailed info on egg donor. Makes no difference now. We have to live with what we have.'

There were more texts and emails but he never got to talk to Shyama directly, despite leaving her regular voice messages. Not that there was anything new to report – every day passed the same way. Mala's bleeding continued on and off so she stayed put; the foetal heart monitor became their reassurance: there he was, tiny horses' hooves galloping their glee. If there was something wrong with this child, he didn't know and didn't care. Toby would bring Mala fruit and magazines and they would eat lunch together, though there was a new formality between them. He kept his conversation light, polite, skimming over the subtext that seemed to underpin every exchange. She held herself carefully all the time now, every shift slow and deliberate. He sometimes had to look away; he did not want to see her tender movements which gave away the unpalatable truth: she was frightened too, because she cared way beyond her job description as womb for hire. How could she not? How could they, any of them, have assumed otherwise?

In the afternoon he would get into the car and drive aimlessly around the country lanes, carefully avoiding any old haunts or places where familiar faces might lurk. Suffolk was a big county but not big enough to lose the fear that clawed at his skin, his chest. A long and at times angry conversation with Mr O'Connell, their obstetrician, the same soothing reassurances, the same tiny note of doubt – he told Shyama all of it and all he ever got back were her typed responses: 'That's fine', 'Agree – go ahead', 'Late here – let u know tomorrow'. The test results, they both knew, would only tell them half the story: Toby's genetic gift or curse. But in the end, did it matter now? They were experiencing the hopes and fears of every parent for the being they had created. And what would they do if their creation turned out to be flawed? Give him back like a faulty product? This child was an x-ray of their shared conscience. If he was anything less than the perfect and carefully chosen baby they had ordered, how they coped with him would expose who they really were: people who wanted to be parents at any cost, or people who decided the cost was now far too high.

Nine days after she had been admitted, Mala was well enough to be discharged. Though it hadn't been a holiday of any description, she looked better, rested; her colour had returned, along with the fresh openness of her face. A kindly orderly had sponged the mud off her maternity trousers. The coat would have to be dry-cleaned.

Despite Dr Pardew's assurances that they could send the test results to London, Toby insisted they would wait for them in Suffolk. If it was bad news, he wanted to be standing on his home soil, pathetic as that sounded. He took Mala back to the nearby hotel where he had been staying, a cheap and cheerful popular chain, clean, no frills, cooked breakfast included. His family farm was less than an hour away. It could have been the other side of an ocean. He tried to imagine Matt's face if he turned up with Mala in tow. He fleetingly wondered when he'd ever be able to pay back that advance.

It turned out that there were no other free rooms on Toby's floor and he worried about Mala being too far away if anything happened in the night. As he had a twin bedroom, he paid a supplement and they stayed in the same room. Only a week ago this would have been wildly inappropriate, but in this strange limbo period it became just another new version of reality. He left the room whilst Mala changed and showered, shivering in the car park as he left another message for Shyama, hoping that this time she would relent and take his call. Mala was asleep when he crept back into the bedroom. She snored gently, while he lay wide awake for most of the night. Once, in the blue light of his phone screen, he saw his child ripple its presence across Mala's stomach. All Toby could hear in his head was, *There were three in the bed and the little one said, 'Roll over, roll over'.*

They got the call to come back in the next day. Toby noticed that Dr Pardew was wearing exactly the same style blouse as when she had discharged them the day before, but in a different colour. It probably saved time, he thought randomly. His knee shook a little as he shifted in the hard plastic chair.

Dr Pardew pushed her glasses on top of her head and smiled. 'Well, I have good news. Firstly, we found the translocation in you but not in Mrs Shaw, so the baby is healthy. There's no abnormality.' She faltered in the ensuing silence. 'Mr Shaw? You do understand, I hope, that the worry is over. I've already let Mr O'Connell know. Horrible that you had to go through the uncertainty, but at least—'

'Sorry,' Toby interrupted. 'I have to tell you something . . . The tests may not be accurate, because . . .' He trailed away. Once said, this changed everything. He looked at Mala, expecting her frightened face to be staring back at him. Instead she seemed at ease, prepared. She laid a firm hand on his knee to still its quaking. He swallowed and continued. 'You see . . . Mala is a surrogate. This child, it's my sperm and a donor egg. From a clinic in India. My wife's out there now, but she wasn't able to find out anything more about the woman whose egg it is, but—'

The doctor raised her fingertips, requesting a pause, looking concerned.

'No, can I finish?' Toby ploughed on. 'It means these tests – they're worthless, aren't they? I should have said. I thought . . . well, I thought you should know.'

Dr Pardew took a moment to scrunitize them both, shuffled her notes and then said, 'I'm afraid that's impossible, Mr Shaw. I won't muddle this with medical terms, but what the tests do show without any doubt is a genetic link between this baby and Mrs . . . and you.' She nodded at Mala. 'It was your egg that grew this child.' She turned back to Toby. 'And as you said, your sperm. You are both its biological parents. One hundred per cent.'

# CHAPTER TWELVE

I THINK I HAVE always known. He is mine. This was Mala's single thought throughout the fog of the next few days. Through-out all the shouted phone and Skype calls, hai, such a *garbard* of slamming doors and Toby stamping like a *balloo*, bear-feet up and down the stairs, throughout the days where she struggled downstairs to make her meals, *theklo*, I am always leaving enough in the pan for him, always finding it uneaten. So much to do now with the sorting of my baba's clothes and toys, working out how to make the seat that goes in the car into a pram, *nahin*, bug-gy. Bug is also an insect, and he will look like a caterpillar wrapped in layers of blankets, a small cocoon with a face peeping out. And yet she couldn't sleep. Every time I lie down, why do you wake up for a dance? But now you are dancing for me, so I will put the second pillow between my thighs, so heavy down there now, you are pressing on my bones, you are coming soon. And she would say it to herself, sometimes silently, sometimes out loud in both Hindi and English. *He is mine.*

She was standing in the garden one morning, watching the steam from her chai curl in clouds through the cold air, when Toby joined her. Someone else also wasn't sleeping: he had red eyes like a night jackal and a smell coming off him like rain-soaked hay going rotten. He carried a bundle of papers in his hands.

'Mala . . .' he began.

'I cannot pay any money. I have to give back. I cannot go back to India alone with a baby. I only know all the things I cannot do, Toby.'

Toby nodded resignedly, unconsciously crumpling the sheets in his hand. 'Shyama,' he began. It hurt him to say her name. 'She's not coming back yet . . . Sometimes she blames Dr Passi, sometimes . . . us.'

Mala nodded. *Leh,* what woman would not think what she was thinking? Maybe this was what happened when people tried to cheat Nature, or maybe it was just that hard-faced doctor who was an A-One cheat all along. They would never have known any of this if Mala had not slipped on the ice. She had never paid much attention to her religious studies in the under-the-tree school in her village. Master-ji seemed to favour any story that warned girls about bad behaviour and the consequences of disobeying their men: Sita kidnapped by the demon Ravan after stepping out of the golden circle of protection drawn for her by her husband, Lord Ram, was one of his favourites. Yet one story had stuck with her. How could it not? That doctor woman had recited it to all the Hindu women who entered her doors.

'Surrogacy is even blessed by our holy book. You have heard about Lord Krishna's own brother, Balarama? He was transferred from the womb of Devaki to the womb of Rohini to ensure his safe birth!'

When Mala had asked why, Dr Passi had given her an impatient look. 'Look it up,' she said, 'and remind yourself that what you are doing is approved by the gods . . .'

But we are not gods, Mala thought sadly, just men and women, and you only need one man and one woman to end up like this.

'I have to ask you something.' Toby broke into her thoughts. He sat on the small garden wall, his eyes crinkling as he looked up at her, the tentative sun behind her like a halo. 'Would you consider keeping our bargain? We will give you double what we agreed.'

'We?' Mala asked. 'Shyama Madam wants this? Is it what you want?'

He did not answer. He could not meet her eyes. She felt a cold fury rising from the soles of her feet, suffusing her whole body.

'All my life I am a thing bought and sold. I thought this is all I would ever be. But you and Shyama Madam have shown me another kind of life. Where honey costs more than gold . . .' Her mother's words came back to her; she wished she could be here to see her now, remembering them – and in English, too. 'You won't believe me when I say I don't care about the money, because that is what you think I only understand. Here I can be someone. And so can my son. You have a price for that?'

Mala took his hand. She ran her fingers over his roughened palms, she felt the weight of his head bent like a tree against the wind. 'You have given me so much. But now we are equal.'

I think I have always known. He was never mine. This was Shyama's recurring thought after that phone call from Toby, the only one she had finally chosen to accept, ready to hear the test results, whether good or bad. Beneath the shock was a jolt of recognition, almost *déjà vu*, the coming together of something inevitable. It walked alongside her in the hospital grounds, in her uncle's house where her parents now stayed as her father recuperated, in the room of the small hotel nearby which had become her refuge. She told the family she needed the space to work, she had some business plans, she may be staying longer than expected. She booked the room for a month.

She wondered if marrying Toby would have made a difference, but she suspected not. She wondered how differently she would have felt about ageing, about having another child, if she had been with a man her own age. His muscles would be softening at the same rate as hers, their temples turning silver together, spidery veins appearing in hidden folds of skin. Keeping up with Toby had certainly kept her looking and feeling young – she'd always enjoyed the surprise on others' faces when they dared to ask how old she was. And it wasn't as if she'd had to go clubbing with him regularly in a mutton-dressed-as outfit or had required the use of an inhaler to beat him at tennis. Their life together had been, in essence, quite staid: good food, supper with friends, cinema, walks. His connection to animals and the land, the fact that he was a country boy at heart, had given him a maturity beyond his years, a solid, old-fashioned air. Even now, she knew he loved her.

But some things are more powerful than love. Just as water always finds an outlet, the same could be said for the urgent desire to procreate, thrusting its roots through propriety and common sense like weeds through paving stones. Shyama remembered those feelings: they had led her to this place, this moment, filling her body with that consuming need for a child, a piece of them both, flesh of their flesh. But it was Mala and Toby who had created a life together, and now that information was no longer a secret, they would share that connection for ever. Oh, she could get Toby back, she was sure of that – his own guilt and sense of duty would keep him with her for a while. But no matter where Mala ended up, no matter who claimed the child, they would be indivisible in thought and memory and longing for what might have been. Mala, Toby and their son.

*

Mala defied the statistics and went two days over her due date before her waters broke without warning as she was making a third round of buttered toast. Toby's first thought was there must be a leak under the sink. And his second that they had better get a move on as it was rush hour. As he waited outside Mala's door, hearing her gasps as she changed out of her wet clothes, refusing his offer of help, he texted Shyama: 'Mala's just gone into labour. You know where we will be.'

Shyama received it just as she was washing her hands in the cramped bathroom of her uncle's extension, about to watch a late-night movie with her parents, who were curled around each other on their bed like speech marks.

Around the same time, less than three miles away from Shyama, a young woman was boarding a bus with her male companion. He was a software engineer, she a physiotherapy student. Her father was an agricultural labourer who had sold land to pay for her studies and worked double shifts to sustain them all; she was the first in her family to attend college. Later her father would say it had never crossed his mind not to educate his daughter as well as his sons, for who could deny a little girl who loved going to school? The two young people had just seen *The Life of Pi* at a cinema complex and boarded a virtually empty bus, their only companions five men and the driver.

Shyama sat on her half-packed suitcase in the darkness of her hotel room, her passport in her hand, unable to move. By then, Mala had reached the hospital, been admitted to her bed, given a hospital gown and attached to a foetal monitor. During the next hour, the young woman on the bus would sustain a gang rape of such brutality that afterwards her intestines were seen looping

402

out of her body. The iron rods used to penetrate her were also used to knock her companion unconscious; he was then bound and gagged as the attack continued. By the hour's end, Shyama had still not moved from her seat in the dark, except to switch off her phone. Mala's pains had begun in earnest; held in the grip of a giant fist, she clenched her teeth so hard that she tasted blood. The midwife urged her to relax and breathe through the pain, as it was only just beginning. At that moment the young woman and man were thrown out of the bus on to a busy roadside; he just managed to pull her body away as the driver tried to reverse over her, before speeding off. It took the young man several attempts to flag down a passing car to get someone to assist them. They were both partially clothed and the unconscious young woman's body was covered with bite marks. By the time she had been put on a life-support machine in Safdarjung hospital with irreparable damage to her womb, intestines and internal organs, and reports of the assault had begun to filter through news and social-media networks, Mala held a son in her arms. He had her eyes and his father's chin, and neither of them could look away from him for a long time.

Tara burst into the room, surprised to see her mother lying on the bed in the same clothes as the night before.

'Have you heard?' was all she said, before she grabbed the remote to switch on the small portable television perched on top of the chest of drawers.

For a few seconds Shyama thought, Toby must have called Tara when he couldn't get hold of me. Maybe he's sent a picture. I have to tell her I would rather not see it. Then the screen blared into life – her parents always had the volume up far too high – just as the headline appeared: DELHI BUS RAPE. The two women said nothing throughout the report, watching with a growing sense of horror and disbelief as the details emerged. There were experts of several kinds, discussing the rise in attacks nationwide, police ignorance and inefficiency, and low conviction rates; politicians supplied soundbites saying that more would and should be done and that the perpetrators would most definitely be caught. And then a short-haired woman talked straight to camera, barely controlled fury spitting through every word.

'You could argue the reason this case has become headline is because the victim is seen as a respectable middle-class college girl, when hundreds of poor and Dalit women, brutalized every day, never make the news. Firstly, every woman should be counted, no matter where she comes from. Second, even I, who have worked for so many years in this field . . . what happened to this woman . . .'

She paused here, struggling to find her flow again – there were no words for what had happened. 'Are we less than human now? What have we become?'

'That's my boss, Kavita,' Tara said quietly. The report ended and Tara switched off the television. Time seemed to have stopped; the silence in the room hung thickly. Shyama had the sensation of being suspended and weightless, looking down at herself looking at her daughter. Her darling daughter, who did not weep or lash out as she would have done not long ago, but who looked back at her steadfastly, her heart wide open, and what Shyama saw there almost made her buckle. She was reminded of a Frida Kahlo painting in which she had painted her body as if split wide open for an autopsy, as exposed as a dissected frog in a school lab. Frida's face held her usual knowing, mischievous look, eyebrows and upper lip defiantly untended, staring straight out of the canvas and right into your soul. Yet her anatomically detailed torso revealed the secrets you would never guess from her expression: the smashed bones, the battered heart, the empty womb. Tara's eyes told Shyama what she should have known – what she would have guessed, if she hadn't been so enveloped in her own blind desires. It wasn't just ideology that had brought her girl to this place; there had been something else, something that had left damage and determination in its wake.

'I can't bear this any more,' Tara whispered, her hands clasped around her body, trying to quell the quaking of her bones, her ragged breath. She managed to make it across the room in wounded, weary steps before she broke on the rocks of her mother's arms. As the sun moved across the room, they talked, their shadows marking out the day like a sundial, every shade and dip of emotion, from grief through fury to an exhausted, tender calm. Shyama could not help touching her daughter, she had to hold her, press into her limbs, bury her face against her chest. She wanted to reach inside and remove every trace of what had hurt her baby, eat it, take it inside herself as punishment, penitence. She would do anything to make her whole and happy again.

'Do you remember,' Shyama asked some time in the late afternoon, 'that time when Uncle Yogi and Auntie Neelum came to visit us? You were about twelve.'

They were both lying on the bed in a nest of damp tissues and empty biscuit packets. Neither of them had wanted to leave the room, so they had simply eaten their way through Sita's emergency snack bag.

'I was thirteen,' Tara said, curling into Shyama's side. 'And how could I forget, such a happy family summer that was . . .'

That had been Yogesh and Neelum's only British visit, and naturally Prem had insisted his beloved brother stay with them, in the days when the illegally occupied flat was an embarrassing no-go conversation topic rather than the brotherly betrayal it eventually became. Shyama had given up her bedroom and shared a bed with Tara for a month, whilst her parents ferried Yogesh and Neelum around various tourist attractions and kitty parties, one day insisting that they visit the area where Shyama would eventually open her salon. Prem had been keen to show their Indian family how London embraced all their needs: no more driving miles to root out a clove of garlic or a green chilli as they had had to do in the seventies, behold the *pukka desi* market in all its noisy glory. Yogesh had beamed and nodded enthusiastically as Prem had walked him past the bustling pavement stalls, all lit up as the dusk crept in, the street-food vendors shouting out their wares.

'*Theklo, bhaiya,*' Prem beamed. 'Now tell me, is this any different to Pusa Road market?'

Neelum had cleared her throat delicately, wrinkling her nose as a particularly strong gust of fried jalebi came her way, her jowls obscuring the heavy diamond and gold choker she'd considered suitable for a wander around a street market. 'Pusa Road was never this dirty. And the clothes! What is it with you Brits and polyester?'

'There are designer boutiques further along, actually,' Sita had said brightly. 'There's one, Zameena, she has made clothes for Cherie Blair.'

'Probably OK for *angrezi* who don't know better, but really, *bhabhi*, aren't you embarrassed by how low-class this all is? This is the kind of market our servants go to. I won't step into any shopping place without air conditioning and a valet-parking man. But this is the problem you have. In this country, they let everyone and anyone in when you came, not like US or Australia, where they only let the educated classes enter. Here every Bihari bus driver and Mirpuri mud cleaner was allowed to come in, and then brought the whole extended family, also. This is why you are getting all the racialism, isn't it? They are painting even decent people like you with the same colour.'

'Brush,' interrupted Tara, whom everyone had forgotten was there.

'What, *beti*?' Neelum smiled. 'Brush what?'

'You say you paint people with the same brush,' Tara had continued evenly, her face deadpan, always a bad sign. Shyama could remember that expression so clearly, even now. She remembered thinking at the time, I probably ought to jump in like a good Indian mummy and clip her round the ear for daring to correct an elder. But she had been fascinated to see what would happen next.

'And in any case,' Tara had continued, 'all the really kickin' stuff in music and fashion and even comedy is coming from here, probably 'cos we're really mixed up together, and, like, I don't know whose mum or dad was a farmer or an "Untouchable" back in India and I don't care either, 'cos we're all seen as brown here anyway. Not like in India, where you treat the servants like crap and let people live in houses that don't even belong to them and won't give them back.'

Shyama repeated the speech word for word, mimicking Tara's thirteen-year-old eye-rolling and sassy head-snapping, making Tara smile, so achingly sweet to see.

'Oh . . . my . . . God! I'll never forget Neelum's face, it was like I'd crapped in her designer handbag and emptied it over her thieving head. And Nanima and Nana were *sooo* embarrassed, they kept saying, "She has a lot of exam stress right now." I cannot believe you . . . how did you remember so much of it . . . all of it?'

'Because I wished I had said it,' Shyama said simply. 'Because that's when I knew you were already braver than I would ever be. And I should have said that then. So I'm saying it now. I am so proud of everything you have been, everything you are, and everything you are going to be.'

Tara shredded the end of a tissue into a tiny blizzard before looking back up. 'Aaah. That may just be my next tattoo . . .'

'Your *next*—?'

Tara smiled again, softer this time, retreating into herself again for a moment.

'We can get him, you know, I can call lawyer Gina right now . . .' Shyama said eventually. 'When you get back we can go straight to the police. You have five years to bring a charge . . .'

'Not yet, Mama. When I'm ready.'

'I wish you'd told me. What kind of a mother am I?'

'Mine. I'm so glad you're mine.'

The whole city held its breath for the two weeks that Nirbhaya clung to life. For legal reasons her identity could not be released to the press, but people needed to name her so that they could claim her as their own and show their support and outrage. Nirbhaya, the fearless one, seemed to be the most popular name. Demonstrations sprang up spontaneously outside the hospital, around India Gate and the Lok Sabha, then spread to other cities – Bangalore, Kolkata, Mumbai, Paris, London – silent candlelit vigils with home-made placards, angry marches with mega-phones; hundreds of thousands joined in on social media, where users replaced their profile pictures with a black dot to symbolize their solidarity and spread the message.

Shyama rarely attended any of these events. She preferred to be in the office, where an extra pair of hands was always welcome, to make tea and bring in food, to answer the constantly ringing phone, to make banners, painting slogans sometimes in Hindi, following the curves and lines of letters she could not read. She would send Tara and Dhruv off with bottles of water and roti rolls when it was their turn to take a shift on a vigil, reminding them every time to stay near each other and keep away from the police. The calm of the empty office after the frantic activity of each day was some sort of balm. Shyama would tidy and wash up, keeping an eye on the twenty-four-hour news channel on the computer screens. Occasionally she would forget for a moment about the three of them back in London, but they were always with her in some way. Well, there were so many children running around wherever you went – there were Tara and Dhruv, so obviously besotted with each other, each private look and coded smile a bittersweet reminder of the love she thought she had found second time around. And then there were the young men – so many of them at every demo and vigil, standing alongside the women, letting the world know: 'Not in My Country' and 'This Is Not Me'. She hoped that one day the boy so far away would grow up to be like them.

By the time the Indian government made the decision to move the gravely ill Nirbhaya to a specialist hospital in Singapore, Christmas had been and gone, barely a blip in Shyama's calendar. Tara and Dhruv had been caught up in a demonstration at India Gate on 21 December which had turned violent and been broken up by water cannon and tear gas, the crowds sick of the continuing apathy of officials in the face of their continual demands for change and action. Five men had been charged, one of them a juvenile of just seventeen, but everyone knew how long getting to trial could take. There were renewed calls for fast-track courts which went unheeded, and feelings were inflamed by comments from one of the accused's defence lawyers, who declared he had never heard of a single incident of rape suffered by a respectable lady, and that furthermore, the victim's male companion was wholly responsible for the attack because he had failed to protect her honour. A prominent holy man suggested the victim herself could have avoided any harm if she had simply chanted God's name, thrown herself at the feet of her attackers and begged for mercy.

Shyama and Gauri had ordered both their children out of their soaked clothes, bathed their swollen eyes and given them ginger infusions for their inflamed throats. Still Tara and Dhruv sat in front of the television and their computer screens with their mugs in their hands, channel hopping and monitoring feeds to check the varying coverage of the incident, occasionally shouting at paraded politicians in hoarse overlapping voices. Shyama wondered if Tara had confided in Dhruv, shared with him the secret she'd kept for so long, which still rose every day at unexpected moments in Shyama's head, a shark fin in a seemingly calm sea. Maybe that's why he was so polite and respectful with her, careful even. Or maybe that's how boys were here. Some boys.

'Look at them both,' Gauri sighed, proud and fearful. Shyama understood that. 'Tara said you might be going back soon?'

'My parents are anxious to return, they've been away some time.'

'She will be fine with us,' Gauri reassured her.

'Oh I know, that's not what I'm worried about.' Shyama sighed. 'Her college course . . . amongst other things.'

'You know, we run a very similar course here at my college. It has an excellent reputation. In some cases, for someone with Tara's grades, we could look into the possibility of a year's exchange. She could apply for financial support via a scholarship scheme.'

'Has Tara been talking to you, by any chance?'

Gauri laughed. 'No, Dhruv has been talking to me. When I tried to raise the subject with Tara, she said she wasn't going to discuss anything before talking to you . . . such old-fashioned respect. What's your secret?'

'Where do you want to start?'

Nirbhaya died on 29 December in Singapore and the streets in so many cities roared in mourning in response. Commentators were calling this India's version of the Arab Spring. The taboo of sexual violence, India's hidden shame, was not so hidden any more, and as people like Kavita continued to stress, not just India's shame. The government hurriedly set up a judicial committee, asking for suggestions from the public as to how they could amend the law to provide quicker investigation and prosecution for such crimes. They received eighty thousand replies.

Shyama had managed to book tickets back to London for herself and her parents on 31 December; it seemed not many people wanted to fly on New Year's Eve. Despite her unashamed pleading with Tara, no amount of bribery or half-hearted emotional blackmail could persuade her to join them. She told her mother it was less to do with Dhruv (did she think she was the kind of woman who would build her plans around a boyfriend?) and more to do with what was happening at Shakti; it felt too momentous to leave Delhi at the moment. Besides, here her shedding of her old skin could continue, along with her acquisition of new landscapes, new faces, new beginnings.

Shyama thought it was fitting to leave on that particular day. She had never been a fan of New Year's Eve parties – too many anti-climactic renditions of 'Auld Lang Syne' in overcrowded sitting rooms, getting kissed by drunk strangers, thinking about how to get a cab home as the last chime sounded. There was always a sense of melancholy mixed in with the mad partying: how quickly the time had gone since last year's awful do at Dave and what's her name's place; all the resolutions made and broken – still smoking, still overweight, still single or married and still not happy about it. But still here, that was something.

The pilot told them they would have the privilege of seeing in the new year a few times as they flew over different time zones – or, the only way Shyama could imagine it, flying backwards against the clock, reversing the hands again and again to welcome in several new years. Prem and Sita were happily seated next to her with their travel pillows and blankets; she had set each of them up with their headphones and personal screens and they were already looking forward to the complimentary salted snacks. They had asked her about the baby some time ago. She had told them what she knew from Toby: he was six pounds exactly and healthy. They had known not to ask anything else. Not right now.

Only once they had taken off did Shyama allow herself to click on the picture attachment on her phone which had been there unopened since she had received it. She could see Mala's arm cradling him against her chest. Toby must have taken the picture – nothing of him except in the child's chin and his unblinking, wise expression. What was she worried about? It was just a baby, after all. Just another everyday miracle. She deleted the attachment and ordered herself a vodka and orange juice. Prem was busy fiddling with random buttons, Sita fussing over his seat belt. Shyama saw her hesitate just once, when Prem turned to look at her – at her hands on his lap adjusting his buckle, and then back at her face, trying to place where he might have seen her before. But before she could be sure, it was gone, as momentary as the fireworks that began to leap up from the ground far below in blazing arcs and fade away as quickly as falling stars.

# ONE YEAR LATER

'G OD, I HATE bloody sat-navs!' Shyama said for the fourth
time as she pulled the car into a lay-by and prepared to
do another three-point turn.

'I offered to drive . . .' Lydia murmured, blowing smoke from
the side of her mouth out of the open window.

'And can't you put that out now? It's freezing in here,' Shyama
moaned as she screeched off in the direction from which they
had just come. 'According to this stupid machine, they live in the
middle of a field . . .'

'I think you might be right there,' Lydia said suddenly. 'Slow
down, there's an opening just here. Turn left . . . *left*!'

'You just said right!'

At the last moment, Shyama managed to manoeuvre the car
on to the rutted track, where it hit a pothole and stalled. She put
the handbrake on and took a deep breath. Beyond the sparse
hedges, sleeping fields stretching for miles, a creased brown
blanket sugared with frost.

'You sure about this, Shyams?' Lydia threw her stub out of the
window and closed it, muffling the distant caw of crows. She
took Shyama's hand, which was cold and clammy, in hers and
rubbed it vigorously.

Shyama nodded.

'Thanks for coming with me,' she finally said.

'I told you, I'm on call. Any time.'

Shyama restarted the car and edged slowly up the lane. She didn't know how she would have got through the past year without Lydia. It mattered less that she happened to be a therapist, more that they had a shared history which needed no explanation. The relief was that she didn't have to talk it all out, she could rely on silent shorthand and get on with other things. In fact, when she had first returned, all Shyama had wanted to talk about was Tara. Had Lydia known? No, but she had guessed something like that might have happened. Shyama had waited for the recriminations, the I-told-you-sos that never came. She had remembered then why she loved Lydia so much. She asked if she would try and persuade Tara to return to the UK and press charges against Charlie, whose name she could hardly bear to say. Lydia repeated what Tara had said: when she's ready, and when she's strong enough to face the inevitably long and painful process, they would all be there for her, armed and dangerous.

Whilst Lydia had appointed herself unofficial nurse and all-round wise woman, Priya had been assigned the role of chief entertainments officer, showing up with tickets for the theatre or an invitation to an art-gallery opening, turning up unannounced with fish and chips and Trivial Pursuit. There had never been much talk about what exactly had gone wrong between Shyama and Toby; it was enough to know that it had, and badly. And because they were women of a certain age and they knew life's curve balls oh-so-well, it was best just to dust her off and get her back to gorgeousness. Or at least functioning, which she had been doing, pretty well.

The phone rang and switched to speaker.

'Mum? Are you there yet?'

'Almost, and you're on speakerphone, before you say something rude in front of your Auntie Lydia.'

'She taught me every rude word I know, so don't worry about that . . . just wanted to know if we should have supper ready for when you get back? Are you staying? Or . . .'

Three dots. An open-ended question. No answer yet.

'I'll let you know soon. How's Dhruv?'

'Right here, Auntie!' She could hear Dhruv making fun of her even from this distance.

'Yes, touch my feet when I get back . . . did you do the open-top London bus tour then?'

'Actually it was so cold . . .'

'. . . we went to the movies and ate two tubs of mixed popcorn. It was extremely cultural, you would be proud.'

They usually finished off each other's sentences. Lydia thought it unbearably cute. Shyama thought it occasionally wandered into just about unbearable, but Lydia said that was because she was turning into a bitter old cow, and when she fell in love again, she would probably do it herself. How I love an optimist, Shyama had told her. What's the alternative? Lydia had replied.

'How's Nana-ji today?' Shyama asked, speeding up a little as the track suddenly widened and the landscape dipped around her; they were going to higher ground.

'He's OK. Had a bit of a slow start this morning, but the carer was great, she got him dressed and by lunchtime he was all there, recognized us all, chatting away. He even helped Nanima with a bit of gardening. We're going to take them to Westfield later on for a walk in the warm . . .'

'Are you mad? It will be rammed, three days before Christmas.'

'Hey, we live in Delhi, we can handle a few pushy shoppers . . .'

'Oh, got to go, sweetie, call you on the way back!'

'Bye!' they both said together before hanging up.

Shyama parked up. She could see the house clearly now. It was really a cottage sitting in a small courtyard with one ramshackle outhouse and a large fenced garden at the back. It must have been cheaper to buy here than down in the village because of its inaccessibility, but the views were impressive and uninterrupted. There was a muddy estate car parked outside the front door, a National Trust sticker on the windscreen. A lit Christmas tree was just visible through the curtains in the front bay window. Shyama reached over to the back seat and grabbed the present, its shiny paper patterned with tiny Santas crackling in her hands. She had chosen one of those educational play centres in bright primary colours with various levers and buttons and scrunchy things to keep little hands and minds busy. She had asked the sales assistant for something suitable and this had appealed to her – she liked anything that multi-tasked.

'I'll walk from here, I think.' Shyama opened the door. Lydia gave her one last searching look. Shyama nodded back her answer and set off for the house.

As the track wound round the curve of the hill, she saw he was in the back garden. Toby had his jumper sleeves rolled up and was tying something to the large tree at the far boundary in that methodical, unhurried way she remembered. He stepped back and straightened out the wooden swing, pulling down on the ropes, testing the weight. It looked like a cradle – a small seat with a back, and holes for legs. He called out something snatched away by the wind, and the boy toddled into view on fat unsteady legs, his arms outstretched in his quilted jacket. She couldn't see much of his face due to the large bobble hat low down on his head and fastened under his chin. She saw strands of dark hair,

416

pale olive skin. Toby lifted him up and kissed him roughly on his cheek, but the boy wriggled away from it, his hands grabbing air, his legs kicking in anticipation. Toby relented and settled him carefully into the swing and gave it a little push. More, higher, she thought she could hear him say, but of course he probably couldn't say much yet. He expressed himself with the grip of his plump hands and bouncing knees.

And then she joined them, a sudden brushstroke of colour on the dun landscape in a sari of pink and blue, a basket under her arm. An exotic flower transplanted to this harsh soil, but she seemed to have taken root and thrived. Mala raised her free hand to wave at the boy. She kept waving each time he swung forward – it must have been a game. Toby kept pushing and Mala kept waving and the boy kept kicking, whilst Shyama crept round to the front of the house and left the present on his car's bonnet. He would read the card much later, then leave it on the kitchen table so Mala could read it herself without watching his face. He didn't want her to see a disappointment he had no right to feel.

*Dearest Toby,* he heard her voice so clearly as he read her words, *I wanted to give Krishan something for his birthday and Christmas – yes, it is one of those combined-present gestures, but hopefully it's big and loud enough to cover both. Apologies if the Teddy Bears' Picnic theme gets a bit wearing, there is a mute button underneath, I checked. Maybe one day you might tell him the story of how his Auntie Shyama helped wish him into the world, but no matter if you don't. I'm so glad he is here. Enjoy every moment, the old clichés are true – it goes in a heartbeat and your heart goes with them.*
*Be happy, always.*
*Shyama.*

Then he had remembered the book Shyama had shown him years ago, that image of a blue-skinned deity with the universe in his mouth. He still wasn't exactly sure what it meant, but as he had stood in the garden afterwards, still watching his son on the swing kicking his heels to the sky, he felt a little closer to the answer.

Shyama drove home with the radio tuned to a seventies golden-oldies station, she and Lydia singing loudly and mostly out of tune the whole way back. Tara and Dhruv had prepared a chicken biryani with a sprig of holly stuck in the top to get everyone into the festive spirit. They discussed their plans for refurbishing Prem and Sita's Delhi flat, where they now lived, handed round the latest printed-up snaps from their engagement party last month, and then Tara filled them all in on how her first term had been at Gauri's college. They took special care to point to everyone in each photo to see if Prem could name them. Every man in them, according to him, seemed to be called Yogesh.

Sita had received one phone call from India in February, when news had reached the family there that Prem was not well. She had recognized Yogi's voice just from his namaste. That was as far as he got before she hung up.

Sitting at the table listening to her family chatter around her, Shyama could scarcely believe that a year had passed since she had brought her parents back to the country they now called home. She, of course, did not know that this time next year, her father would no longer speak, but that she would cherish the touch of his hand in place of her name. That her daughter would announce that Shyama was soon to be a grandmother and that if she was to have any chance of finishing her degree, her mother

418

would have to come over and do some seriously hands-on childcare. That there would be someone else in her life who she thought she could love, but that she was quite happy to wait and see. That her parents would never visit India again. All this was still to come, unknown and unnamed, waiting to be lived.

# ACKNOWLEDGEMENTS

Huge thanks firstly to the Transworld team for their patience and for cheerfully waiting so long for this book. In particular, Marianne Velmans, for her unending encouragement and faith, and Jane Lawson, for her insight and forensic attention to the text.

Special thanks are due to Dr Anand Saggar for all his medical advice and expertise, often at the most unsociable hours of the day.

Deepest thanks to K and N for sharing their remarkable story and for opening up their hearts and meticulous records for me. I am so glad your journey ended with a family.

And finally, thank you to my parents, though those words will never be enough, measured against what you have always given me and continue to give: wisdom, conscience, purpose, love.

## A NOTE ABOUT THE AUTHOR

**Meera Syal**, CBE, is one of the most acclaimed actors and writers of stage and screen. She starred in two hit comedy series, *Goodness Gracious Me* and *The Kumars at No. 42*. Her theatre work includes Beatrice in the RSC's *Much Ado About Nothing*, Shirley in Willy Russell's *Shirley Valentine*, and Zehrunisa in David Hare's play *Behind the Beautiful Forevers*. Syal is also known for her funny, sharp and provocative fiction. Her two earlier novels are *Anita and Me* and *Life Isn't All Ha Ha Hee Hee*.